Lamps OF COURAGE

Four Novellas
Honoring the Valor of Nurses
Who Served Both God and Country

Renee DeMarco
JoAnn A. Grote
Colleen L. Reece
Janelle Burnham Schneider

BARBOUR
PUBLISHING, INC.
Uhrichsville, Ohio

By Dim and Flaring Lamps ©2001 by Colleen L. Reece.
Home Fires Burning ©2001 by JoAnn A. Grote.
A Light in the Night ©2001 by Janelle Burnham Schneider.
Beside the Golden Door ©2001 by Renee DeMarco.

Illustrations by Mari Goering.

ISBN 1-58660-229-2

All Scripture quotations, unless otherwise noted, are taken from the King James Version of the Bible.

Scripture quotations marked NIV are taken from the HOLY BIBLE, NEW INTERNATIONAL VERSION®. NIV®. Copyright © 1973,1978, 1984 by International Bible Society. Used by permission of Zondervan Publishing House. All rights reserved.

Published by Barbour Publishing, Inc., P.O. Box 719, Uhrichsville, Ohio 44683 http://www.barbourbooks.com

 Member of the
Evangelical Christian
Publishers Association

Printed in the United States of America.

INTRODUCTION

By Dim and Flaring Lamps by Colleen L. Reece
Lucy Danielson longs for just two things in life: to ease pain and suffering alongside her doctor father and to marry Jeremiah Cunningham. But Jere's father wants him to marry a more influential young woman and serve with the South against the tyranny of the North—or be disinherited. What paths will Lucy and Jere decide to take when the Civil War erupts?

Home Fires Burning by JoAnn A. Grote
Glorie Cunningham thought it would be wonderful to serve her country on the European front during the Great War, but she is assigned at an army hospital in her hometown. Her work seems to be the mundane battle against the flu epidemic—until Armistice Day and soldiers start pouring into the hospital for rehabilitation. She knows she shouldn't allow it, but she can't fight an attraction to a certain patient suffering effects of mustard gas. Will her heart get irrevocably tangled?

A Light in the Night by Janelle Burnham Schneider
Elisabeth Baker is a Red Cross nurse who doesn't particularly enjoy being called to work for the U.S. Army at a remote post in Labrador. She's hoping for a quick end to the Second World War, and is not allowing herself to get too attached to anyone. Then she meets a Canadian pilot whose gentle friendship tugs at her heart. Can she risk opening herself up to love? What if she loses him to the awful war?

Beside the Golden Door by Renee DeMarco
Just three short internships, then Kiersten Davis will sign up to serve her country in the war-torn areas of the world. Working with drug addiction, alcoholism, and cases of abuse was not in her plans. It is hard for her not to get judgmental—until she makes a very embarrassing judgment call and meets Brett Lewis. Can he help her see a different side to her patients and their circumstances?

Lamps
OF COURAGE

AUTHORS' FOREWARD

The year 2001 marked the exciting 120th anniversary of the founding of the American Red Cross and the 100th anniversary of the Army Nurse Corps. The year 2002 commemorated the 120th anniversary of the United States' ratification of the Geneva Convention treaty, which calls for humane treatment of sick and wounded soldiers, prisoners of war, and others during wartime.

These historic events became possible because of one woman's perseverance and valor. Clara Barton (1821–1912) carried supplies to the front lines and nursed wounded soldiers during the American Civil War. Her acts of mercy attracted the nation's attention, won its gratitude, and earned for her the title *Angel of the Battlefield*.

In 1869, Clara went to Switzerland and served as a battlefront nurse in the Franco-Prussian War. The work done by the International Committee of the Red Cross impressed her deeply. She returned to America in 1873 and tirelessly campaigned until the American Association of the Red Cross was established in 1881. Clara served as president from 1882–1904.

Clara Barton's relentless mission finally goaded President Chester A. Arthur and the U.S. Senate into unanimously signing the Geneva Convention Treaty in March 1882. The *Angel of the Battlefield* made a life-and-death difference in the lives of all those who serve in times of war.

Although Clara Barton accomplished a great deal, the honor of being the founder of modern nursing belongs to Florence Nightingale (1820–1910). She courageously determined to change existing hospital conditions where drunken, unfit women often served as nurses. She shocked society and her wealthy British parents by renouncing her social position and going into training. There she learned the crucial need for sanitation in caring for the sick.

During the war in Crimea in 1854, Florence and thirty-eight assistant nurses fought their own war in old, dirty, unfinished Turkish barracks. She enlisted patients well enough to work and set them scrubbing. Florence and her faithful assistants struggled with the lack of food, bedding, and medical supplies—including bandages—and battled doctors who openly resented being dictated to by any woman. She refused to compromise and badgered British military officials until she got the desperately needed food and supplies.

Florence walked four miles of corridors every night to check on the wounded. Grateful British soldiers called her the *Lady with the Lamp*. Henry Wadsworth Longfellow wrote of her in "Santa Filomena" (1858, selected verses):

> The wounded from the battle-plain,
> In dreary hospitals of pain,
> The cheerless corridors,
> The cold and stony floors.

> Lo! in that house of misery
> A lady with a lamp I see
> Pass through the glimmering gloom,
> And flit from room to room.

> And slow, as in a dream of bliss,
> The speechless sufferer turns to kiss
> Her shadow, as it falls
> Upon the darkening walls.

As if a door in heaven should be
    Opened, and then closed suddenly,
The vision came and went,
    The light shone was spent.

A lady with a lamp shall stand
    In the great history of the land,
A noble type of good,
    Heroic womanhood.

No one will ever know how many lives were saved because of the difference the gallant *Lady with the Lamp* made.

The four dedicated nurses in *Lamps of Courage* also make a difference. Each fights a different type of war, depending on the era in which she lives. All battle sickness, disease, and prevailing world conditions: on the front lines, on the home front, in hospitals, clinics, or wherever needed. These fictional characters represent the great army of nurses who have and will continue to serve and follow the path of Jesus when He said,

> *Inasmuch as ye have done it unto one of the least of these my brethren, ye have done it unto me.*
> MATTHEW 25:40

By Dim and Flaring Lamps

by Colleen L. Reece

Author's Note

The Civil War, also called "The War between the States," divided families and pitted brother against brother. Each side fought for a *cause:* the North to free the slaves and preserve the Union, and the South to maintain a way of life begun by those who pioneered and won their lands against immeasurable odds.

Some incidents in *By Dim and Flaring Lamps* are based on stories handed down in my family for more than a century—legends of boys in their teens and grizzled men who, at day's end, often laid down their weapons and crossed battle lines. They played cards, swapped tobacco, and told stories about their homes, all the time knowing the next day they would again fight one another.

Music played an important part in the conflict. Southern Johnny Rebs lustily sang, "Oh, I wish I was in Dixie. . ."—a song used against Abraham Lincoln when he ran for president in 1860. (Five years later, after the Civil War ended, Lincoln had a band play "Dixie" at the White House.)

Julia Ward Howe gave the North "The Battle Hymn of the Republic," inspired by visits to military camps near Washington, D.C., shortly after the war started.

Colleen

Chapter 1

Thy word is a lamp unto my feet, and a light unto my path.
PSALM 119:105

I have seen Him in the watchfires of a hundred
    circling camps;
They have builded Him an altar in the evening
    dews and damps;
I can read His righteous sentence by the dim
    and flaring lamps,
His day is marching on.
        —"Battle Hymn of the Republic"
      by Julia Ward Howe; 2nd stanza; 1861

Hickory Hill, Virginia
October 25, 1860

An inquisitive, late-afternoon sunbeam sneaked between the thin muslin curtains of the upstairs hall's west window in Dr. Luke Danielson's modest but spotless home. It roved over plain white walls brightened by occasional watercolor landscapes, and highlighted a cross-stitched sampler that read: *How far that little candle throws his beams! So shines a good deed in a naughty world.* * The sunbeam danced on until it reached a heavy mirror mounted on the wall next to the staircase leading to the ground floor. There it lingered, for all the world as if it had finally found something worthy of its full attention.

The massive mirror gave the slim, blue-calico-clad figure poised at the top of the staircase an auburn-haired twin, a twin with sparkling blue eyes that often changed to mysterious green, depending on the wearer's gown. Both image and original displayed a few tiny, gold-dust freckles on their lightly tanned, tip-tilted noses—the result of forgetting to shade creamy skin from the sun by wearing tiresome hats.

The gleaming glass also reflected Lucy Danielson's right-hand grasp of the smooth, highly polished banister rail, a definite threat to good intentions. "Young ladies should rest one hand lightly and sweep down the stairs," she muttered.

Knowing she should put aside her childish ways on this, her fifteenth birthday, Lucy loosened her grip. She was almost a woman. Why, some of her friends were married and taking on airs. Lucy grimaced. *She* would never do so. "I may become a woman, but I won't stop being a girl," she vowed.

She sighed, then with a quick change of mood, curved her left hand, smirked, and took a single mincing step forward. The next moment, she made the mistake of allowing her gaze to linger on the tempting banister. Its beautifully grained surface served as a silent reminder of countless journeys made since Lucy first eluded Mammy

*William Shakespeare

Roxy's watchful care and discovered the new, wonderful means of descent. Numerous scoldings and threats (that never materialized) to tell the child's beloved father, "Daddy Doc," hadn't kept Lucy from engaging in the forbidden activity.

She closed her eyes in order to better fight temptation. A girl who had accompanied her father on his rounds ever since she was old enough to sit in the buggy beside him had no business sliding down banister rails. Lucy laughed. The joyous sound echoed in the quiet hall. How many times had Mammy scolded, "It ain't fittin' for you to be takin' that chile into all kinds of unsav'ry places, Dr. Luke. It just ain't fittin'!"

Lucy's big, blond, Scandinavian father always just laughed. He usually listened to Roxy, who had become nurse and substitute mother on the day Dr. Luke's cherished wife died while birthing their only child. Yet on this one thing he remained firm. "I don't take Lucy anywhere that will endanger her health," he patiently explained over and over. "It's also the only way I can be with my daughter. Hickory Hill folks run me ragged; you know that." He covered a yawn with the strong hand, which could be gentle as a mother's touch when needed, and smiled at Roxy.

"Those same folks is plumb scandalized," Roxy reminded him. She rolled her dark eyes. "Just last week Miz Tarbell said 'twas plain shockin' to see a girl-chile sittin' on the seat of a doctor's buggy and goin' into sickrooms."

"That was last week." Dr. Luke grinned like an urchin triumphantly harboring a secret weapon. "A few days later, that same Miz Tarbell admitted Lucy's small but firm hands 'do a powerful lot to ease away miz'ry in the head.'"

Roxy threw her voluminous white apron over her head, and the doctor added, "Don't worry, Roxy. Lucy has wanted to be a nurse for as long as either of us can remember." His blue eyes glistened. "She will make a fine one. The child brings light and happiness simply by stepping into a room. She comes by it naturally. Both of our names mean 'bringer of light.'" His face turned somber. "Would that we could bring even more light into the darkness! Doctors and nurses fight ignorance and superstition as much as actual illness."

✻

The distant slam of a door returned Lucy to the present. She blinked moisture from her uselessly long lashes. A rush of love for her father and Mammy Roxy swept through her. Would she ever be as good as they thought she already was?

Probably not. She had inherited too much of her carefree Irish mother's bubble and bounce.

She glanced at the tempting rail again, intending to overcome its silent invitation. Instead, she recalled the exciting *whoosh* created by her rapid downward progress—her momentary kinship with birds flying wild and free. Most of all, she remembered the satisfying *thud* of her slippered feet when she landed in the small, sunlit entryway below.

The memories proved Lucy's undoing. She glanced to her right. To her left. She looked out the sun-touched window and made sure no one was entering or leaving the adjoining single-story building her father used for his medical and surgical practice. October lay over the land like a benediction, warm and soft as the feather bed in which Lucy slept. Good. No one was in sight. Her father had been called out earlier but refused to take her with him. "Birthday girls need to be home getting beautiful," he had teased.

"My stars, who can be beautiful when they have red hair?" Lucy had burst out.

"Your mother was. *Fiona* means fair. She was and you are. Inside and out."

His words pounded in Lucy's brain but were soon vanquished by the desire for mischief that surged through her. This time she made no attempt to squelch it. The "almost a woman," who planned to never cease being a girl, bundled her wide skirts and many petticoats around her. She catapulted down, down, down in a ride more glorious than any she remembered.

"Honeychile? Is that you?"

The rich voice, followed by heavy footsteps, drowned out the sound of Lucy's landing *thud*. She set herself to rights and whispered an unrepentant prayer of thanks for not being caught. An irreverent thought followed. Did God have banisters alongside the heavenly golden stairs Roxy and her caretaker husband, Jackson Way, sometimes sang about climbing?

The door leading to the large Danielson kitchen opened. A massive woman stepped into the hall. The dark face beneath Roxy's spotless white turban held suspicion. So did the folding of her hands across the familiar white apron that protected her print work dress. "What you up to, Miss Lucy?"

Oh dear. Mammy seldom called her charge Miss Lucy, except to strangers. *Better try to distract her.* "Nothing important. Mammy, will you please tell me The Story before it's time to dress for my birthday dinner? Who is coming, anyway?"

"Who says birthday dinner?" Roxy planted her hands on her hips and glared, but her twitching lips betrayed excitement at what Lucy knew lay ahead. "If you was havin' a dinner, and I ain't sayin' so, who d'you think would be comin'?"

Lucy swallowed a grin at the success of her diversionary tactics and tried to suppress the blush she felt creeping up from the soft white collar of her gown. "You 'ain't sayin' ' not, either," she mimicked. "Why else did you order me out of the kitchen and dining room today? I'll wager the table is already set." She danced across the hall in a whirl of skirts and threw her arms around her nurse and friend.

She waltzed Roxy across the hall until the older woman protested, "Stop, Chile! You'll be the death of me yet." She pulled free and rested one hand on Lucy's shining auburn hair. The corners of her mouth turned down. "Tryin' to s'prise you's like tryin' to put salt on a bird's tail. And the same folks've been comin' year after year."

"I know," Lucy admitted. She felt a rush of tears crowd behind her eyelids, as they did each time she wheedled Roxy into repeating the tale more romantic to her fifteen-year-old heart than those in any storybook or novel. "Tell me The Story again, Mammy. It's the best birthday present of all."

"I done tol' you that tale more times than there's stars in the sky," Roxy protested. Yet a special look came into her eyes, and she allowed Lucy to lead her into a small, carpeted sitting room, made bright with fall foliage Lucy had gathered and arranged earlier in the day. She plumped heavily down on a settee and smiled at her charge.

Lucy dropped to a tapestry-covered footstool and leaned against Roxy's knee, her favorite position for The Story. "Now, Mammy." She closed her eyes, listening for words she knew by heart.

❋

The day Laird and Isobel Cunningham's only son was born, the prosperous Virginia plantation owner devised a

plan cunning enough to make his frugal Scottish ancestors chortle with glee. He would begin searching at once
for a suitable wife for young Jeremiah, thereby ensuring a
large dowry for the Cunningham coffers and expanding
Hickory Manor's wide borders.

But, alas, his son's first glimpse of Lucy Danielson
dealt a deathblow to Laird Cunningham's hopes. Jeremiah
gazed at Lucy's fair skin, shining red curls, sometimes blue,
sometimes sparkling-green eyes—and promptly declared
his intentions to marry her!

At this point in the story, Lucy felt the same thrill she
experienced no matter how many times she heard about
that fateful day. Her heart pounded, thinking of Jere
Cunningham and his daring.

Roxy's body shook with mirth when she said, "Honeychile, you took one look at Master Jere when he come in
the room and honed in on him like a bee heads for a
flower. When your fingers touched his hand, why, they just
tangled themselves round and round his heartstrings."

"Shameless," Lucy put in from the depths of Roxy's
capacious lap, where she had hidden her burning face.
"Why didn't you teach me better?"

Roxy's deep laughter sounded as if it came from her
toes, as Dr. Luke wrote that it must. She ignored the question she had heard a hundred times before and continued
with The Story. "Folks gathered round laughed and
laughed, your daddy most of all."

"Why, Mammy?" Lucy asked, as usual.

"You already knows," Roxy scolded, also as usual.
"Master Jere were only six and it were only your first
birthday."

Lucy wondered if Roxy could hear her wildly thumping heart but remained silent. A gentle hand smoothed

the rebellious auburn curls that insisted on going their own wayward way. The older woman's rich voice went on. "Chile, that were fourteen year ago." She hesitated, then added significantly, "Folks done stopped their laughin' a long time ago."

Lucy looked up in time to see Roxy nod and to catch the knowing expression that filled the shining face. "You young 'uns ain't changed a mite. There ain't nothin' in this world goin' to sep'rate you."

A feather of fear brushed the listening girl's heart, which skipped a beat. "Laird Cunningham would, if he could. *He* didn't laugh that day."

The life-wrinkles at the corners of Roxy's expressive mouth deepened, and she shook her head. "Hmp-um. I reckon the milk of human kindness done soured in that man. Now Jackson Way heard tell he's already combin' the countryside lookin' for suitors for Miss Jinny." Roxy rolled her eyes and grunted, "And her not yet fourteen."

Lucy sat bolt upright. "Suitors? Jinny? *I* never had suitors."

Roxy's laugh rolled out again. "That's 'cause all the boys know you belongs to Master Jere. Ain't he been takin' you ridin' and sleddin' and lookin' after you since you could crawl? Whyfor you want suitors? Hmm?"

Lucy cocked her head to one side, a habit that signified deep thought. "I didn't say I *wanted* suitors, Mammy. Just that I didn't have any." She grinned at the answering frown.

"Don't you go hankerin' after brass when you done got pure gold," Roxy warned. "Ain't no boy round Hick'ry Hill better than Master Jere."

Lucy felt warm blood course through her veins. A tantalizing image of the tall young man her childhood playmate had become crept into her mind. "I know," she whispered.

The sound of buggy wheels shattered the special moment they had shared and sent Lucy flying to the window. "My stars! Daddy Doc's home already." She leaped to her feet and hurled her disheveled self through the hall and out the front door, to enthusiastically welcome home one of the two men most important in her charmed, secure world.

Chapter 2

A war-cry yell like those heard in battles between early Virginia settlers and Indians mingled with the steady drum of hooves beating on the well-traveled road from Hickory Manor to Hickory Hill. The next instant, a magnificent black stallion with a rider bent low over his neck topped a knoll overlooking the plantation. They stopped, turned, and faced the wide valley below, as they always did on their way to and from the village.

"Good boy." Jere Cunningham relaxed his set jaw, patted his thoroughbred's neck, slid from the saddle, and tossed the reins over Ebony's head. No need to tie the horse taught as a colt to stand with reins hanging. One arm thrown across Ebony's neck, the strong young man surveyed the land he loved.

Horse and rider's vantage point offered an unsurpassed view. The three-story mansion, in all its white-columned glory, crouched amidst manicured lawns, well-cared-for flower beds, and a stand of hickory trees from which the plantation took its name. Late afternoon sunlight gilded the walls of Jere's home. It changed glistening white to soft gold, enhancing the beauty. Pride stirred within his heart.

"Mother's doing," he muttered to Ebony, who nickered and nosed him in response. "Father cares far more for land than for buildings. Land and money," he bitterly added. Yet the familiar sense of permanency emanating from the heart of Hickory Manor swelled within him. Anger over Jere's recent confrontation with his father lessened. The peace he always experienced in this particular spot gradually stilled his twanging nerves.

A vision of his lovely, patrician mother danced in the still air. Jere drew in an unsteady breath and shot a silent prayer of thanks upwards. How much Isobel Cunningham had passed on to her son! From her had come the crisp, golden brown locks that waved across his wide forehead. The ruddy color in his cheeks that even his deep tan couldn't hide. The farseeing eyes that stole their brightness from Scottish lochs reflecting the bluest heavens.

Jere had also inherited his mother's love of books, especially the "Auld Book," as his Scottish ancestors called the Bible. Most important, she had led Jere to the Lord when he was first old enough to understand God's infinite love. "If you had been the only person who ever lived, Jesus would still have come, so that you might one day live with Him," Isobel quietly told her listening son.

Jere never forgot the childish words with which he asked Jesus to live in his heart and help him to "be a good boy." They served him in good stead when trials came. The stern control Laird Cunningham exercised over himself, his household, the many slaves who served him, and especially his only son seldom slipped. The occasions when it did were legendary.

The elder Cunningham unfortunately bequeathed both his love for the plantation and his stubbornness to his only son. Many times Jere flinched at his father's rock-hard determination to control his life. Jere never let it show. Laird Cunningham despised weakness and rode roughshod over opposition, believing he was duty-bound to direct others in the way they ought to go.

On most such occasions, Jere silently met his father's stern gaze, then went his own way. Today in the drawing room had been different. Jere shrank from the memory raw in his mind and deliberately concentrated on the vast Cunningham domain. It stretched as far as he could see in every direction. Beautifully cared-for fields ribboned with lazy streams swept to low hills that were backed by distant mountain ridges. The hum of bees heavy with pollen harmonized with voices from the whitewashed cabins that housed the Cunningham slaves. Voices now raised in a familiar spiritual. No ramshackle dwellings marred Hickory Manor. Each tidy cabin had its cow, garden, and patch of flowers.

Jere turned up his nose in disgust. Some of the neighbors' slave quarters were disgraceful, little more than shacks. He furrowed his brow. The one time he protested the deplorable conditions to his father, Laird Cunningham shook his head and sternly reminded, "How he treats his slaves is each man's responsibility. We treat ours well, but we are not our brothers' keepers."

We should be. The words remained unspoken but never completely disappeared into the land of forgotten conversations. They popped up at odd times, leaving Jere depressed without knowing what to do about his feelings.

A cloud slid across the sky, blotting out the sun and Jere's temporary peace. He sighed, unable to laugh off or ignore the incident that had sent him galloping away from home and his father's presence. Resentment rose like bile. Jere flung his head back and stared at a distant, blue-hazed mountain. "Sorry I couldn't hold my tongue, God. I can't and won't marry Harriet Conrad, even though she would bring a dowry as large as her feet to the house of Cunningham."

He paused, wishing God would tell him, *I don't expect you to marry her.* The heavens remained silent. Jere chuckled. What had he expected? A lightning bolt? Why ask for reassurance when he already had it? His heart had confirmed his convictions a hundred, nay, a *thousand* times since the day he would remember if he lived to be older than Methuselah. In the space between heartbeats, he had taken measure and staked his claim to Lucy Danielson. For fourteen years he'd remained unshaken in the face of his father's continuing disbelief that a six year old's fanciful attachment would be strong enough to carry into manhood.

Jere expelled an exasperated breath and set his mouth in a grim line. Father had brought the subject up again today. His steely gaze had bored into his son, who dreaded hearing the timeworn arguments and accusations he knew by heart.

"You're twenty years old," he stated through thinned lips, paying out the words the way a miser reluctantly parts with his gold. He glared at Jere, seated in the richly upholstered chair on the opposite side of the great marble fireplace. "Old enough to put aside this abominable obsession with the Danielson child, and—"

Jere closed his mind against the rest of the speech. *Child? In many ways,* he admitted to himself. A hundred glimpses of her laughing face when she followed or led him into mischief flooded his brain. Lucy calmly removing her shoes and wading stocking-footed in the creek when she knew it would scandalize Mammy Roxy. Lucy sneaking tidbits to a mongrel dog through the open window behind her at a formal dinner. Lucy filling his heart with her antics and obvious adoration. Even though no vow of love had been declared between them, her incredible blue-green eyes showed awareness of the bonds that shut out any possibility of either Jere or her marrying anyone else.

His father's grating voice interrupted the thought. "Can you imagine *Lucy Danielson* as mistress of all this?" He carelessly gestured around the tastefully furnished drawing room. "Unless she changes completely, and I see little hope of that. . . ." He paused and raised a skeptical eyebrow. "She will never be mature enough to properly grace any man's home, let alone a man of your station."

The sleeping protest Jere had stifled more times than he could remember roused, shook itself, and roared like a cannon. "Mature enough!" Jere felt his eyes burn and knew they flashed blue fire at his father. "She's mature enough to accompany Dr. Luke on his rounds. Mature enough for everyone in Hickory Hill and miles around—except you—to recognize that she has been given the gift of healing! Mature enough to know from childhood that nursing is her calling and to have studied all she could get her hands on, plus learning from Dr. Luke." Pride choked off his tribute. He observed the consternation in his father's face at the unexpected outburst but retrieved his voice and heedlessly rushed on.

"Every day Lucy tries to live up to the standard set by her heroine, Florence Nightingale. You must know the courageous 'lady with the lamp' and her assistants overcame unspeakable conditions in the Turkish barracks used as a hospital during the Crimean War. Miss Nightingale saved the lives of countless British soldiers." He paused. "Lucy has already helped save lives right here."

"The Nightingale woman disgraced her father and broke his heart."

Jere sprang to his feet so abruptly, his heavy chair crashed to the polished floor. He stepped forward, unable to hold back words he had wanted to speak a million times. Words he had swallowed because of the commandment to honor his father and mother. "Thank God Dr. Luke isn't such a man! He respects his daughter enough to let her choose her own life."

The older man slowly and deliberately raised himself from his chair. His fixed gaze never wavered from his son's face. "Some of us can afford to be more choosy," he grimly pointed out. "Lucas Danielson has little land and fewer possessions to leave future generations. Your mother and I have given our lives to the establishing of Hickory Manor. In many ways, it *is* our lives."

Yours, not mother's, Jere thought. *She would be happy no matter how little she had. Although she enjoys her home, what really matters to Mother is serving God and her family.*

"Jinny will be suitably betrothed at the proper time," Laird droned on in a voice as devoid of emotion as if he were describing the selling of a farm animal.

Jere opened his mouth to protest, then shrugged. Why bring his younger sister's future into the argument? Doing so at this point meant prolonging Father's tirade, something Jere hated and avoided whenever possible.

Today it wasn't possible. In the same calculated tones, the master of Hickory Manor announced, "You will be twenty-one next August. As you know, you stand to inherit a goodly section of land. If between now and then you consent to wed Harriet Conrad, all will be well. I have approached her father on your behalf." The words fell like cold, hard pebbles into the pool of silence that Jere stonily maintained. "Conrad and his daughter are both agreeable to the union."

"Agreeable?" Furious at the suggestion, Jere lost the last of his self-control. "Not to me. I absolutely refuse to marry that simpering lummox!"

Laird's great hands balled into fists. His face grew mottled. "Enough! No woman will be spoken of so in this household."

"You are right, Sir. I shouldn't have ridiculed Miss Conrad, any more than you should belittle Lucy Danielson." He hesitated, then decided that since all-out war must ultimately be declared, it might as well happen. Father could never be any angrier than right now, after having had his principles thrown into his teeth.

"I'm sorry I can't live up to what you expect of me, but I wouldn't marry Miss Conrad if she were the only woman on earth. I will also never marry in order to increase our holdings. You married for love. So will I." Jere searched the granitelike face for any sign of softening. He found none. Years of pride and ambition had evidently erased Father's memories of the young man he once was.

Jere took a deep breath and freed himself from the invisible shackles he'd felt tightening around him ever since the conversation began. Should Father carry out his implied threat of disinheriting, perhaps even disowning, his natural heir, it meant losing both land and dreams. Yet something deep in Jere's soul compelled him to say, "I've loved Lucy Danielson since childhood. I always will. Marrying another would be akin to sacrilege. God and Dr. Luke willing, I plan to offer Lucy a betrothal ring one year from today."

His father laughed unpleasantly. "Which she will naturally accept. What girl wouldn't leap at the opportunities you offer?" He ignored Jere's murmur of protest. "I repeat my ultimatum. Either you marry Miss Conrad on or before your twenty-first birthday, or I shall not be responsible for the consequences."

Jere didn't trust himself to say more. He bolted from the room and from the house as if pursued by a thousand devils. A few minutes later, he mounted Ebony and galloped away, seething with the unfairness of it all. Just before he reached the rising ground leading to his favorite knoll, his pent-up emotions exploded into a war cry that echoed across the valley and bounced off the distant hills.

✳

Ebony poked his nose against his master's shoulder and whinnied, shattering Jere's reverie. How long had he been standing atop the knoll? He gazed at the westering sun. Rose-purple streaks heralded the near approach of dusk. Jere vaulted into the saddle and headed for Hickory Hill. Should he remain in the village after completing his errand and go straight to the Danielson home at the appointed time, thereby escaping another meeting with Father?

A hasty survey of his rumpled riding clothes scotched the idea. No gentleman would appear at his ladylove's birthday soiree in such condition, even though she had seen him far more disheveled many times. *Social conventions sometimes bring more trouble than they are worth,* he thought bleakly.

"Nobody knows the trouble I've seen," Jere sang mournfully, urging Ebony into a ground-devouring trot, then a canter, followed by a gallop. "Nobody knows but Jesus. . . ." He thought of the many times he'd heard field hands sing the haunting words, supposedly written by an unknown slave or slaves. Somehow their poignancy had never touched him as much as they did now. He sang on,

"Sometimes I'm up, sometimes I'm down,
Oh, yes, Lord;
Sometimes I'm almost to the ground,
Oh, yes, Lord."

Inexplicably comforted, Jere reached the outskirts of the village. He slowed Ebony to a trot and turned him toward the least likely place one would expect to find a gift for fifteen-year-old Lucy Danielson's birthday: the blacksmith shop.

Chapter 3

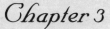

T he grime-covered face of the village blacksmith brightened when Jere and Ebony halted before the smithy. A wide smile broke out, like white-caps against a dark reef. "I was beginning to wonder if you'd forgotten our little secret." He removed a bulky package from the corner. "It's just as you wanted it."

Jere's usual high spirits returned. He leaped from the saddle and eagerly accepted the package, hefting its weight and grinning. "How did it turn out?"

"Perfect. Just perfect." The smile grew even larger. "Miss Lucy's gonna get the surprise of her life." The black-smith chuckled gleefully and rubbed his hamlike hands, obviously enjoying the conspiracy. "Smart as she is, I predict that little lady will never guess what's in the package—not the way you had me wrap it. Your folks coming in for her birthday supper, as usual?"

"Yes." Jere tucked the heavy package in his saddlebag and paid the previously agreed-on price for his purchase. "As usual."

"Lemme see; it's been nigh onto fourteen years, ain't it?" Rolls of flesh nearly hid the twinkling eyes. "Folks ain't forgot the way you stood there straight as a wooden soldier when Miss Lucy toddled over to you. Or how you

told the world what you wanted, right then and there."
His joyful bellow rang out louder than the sound of
hammers and anvil with which he plied his trade. He
slapped his leather apron. "I hear tell you ain't changed
your mind."

"Would you?" Jere demanded, already knowing the
answer.

"No, siree. You're the second luckiest feller around."

"Second luckiest? Why not the luckiest?" Jere
demanded.

"The way I figure is, I got me the best lass in the
world. I've had her for more than thirty years. That
makes Miss Lucy second." He scratched his balding head
and his expression changed. "My wife wouldn't have made
it through that bad spell of ague if it hadn't been for that
child, which she ain't anymore. Dr. Luke was run off his
feet taking care of sick folks. He didn't have time to stay
with just one person. Miss Lucy waltzed into our house
like she owned it. She told me what to do and made sure
I did it." Gratitude added a touch of beauty to the rugged
features. "There's nothing I wouldn't do for her. The
whole village feels the same way." The big man cleared
his throat. "That goes for you, too, Son."

A bittersweet feeling threatened Jere's composure.
Why couldn't Father admit Lucy's worth, when so many
others recognized it and loved her for serving? *Or mine,* he
mentally added. Family loyalty sealed his lips from utter-
ing words that would betray the lord of the manor's attitude. Besides, folks—including the blacksmith—would
find out soon enough. He'd wager Ebony against a sway-
backed nag that before morning, news of the heated argument with Father would romp through the peaceful valley
on tattletale feet. Each telling would add spice and lurid

details until the tale had only passing acquaintance with truth.

Jere grinned in spite of himself. By the time the story traveled full circle through village and neighboring plantations then back to Hickory Manor, he'd be cast as everything from the Prodigal Son to Sir Galahad, depending on who repeated the gossip and how many times.

He gripped the blacksmith's hand, then swung into the saddle. "Thanks. I couldn't have done this without you, but you already know that."

The blacksmith swiped one hand across his face. "Yeah, but it won't be me who gets Miss Lucy's undying gratitude." His eyes glistened. "Wish I could be a mouse in a corner when she starts peeling away that paper."

His laggard customer just laughed. A touch of heels to Ebony's sides sent them racing down the wide street toward home. The last thing he needed tonight was another lecture about cutting the family's time for leaving short. "This is Lucy's birthday, and she has a right to be happy," he told the stallion.

Ebony snorted, extended his powerful legs, and headed for Hickory Manor.

They reached the stables at last light. Jere tossed the reins to a waiting stable boy, hid his package in the carriage the family used for more formal occasions, and hurried toward the house. He reached his room undetected and rang for hot water. After his bath, the dark-suited gentleman with the gleaming white shirtfront who stood brushing his sunny hair before the glass atop his chiffonier, bore little resemblance to Ebony's carelessly attired rider. Jere admitted without conceit that he would do and bounded downstairs after a servant tapped at his door and informed him the family was ready and waiting in the "libr'y."

Laird Cunningham raised one eyebrow but said nothing. Isobel, lovely in pale blue, smiled a welcome. Jinny curtseyed, her rose pink skirts swaying with the motion. Alerted by his father's coldly stated plan for Jinny, Jere felt a protective surge of concern. He silently vowed she would not be sacrificed on the altar of greed. If Father ever attempted to force Jinny into a marriage not of her own choosing, Jere would thwart his plans. Even if it meant carrying her so far away that Father would never find her. God forbid it would come to that.

"You're staring at me as if you'd never seen me before," Jinny accused.

"I've never seen you look so beautiful," her brother told her.

She blushed until her surprised face matched her gown. "Why, Jere! You never use pretty words to me. Is it because—I mean, you act different."

"I never before realized how quickly you are growing up," he said soberly, wondering if his fear for her future showed in his eyes or in his voice.

Perhaps it had, for some of Jinny's radiance dimmed. Uncertainty crept into her face, and her gaze followed Jere's quick look at their father. With a rustle of skirts, she ran to Isobel and unnecessarily smoothed a wisp of her carefully arranged hair. "You're the one who looks beautiful. Doesn't she, Father?"

Jere hated the appraising look that came into his father's eyes before he bowed to his wife and said, "Mrs. Cunningham is always pleasing to behold." Why didn't he admit Mother was even lovelier than Jinny?

Jere held his sister's cloak while his father did the same for Mother. Donning his own, Jere trailed the others out the front door and down the steps to the waiting carriage. At first, Jinny excitedly chattered about the evening ahead. Her father's rigidity and lack of response soon silenced her. The rest of the journey was accomplished in total stillness, broken only when they reached Hickory Hill.

"I hope you acquired a gift suitable for the occasion," Laird Cunningham said in a voice that showed he had grave doubts about that very thing.

Jere knew the comment was directed at him but clung to his determination to make this a happy occasion for Lucy and refused to rise to the bait. Jinny quickly replied, "Oh, my, yes! Mother and I sent away for a copy of Mr. Dickens's *A Christmas Carol*. Lucy has read her copy so many times, it is almost worn out."

"A quite suitable gift," her father mocked. "Especially for one obviously fond of frittering away valuable time on idle tales."

"That will be quite enough, Mr. Cunningham," Isobel said in a voice cold enough to freeze icicles. "*A Christmas Carol* is no idle tale. It offers great value to those who read it. I suggest you do so before criticizing those who have."

Jinny gasped. Jere wanted to cheer. He could count on one hand the times his mother had stood up against her husband in their children's presence. The last time had been so long ago, Jere couldn't remember the reason. He did remember shock at his father's reaction. A cool stare, then, "As you wish, my dear."

How would Father respond this time? Jere's lips twitched when Laird Cunningham hesitated, then said in a colorless voice, "As you wish, my dear," before irritably telling Jinny, "If you must make rude noises, Virginia, do cover your mouth."

A lace-adorned hand flew to obey, but Jere gave

wordless thanks for the darkness he felt sure hid satisfaction dancing in his sister's expressive eyes.

His suspicions were confirmed when they reached the
Danielson home and he helped Jinny from the carriage.
She lingered long enough for their parents to reach the
porch door and be out of earshot, then giggled and quoted,
" 'The smallest worm will turn being trodden on. . . .' "

Jere squeezed her arm in relief. "Lord Clifford to the
king in *Henry VI, Part 3.*" Jinny was growing up, but she
hadn't completely crossed the borders of childhood. Yet if
she were still a child, why did he feel he had gained an
ally, a staunch friend who would prove herself invaluable
in coming days?

Pondering the strange thought, Jere ceremoniously
followed his parents into the Danielson entryway, where
a beaming Jackson Way took their cloaks. A loud gasp
turned all heads toward Jinny, staring openmouthed at
the staircase leading to the upper floor.

"What did I tell you, Virginia?" Laird Cunningham
hissed, face red with annoyance. "Have you no manners
whatsoever?" The next moment, his gaze followed his
daughter's. His jaw dropped. He rubbed one hand across
his eyes like someone awakening from a deep sleep and
being unsure of his surroundings.

A small smile played over Isobel's sensitive lips. She
laid a gentle hand on her son's dark sleeve and unobtrusively pointed with the other.

Jere turned his back on his thunderstruck father and
looked up. In the next few seconds, he felt himself running a gamut of emotions, from shock to wonder, pride
to humility. Two long strides put him at the foot of the
staircase. He rested a strong hand on the carved top of
the newel—and waited.

❋

A short time before Jere Cunningham stepped into the family carriage at Hickory Manor, Roxy reverently held up a gown the same hue as November sunlight and Lucy's bedroom walls. "Mmm, mmm, this do be fine," she crooned. "The finest ever you had." She carefully dropped the garment over Lucy's head and fastened the row of tiny buttons from the modest neckline to the girl's slender waist. She spread the gown's ruffled skirt over her charge's many petticoats. Lucy scorned the heavy wire and whalebone crinolines her friends wore. She claimed they "squished her innards," and she absolutely refused to put herself through such torture for the sake of fashion.

Roxy leaned against a dark wooden bedpost. "Honey-chile, 'twouldn' s'prise me if your real mammy is lookin' down from heaven this very minute. I s'pect Miss Fiona's bustin' with pride and pointin' you out to the angels."

Lucy gazed at the silken-clad figure in the bedroom mirror. "Do you really, truly think so, Mammy?" Her lips trembled. She tried to blink back tears conjured up by the precious image of a mother she only knew through pictures and what she'd been told by others. Despite her best efforts, one spilled.

Roxy brushed it away with a gentle dark finger. "I does, and I reckon Master Cunningham's goin' to think you're just as fine." She pursed her lips. "Only trouble is, my chile's done gettin' all growed up." A shadow crossed the face peering over Lucy's shoulder and into the mirror. A sigh escaped.

"Don't you want me to grow up, Mammy?" Lucy tremulously asked.

"I does and I doesn't," was the cryptic answer. "Now

run along. It's time for the comp'ny." She placed her hands on her hips and stood with arms akimbo. "And don't be forgettin' what Dr. Luke always says."

"I won't." Heart overflowing with happiness, Lucy whirled toward Roxy and mimicked Dr. Luke, " 'Handsome is as handsome does.' " The sound of carriage wheels set her heart to thumping. "They're here, Mammy!" She ran into the hall and rustled her way to the top of the staircase, with Roxy close behind.

"No slidin' down, you hear?"

Lucy's imp of mischief, perpetually poised for action, tempted her to do just that. She'd love to see Laird Cunningham's face if she landed at the bottom just as he stepped inside the front door! Lucy firmly shook her head. Tonight, she would be a lady. She wouldn't embarrass Daddy Doc before a man he persisted in keeping as a friend, although Lucy couldn't for the life of her see why.

One hand lightly touched the railing. One dainty slipper reached for the first step, then hesitated. Something about the moment made her long to hold it close forever. To stay at the top of the stairs, secure in Mammy's care. To savor the aroma of roasting meat, the tang of wood smoke from the fireplace, and the bustle in the entryway below, as Jackson Way proudly took away the guests' cloaks.

Don't be foolish, she told herself. *This is just another birthday, even if you do have a new, becoming gown. You're as bad as Mammy with her does and doesn't want you to grow up. Next thing, you'll be having the vapors.* She laughed and shook her head so vigorously, the curls Roxy had insisted on pinning into a cluster threatened to escape their moorings and come tumbling down. The action freed her senses, and her reluctance to move vanished.

A loud gasp from below caught Lucy's attention. She

gazed down at Jinny, lovely as a wild rose. At frowning Laird Cunningham, whose change of countenance more than repaid the forfeiture of a downward plunge. At his wife, whose smiling eyes and mouth warmed Lucy's heart.

Last of all, she faced Jere, standing next to the newel. Lucy had never seen him so elegant and refined. Where was her playmate of former years? Gone forever, replaced by the man whose hair looked molten gold in the lamplight; whose blue eyes held admiration and love.

She caught her breath at the indescribable sweetness of the look. A feeling far stronger than all the comradeship and adoration she had freely given her friend stirred in Lucy's heart. She squared her shoulders and, step by graceful step, made her way downstairs to take her place where she knew she belonged: at Jere Cunningham's side.

Chapter 4

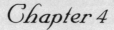

It came like a storm in summer. Unexpected. Unwanted. Unnecessary. Afterward, Jere censured himself for failing to observe small-cloud warnings, starting with his father's expression when Lucy first appeared. Never again could he dismiss her as a child. In all probability, she would continue to lapse into childlike behavior now and then, but the radiance and grace shown tonight proved her worthy of the heir of Cunningham.

Jere noticed little else. The change in Lucy's dress and demeanor were enough to distract any man. Her modest home sparkled with lamplight and laughter. It provided a fitting setting for the capable young woman at the opposite end of the table from Dr. Luke. Quiet orders to Jackson Way resulted in a succession of vittles. Great platters of pink Virginia ham. Luscious yellow sweet potatoes. Collard greens. Beaten biscuits light enough to float from the lace-covered dining room table, accompanied by home-churned butter and a variety of preserves. Jackson Way beamed and kept a seemingly endless supply coming until all at last protested they could eat no more.

As if on cue, Roxy demoted her husband from the role of waiter to table clearer. She herself carried in the *pièce de résistance*—Lucy's birthday cake. Seven layers high and swathed in delicate frosting whiter than Roxy's turban, it even brought a grunt of approval from Laird Cunningham.

"Roxy, you've outdone yourself," Dr. Luke solemnly told her after his first generous bite. "Every year your cake gets better. This one really is the best."

She beamed, spoiling any attempt at modesty. "Mmm, mmm. Strange how folks be so full, yet have space for cake." A burst of laughter greeted her sally. Roxy bowed her head and backed out of the room, voice swelling in song.

> "My Lord calls me,
> He calls me by the lightnin';
> The trumpet sounds within-a my soul,
> I ain't got long to stay here."*

The rich voice faded kitchenward.

Laird's features congealed. "How dare she sing that abominable song? When are you going to sell her and Jackson Way and get decent house servants?"

Dr. Luke laughed outright. "Lucy and I prefer loyalty and excellent service, music included. We couldn't get along without Roxy and Jackson Way." He smiled down the length of the table at his daughter.

Laird raised an expressive eyebrow. "She shows insolence and lack of respect to you and your guests," he carped. "Correct me if I'm mistaken—I'm sure I am not; that song was first used during the Nat Turner Rebellion, right here in Virginia in 1831. It was and continues to serve as a signal for secret meetings of slaves, escape plans, and other nefarious behavior."

---

*Negro spiritual, chorus

Consternation choked off Jere's protest. How despicable of his father to introduce such an unpleasant topic of conversation at such a time!

Laird continued, lecturing as if the others were historical illiterates. He sounded like he was reading from a textbook. "It's one of the biggest blots on Virginia history. A black slave and preacher, leading sixty to seventy slaves. Sixty whites died, including the family of the man who owned Turner!"

"Let's not forget the one hundred innocent slaves killed by angry whites," Dr. Luke quietly reminded. "Including everyone in Roxy and Jackson Way's family. The two of them barely escaped with their lives. Now I believe it's time to repair to the parlor for coffee. I must confess that I prefer the small sitting room, but this is an occasion. We shall do Lucy honor by sitting on less comfortable chairs."

"Not at all," she protested. Laughter swept color back into the cheeks that had turned pale a few minutes earlier. "We will use the sitting room, as usual."

"Good." Dr. Luke stood. "Ladies, if you please. Come, Laird."

Jere felt reprieved. Tonight wasn't the first time the lord of the manor had publicly objected to Dr. Luke about Roxy and Jackson Way's lack of formality.

Yet he had never before gone this far. Mother's set face and tightly compressed lips betrayed the fear she would say far too much if she stepped in. If only Father would hold his terrible tongue! Jere had little hope of such a miracle. Laird Cunningham hated not having the last word.

It happened as Jere feared. Minutes after the party seated themselves in the other room and Lucy served coffee from the polished tray that awaited them, Laird returned to his obsession like a deer to a salt lick. He took a sip of midnight black liquid and declared, "Really, Lucas. You *must* do something about this impossible situation."

He paused to let the command sink in. "If not for your sake, then do it for the the rest of us. There's already unrest in the slave quarters. The shameful way you allow your blacks to rule the roost is common talk. It can't help encouraging rebellion in others. God knows we have more than enough of that, ever since the pack of lies called *Uncle Tom's Cabin* was published eight or nine years ago.

"The way I hear it, the Stowe woman came prancing down here breathing fire and chock-full of her Northern ideas.* She poked around until she found a few mistreated slaves, which, unfortunately, can be done if you look hard enough. Then she headed back to where she should have stayed in the first place and wrote the book." He clenched his free hand. "I tell you this. If war between North and South ever comes, it will largely be that meddlesome woman's fault!"

Lucy stirred in her chair and started to speak. Dr. Luke warned her with the look Jere had seen dozens of times before in volatile circumstances. A muscle twitched in his cheek. He ignored the latter part of the tirade and addressed Laird's earlier comments. "You call my treatment of Roxy and Jackson Way shameful. Hardly." His Scandinavian blue eyes flashed, but his impeccable manners held. "It is true they serve us, but there is neither bond nor free in this household."

A triumphant smile curled Laird's thin lips. "You inherited Roxy and Jackson Way from your parents. Call them anything you like. They are still slaves."

"No, they are not." The flat denial hung in the tense

*Harriet Beecher Stowe (1851–52)

air. "Slaves are subject to their masters. Servants choose where and whom they will serve."

Match to powder keg. Laird looked jolted. Coffee spilled from the cup he clutched in shaking hands. "Sir, *don't tell me you've freed Roxy and Jackson Way!*" Horror punctuated every word.

"I have. They've had their manumission papers for years. They are free to go at any time." Dr. Luke's eyes glowed. "Thank God there has never been any question about them wanting to leave Lucy and me. They consider us the family they lost through revenge."

Laird Cunningham looked dumbstruck. Jere silently compared him with Dr. Luke. Both God-fearing. Both hardworking. Yet one lived by the letter of the law, one by its spirit. It made the latter the stronger man.

For the second time that day, Isobel Cunningham asserted herself, in the same steely voice she had used a few hours earlier. "Gentlemen, we will speak of other things." Her tone permitted no disagreement and was in sharp contrast to the loving smile she aimed at Lucy. "Today should be happy, my dear, not a time for airing grievances. You must open your presents before we take our leave. Jinny, I believe you insisted on carrying ours in your reticule?"

"Y—yes." She shot a frightened glance at her father and scurried to get it.

Jere watched Lucy unwrap her gift, hoping with all his heart the evening would end without another incident. His heart went out to Lucy, valiantly attempting to gather the remaining fragments of her birthday joy into a semblance of the real thing.

"Thank you so much," she said, clasping *A Christmas Carol* with both hands. Honest pleasure shone in the eyes more blue than green tonight, because of her pale yellow gown. Her few tiny freckles glinted like specks of gold. "Now I know why Jinny stared so at my tattered copy some time ago."

Jere bit his lip. How gallantly she carried on! *She always will,* a small voice inside him reminded. *No matter where she is or what she faces, Lucy Danielson will carry on, with banners.*

Isobel turned to her son. "I believe Jere has a gift for you, as well."

He had purposely left it in the carriage, planning to bring it in at the proper time and bestow it on the girl he loved. Now Jere rebelled at the idea. In spite of the Danielsons' efforts to restore normalcy, tarnish lay over the celebration. He could not bear to present the special gift on which he had spent so much time and effort in such circumstances. If Father dishonored his choice, Jere would not be able to control his temper. Lucy and Dr. Luke had gone through enough tonight. They should not be forced to endure a row that would make the Cunningham men's earlier altercation pale by comparison.

Laird spoke for the first time since his wife intervened. "Well?"

A quick glance around the room alerted Jere to the fact everyone present recognized it as a challenge. He rose to his feet and forced a smile. "Sorry, Lucy. I don't have your gift with me." He didn't. It was still in the carriage.

Quick understanding sprang to her eyes. "It's all right. You can drop by tomorrow. It will give me something to look forward to."

He had never been prouder of her than at that moment. Not even when he stood at the bottom of the staircase and watched her come down and stand beside him. He stood, took her hand, and formally bowed. "Until tomorrow."

"Must you go? You haven't seen Daddy Doc's gift," Lucy said reproachfully. Some of the sparkle came back into her face. "It's a book, too. A wonderful book about famous persons, such as George Washington, Thomas Jefferson, and Benjamin Franklin. It also has stories about people who are important right now, such as Abraham Lincoln."

Jere cringed. In her eagerness to ease the tension, Lucy had unwittingly chosen the worst subject possible. Laird Cunningham hated and feared Lincoln, an antislavery Republican. He idolized Democrat Stephen A. Douglas, who contended each state or territory had the right to choose whether they would be slave or free. Great had been Laird's rejoicing when Douglas defeated Lincoln for a United States Senate seat in 1858. Loud was his outcry after the May 1860 Republican national convention chose Lincoln as their candidate.

To make matters worse, the Democratic party had been weakened by splitting into factions. Northern Democrats nominated Douglas for president. The Southern proslavery wing, angry with Douglas, nominated Vice President John Breckinridge, now serving with President Buchanan. A fourth party, the Constitutional Union party, nominated former Tennessee Senator John Bell.

For months, Laird Cunningham and other concerned plantation owners made dire predictions about the future if Lincoln became president. Now only twelve days remained until the November 6 election day. Jere shuddered to think what his home atmosphere would be like should Lincoln win. Or what struggles Virginia and the rest of the country would face. Talk of secession by several Southern states already ran rampant. What would Lincoln do if the South rose up in defense of her way of life and tried to leave the Union?

Jere thought of the warning given in Matthew 12:25. *"And Jesus knew their thoughts, and said unto them, Every kingdom divided against itself is brought to desolation; and every city or house divided against itself shall not stand."*

A hollow feeling grew in him. Tonight had seen the fulfillment of the Scripture in small part. Laird Cunningham's attitude had created a rift in the two families' long-held friendship. Lucy's innocent remark had widened it. Now more than ever, the lord of the manor would vehemently oppose any alliance between the houses of Cunningham and Danielson.

At last they were in the carriage and headed toward Hickory Manor. Laird unclamped his tight lips and said, "You made a fool of yourself tonight, Jeremiah. Only a simpleton attends a birthday celebration empty-handed. Not that the girl needed anything from you. She appeared perfectly satisfied with your mother and sister's gift. And of course, her book about Lincoln." He spat out the name like a morsel of spoiled food.

Jinny clutched her brother's arm, but Isobel sat up straight. "It is not my son who played the fool, Mr. Cunningham. No *gentleman* transgresses the laws of hospitality as you did tonight." Her stinging words fell like ice pellets.

Jere waited for the inevitable explosion. Stopping an unpleasant conversation was one thing. A slur against Father's conduct was far more serious. The blood of proud Scottish chiefs flowed in his veins, and his greatest vanity lay in being considered every inch a gentleman.

"How dare you speak so to me?" Laird inquired in a deadly voice.

She didn't give an inch. "I dare because I must. No

man should be allowed to act in such a manner. We shall continue this discussion in private."

Jinny was right. For better or worse—and all indications pointed to the latter—the worm had turned. For the second time that day, Jere Cunningham wanted to stand up and cheer.

Chapter 5

Hickory Hill, Virginia
April 12, 1861

L ucy Danielson fingered the collar of the simple dark cotton dress she wore when assisting her father. Her hands dropped to the towering stack of sun-dried sheets and towels fresh from washing in strong soap and boiling water. Her mind far away, Lucy automatically began folding them and stowing them away in the storage area adjoining her father's examining room.

She looked out the open window, rejoicing in the warm April day. How long ago her disastrous fifteenth birthday celebration seemed! " 'Weeping may endure for a night, but joy cometh in the morning,' " she softly quoted. "Psalm 30:5."

Her hands stilled. A small smile tugged at her lips. Joy hadn't come on the morning of October 26 as she had expected. All day she waited for Jere Cunningham to keep his promise and bring her gift. She had almost given up on him when he and Ebony dashed into the Danielson yard in the late afternoon. Storm clouds darkened his blue eyes as he stepped inside the front door. "I'm sorry.

I couldn't get here any sooner." Lucy suspected from the firm set of Jere's lips and jaw that there had been another altercation with his father, perhaps concerning a certain red-haired Danielson girl. She was incensed. Why must Laird Cunningham be so set against her? So what if she didn't have wealth and lands? Wasn't a heart full of love enough? She felt a blush begin at her collar and move upward, so she quickly led Jere into the small sitting room. "It's all right. I'm just glad you came." In an attempt to erase the anger in his face, she planted her hands on her hips and demanded, "All right, Jeremiah Marcus, Jerabone, Markabone, Napoleon Bonaparte Cunningham, where's my present?"

Her tactic worked. Jere threw his head back and snickered loudly. "Aren't you ever going to forget that?"

"No one in Hickory Hill except your father is ever going to forget it," she taunted. "I never did understand how he kept from hearing about it." She bit her lip. She actually did know. Village sympathies had always lain with son, not father. In addition, few people cared or were brave enough to risk the lord of the manor's wrath by reporting Jere's shortcomings.

Lucy returned to her attack. "The idea! Telling the brand-new schoolmaster your name was Jeremiah Marcus, Jerabone, Markabone, Napoleon Bonaparte Cunningham on the very first day he walked into the classroom and took roll."

Jere's eyes gleamed with memories and mischief. "Don't scold. I was only ten. Besides, I couldn't resist testing the new schoolmaster."

"You didn't even *try* to resist," she accused. "It's a wonder he didn't punish you severely."

"He was a good scout." Jere chuckled, the last shreds

of trouble disappearing from his face. "He just stood there all solemn and tall until everyone stopped laughing. Then he quietly said, 'That's an awfully long name, Jeremiah. Do you mind being called something shorter?'"

Jere grinned sheepishly. "No one moved a muscle. I felt like crawling under a table but managed to mumble, 'Call me Jere, please.'

"The teacher's mouth twitched. 'Very well,' he said. Then he grinned and began laughing. The whole room joined in." Jere smiled at the memory. In an apparent burst of high spirits, he grabbed Lucy's hands and whirled her around the entryway.

"Stop stalling," she told him after she caught her breath from the wild dance and could speak again. She pulled her hands free and scowled, knowing her uptilted lips spoiled any attempt at sternness. "I want my present. Now."

Jere folded his arms across his chest. His eyes sparkled with the ten-year-old mischief that had prompted the schoolroom incident. "Really, Miss Danielson, your curiosity is mighty unbecoming for a proper young lady."

"So when have I ever been a proper young lady?" she asked.

He gave her a dazzling smile. "You were last night. Surely Roxy and Dr. Luke told you that, as well as your mirror. 'Mirror, mirror, on the wall, who's the fairest. . . ?'" He bowed from the waist in a grandiloquent manner.

Lucy's heart bounced at the open admiration in his gaze when he straightened up. "Thank you ever so much, kind sir." She spread her green-checked gingham skirts and curtseyed low in imitation of a coy Southern belle. "I do declare, Sir. I remember a certain gentleman promising that same proper young lady a present." Lucy fluttered her eyelashes. Ugh. How could her girlfriends bear to act so? It made her feel like a ninny.

Jere threw his hands into the air. "I surrender. Sit down and I'll bring it in."

He strode out and returned a few minutes later carrying a good-sized package, which he carefully deposited in her lap.

Lucy touched it with an exploring finger. "It's heavy." She took off the outer wrappings and revealed a box. She opened it and found more wrappings. Another box. "What is this? A treasure hunt?"

"You might say so." Jere chortled. A suspicious glance showed he was thoroughly enjoying her bewilderment.

Lucy continued removing wrapping and boxes until, "A brick?" she said disbelievingly. "You gave me a *brick* for my birthday?" She stared at the heavy, offensive object lying off-center in the bottom of the last box.

"You mean you don't like my present?" Jere laughed until tears rolled. "You could at least be polite and pretend."

Lucy cocked her head to one side and silently surveyed his oh-so-innocent face. Did the silly brick hold a special significance? Was it his way of hinting that someday they would build a home together, using the brick for a cornerstone? The thought sent another rush of blood to her already overheated cheeks. "Is it. . .does it. . .I mean, is there a reason for giving me a brick?" she finally asked in a very small voice.

He lifted one eyebrow. "Oh, yes. A very special reason."

Lucy couldn't move. *My stars. Is Jere about to declare his intentions? Again? If he does, what shall I do? What should I say? Heroines in novels faint at such moments, but I can't imagine myself swooning.*

She was spared the painful decision of how to answer

when after a long pause Jere told her, "The brick is actually camouflage for your real present."

Lucy didn't know whether to be glad or relieved. The strange new feelings of the night before suffered a setback and mild disappointment, but part of her didn't want things to change between them. "There's nothing else in the box."

"Oh, but there is. Reach to the very bottom, alongside the brick," he said in a voice that showed he was as excited as she. Lucy obeyed and took out a hard something swathed in more paper. She discarded the final wrappings and a small box appeared. Lucy hesitated, heart pounding. The box was just large enough to hold a ring. Lucy swallowed. Now what? *Please, God, help me to not make a fool of myself,* she prayed.

"Open it, Lucy," Jere whispered.

With trembling fingers, she followed directions. The contents of the box made her gasp. A small brooch lay on a nest of soft cotton. Not a jeweled or antique brooch, but one far more precious to Lucy—a tiny lamp hammered from metal and burnished to a soft glow. The pin was a miniature replica of the lamp carried by Florence Nightingale that Lucy had seen in pictures. She picked it up and held it in the palm of her hand. "Oh, Jere!" Tears spilled. "How could you ever find such a perfect gift?"

"I didn't find it. I made it for you." His intense blue gaze never left her face. "I've been working on it for months, whenever I could steal a few minutes from chores at Hickory Manor. My friend, the blacksmith, taught me how and kept my secret." He cleared his throat. A slight uncertainty crept into his face.

"The blacksmith says I crafted it so well, it will last forever. You can pass it down to our—your children and grandchildren." Color crept up to the golden brown hair across his forehead.

Lucy knew that if she didn't do something, anything, she would burst into tears of joy and be unable to tell Jere why. She quickly pinned the brooch just above her heart and impulsively sprang from her chair. A few steps took her to Jere. She threw her arms around him, rose to the tips of her soft-soled slippers, and kissed him. Then with a gasp at her brazen action, she darted into the entryway, unceremoniously leaving her astounded guest frozen to the spot.

※

A flash of red and the call of a cardinal to his mate just outside the open window rudely interrupted Lucy's woolgathering. Her face burned, as it did each time she remembered the kiss. Her fingers stole again to her collar and gently stroked the tiny lamp's smooth surface. She had worn the brooch day and night since the day she received it.

Lucy chuckled to herself. The kiss wasn't all she remembered about that fateful afternoon. Or the lamp pin. Jere's dumfounded expression when she kissed him never failed to bring a smile to her heart and lips. Thank goodness Jere was gentleman enough not to remind her of how forward she had been! She knew he hadn't forgotten the incident, any more than she could forget. His just-biding-my-time expression and occasional comment that sixteen was a good age for a girl to become betrothed, preferably to someone a few years older, made clear his love for her, without pledging vows of eternal devotion. The love that hadn't changed since he was a boy of six.

"I'm the one who has changed, God," she whispered. "I feel years older than I was just six months ago. If Jere brings me a ring on my next birthday and Daddy Doc agrees, I'll be the happiest girl who ever lived. You've blessed me so much. Help me be worthy of Jere and a good mother to his children."

She hesitated, wanting to cling to the sunny moment, knowing only too well that shadows and perhaps darkness lurked just around the next bend in life's road. "Father, so much has happened in such a short time that sometimes I feel the world has gone crazy."

When had the fog of anxiety first begun to cloud her normally bright skies? Lucy thought back to her birthday dinner. Laird Cunningham had all but accused Mammy Roxy and Jackson Way of being part of some dark and devious plot. To do what, Lucy had no idea. Escape? Hardly, when they were free to leave anytime they chose. Slaves, including some on neighboring plantations, might use the song "Steal Away" as a signal. Not Mammy. When she sang about the Lord calling her and a trumpet sounding in her soul, she expressed the deep faith she had passed on to her charge in good measure. The words, *I ain't got long to stay here,* reflected her yearning for heaven and the family who had been so cruelly torn from her and Jackson Way long ago.

The seeds of depression planted in Lucy's heart that birthday evening had been temporarily overshadowed by the gift of the lamp pin. Yet they sprouted alarmingly on November 6 when Abraham Lincoln won the presidency of the United States. Consternation sped through Hickory Hill. Talk of Virginia leaving the Union intensified, especially after South Carolina actually seceded. A month later, Alabama, Florida, Georgia, Louisiana, and Mississippi followed suit.

The flames of independence flared even higher when

the six states sent representatives to Montgomery, Alabama in February. There they formed the Confederate States of America and elected Mississippian Jefferson Davis as their president. Two days before Lincoln was inaugurated in March, Texas became part of the Confederacy.

In his inaugural address, Lincoln wisely omitted any mention of threatening immediate force against the South. However, he firmly stated that the Union would stand forever. He would use the nation's full power to hold federal possessions in the South. This infuriated many. Virginia teetered on the edge of secession.

The tenth state to be admitted to the Union was greatly divided on whether to remain with the Union or join the Confederacy. So was Hickory Hill. Secession became such an issue between families and friends that many "done chose up sides and are about to start throwin' rocks at each other," as Jackson Way put it.

Lucy and her father kept their opinions to themselves. "I'm a physician, not a politician," Dr. Luke protested, when pressed by warring factions. "God put me here to patch up folks. He gave me Lucy to help. We have a full-time job, just doing what we're meant to do."

Yet just the night before, the troubled doctor had privately confessed to his daughter, "I don't know how much longer Virginia will remain neutral. We have hotheads on both sides." A somber hue marred his usually cheerful countenance. "It's like the sword of Damocles, suspended over our heads and hanging by a single hair. It won't take much to break the hair and free the sword. I fear what will happen when it comes plunging down."

Lucy suddenly felt cold, even though sunlight streamed in the window as brightly as ever. A long time ago, she'd heard a granny-woman say she felt like something was walking across her grave. Lucy hadn't understood what the woman meant. Now she did. If the sword fell, it could destroy all she held dear.

A few hours later, her worst fears were realized.

Chapter 6

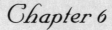

Footsteps in the entryway outside the cozy sitting room where Lucy sat reading took her away from King Arthur's court and into the present. She raised her head and frowned. The steps sounded shambling, not sure and crisp, like Daddy Doc's firm stride. Was something wrong with him?

The door flew open. Lucy jumped to her feet as her father reeled into the room, blond hair awry, face whiter than the sheets and towels Lucy had folded earlier. A tornado of dread swept through her. "What's wrong? Are you sick?"

"Sick at heart." Pain contorted his face and dulled the blue of his eyes to gray. Lucy recognized the look from times she had seen her father give the best of his skills in an attempt to save a life, only to face defeat in the end.

Her father dropped heavily into a chair. He stared straight at Lucy, but she felt he wasn't really seeing her. "Word just came. The Confederate forces have fired on Fort Sumter, the federal military post in the Charleston, South Carolina, harbor."

Lucy felt herself stiffen. "What does it mean?"

A glazed look further dulled his eyes. "War. Misery,

suffering, needless death. North against South. Brother against brother. Friend against friend. God help us all— and forgive the sins that have led to this terrible thing!"

His outburst shocked Lucy to the core. Even in critical situations, she had never heard him speak so. "Why?" she cried. "There must be a way to stop it."

"The time for that is past. It ended with the firing of the first shot."

Horrified by the hopelessness in his voice, a sob rose to Lucy's lips and escaped. She blindly fled to her father, who opened his arms and encircled her. She felt the peace of his embrace—along with something else: his need to receive comfort, not just give it. "God won't allow war to come," she faltered, desperately trying to reassure herself as well as her father but knowing how unconvincing she sounded. "He doesn't want people killing each other."

The arms about her tightened. "No, Lucy. He doesn't. Yet men choose to take control instead of leaving the world in His hands. God gave us agency. When we make terrible choices, He stands aside and lets us suffer the consequences."

"Sometimes He intervenes."

"Yes." Dr. Luke held her away from him and looked down into her wet eyes. "We can pray this will be one of those times." His lips thinned to a straight line. "It's hard enough fighting ignorance and superstition and sickness. If war comes, we will be forced to tend hundreds of victims of man's folly."

"You don't think war will come to Hickory Hill!" Lucy freed herself and slid to her knees in front of his chair. "It can't. It just can't," she brokenly protested. "Our valley is so peaceful." She put her hands over her ears, vainly attempting to silence the imagined sound of cannons, the cries for help from the wounded.

Dr. Luke gently removed her hands and cradled them in his own. "I'm terribly afraid today's action by South Carolina will inflame Virginians to the point of secession," Dr. Luke told her. "The worst thing is, both North and South believe they have a cause worth fighting for, even dying."

"Who cares about causes?" Lucy flared. "We are all part of the same country. How can a cause be important enough to make us go to war against ourselves?" She anxiously searched her father's face for help in understanding the precarious position into which the country she loved had fallen.

"Many wonder the same thing," her father said. Some of the blue returned to his eyes, but none of their usual sparkle. "It is a dangerous thing when both sides believe they are right. That is what's happening now. The North is committed to freeing the slaves and preserving the Union. The South will fight to maintain a way of life begun by those who pioneered and won their lands through suffering and hardship. Only God knows how or when it will end."

He dropped Lucy's hands and stroked her hair. "You need to face the worst. If war comes, as I feel it will, our lives will never be the same." He paused before adding, "Neither will Jere's. If I know Laird Cunningham, and I believe I do, he will move heaven and earth to ensure his son fights for the Confederacy."

"No!" Lucy shrieked. She bounded to her feet and glared down at her father. "If he wants war, *he* should be the one to go fight it, not his son. Jere can't go. I won't let him!" More protective of the man she loved than a wildcat guarding her cubs, Lucy felt herself wave good-bye to lingering childhood.

"How does Jere feel about it?" Dr. Luke asked.

Lucy's defiance crumpled. She would fight Laird Cunningham to the death, but if Jere chose to go, she would be helpless. "I don't know. Oh, Daddy Doc, how can such things be?"

✳

Lucy's poignant cry resounded across the valley and echoed off the distant ridges above Hickory Hill. They grew even louder three days later when Lincoln ordered Union troops to reclaim Fort Sumter. The South saw it as a declaration of war. Soon Arkansas, North Carolina, and Tennessee joined the Confederacy.

So did Virginia, in spite of vehement protests by those in the western counties. Strongly loyal to the Union, they threatened to leave Virginia and become a separate state.* Southern patriots branded them as traitors.

Once Virginia joined the Confederacy, Jere Cunningham's life became a living hell. Laird Cunningham continually harped on the need for Jere to enlist in the "Cause."

"Would to God I weren't desperately needed here," he lamented. "Since I am, you must go in my place."

Jere didn't know what to do. The desire to please his father for once in his life warred with his own convictions. "Or lack of convictions," he told Dr. Luke one day while waiting for Lucy to come downstairs. "I see right and wrong on both sides." He buried his head in his hands. When he raised it, he felt his mouth twist into a grimace. "Our preacher told me it was my duty to serve. He said God would give the South victory over the oppressors. My God isn't Northern *or* Southern. Claiming He is on one

---

*This separation led to the eventual statehood of West Virginia in 1863.

side is simply an excuse to justify war."

"My heart goes out to you," Dr. Luke quietly told him. "I wish I had the answer. Instead, I struggle over my own place of service. I'd like nothing better than to stay right here. I doubt it will be possible." He gripped Jere's hand.

Lucy's quick footsteps on the stairs effectively ended the conversation, but not Jere's dilemma. It worsened one afternoon a few weeks later when his father called him into the drawing room. In the past months, Jere had grown to hate the room that had seen so many quarrels. Every tick of the mantel clock prolonged the battles. Strange. Until now he had never noticed how relentlessly it marked time. Now he groaned. What new torment had Father dreamed up?

Laird Cunningham's latest ploy far exceeded Jere's wildest fears and imaginings. He carefully seated himself in the chair across from the one his son occupied. His colorless eyes gleamed. "I have a proposition for you, Jeremiah." He fitted the tips of his fingers together and made a teepee before aiming a calculating look toward Jere. "Do you still hope to marry the Danielson girl?"

Jere clutched at his frayed temper with all his might. "Yes, I intend to marry *Miss Danielson,* when the time is right for both of us."

"I am ready to withdraw my objections—on one condition."

Jere's heart leaped at the first statement, plummeted with the second. Father never traded unless sure he would best his opponent. "That condition is. . . ?" He marveled that the words could crowd out of his suddenly dry throat.

Another long, searching look probed the depths of

Jere's soul. He had the feeling eternity hung in the balance. Then Laird said, "If you will enlist and serve your country, I will no longer oppose your ill-advised choice of mate. It will not take long for the South to drive the enemy from her lands. I fully expect this ill-conceived impertinence to end long before your birthday in August."

He paused to let his proposition sink in before folding his arms across his chest and tucking his stubborn chin deeper into his high collar. "You will come home having done your God-given duty. You will be twenty-one. The land set aside for you will be ready and waiting. If you present the betrothal ring as planned, Dr. Danielson will insist on his daughter having a year in which to prepare for her marriage. During that time, you will build a fitting home for the woman you intend to wed."

Once long ago, Jere and Ebony had been caught in a hailstorm that pelted them with ice balls the size of walnuts. In the few minutes before they reached shelter, both were bruised and battered. So it was now. Each word bruised Jere's spirit and battered against reason. What a diabolical plan, yet how canny! With his usual unerring instinct, Father had ferreted out Jere's weak spot: Lucy. Now he had made clear that he intended to use it to conquer his rebellious son.

"Well?" The word cracked like a horsewhip.

Jere steadily eyed the father he loved but could not please, no matter how hard he tried. What if he acceded to the lord of the manor's wishes and enlisted? What if he refused? The questions smoldered in his soul, then burst into a raging flame. He had to know the answers, no matter how terrible they might be.

"Speak up, Boy. What's it to be? Will you do as I command?"

Jere took a deep breath, held it, then slowly expelled it. "If I refuse. . . ?"

Rage changed the granite-hard face to an ugly mask. "Should you be half-witted enough to cross me in this, you will henceforth be no son of mine. I will have no part of you. The land earmarked for you will be given to the man Jinny marries." Laird stood and strode to the door on giant steps, turned, and flung back, "You have one week to decide. Seven days from now you will pack and leave Hickory Manor. Either you will take up arms for your country or go wherever you choose, so long as it is out of my sight. I cannot force you to leave Hickory Hill, but I give you fair warning."

He shook a long, bony finger at his son. "If you stay, no neighbor will hire you. I will see to that. If we meet on the street, I shall neither recognize you nor speak." Again he paused, then fired the most significant weapon in his arsenal. "I shall also forbid your mother and Jinny to have anything more to do with you."

White-hot fury brought Jere to his feet. "Only a coward threatens from behind women's skirts." Scorn underlined each word. "Nothing on earth, including you, can keep me from Mother and Jinny. Do you think they will allow it? Lord of the manor you may be; lord of creation you are not." His voice rang in the silent room. If the truth sounded a death knell to reconciliation with Father, so be it.

Laird Cunningham turned apoplectic. "How dare you speak to me like this?" he thundered. "It is a commandment of God that you honor your father.* I myself taught you His precepts."

---

*Exodus 20:12

Jere didn't give an inch. "They also require me to honor my mother. Forsaking her would not show honor." Another accusation poured out. "The Bible also warns, 'Fathers, provoke not your children to anger, lest they be discouraged.' "*

His father remained rigid, yet Jere had the feeling he had suddenly shrunk in stature and grown hollow. Pity welled up in Jere. It softened his voice. "Father, I haven't yet said I won't fight." He ignored the hope flickering in the watching eyes. "I know your offer to set aside your feelings about Lucy was not easy. I thank you for making it. On the other hand, she can't be a pawn. Or a carrot dangled before my nose to make me do your will." He spread his hands wide.

"Don't you see? I have to decide my own course. We are talking about my conscience and my life, Father. Consider. What if you send your only son into battle and he comes home to lie in the family plot? How will you feel?"

Laird straightened his shoulders. The look of a fanatic came into his face. "If that comes to pass, and I pray to God it never shall, I can always be proud I had the courage to do what was right. You have one week to decide." The first hint of emotion he had shown during the entire conversation roughened his voice. "If you cannot serve for the girl's sake or for that of your country, go for your mother and sister. If war reaches Hickory Manor and I am killed, they will not be safe from invaders." He turned on his heel and marched out, closing the door behind him as firmly as he'd closed off any chance of compromise.

Jere could not help respecting his father for the

---

*Colossians 3:21

valiant fight he was making on behalf of what he undeniably believed was right. He walked to the fireplace, cold and empty now, and leaned his head against the mantel. If only Father's passion were directed toward anything but "the Cause"!

The door opened behind him. *Please, God, don't let it be Father,* Jere silently pleaded. *I can't talk with him any longer just now. I must have time to think.*

A rustle of silken skirts brought his head up. He turned. His mother stood at his side. "Jeremiah, you must follow your heart." Her soft lips quivered and the hand below her lace-edged sleeve found its way into her son's. "No matter how high the cost, *you must do what you believe is right.*"

He clutched her fingers, wishing he were a carefree child again, not a man facing the hardest, most important decision of his life. His cry of despair rose to the high drawing room ceiling. "What *is* right? If I only knew!"

Isobel Cunningham mournfully shook her head. The mantel clock continued its merciless ticking. Seconds. Minutes. Hours. Each pushing the troubled son of the house of Cunningham closer to his moment of decision.

Chapter 7

Late in the afternoon of the sixth day following Laird Cunningham's edict, Jere and Lucy rode to the knoll overlooking the peaceful valley they both loved. Dismounting, they stood side by side, united by years of companionship. Hickory Manor lay tranquil in the sunlight. At that moment, the possibility of battle one day marring its serenity seemed unreal.

Long moments passed before Lucy turned to the tall young man who had transferred his blue gaze from the valley to her face. So much love and pain showed in his eyes, she wondered how her heart could go on beating. At last she spoke. "You know what your decision means."

"I know."

She didn't cry out or attempt to sway him. She didn't know if his choice was right or wrong. She only knew the boyishness he had retained in spite of reaching manhood was gone, perhaps forever. She mourned its passing, even while recognizing that the upheaval of their secure world required both Jere and she herself to put aside childish things and become man and woman.

Jere had not told her of his soul struggle and night-long vigils. Lucy had also kept vigil in the sleepless hours, not knowing what to say to God at this momentous time. The night before, she stole from bed in the darkest hour and made a light. She returned to her pillowed nest with her Bible. It fell open to Psalm 119:105—"Thy word is a lamp unto my feet, and a light unto my path." Again she tried to pray, to ask for that light. She felt her petition barely reached the ceiling.

"Please, God, help me," she whispered. After a short while, something Daddy Doc said long ago crept into her troubled mind. Lucy remembered the day as clearly as if it were yesterday. She sat next to her father in the buggy, a small child content to be going on rounds with him. She was curious about the world and God and Daddy Doc's faith in Someone he couldn't see. "Does God hear every prayer? Even the littlest, tiniest one?" she anxiously asked.

"Oh my, yes," her father told her. "He hears all kinds of prayers. Ones we speak, and ones we just think and don't say out loud." Dr. Luke chuckled, a sound as warm as the sunlight on his fair hair. "God hears written-down prayers, too. Many of the songs we sing are really prayers." He began to sing.

"O God, our help in ages past,
    Our hope for years to come,
Our shelter from the stormy blast,
    And our eternal home!"*

Lucy never forgot that special moment, with sunlight on her face and Daddy Doc close beside her. Every re-membrance of his rich voice raised in a hymn of praise,

---

*Isaac Watts (1674–1748)

which she felt surely reached the heavens, set chills playing tag up and down her spine. Now she idly turned the pages of her Bible, reading verses here and there until one Scripture leaped from the page and etched itself into her brain.

"And the Lord answered me, and said, Write the vision, and make it plain. . . ."*

The rest of the sentence blurred. Lucy's heart threatened to burst from her chest. She had prayed for help. Was this God's answer?

She scrambled from bed, heedless of the cool breeze blowing in the open window and fluttering the thin sleeves of her nightgown. She dared not chance disturbing her father, so she crept down the hall guided by pale moonlight streaming in the window near the head of the staircase. For once, Lucy didn't even consider sliding to the entryway below but descended step by cautious step.

A few minutes later, she gathered writing materials and curled up in her favorite chair in the small sitting room, not bothering to close the door. What she planned to do wouldn't rouse her father. A thick book with blank pages lay in her lap, one she had intended to use for recording patient visits. Daddy Doc wouldn't care if she used it for a worthy purpose. After a time of thought, Lucy started writing.

> *Dear God,*
>   *Daddy Doc says songs are written-down prayers, and that You hear every one. I am having a hard time telling You how I feel, so I was just wondering: Will You hear my prayer if I put it in a letter to You?*

---
*Habakkuk 2:2

71

A little while ago, I asked You to help me, and I found the verse about writing. I don't know if it is Your answer, but right now it is so much easier to talk to You on paper. Everything is so confusing. The war. Jere and his father. Even Hickory Hill has changed. At church last Sunday some of the families who have always sat together took seats as far away from each other as possible and scowled across the aisle.

Lucy was so engrossed in her task, she didn't realize she was no longer alone until a slight sound drew her gaze to the open doorway. Her father stood rubbing his eyes in amazement. "I thought I heard a noise. What is Miss Nightingale Danielson doing out of bed in the middle of the night? Doesn't she know my best nurse needs her rest?" He looked at the blank book. Understanding came into his eyes. "A letter to Jere?"

"No. A letter to God." She waited, hoping he would grasp what she couldn't fully explain, even to herself.

"A fine idea, Lucy. I am sure any means that helps us approach our heavenly Father is acceptable to Him. Go on with your letter." Dr. Luke cleared his throat and quietly left the room.

In the wee morning hours, Lucy slipped back to bed, carrying the book. Little did she realize she'd just written the first of many letters to God, letters that would sustain and give her hope in the perilous times ahead.

※

The last six days had also taken their toll on Jere. Keenly aware of his father's marking time, he spent hours alone with Ebony on their favorite knoll. He watched the slaves on the plantation, noting how well-cared-for they were. What would happen should they be freed? Used to others being responsible for their welfare, could they survive if set adrift? Yet Jere's soul rebelled at taking up arms against the Union, even in defense of the only way of life he knew.

He turned to the Scriptures for help and found it in James 1:5, a familiar verse: "If any of you lack wisdom, let him ask of God, that giveth to all men liberally, and upbraideth not; and it shall be given him." Instead of stopping, as he usually did, he read the next verse. "But let him ask in faith, nothing wavering. For he that wavereth is like a wave of the sea driven with the wind and tossed."

The words haunted him. What would tomorrow and all the tomorrows bring? To him, to Lucy, to North and South? He ceased to waver and made his choice.

Only God could know the outcome, but Jere shuddered just thinking about it.

Now he laid his arm across Lucy's slim shoulders. "It means separation," he quietly told her. "No one can predict for how long." His heart quelled at the thought. How could he stand days and months apart from the bright-haired lass he loved more than anything in the world except God? "I'll come back, Lucy."

"I know." She turned from the valley and looked into his eyes. "I'll be here waiting." Her voice broke.

Jere gathered her into his arms and bent his head. How ironic! Their first mutual kiss—bittersweet with memories and fear of the future—was also good-bye. Lucy clung to him for a moment, then freed herself and stumbled to her horse.

They silently rode from their meeting place to Hickory Hill, Lucy's promise warm between them. The tiny lamp pin glinted on the collar of her blouse. Neither spoke when Jere wheeled Ebony in front of her home and goaded him into a dead run. Yet if he lived to be a hundred, he'd never forget his last blurred sight of her. Head high, although Jere knew her heart was breaking, Lucy flung one hand toward the sky in a valiant gesture of farewell. Only the knowledge that he had chosen the one course open to him kept Jere from turning back.

❋

Supper at the Cunninghams' that night was a miserable affair. Jinny poked at her food until Laird ordered, "Either eat it or let the servants take it away."

Jere longed to defend his sister but refrained. Tension in the dining room was already thick enough to slice. With a reassuring glance for his drooping sister and a prayer for the coming interview, Jere said, "I'm finished, as well."

His father threw down his linen napkin and rose. "Then I suggest we excuse ourselves from the ladies and repair to the drawing room. Tomorrow is the seventh day, as I'm sure you recall."

Jere searched the stern face for any sign of weakening. There was none. He sighed, stood, and opened the fray. "Mother, Jinny, I want you to be present."

Laird's eyes darkened. "As you wish." He led the way to the scene of so many recent battles between father and son. Isobel and Jinny sat side by side on a settee. Laird seated himself in his usual chair. After a moment's hesitation, Jere took the one opposite. He preferred to stand, but it would not be permitted. Doing so would offer too much advantage over his opponent. Regret went through him. And anger. Why must Father be considered an enemy? Jere jerked back to the present. Now was no time to ponder long-held resentments and wrongs.

Every tick of the clock beat into his brain. "Sir, I ask

you to do me the courtesy of hearing me out before speaking." His father folded his arms across his chest and nodded, but the grim set of his jaw warned that storms lay ahead.

With another quick prayer for help, the impassioned feelings built through six long days of inward strife rolled out. "You have ordered me to fight for my country. This I am prepared to do. I will live up to the letter of the law in your command, but not the spirit." Jere saw the quick relief that sprang to his father's watching eyes, then died aborning.

"The word 'country' means more than just the South to me. America is my homeland—a nation forged by all those who gave their lives to settle it. How can I fight men whose ancestors died the first hard year at Plymouth? Or at Valley Forge?" He paused for breath, then rushed on. "Jesus said, 'Every kingdom divided against itself is brought to desolation; and every city or house divided against itself shall not stand.'* Father, if this country is split in two, it shall surely fall, perhaps to foreign powers. I cannot be part of its destruction."

Slow understanding crept into Laird Cunningham's stone gray eyes. His face congealed. "You, my only son, intend to turn traitor and join the Yankees? To arm yourself and perhaps kill friends and kin, as others are doing?" A hint of froth came to his lips. "*Would to God I had never lived to see this day!*"

Jere leaped to his feet and forestalled the tirade he knew would come. "Never! I shall join Northern forces with the stipulation I shall not be forced to bear arms. Thanks to Dr. Luke and Lucy, I know the rudiments of

---

*Matthew 12:25

medicine. I can bind up wounds and care for the injured. I am strong and can carry litters. By serving my country this way, I will be saving life, not taking it."

Laird Cunningham stood. "Do you honestly think you will be allowed to play war under your own terms?" Scorn dripped from every word. "What a fool! The first time you refuse to carry a weapon *and to use it against your own,* you will be court-martialed. Or shot without the formality of a court-martial."

Jere didn't budge. "Were I to fight for the Confederacy, I'm sure that would be true. However, I am voluntarily enlisting under the explicit understanding I will not bear arms. I will also demand and receive a written, signed statement to that effect from a commander in charge. Otherwise, I shall not enlist. Conscientious objectors have been exempted to noncombatant positions since Colonial times, when men were forced to serve in their colony's militia."

"Are you such a dunce that you aren't aware you must belong to some pacifist religious group to claim such status?" Laird taunted.

Jere deliberately kept his voice steady. "Under normal circumstances, yes. In my case, no. I cannot and will not break God's commandment not to kill."

His father squared his shoulders. "Conscientious objectors. They are even worse than Yankees! Cowards, all of them, unwilling to fight like other men. . . ."

Isobel Cunningham rose with a rustle of skirts. Her face was whiter than her delicate gown. "Be still!" she commanded in a voice like low, rolling thunder. "You shall not say such things in my presence. No man willing to carry the wounded from the front lines of battle is a coward! Far from it. It takes more courage to go armed with nothing save the protection of Almighty God, than equipped with weapons." Twin spots of red burned in her cheeks like circles of paint on a stark white ground.

"Mr. Cunningham, I wish to speak with you alone and at once. Virginia, Jeremiah, you may be excused."

Brother and sister somehow made it out of the room. Jere regained his wits enough to say, "Father may forbid contact with me once I leave the house. Tell Mother I will send word through the blacksmith." He embraced Jinny. "Hurry upstairs and don't come down in the morning. I couldn't bear it."

"All right." She kissed his cheek, leaving a wide wet streak, then fled.

Jere never knew what his mother said to the lord of the manor. Only Isobel appeared the next morning to wish her son Godspeed. But before nightfall, the valley grapevine had reached into every hut and mansion with its shocking news: Jeremiah Cunningham had ridden away to join the Union army.

Chapter 8

Lucy Danielson did not receive an engagement ring on her sixteenth birthday. Caught in the upheaval of the world she had taken for granted, the significance of the day she had looked forward to dwindled. How could she be happy with Jere far away?

It was all Lucy could do to poke down Mammy Roxy's delectable fried chicken and luscious cake. She pasted on the best smile she could manage for the sake of Daddy Doc, Mammy, and Jackson Way, whose anxious gazes betrayed their deep concern for her. Yet all the while, she missed Jere Cunningham so badly she wanted to cry.

Lucy had received a few scrawled letters from Jere. Knowing him as she did, she saw beyond the forced cheerfulness to his turmoil of soul, his rebellion against the conflict rending country and families. Lucy filled her answers with hope that the fighting would soon end, although Daddy Doc warned her it wouldn't happen. Both sides had too much at stake to allow a quick end to the war that should never have begun.

After supper, Lucy and her father settled down in their cozy room. A bright fire crackled and cast an orange glow on the walls. Peace slowly stole into the troubled girl's heart. The next moment, a quick look into her father's grave face made her sigh. "What is it?" she asked.

Dr. Luke didn't act surprised at her perception. He leaned forward and fixed his steady gaze on his daughter's face. "I've fought it for weeks, but now I know what I must do, Lucy. I have no choice but to leave Hickory Hill and serve at the front." His somber face showed the struggle he had gone through. "I also feel I should not go alone."

Lucy sat up straight, heart pounding. "You mean. . . ?"

"I believe you will be safer with me at the front than if I were to leave you here. God knows I can make use of your willing hands and heart." A twisted smile came to his lips. "This is your chance, Miss Nightingale Danielson. Will you go serve with your father and help him patch up the wounded? It won't be easy."

"I will," Lucy vowed. She slipped from her chair and knelt beside him.

Dr. Luke's strong hand rested on her shining head. "There's a catch. You are far too young and lovely to be a regular nurse. You must dress as a boy." He tugged at a curl. "Are you willing to sacrifice your beautiful hair?"

Lucy blinked hard and she sprang to her feet. "Do you think I'd let any silly curls keep me from serving, when Jer—that is, others—are giving up everything?" she fiercely demanded. "I'll have Mammy cut my hair tomorrow." She laughed. "It will hurt her more than it will me!"

Lucy predicted wisely. Roxy was scandalized when Dr. Luke told her what he planned. She threw her hands into the air and exclaimed, "You're takin' my chile off to the *war?* Lord have mercy on us all!" She sniffled with every snip of the scissors and bathed her charge's shorn head with her tears.

A few days later, Dr. Luke and Lucy rode away in their well-equipped buggy, leaving their loyal servants to look after things. Dr. Luke's parting orders were, "If you are ever in danger, don't try to protect the property. You're far more important to us than the house or even my offices."

Lucy waved until they reached a bend in the road, then set her face forward. How long would it be before they returned? Weeks? Months? *Years?* her heart questioned. For one traitorous moment she wanted to stop the buggy and go back. Plenty of folks in Hickory Hill needed their skills. Why should they leave their own people to the uncertain ministrations of the retired doctor who had reluctantly agreed to carry on while the Danielsons were gone?

Daddy Doc evidently sensed her hesitation, for he said, "It isn't too late for you to turn back, Lucy. I can make arrangements for you to leave Virginia and stay with friends where there is little likelihood of fighting."

"Would you go with me?" she burst out, ashamed, but knowing she must ask.

He shook his head. "No. Our heavenly Father has called me to serve according to His will. I can do nothing less than obey Him."

A wave of love drowned Lucy's fears. She would not desert Daddy Doc. " 'Entreat me not to leave thee,' " she shakily quoted, " 'or to return from following after thee: for whither thou goest, I will go. . . .' "*

One hand left the reins and patted Lucy's hand. "Thank you, my darling." Dr. Luke lightened the emotion-charged moment by adding, "We have to decide what to call you. I don't know any boys named Lucy. Hmmm. We're Danielson and Danielson. I'll call you by our last name."

---

*Ruth 1:16

"All right." Lucy removed the wide-brimmed hat that shaded her eyes and let the cool late-fall air riffle her short hair. New name. New haircut. New life. The future was irrevocably sealed. She would look back no more. She bounced on the buggy seat, some of her naturally high spirits returning. "All my life I've wanted to help make a difference," she confided to her father. "Now I will have the chance." She shivered. "I only hope I can meet the test."

"You can and will," he reassured. "God will give us strength to accomplish whatever tasks we face and help us keep on giving our best long after we feel we can do no more."

✹

Dr. Luke's words stayed with Lucy. She clung to them, as the Southern field hospital unit she and her father had joined followed the sounds of battle across the Virginia landscape. Lucy sometimes felt if she had to watch the tents come down one more time, then wearily crawl into the Danielson buggy and relocate closer to the ever-shifting front, she would scream.

She never did, although the excellent training she had received from Daddy Doc a lifetime earlier hadn't prepared her for the ravages of war. Many times Lucy was sickened by what she was called on to do. She often responded to her father's quiet, "Danielson, I need you" purely from habit. Yet again and again, God provided the strength to keep on, to care for the wounded and comfort the dying.

Had Florence Nightingale felt the way Lucy did when she made her nightly rounds with her dim lamp? Powerless to stem the tide of injured but glad for the solace she could offer? The thought brought consolation and a renewed determination to give her best to men and boys, some no older than she. She faithfully followed her father's orders, and those given by Mary, the crusty, gray-haired nurse who had automatically assumed command over the newcomer when the Danielsons arrived at the front.

Months later, Lucy wiped sweat from her forehead and stumbled to her blanketed cot. She had just finished assisting Daddy Doc and Mary with a nasty piece of surgery, one a less-skilled surgeon would never have attempted. Because of the three dedicated workers, a young soldier's life had been saved.

For what purpose, God? Lucy wrote in her journal later that night. *We dress their wounds, set their broken limbs, patch them up, and send them back into battle. The boy we saved today was brought in a few weeks ago. We did our best, then and now. Others we care for don't return. Is there really any use in saving lives that will only be lost in the end? I secretly rejoice when those we care for are disabled enough to be sent home, at least for a time. There is always a chance the war will end before they are healed enough to be able to fight again.*

Lucy slowly closed her journal. Some of her greatest help came from two sources: her letters to God and the fact that she saw Jere Cunningham's face superimposed on every suffering Confederate or Yankee soldier she treated. One night, when she was so weary she could barely keep her eyes open, Lucy fancied she saw the face of Christ looking at her from a nearby cot, waiting His turn for the help she could give. Daddy Doc wept when she shared the experience, and he reminded her that all they did for those in their care was also done for Jesus.

Somewhere in the second—or was it the third?—year of the war that Lucy felt had begun an eternity earlier, the tired nurse lost track of what day or week it was. Hickory Hill had receded into the mists of the past, real only when rare news came. Jinny Cunningham wrote that her father had sent her and her mother north to keep them safe from possible danger. She thought it hypocritical of him to seek the North's protection for his family while condemning the North for the war.

Jere's blacksmith friend later sent word that Hickory Manor had been stripped by the Billy Yanks, although the mansion itself still stood. No one knew what had become of Laird Cunningham. The blacksmith added that Hickory Hill had so far escaped invasion. Roxy and Jackson Way were keeping the Danielson home in such a constant condition of readiness, one would think they expected Dr. Luke and Lucy home any minute.

The news about the Cunninghams saddened Lucy, but some of her old grin returned when she told her father the part about Mammy and Jackson Way. His sudden smile brightened Lucy's day.

The war ground on. Both North and South instituted a draft system. Once enthusiasm for the war faded, volunteer enlistments had dramatically decreased. Persons and places were in the news. Northern generals Ulysses Grant and William Sherman. Southern counterparts Robert E. Lee and Stonewall Jackson. Chilling tales of battles ran rampant. Bull Run, also known as Manassas. Shiloh. The gory battle of Antietam. Fredericksburg and Chancellorsville. Gettysburg. A never-ending stream of wounded and dying poured into the Danielsons' care.

Other news trickled to the front. Lucy and Dr. Luke laughed when hearing the qualifications from a circular: "No woman under thirty years need apply to serve in government hospitals. All nurses are required to be very plain-looking women. Their dresses must be brown or black, with no bows, no curls or jewelry, and no hoop skirts."

"Wonder what the recruiter would think of you?" the good doctor teased.

Lucy ruefully looked at her worn clothing. "Not much, I'm afraid." She turned toward him, noting the fatigue in his face, the early streaks of gray in his hair. The sparkle in his fine eyes remained undimmed, however. She sighed in relief. As long as Daddy Doc could keep going, so could she.

Women were also making their mark. Mary ("Mother") Bickerdyke went to the front wearing a calico dress, heavy boots, and sunbonnet. According to rumor, when she was challenged about not having an official commission, she retorted, "I have received my authority from the Lord God Almighty." Officials dared not dispute her claim.

Florence Nightingale remained Lucy's heroine. After serving in Crimea, Miss Nightingale had become a world authority on the scientific care of the sick. The United States sought her advice on setting up military hospitals.

Another selfless woman offered further inspiration to Lucy. Clara Barton, also without an official commission, began carrying supplies to the front and nursing the wounded on the battlefields soon after the war started. Her work gained national attention and appreciation. She was given the title *Angel of the Battlefield*. Garbed in a plain skirt and jacket, she was determined to serve but struggled. She was quoted as saying she had contended long and hard with her conscience. The appalling fact that she was a woman whispered in one ear; the groans of those who needed her thundered in the other.

Lucy understood her feelings. If Mammy could see her "honeychile" in the primitive surroundings where need overcame maidenly modesty, she would roll her eyes and throw her apron over her head!

⌘

Jere's letters became more despondent and less frequent. He no longer attempted to hide his true feelings. One letter almost broke Lucy's heart.

> *Tonight some of the Johnny Rebs crossed the lines after the fighting ended for the day. We gathered around our campfires. Some swapped tobacco and played cards. Others simply talked. Of home. Of families. There was little speculation about when the war might end or the war itself.*
>
> *I thought I would die of pain when they left. Tomorrow, or the next day, I may be called on to bind up the wounds or help set the shattered bones of some of those here tonight. My countrymen, whose only desire is for this to be over so they can go home. Oh, Lord, how long?*

Jere's cry of despair echoed in Lucy's heart. She kissed the single page and tucked it into her journal next to his previous letters, worn thin from handling. How thick her journal had become. How revealing. Brief notes about the war and the Danielsons' place in it snuggled among rare bits of humor and Lucy's precious letters to God. Together they painted a painfully accurate picture of life since she left Hickory Hill.

Lucy clutched her journal, knowing she would keep it long after the war ended. Someday she would pass it on to future generations. God forbid any of them would face experiences similar to her own! If they did, perhaps the precious journal would offer the same strength to them as it had to her.

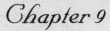

Chapter 9

It was Jere's last letter. Plagued by fear, Lucy continued to write to him. Was Jere dead, victim of a bullet fired by a Johnny Reb with whom he had spent the evening? Struck down by a Billy Yank's stray shot?

The thought terrified Lucy more than the war raging around her. She spent every free moment in prayer. She searched the Scriptures and clung to the Twenty-third Psalm, receiving comfort each time she quoted it to those in her care.

The fourth verse, "Yea, though I walk through the valley of the shadow of death, I will fear no evil: for thou art with me; thy rod and thy staff they comfort me," took on special meaning. The shadow of death hung low. Yet Lucy knew God was still in control. His rod, a shepherd's cudgel, was stout enough to drive off enemies; His staff, far-reaching enough to pull His children back from danger. No harm could befall them unless God permitted it.

Lucy shared her deepening faith one evening when she and Daddy Doc had a few minutes free. "Knowing God really is in control changes everything," she said. "That's what keeps you going, isn't it?"

Dr. Luke gathered her in his arms and held her close.

Hot tears fell on the kerchief that kept Lucy's curly hair out of her eyes. She had discarded her disguise soon after reaching the front and proving herself so invaluable, no one, not even Mary, protested her presence. She regretted abandoning the more practical male attire but soon discovered the wounded often appreciated a woman's presence, even one clad in simple dark dresses with white collars and cuffs.

"No man ever had a better daughter," Dr. Luke said hoarsely. "I am proud of you. I know God must be, too." He released her and stumbled away.

Lucy watched him go with brimming eyes. It was the first time she had seen him shed tears. Her work-worn fingers stole to her collar and the tiny lamp pin that adorned it. She needed no mirror to picture its glow, bright through constant touching. It warmed her fingers and her soul.

Just like the service we give for Christ's sake, her heart whispered. Tears gave way to peace, and that night Lucy slept deeply. It was well, for the rest and peace fortified her for what was yet to come.

A few days later, she received a long-delayed message from the Hickory Hill blacksmith. Jeremiah Cunningham was officially listed as missing in action.

A time of waiting began. A time of "hanging onto God's coattails for dear life," as Lucy wrote in her journal. A time of losing her life for the sake of others and finding it again; of sensing that Someone walked beside her. A time of predictions that the war must soon end. The Union army supposedly had grown to more than a million soldiers, five times the number of Confederate soldiers. Rumor claimed that a full 10 percent of those on both sides had deserted. Sickened of fighting, they simply laid down their arms and started their long journeys home.

A bedraggled letter from Jinny Cunningham brought both hope and fresh concern. Jere and several comrades had been captured and sent to a prison camp. Some had been wounded, but Jere had miraculously escaped injury.

Lucy saw her father's worried look. Survival in the pest-ridden camps was as precarious as on the battlefield. "Jere has something in his favor," Dr. Luke comforted. "Prison camps can always use those with medical knowledge." He smiled. "At least you know where he is. Now you can write to him."

"Yes. Except Jinny's letter is dated weeks ago." Still, hope fluttered in Lucy's heart like a moth dancing in the wind that night when she wrote her letter. It overflowed with joy for Jere being alive. Lucy forced back sleep and didn't stop writing until her lamp dimmed, sputtered, and went out. Her last waking act was to smile and touch her own lamp, carefully pinned to her high nightgown collar.

✳

Jere Cunningham slowly pulled a worn blanket over a dead soldier's face, one of a half-dozen lads in their teens who had died that week. Confederate gray or Union blue, the same red blood spilled on the battlefields and stained the nation.

What felt like an eternity earlier, Jere and his friends had been captured in a surprise attack. Jere cocked an eyebrow. In the time it took to reach the Southern prison camp, at least he'd be free from the stench of powder and death.

Unfortunately, the long, jolting ride also provided time for Jere to relive the past. It unrolled like a scroll in his mind. How sure of himself he had been that final morning at Hickory Manor. How cocky to think he could dictate to the Union army! Except for the grace of God and a Northern surgeon. . .

Jere grinned. He and Ebony had headed straight for the closest Union encampment. In accordance with Jere's well-laid plan, they were captured. "I came to enlist," Jere said. "Take me to your commanding officer."

The patrol who had discovered him gaped. Their leader sneered. "Count on it." He led the way, with Jere sandwiched between him and his men.

Once in camp, Jere stepped from the saddle. A grizzled sergeant approached him after a rumbling exchange with the patrol. "You want to enlist, you hightail it to the other side of the war, Sonny." He cursed.

"No, Sir," Jere said in a loud voice. "My conscience doesn't permit me to bear arms for either side. I won't take life, but I can help save it. I know basic medicine and can serve as a litter bearer or surgeon's assistant."

"Just what might your name be?" the sergeant demanded in icy tones.

Jere stifled the perverse desire to retort, "It might be Tom Thumb or Jeremiah Marcus, Jerabone, Markabone, Napoleon Bonaparte Cunningham, but it ain't."

He disciplined a grin. The doughty sergeant was no good-natured schoolmaster with whom to trifle. "Jeremiah Cunningham. Hickory Hill, Virginia."

"Well, Mr. Jeremiah Cunningham, what makes you think the Union army can be told what to do by a Johnny Reb?" the sergeant barked.

"If I were a rebel I wouldn't be here."

Mistrust sprang into the pale eyes. "You would if you were a spy." He spat. "I'm betting that's what you are."

"I am no spy." Jere raised his voice until it rang throughout the encampment. "I demand to see your commanding officer. *Now.*"

Pitting belligerence against belligerence followed by a

silent prayer had paid off. A camp doctor clad in blood-stained clothing erupted from a nearby tent. He had obviously heard the altercation. "For the love of God," he yelled, "if this man has medical skill, I don't care if he's Southern or purple! I'll take full responsibility for him!" He gripped Jere's shoulder and unceremoniously shoved him into the commanding officer's tent.

Gimlet eyes must have seen Jere's sincerity. A half hour later, he was given an ironclad, special-consideration contract with the Union army.

Heartaches and horrors followed, tempered by joy over saved lives. The thought of Lucy facing the same situations gripped Jere's heart and gave him strength. Days and months limped into a blur of years. The loss of Ebony to a covetous officer hit Jere hard. He couldn't speak of it, even to Lucy, whose letters he read until they fell apart at the creases. He memorized what his weary brain could retain, preparing for a time when no letters came.

Now Jere bowed his head, wondering, as he had done the fateful day he was captured: Could even the Almighty salvage anything good from the carnage? He pondered the question until one day a startling thought came. Wasn't his being in the prison camp proof God cared for the sick and dying? Cared enough to send Jeremiah, "appointed by Jehovah," to give soul comfort, even when the lack of medicine and supplies hampered proper physical care?

The conviction revitalized him. He began to share his faith with all who would listen. "God loves us so much He sent Jesus to die in our place," he stated. Truth rang in every word. "If we accept God's gift and invite Jesus into our hearts, our souls will never die." Jere threw his head back and laughed. Laughed at the squalor, the privation, the misery. "Men, *we will never have to fight again.*

We will live in heaven in peace. Forever."

Some responded to the sheer force of Jere's belief. Conditions in the prison camp worsened, but a powerful new influence was at work. No walls could keep out the hope of the gospel of Christ when preached by a man who knew and loved his God. Was it for this Jere had ridden away on his faithful horse, Ebony? Could this be the good God had foreseen during all Jere's terrible arguments with Father, the agonizing years of war, his separation from family and Lucy?

Jere felt reborn. Like a child who discovers a bright new world outside his doorstep, his first thought was: *I must go tell my father.* He could not. Shackled by duty, he pushed himself even harder to relieve suffering. One day he collapsed, victim of the unspeakable conditions. He didn't know or care that General Robert E. Lee formally surrendered to General Grant at Appomattox on April 9, 1865. Five days later, the world reeled from the news of President Lincoln's assassination. Jere's world reeled with fever, so high and debilitating, the grave-faced doctor who finally came shook his head and moved on. Jere didn't know how or when he was removed from the prison camp to an overflowing hospital that offered a shade better care than the camp.

Deep inside his tortured body, a spirit made strong by trials refused to give up. Jere slowly began to rally. At last he opened his eyes and stared at the unfamiliar ceiling, then dropped into a natural sleep. He awakened to find a man at his bedside. Jere recoiled, certain he had lost his sanity and was seeing ghosts.

The man knelt by his bed and took Jere's wasted hands in his. A voice Jere had never forgotten spoke in a tone he'd never before heard. "Jeremiah. Son. God knows you have good reason, but please, don't turn away from me!"

You? Here? It was too much to comprehend. Weakened by all he'd gone through, Jere bowed his head. The dam that had withstood coldness and injustice broke. A flood came, carrying away the debris of bitterness.

Later, he learned his father's story. When the invaders neared Hickory Manor, Laird took refuge in a large hickory tree. He watched his home being stripped of all but the family silver, previously buried. A former slave, now wearing Union blue, shouted, "We'll show old man Cunningham. Burn the house!"

"Hold it!" a grizzled sergeant had barked from below Laird's perch. "There's a surgeon's assistant at my former company named Cunningham. He's from around here. Good man. Saved a lot of Yankee lives. March on!"

Jere gasped, but his father continued. The enemy rode away. In the dead of night, Laird dug up as much of the family silver as he could carry. He made his way to Boston. Isobel and Jinny had just learned of Jere's whereabouts. "I spent weeks trying to obtain your release," he brokenly said. "Now the war is over. God has forgiven this stubborn Scotsman. So have Isobel and Jinny. Can you?"

"I forgave you the moment I realized God brought good from our conflict."

Laird smiled. "As soon as you get well, we'll go home. If the government confiscates Hickory Manor, as it may, so be it. We'll start over." A twinkle brightened his gray eyes. "With a new redheaded member of the family."

❋

The war was over, but nineteen-year-old Lucy's battle raged on. Where was Jere? Her letters to the prison camp had come back unopened.

After the Danielsons' last patient was gone, they packed the buggy and left for home. Lucy dreaded going. Would they find desolation, ruin, a town ravaged by war like the ones they passed? Finally realizing that no more wounded and dying pleaded for her help, Lucy closed her eyes and asked for strength before they reached the village.

"Wake up, Lucy. Look. Oh, Lucy, look!" Dr. Luke's voice broke.

She opened her eyes and stared toward Hickory Hill. It had been spared and lay peaceful in the sunlight. They reached the Danielson home. The fragrance of roses and beeswax greeted Lucy when she rushed into the entry hall. "Mammy?" she screamed. "Jackson Way?"

"Honeychile, is that *you?*" Roxy stepped into the hall and clasped Lucy to her white-aproned bosom. "The Lord be praised!" she shouted. "Your mammy was afeared she'd never see her chile again!"

"I'm home, Mammy." Blinding tears choked off Lucy's words.

She heard steps behind her, then a laughing voice said, "My name is Jeremiah Marcus, Jerabone, Markabone— oh, hang it all, Lucy, the fighting's over, with Father as well as the country. When will you marry me?"

She tore herself free from Mammy's arms and whirled. The man she loved stood just inside the doorway. She searched his face. Laughter couldn't hide how he had aged, but the love in his blue eyes shone steady and true.

Lucy slowly removed the lamp pin from her collar. She pinned it on his ragged shirt. "Soon, Jere," she whispered. "Very soon."

COLLEEN L. REECE

Colleen, born in a small, western Washington logging town, describes herself as "an ordinary person with an extraordinary God." As a child learning to read beneath the rays of a kerosene lamp, she dreamed of someday making a difference with her writing. Yet she never dreamed she would one day see 120 of her "Books You Can Trust" (motto) in print; more than three million copies sold.

Several of Colleen's earlier inspirational titles have been reissued in Large Print Library Editions. She is deeply grateful for the many new readers who will be exposed to the message of God's love woven into her stories. In addition to writing, Colleen teaches and encourages at conferences and through mentoring friendships. She loves to travel, and is always on the lookout for fresh, new story settings, but continues to live just a few hours' drive from her beloved hometown.

Home Fires Burning

by JoAnn A. Grote

*And the bow shall be in the cloud; and I will look upon it,
that I may remember the everlasting covenant between God
and every living creature of all flesh that is upon the earth.*
GENESIS 9:16

Keep the Home-fires burning,
    While your hearts are yearning,
Though your lads be far away
    They dream of home;
There's a silver lining
    Through the dark cloud shining,
Turn the dark cloud inside out
    Till the boys come home.
              —From *Keep the Home-Fires Burning,*
              by Lena Guilbert Ford, 1915

Author's Note

H*ome Fires Burning* is set at the World War I military hospital at Fort Snelling in Minnesota. For years before the war, the Red Cross had kept a roster for the surgeon general of qualified nurses who agreed to work for the United States military in times of emergency. Women responded wholeheartedly to the United States' need for nurses in World War I. In March 1917, just before the United States entered the war, 403 nurses were on active duty. On Armistice Day, November 11, 1918, 21,480 women were members of the Army Nurse Corps.

No nurses were killed by enemy fire in the war. Even so, the first United States war casualties were two nurses. The Base Hospital Number 12 unit was aboard the SS *Mongolia* on its way to Europe in April 1917, when one of the ship's guns misfired, killing the two nurses and wounding a third.

Most Army Corps nurses who died in World War I were victims of the epidemic of influenza commonly called the Spanish flu. Almost all of the 102 nurses the surgeon general reported as dying overseas during the war were killed by the flu. One hundred twenty-seven

Army Corps nurses died of the Spanish flu while serving in home-front military hospitals.

More American servicemen also were killed by the flu than by the enemy in World War I. The disease killed more than 500,000 American civilians and servicemen, more Americans than died in all the wars of the twentieth century.

Following the war, home-front military hospitals centered their efforts on helping wounded servicemen rebuild their lives. When a Red Cross nurse joined the Army Nurse Corps, she was technically no longer a Red Cross nurse but a member of the military. In many people's minds, the Red Cross was so interwoven with the Army Nurse Corps that they were one organization. Captain C. Arthur McLeod praised the work of nurses in World War I with these words: "We breathe a prayer of thankfulness for her presence among us—bend down in fullest veneration of her marvelous work and challenge the race to find her equal. ATTENTION!!! The world! Salute the noblest creation of the boundless love of God for His creatures, perfect and imperfect—the Red Cross Nurse."

JoAnn

Prologue

October 14, 1918, early morning
Fort Snelling, Minnesota

P*ray."* Glorie Cunningham's eyelids flew open. She stared into the dark of the nurses' quarters and held her breath, listening. There was no sound but the even breathing of the nurse in the next bed and the clock on the bedside table.

Had the voice been part of her dream? Unlikely. In the dream she and her brother Fred were playing together as children.

Fred. The fog of sleep evaporated from her mind. Fear gripped her, squeezing her heart. Fred was in France, on the western front. She shut her eyes tight against images of inhumane conditions on the battlefields and the terror of attack.

I should be there, not serving on the home front. From the time America joined the war it had been her desire to nurse at the front, as her Grandmother Lucy Cunningham had done in the War between the States.

Pray. Glorie prayed—prayed for Fred and the men who fought with him, and the doctors and nurses who cared for the wounded. She prayed until she fell again into a restless sleep, exhausted from her twenty-hour shift caring for soldiers on the home front who were battling the Spanish flu.

October 14, 1918
France

"Busy evening, huh?"

"I'll say," Johan Baker yelled in response to the soldier beside him.

The enemy had kept a steady barrage of fire directed at the artillery. The cold and rain and mud and worn-out horses didn't help the Americans, who were trying to get shells to the large-gun positions. On top of that, today the division experienced some of the heaviest fighting since its arrival in France, and that was saying a lot for the tough Rainbow Division.

A screeching shell sent the two soldiers heading pell-mell toward a trench, slipping and sliding in the mud. Johan dove into the hole headfirst. He rolled over. Where was the soldier he'd just spoken to? Johan popped his head up over the edge of the trench. Twenty yards away, on the edge of the makeshift road, the shell burst. *P–bl–uup.* The typical silly little sound didn't do justice to the toxic cloud of gas that rolled out.

He shoved off his tin helmet, forced his gas mask over his face, and slammed his helmet back on, all the time scanning the slope. Where *was* that man? A shell bursting in the distance outlined the soldier, stuck in mud up to his knees and not wearing his mask.

Johan slithered out of the trench and over to the man.

He grabbed the soldier's gas mask. The soldier pointed to a puncture. Johan's chest deflated. The mask was useless. The cloud would reach them any second. There wasn't time to get his companion out of the mud and find another mask.

Frustration ripped through him. He tore off his own mask and started pulling it over the man's head. "No!" The man struggled against it.

Johan let go, grabbed the soldier's damaged mask, and rolled away from him. He stuck a handkerchief in the puncture. It wouldn't help much, but it might give him a minute or two. The cloud was on them. *Too late*. The words blazed through his mind as he tugged the mask over his face. He slid into the trench and looked back. Thank God, the soldier had put on the good mask.

Chapter 1

The whistle warned him.

Johan dove into a nearby shell hole. He pressed his body against the mud wall, making himself as small a target as possible. *Little good it'll do if that bomb has my name on it.* He grabbed the gas mask attached to his belt. The hose was torn. Despair washed over him. He shoved his face between his arms until he felt the cold earth against his cheek, could almost taste the mud.

Someone shook him. He shoved the hand away from his shoulder.

"It's all right. Nothing can hurt you anymore." The soft voice filtered through the explosions and screams of battle. The gory scene disintegrated. Johan opened his eyes. His mind registered the fact that he'd been dreaming, but his heart still thumped hard and fast against his ribs. That battle was a dream, but the battle that landed him here at Fort Snelling had been real. The knowledge prevented relief on wakening.

Two identical women in their early twenties stood beside his bed. Identical red hair swept neatly back from identical freckled faces. Two pair of identical green eyes stared at him in concern and sympathy. Either the dream continued or he was seeing double.

He rubbed his eyes with his thumb and index finger, then looked again. The women were still there, both dressed in white, one wearing a small nurse's hat.

The woman beneath the hat smiled. "Your vision is fine, Lieutenant Baker. There are two of us. I'm Nurse Gloria Cunningham. This is my twin sister, Grace Holt."

He recognized the gentle voice that had drawn him from the dream.

Grace held up her left hand and wiggled her red-tipped fingers. A diamond flashed, reflecting the sudden amusement in her eyes. "Mrs. Daniel Holt."

Johan grinned. "For a moment I thought the war left me with double vision. Seeing two of every beautiful woman wouldn't be a bad way to go through life." As usual, his voice, the legacy of mustard gas, came out as though he was a frog with laryngitis.

Grace smiled and shook a finger at his not-so-subtle flattery.

The edges of Nurse Cunningham's lips hinted at a smile. She held up a white pitcher. "Would some ice water taste good, Lieutenant?"

He nodded. Clear, cold water still seemed a luxury. In France there'd never been enough to drink, or bathe in, or for the field hospitals' needs. Filthy water, on the other hand, was everywhere, especially in the trenches.

Johan's fingers met the nurse's lightly when he took the glass. The simple touch sent a jolt of awareness through him. He'd been too ill from the gassing to pay the nurses in France much attention. *Why, I haven't held a woman's hand since leaving for France,* he realized.

That was not the place to allow his thoughts to travel. Half the hospitalized doughboys fell for their nurses. He wasn't going to be one of them.

The water felt good on his throat. His voice had returned only a few days ago, and he'd talked too much today. When he indulged in speaking, he paid for it with searing pain. But who could refrain from cheering a mite when the Allies were finally victorious?

His gaze followed Nurse Cunningham as she turned her attention to the soldier in the next bed. He glanced up at Grace. "Twin nurses; that's unusual."

"I'm not a nurse." Grace waved her hand toward her sister's back. "Glorie's the Florence Nightingale. I'm but a humble Red Cross volunteer." She lowered her lashes.

Her feigned modesty brought a chuckle from Johan. A Red Cross girl. He should have recognized the high-buttoned white dress, but she wasn't hiding that fabulous red hair she shared with her sister beneath the traditional Red Cross headpiece.

The captain in the next bed peered around the nurse. "A Red Cross girl brought us lemonade in the middle of a battle. You'd have thought we were on the beach at Cape Cod, for all the notice she gave the bombs and bullets. Red Cross girls are okay in my book."

The patients who overheard him agreed, giving Grace a "hip-hip-hooray!" She flushed with obvious pleasure.

Johan observed the captain with reservations. He wondered how Captain Smith had ended up in the next bed. Johan avoided Smith whenever possible. He was an intelligent, loyal officer, but his hatred of Germans extended way beyond German soldiers. Still, Johan agreed with the captain's appreciation of Red Cross girls.

"Why aren't you out celebrating Armistice today with the rest of the city?" the captain asked.

Grace propped her fists on her hips and gave him a

saucy look. "What better place to celebrate than among the men who won the peace and took the curl out of Crazy Bill's mustache?"

Her implied praise of the doughboys and belittling reference to the kaiser brought huzzahs and cheers from the patients.

A moment later, a thin soldier with brown hair parted in the middle and a black patch over one eye, broke into song. "Johnny is marching home again, he's finished another fight." Before the end of the second line, most of the soldiers had joined him.

Singing was beyond Johan's capability. To try it would be to tear open the lesions in his throat, which were finally beginning to heal.

Listening to Joe's patriotic enthusiasm brought a lump to that throat. Joe would never again see with the eye beneath that patch, but that fact didn't lessen his love for his country.

A doctor walked into the room, wearing a typical olive green army medical officer's jacket. Johan's gaze immediately sought his shoulders and standing collar for brass; a lieutenant colonel, likely the top medical officer on the post. Johan's back stiffened and he started to sit up, then remembered he didn't need to snap to attention in a hospital bed.

A toddler in a yellow dress entered hand in hand with the doctor. Her hair was hidden by an oversized Red Cross headpiece. She tugged her hand from the doctor's and marched down the aisle separating the two rows of white metal beds. Her arms and knees pumped as she sang the popular song with the soldiers.

Patients continued to sing, their eyes dancing with laughter.

Johan's gaze immediately sought the quiet Nurse Cunningham, to see her reaction. She was speaking to another patient, her lips close to his ear because of the din. The patient's eyes were bandaged. Johan couldn't hear what she said, but when the patient laughed, Johan was sure she'd described the little girl's march.

He liked the nurse's thoughtfulness. There were two other nurses in the ward, but something about Nurse Cunningham's sweet reserve caught his interest.

The little girl stopped beside Grace and grasped the blanket at the bed's edge. Her blue eyes looked right into his. "Hewwo."

"Hello yourself, Miss." It was easy to see from the girl's round face that she belonged to Mrs. Holt or Nurse Cunningham. His heart skipped a beat. Why hadn't he thought to look for a wedding band on the nurse's hand? *You're out of practice, Soldier,* he scolded himself, then remembered he'd pledged not to fall for her.

"I'm 'Lisbeth. Who're you?"

"Elisabeth." Grace spoke in that warning voice mothers use to gently let their children know their behavior isn't proper.

The mother, he thought before answering. "Johan."

"Lieutenant Baker," Grace corrected.

He held out a hand to Elisabeth. "You can call me Johan."

She shook his hand gravely. "You talk funny. Do you have a cold?"

"Elisabeth." This time Grace's warning was louder.

Johan ignored Grace and smiled at Elisabeth. "Something like that." He caught Grace's glance and nodded at the doctor the girl had walked in with. "Is that the honorable Daniel Holt?"

Grace shook her head. "No. The military wouldn't take Daniel. He had scarlet fever as a child. It left his heart too weak for fighting."

"Are you wearing your mother's Red Cross hat, Elisabeth?"

She nodded and stroked the white cloth as though it were silky hair. "Isn't it pwetty?"

"Very pretty." Wisps of short red hair curled out from beneath the white cap, framing the cherub's face. The symbolic red cross was slightly askew in the middle of her forehead above curious eyes. The folds of the hat hung down her back like a veil.

"When I don' feel good, Mommy weads me stowies. Would you like me to wead you a stowy?"

It brought a lump to his throat, which made talking even more difficult than usual. He nodded.

"I'll bwing my stowies."

Grace indicated the notebook she carried. "I'm making a list of soldiers' requests. I visit the hospital regularly as part of my Red Cross duties. Is there anything I can bring you?"

A hunger ate at his insides, just looking at her pad of paper. "A sketch pad, please, and some charcoal pencils if you can find them."

"I'll find them." Her pencil scratched across her pad. "I'm quite the detective when it comes to searching out things for our men."

Nurse Cunningham stepped quietly up beside Grace. He liked the graceful way the nurse moved. She laid a hand gently on his shoulder and smiled into his eyes. His insides turned to mush. A hint of spring flowers lightened the hospital's disinfectant odor.

"You need to stop talking for awhile, Lieutenant,

and rest your throat."

He nodded. At least he didn't need to communicate with sign language and paper and pencil the way he had for awhile. The first two weeks, he'd been blind as well as mute and couldn't communicate at all.

She lifted her hand. He held back the absurd desire to grasp it and ask her to stay, to simply talk to him awhile, talk about anything at all. He just wanted to look in those sweet eyes and hear that reassuring soft voice.

Instead, he watched her leave the ward with Grace and Elisabeth.

What was the nurse's first name? It started with "G" like Grace—Gloria, that was it. Gloria reminded him of a sky filled with angels singing praises to God. A nice image but too noisy for someone as quiet as this nurse. Glorie, the name Grace called her, suited her better. The two looked alike, but talk about opposite personalities!

Johan laid back on the bed, suddenly exhausted, amazed at how it tired a body to fight for health. His gaze drifted over the white-walled room. The sense of light and cleanliness rested him after the year of mud and filth. Everything here was white: walls, ceiling, floor, metal beds, bedside tables, nurses' uniforms, sheets. Clean sheets were a luxury barely known in the field hospitals in France.

The quiet was heavenly. No bombs, no machine guns, no rifles, no train or ship engines. The usual hospital odors had already dispelled the fragrance of flowers Nurse Cunningham carried with her, but even the smells of the hospital were preferable to the sweet, sickening smell of gas.

He'd gone to war with the attitude expressed in the popular song: "We won't be back 'til it's over Over There." He'd hated coming back before it was over. *But today is*

Armistice Day. The buddies I left behind are done fighting, too.
   A peace came over him. His muscles relaxed against the mattress as he drifted toward sleep. He was home. The war was truly over.

Chapter 2

Once out of the ward, Elisabeth spotted another nurse she knew and sped down the hall to say hello.

Glorie moved quickly to the wall and sagged against it. She wrapped her arms over her chest, trying to hold in the pain that threatened to burst through.

"Are you all right?" Grace's voice mirrored the worry in her eyes.

"Yes." Glorie didn't feel "all right." Waves of sympathy and horror washed over her, threatening to knock her off her emotional feet. But she had to be "all right" for those brave men. "It's just. . .so much at once. These men—our first overseas men arriving, 150 of them, men who went away strong and healthy, and now. . ."

Grace rested a comforting hand on Glorie's arm. "You're exhausted, that's all. You were up before dawn helping prepare the celebration for the wounded, whose train arrived with them at eight, and you've been working with them all day since then."

"The wounded." Glorie repeated the words softly. "Before this, patients were the ill or accident victims, never 'the wounded.'"

"You're just tired," Grace repeated. "Things will get better."

Things wouldn't get better, of course. Glorie knew it, and she knew Grace did, too. More wounded would arrive every week until the hospital was filled with them, twelve hundred or so.

It was true she was tired. The influenza epidemic had worn out all the staff, not only here, but in civilian and military hospitals around the world. The first person to die of the flu in St. Paul was a lieutenant here at Fort Snelling. The hospital had overflowed with patients. St. Paul was closed down because of the flu. Restaurants, churches, schools, pool halls, saloons—all were closed in an effort to keep people from gathering in places where the deadly disease could easily spread.

At least the places were ordered closed. Today people flooded the streets, celebrating Armistice.

The first overseas men had been scheduled to arrive at the fort back in September. The flu changed the plans. Finally the flu here at the fort had abated to the point that it was believed safe to allow the wounded to be brought in. The few remaining flu patients were in a separate building, the fort's contagious-disease ward.

"We nurses encouraged our flu patients to get better so they could go overseas to fight, Grace. Did you know that?" A shiver ran along Glorie's spine at the memory. "We'd stand in the middle of the ward and call out, 'Where do you go from here, boys?' and they'd answer in a batch, 'Over There.' None of them made it over there, of course. The war ended too soon for that."

"They wanted to go. They knew what might happen."

Glorie shook her head fiercely. "No. They wanted to be heroes to impress their friends and families and girls.

They were frightened of dying in war, though they blustered that they weren't. They didn't want to die at home of the flu. I doubt they believed they'd return like the overseas men here today."

"No one thinks horrible things will happen to them. Soldiers aren't alone in owning that illusion."

Glorie pushed herself away from the wall. "For most of the world, the war is over. For me and the rest of the medical staff, our war is just beginning."

"Excuse me."

Glorie turned toward the male voice with the heavy German accent. Blue eyes danced in a middle-aged man's narrow, deeply wrinkled face. Beside him a woman with round red cheeks and blond hair had equally happy eyes.

An answering smile spread across Glorie's face. "May I help you?"

The man doffed his hat and held it against his chest. "Our son is here. He's back from the war, a patient, Lt. Johan Baker. Do you know where we can find him?"

"He's right through these doors. Let me show you." Glorie opened the ward door.

The couple followed, thanking her. The mouth-watering aroma of fresh-baked bread brought Glorie's attention to a large basket the woman carried. A white linen towel covered the contents. "Oh, he can't. . ." Glorie hesitated. She'd started to tell them Johan couldn't eat solid food yet. How much did they know about his injuries?

They hurried past her and down the aisle toward his bed in the middle of the ward. She trotted after them, smiling at their eagerness.

The conversation and laughter of the other patients died as the soldiers watched the couple approach their son. They stopped beside his bed. Johan was sleeping again. The couple's gaze moved from Johan to Glorie. She saw fear in their faces. *They don't know how he was injured,* she thought. "He's only sleeping. It's fine to wake him, but you mustn't let him talk much. His throat is still healing from the lesions caused by mustard gas."

Mrs. Baker's eyes widened.

"It will be fine eventually," Glorie rushed to assure her, "but for now he needs to let his throat rest. As you might imagine, he's had a hard time keeping quiet and not celebrating the Armistice."

The Bakers' faces relaxed into smiles.

"Why don't you wake him?" Glorie suggested to Mrs. Baker.

The woman set the basket on the floor, laid a hand on Johan's shoulder, and leaned close to say in a soft German accent, "Johan, it's Mother."

Johan moved slightly in his sleep. A small smile formed.

Mrs. Baker shook his shoulder lightly. "Wake up, Son."

This time Johan obeyed. The surprise in his eyes was greater than when he'd awakened to see Grace and Glorie. He bolted to a sitting position and threw his arms around the woman's neck. "Mother!"

Glorie blinked back sudden tears. Even through Johan's scarred throat, even though it was barely more than a cracked whisper, the word held a world of love.

"Father, you're here, too!" The men gripped each other's hands. Tears streamed down all three faces.

Glorie turned discreetly away. The room had gone from its first hushed notice of the couple to complete quiet. She glanced at the men. Each one watched the meeting. Tears sparkled in more than a few eyes. A couple of men dashed away tears from their cheeks. One corporal pulled out a khaki handkerchief and blew his nose loudly.

The men who earlier appeared tough, courageous, even cheerful in facing the future with the handicaps war had bestowed on them watched the family wrapped in each others' arms. *This is what they're all waiting for—to be home, all the way home, with their loved ones.* She swallowed the lump the scene brought to her throat and unnecessarily started down the row straightening blankets. It wouldn't do for the men to find her staring at them.

"Hip-hip-hooray for you, Johan," one soldier whispered through a throat as scarred as Johan's.

Only Glorie heard him. "Amen," she said softly.

She glanced back at Johan. His mother, beaming from ear to ear and with eyes only for her son, was seated on his chair. She held one of his hands in both her own. A soldier climbed out of bed and brought another chair for Mr. Baker.

Glorie continued straightening blankets and began a conversation with two soldiers. The other patients cleared throats and turned away to give the Bakers privacy.

Even so, Glorie heard pieces of the family's conversation. Johan's questions were those of any family member away for a time—about relatives and friends. The news that an uncle had died in the flu epidemic brought a stillness to the room again, but only for a moment.

Mr. Baker told how the family dog carried one of Johan's shoes everywhere he went. "Even sleeps on it, like a pillow."

Glorie thought she wouldn't be surprised to learn that Mrs. Baker, too, kept something of Johan's with her all day and all night. Glorie herself kept a picture of her brother, Fred, on her bedside table.

She started back toward Johan's bed. She hated to cut the visit short, but Johan shouldn't be talking so much. When she'd almost reached them, she heard Johan say, "Where's the bread? It isn't my imagination that I smell it, is it?"

Mr. Baker grinned and lifted the basket. "We made your favorite sweet buns."

Mrs. Baker folded back the linen towel and displayed the golden bread.

Johan reached for a bun. Glorie grabbed his hand and smiled at his parents. "I'm afraid Johan can't eat that yet. He's on a liquid diet until his throat is better."

"Can't I keep it just to smell?" Johan gave Glorie such a beseeching look that she laughed out loud.

"I'm afraid not, Lieutenant. No doubt you have strong willpower, but these wonderful buns would be far too tempting for any man."

He pretended to pout. "I dreamed of these during every one of those meals of beans and mush in France."

"We own a bakery, Nurse," Mrs. Baker explained. "My husband's people have been bakers for generations. That is why our name is Baker."

"Our son will not be a baker." Mr. Baker lifted his chin in pride. "Johan will be attending the university."

"Schooling won't take away what you taught me," Johan said. "I'll still make a great batch of bread." The last word was strangled in the beginning of a cough that continued for too long.

His parents leaned toward him, concern written in their eyes.

"I'm afraid you must end your visit for today. Johan, Lieutenant Baker, must rest his throat." Glorie felt a wave of color flood her face. The nurses never called any of the soldiers by their first names. She tried to cover her slip with a question for his parents. "Do you live nearby?"

"Not far," Mr. Baker replied. "Our bakery is in downtown Minneapolis."

"As soon as I can eat solid food, I expect a basket of buns and bread each day," Johan challenged. Again a cough erupted, smothering the smile his words brought to his mother.

"That won't be too long," Glorie assured while pouring a glass of water from the pitcher on the white bedside table. "If he learns to stop talking so much." She smiled sweetly at the dirty look he gave her across the glass he accepted.

Mr. Baker took the basket from his wife and set it on the chair. "We'll leave this for the other patients."

Glorie hesitated. She wasn't sure it was fair to share it with only a few, but she didn't want to hurt their feelings.

"We don't want anything made by a dirty old Hun," Captain Smith spat out.

Glorie spun to face the man sitting up in the next bed. "Captain!" Hatred burned in his eyes and so changed his features that she barely recognized him.

He grabbed a bun from the basket and hurled it. It bounced off the wall and hit Mrs. Baker's cheek.

"Stop!" Glorie yanked back the basket before the captain could reach another bun.

A roar came from behind her. A second later Johan burst from his bed. He lunged toward Captain Smith.

Glorie tried to throw herself between the two. The basket which made her hands useless added to her effectiveness as a barrier.

Other patients hurried to the fray. Joe grabbed Johan's arm, and two men pressed Captain Smith back against the mattress.

"You can't insult my folks that way." Johan's attempt at a yell came out a scratchy growl.

Glorie's own throat hurt for the pain she knew he must be feeling, both physically and emotionally. "Lieutenant, please, remember your throat."

"She's right," Joe told Johan. "Besides, the captain outranks you. We might be in a hospital, but we're still in the army."

The satisfied glint in Captain Smith's eyes sickened Glorie. There wasn't an officer of higher rank in the ward at the moment. Surely that wouldn't allow him to get away with such behavior. "Assault on a civilian isn't acceptable no matter what an officer's rank." The command in her voice surprised her.

It obviously surprised the captain, too, from the look on his face when his gaze jerked from Johan to her.

Glorie hurried around the end of Johan's bed. Mrs. Baker held a hand to her cheek. Tears pooled in her eyes, but they weren't tears of joy this time. Mr. Baker had an arm around her waist. "Are you all right, Mrs. Baker?"

"Yah."

"We're used to worse than this." Mr. Baker glared at Captain Smith. "We didn't expect it from the soldiers Johan fought beside."

Glorie walked with them out into the hall. "I'm so sorry Captain Smith ruined your visit."

Mr. Baker shook his head. "To see our boy back, to know he is going to be well. . .nothing could spoil that."

"He isn't our boy any longer, Father," Mrs. Baker said softly. "Didn't you see his eyes? He has his father's eyes now, old eyes, the eyes of a man who has seen too much." She turned her hands palm up and stared at them. "When I fed him as a babe, he'd hold my little finger. It filled his entire hand. When he was a toddler, I'd wrap his blond curls around my fingers when I brushed his hair." Her sorrow-filled gaze met Glorie's. "Our boy went to war, but a man came home."

Mr. Baker laid an arm around his wife's shoulder. "Come, Mother. Let's go home."

Glorie held out the basket.

"You share it with the other nurses."

"Thank you."

Their steps were slow and they leaned against each other, a different image than the eager couple who'd arrived a short time ago.

The memory of Johan's face when Captain Smith shot his ugly words and threw the bread cut into Glorie's heart. She sighed and sent up a prayer for both young officers.

The war was over, but it left a bottomless lake of hate behind. She and the rest of the medical staff would give their all to help the soldiers' bodies mend, but only God could mend men's souls.

The Bakers disappeared around a corner, and Glorie threw off her dismal thoughts. She hurried to the ward station. Relief flooded over her when she saw the ward officer there. She described the situation between Captain Smith and Lieutenant Baker.

"I'll take care of it," the ward officer assured her. "Wouldn't you know trouble would break out between officers and not enlisted men? Poor example, I'd call it."

The next morning Glorie found Joe assigned to the bed Captain Smith previously occupied. The captain now resided in the bed at the far end of the row. This wasn't a permanent answer, of course, but at least it put some distance between the barb-throwing captain and the lieutenant.

Johan managed a smile when she approached his bed, but he didn't attempt to speak. She could see by his eyes that he was in physical pain. All the talking and yelling yesterday likely tore at the throat lesions that had begun to heal. Her own throat tightened in empathy as she took his wrist to check his pulse.

When she returned later, she brought a pad and pencil. "In case you want to say anything," she said, handing them to him. She poured aspirin powders in a glass of water for him. It wouldn't alleviate all his pain, but it would help a little.

Glorie dreaded changing the dressings on the blisters caused by the mustard gas, but it had to be done. She was as gentle as possible. Still, she wondered whether her attempts were clumsy and knew they were hurtful. The blistering was similar to that experienced with first- or second-degree burns.

The blisters had broken on his trip from New York to St. Paul. Now it was important to prevent infection from setting in. She knew if that happened, it would add five or six weeks to his recovery. As usual with mustard gas burns, the blisters were the worst in places where there was the most body friction, like the armpits and behind the knees.

He flinched when she removed the last old dressing.

Glorie gasped, dropped the dressing, and stepped back. "I'm sorry."

Johan scratched something across the pad, then turned it toward her. In bold capital letters he'd written *OUCH!*

A giggle escaped her. Guilt followed on its heels. "I'm sorry," she repeated, though she couldn't discipline her grin.

He smiled back.

She returned to the dressing with a lighter heart,

knowing he'd intended to make her laugh. The pain she'd caused him was real; she'd seen the glint of a tear at the corner of one eye. Yet he wasn't about to wallow in his pain or allow her to feel guilty about it.

Her exposure to the effects of gas warfare made her profoundly grateful for the thousands and thousands of peach pits scouts had collected during the war. The pits had been ground and used in making gas masks. She'd grown so tired of eating peaches and canning peaches and even *seeing* peaches that she'd remarked to Grace, "I'm surprised God made them yellow instead of red, white, and blue."

Treatment of the blisters required frequent dressing changes. The second time Glorie changed them, Johan showed her two sketches. The first was a stick man with a sad face. An arrow pointed from a notation to the man. The notation said, "Me after weeks on a liquid diet." The second sketch was a handsome, muscled, smiling man beside the words, "Me before the liquid diet."

She chuckled and reached for the first dressing.

He scribbled something else. She glanced at it. Beside the sketch of the handsome man he'd written, "Aren't you going to tell me how good-looking he is?"

Her gasp was a mixture of surprise and laughter. Turning her gaze and hands to the dressing, she replied with intentional primness, "Mother always said, 'Handsome is as handsome does.' "

When she chanced a glance back at his face, he was grinning.

On night duty, Glorie discovered that Johan wasn't the only patient experiencing nightmares. Every night at least a half-dozen men thrashed about or awoke screaming. She'd hold their hands, bathe the sweat from their

faces with a cool cloth, and speak to them in low, soothing tones until they fell back asleep. But their screams
awoke others who lay tense, staring into the darkness, not
needing sleep to produce nightmares.

Glorie stopped in surprise beside Johan's bed a couple
of days later. He was sitting up, his sketch pad resting
against his knees. His face was covered with white cold
cream. He'd exaggerated and thickened his eyebrows
with a charcoal pencil. A clownlike broad band of a red
smile covered his lips and more. "What on earth. . . ?"

Johan's eyes glinted in a smile. He lifted his hands,
opening them wide to frame his face, and she saw that he
wore white gloves. He pointed to the next bed. Joe wore
the same gloves and face covering.

Joe pretended to hit a badminton shuttlecock to
Johan. Johan hit it back. Joe returned it. Johan slapped a
hand to his forehead, as if he'd been hit. A white finger
scolded Joe.

"You're mimes," Glorie exclaimed in delight. The
other nurses and most of the patients joined her in laughing at Johan and Joe's show. After the game of volleying,
they performed a tug of war until Johan was tugged out
of bed. He brushed himself off thoroughly, while casting
dirty looks at his gleeful opponent.

"Charlie Chaplin better watch out or you two will
replace him as America's favorite comedian," Glorie
quipped when Johan finally settled back into the bed.
"Before we change your dressings, we'd best get that cold
cream off your faces. The cream isn't good for blisters,
you know. Good thing the blisters on your faces are dried
up and almost healed." There wasn't the friction on the
face skin that caused such severe blistering elsewhere, she
remembered. She leaned closer to Johan's face, studying his

clown mouth. "Where did you get the lipstick?"

He jotted down the answer.

"From Grace. So my own sister is plotting with you. I can see I'm going to have to watch the two of you like a hawk."

The clown smile grew very wide.

❇

The days soon fell into a routine for the medical staff and patients at Fort Snelling. Each morning, promptly at seven—or 0700 in army parlance—the nurses entered the wards. Any fatigue or self-centered pettiness they possessed fled in the face of the patients' situations and cheerful courage in facing their wounds.

The nurses awakened the soldiers with sunny greetings, took vital signs, and wheeled in curtained dividers that were placed between beds for privacy when the patients were bathed. Then came the more challenging duties. Changing dressings was the most painful task, for both patient and nurse.

Convalescing soldiers often preferred to sleep in, but such laziness wasn't allowed. "Muscles need use to heal properly. You want them built up nice and strong for the girls back home, don't you?" Glorie wasn't above needling. Her approach usually brought the desired result. The chaplain doubled as the athletic officer. He made sure the men who were physically able exercised daily, building up their strength slowly.

Next the nurses prepared for the ward officer's 0900 inspection. After the ward inspection, the nurses brought meals to the patients unable to eat in the mess hall.

Each week, another 150 men came for reconstruction and convalescence. *Reconstruction is such an impersonal word,* Glorie thought, wheeling a patient in a high-backed cane wheelchair to a physical therapy session. *It's a term for repairing buildings, not bodies.* Yet that was the term coined for the medical help she and her coworkers provided the soldiers.

Aides in dark dresses and white aprons took over for nurses and doctors in the physical therapy rooms. A soldier flirted with a smiling aide while she massaged his arm. Glorie waited while another soldier completed his hot water treatment, his leg in a tall, round canister that looked like a metal wastebasket. The patient she'd wheeled down would receive the same treatment on a leg amputated just above the knee.

She wheeled another patient back to his ward. They met a group of ambulatory convalescent patients returning from an outdoor exercise session, not looking at all like patients in their sweaters and wool slacks.

One of the men grinned at her patient. "How do you rate, Tom, riding and with a beautiful woman at your service? I've only these ugly doughboys for company."

The wheeled man spread his hands and shrugged his shoulders. "Ugly attracts ugly, and good-looking—"

The men hooted and continued on their way.

The patients' good cheer continually amazed Glorie. They seldom allowed themselves the luxury of self-pity, and they didn't treat each other with pity, either. She and the other nurses followed the men's example to the best of their ability.

After delivering the man to his ward, Glorie headed for the officers' dayroom. Grace was scheduled to read to some of the blinded men and had asked Glorie to join them if she could get away. Their war duties kept them so busy, they seldom saw each other, compared to Glorie's prenursing days.

She was thankful for the busy hours. The joy of Armistice had tarnished with news that her brother Fred was missing in action in the last offensive. She swallowed the painful lump of fear, said a prayer, and forced her thoughts away from the worst.

Her steps slowed when she neared Johan's ward. She hadn't seen him in almost two weeks, not since she'd been reassigned to surgery. She often wondered whether the humorous soldier was healing well. Unless he had another episode with the callous Captain Smith or his friends, Johan's throat and blistering should soon be healed well enough for him to be discharged. She felt a slight twinge in her heart at the thought.

She toyed with the possibility of stopping to say hello but tossed the idea aside after a moment. Fraternizing with patients was discouraged. Patients often developed fond feelings for their nurses.

Glorie sighed and forced herself to pass the ward doors. It wasn't the patient whose heart was endangered; it was hers. She wasn't sure why Johan drew her interest more than any of the hundreds of other men, but he did. Certainly his humor helped, though other men joked and teased, too. Whenever she recalled his face and voice when he'd greeted his parents, the memory warmed her like a blanket. It was like a gift, seeing his heart open in that intimate way. All the patients were courageous men, but few allowed others to see their vulnerable side. Perhaps Johan would have hidden his emotions if his parents hadn't surprised him.

Outside the officers' dayroom she stopped to take a deep breath and put on a smile. She could hear Grace's musical voice through the door. When Glorie entered, the first person she saw was Lt. Johan Baker, seated in a leather mission chair near the stone fireplace. He glanced up. A smile leaped to his eyes, sending shivers of joy through her.

He and the other officers started to rise.

Glorie shook her head. "Please, continue with what you are doing."

Their activities were varied. Captain Smith and a major played chess in one corner. Another major read a book. A lieutenant sat at an oak table writing a letter on familiar YMCA stationery that bore a printed heading which stated that he was proudly serving in America's armed forces. A deck of cards in the middle of another table showed how others spent time. The new tune "Everything Is Peaches Down in Georgia" filled with cheer the corner where a nurse and colonel looked through the record collection beside the Victrola.

A calendar hung above the Victrola, picturing a child Elisabeth's age with short blond curls. Beneath her image was the caption, "Guess what Daddy bought me for my birthday. A Liberty Bond!" Glorie tried to imagine Elisabeth happy about a bond for a gift and failed.

Grace's voice rose and fell while she read the day's *St. Paul Pioneer Press* to a blinded captain. She and the captain were seated in overstuffed chairs near the fireplace.

Elisabeth rose with a gasp of delight and raced to Glorie. The white veil of a miniature Red Cross headpiece Grace had finally made the girl floated out behind her. Glorie knelt to receive the little girl's hug. "Hello, Elisabeth. Are you having a good time?"

"Yes. Muvver is weading, so I must be quiet like my kitty when she naps," Elisabeth informed her in a stage whisper. She took Glorie's hand. "Come sit with me."

Glorie followed obediently. Elisabeth sat on the rug

before Johan's chair. She indicated that Glorie was to sit down beside her.

Immediately Johan stood and waved his sketch pad toward his seat. "Take my chair, Nurse Cunningham."

"I'm accustomed to sitting with Elisabeth, thank you." She lowered herself as gracefully as possible beside her niece, trying to ignore the awareness of Johan's presence, which made every movement feel exaggerated and clumsy.

Johan sat down beside them, crossing his legs.

"Shh." Elisabeth held a stiff index finger to her lips.

"Sorry," he mouthed.

"Your voice sounds much stronger," Glorie whispered.

"I've a lot of practice whispering," he said with a straight face.

She giggled. "I meant when you spoke normally."

"The doctors say they'll discharge me any day now. My throat and the lesions are almost healed."

"That's wonderful."

"Here's some great news, everyone." Grace raised her voice for the entire room to hear. "Sugar allowances have doubled. We're now allowed eight teaspoons a day. It's about time. I'm simply wasting away with so little sugar and real flour. Soon Fuelless Mondays, Meatless Tuesdays, and Sugarless Fridays will be behind us. But they were worth it. It says here that Minnesotans saved thirty-six million pounds of sugar and three million bushels of wheat for the Allies. Hooray for us!" She returned to reading articles for the officer beside her, and her voice moderated. The others in the room returned to their occupations, too.

"You've bobbed your hair," Johan remarked, studying Glorie.

Her hand went to the marcelled waves framing her face. "Yes. I thought it would be easier to care for now that I'm so busy."

"I like it."

His approval warmed h   t
that it shouldn't give her so

Elisabeth tired of not receiving their attention. She leaned toward Johan. "Are you done drawing me?"

"Almost." He added a few strokes. "There." He handed the pad to Elisabeth.

She beamed in delight. "Look, Aunt Glorie."

The sketch caught Elisabeth's intensity as she comforted a bandaged doll in her arms. "You're very good," Glorie told him, her gaze and emotions riveted on his sketch.

He took the tablet from her without comment.

Glorie lifted the real doll from Elizabeth's lap. "What happened to your baby?" It appeared almost mummylike, with only its porcelain cheeks and a few stray brown curls peeking out from the gauze.

"She was wounded in the war." The statement came out short and matter-of-fact.

"Is she a soldier?" Johan asked.

"No, Silly." Elizabeth shook her head vigorously. "Girls aren't soldiers. She's a nurse."

Glorie wondered where Elisabeth came across the idea the war endangered nurses the same as soldiers. True, the flu epidemic killed many nurses. Those near the front lines were sometimes injured, but none had been killed in battle.

The Victrola sent out a new song. Elisabeth jumped up, eyes gleaming. "That's my favowite song. K–k–k–katy," she sang as she skipped across the room to the couple playing records.

Glorie glanced at Johan, and they shared a laugh at

the girl's enthusiastic rendering of the popular tune. When the laugh died, they were still staring into each other's eyes. Glorie wondered what he thought and felt inside, in that place with war memories he didn't share with anyone. She had the sudden, aching wish to hold him, her arms absorbing all the awful pictures, all the horrible and painful memories.

It almost took a physical effort to pull her gaze away. Her cheeks felt warm. Had he seen her thoughts in her eyes?

"Are you changing the doll's dressings?" Johan's teasing tone made her aware she was picking at the doll's bandages.

"Grace says she tore up an old sheet for Elisabeth to use, as she's bandaging everyone and everything. She bandaged their cocker spaniel." She liked the chuckle that rewarded her tale. "That wasn't the worst of it," she continued. "A few nights ago, while her father napped after dinner, she wrapped his feet—wrapped them together. Grace had to cut the makeshift bandages off."

The chuckle became a guffaw. "Wish I'd seen that. Did you know I met her husband? Daniel is one of the volunteers who take us restless convalescing soldiers for Sunday drives. I liked him."

"He's a fine man." Glorie sometimes envied Grace her pleasant married life, with a man who thought the sun rose and set in her and a daughter who lit up her heart. *But I've never met a man I wanted to spend my entire life with,* she thought. *Besides, if I'd married, I wouldn't be here now, helping the soldiers. Grace gave up her dream of nursing for a dream more important to her, building a life and family with Daniel. Until I meet a man I'm that crazy over, I won't marry.*

Johan took the doll from her and looked down at it as though it had secrets to tell. "The men love it when Elisabeth visits. In France, when a little girl was in the hospital she was injured. The war wasn't limited to soldiers."

Glorie's chest constricted at his words. She closed her mind against the image of children with the same grievous wounds as the soldiers at Fort Snelling.

"The day always seems brighter after seeing Elisabeth," he continued. "Have you noticed the way the mood seems lighter in a ward when she's there? She reminds us of that sweet world waiting for us when we leave here. Perhaps we're selfish, grasping for the life she brings." He ran a thick index finger over the wrapping binding the doll's head. "No child should see all the carnage she's seen here."

"No one any age should see or experience it." Glorie stopped his finger, laying her hand lightly over his. "Children are stronger than we think. The children in France have seen worse things. Wouldn't it be wonderful if the Great War turned out to be what President Wilson called it, a war to end war?"

"An end to war. I wish we could make that happen." His voice was low, the passion causing it to reverberate like distant thunder.

"That'll be the day." Captain Smith's harsh comment crashed through the world that had included only Glorie and Johan.

Glorie snatched her hand away from Johan's. The gesture that had been only a natural reaching out to comfort another, suddenly appeared forward and ugly when reflected in the captain's glaring eyes.

The captain's lip curled. "The whole world fought together to put Germany out of business. As long as one German remains alive there won't be a chance peace will last. The Allies shouldn't have agreed to peace. We should keep fighting until the earth is wiped clean of filthy Huns."

Glorie could see Johan struggling to keep his temper. Music continued to roll out from the Victrola with inappropriately cheerful lyrics, but everyone but Elisabeth was watching the two officers. Glorie wanted to lay her hand on his again, to tell him the captain's taunts weren't worth challenging, but she clenched her hands tightly in her lap and sent up a prayer instead.

"You're right that Germany was the aggressor," Johan said through tight lips, "this time."

"You can't weasel your fatherland out of guilt just because there are wars your country didn't fight in."

Johan pointed to a print on the wall beside them, a picture of an American Indian warrior slumped on the back of a horse after battle. "Your fatherland was the aggressor against this nation, wasn't it?"

Captain Smith snorted. "You can't compare the two."

"Why not?" Johan asked softly. "The English and French wanted to take the land from the American Indians. The Germans in this war wanted to take land from the French."

"Are you saying the Germans were justified in invading France?" The captain braced his arms against the back of a chair and leaned toward Johan. Glorie sensed menace in the line of his body.

"No." Johan stood up, the bandaged doll hanging from one hand. "I'm saying evil doesn't exist only in the people of one country. I'm saying a war started for the wrong reasons doesn't justify condemning an entire people for all time, doesn't justify forgetting the good things they've given the world."

Glorie hadn't been aware that the colonel had left the

Victrola and now approached them, until he spoke from behind Johan. "Put a lid on it, officers. There's ladies and a child present. If you want to continue your private war, do battle elsewhere."

"Yes, Sir." The captain's back straightened.

"No need for battle, Sir." Johan's eyes challenged Smith to refute him.

"That's right, Sir." Smith's look said the words were a lie.

When Smith had left the room, the colonel faced Johan. "A word of warning: Take care how you express your feelings about the war. I know you are a loyal American and fought hard for us, but there are those who won't take that into account. They'll remember that your people came from Germany and interpret your words according to their preconceived ideas. They want someone to blame for their sons coming home like this." He rested his left hand on the prosthesis that replaced his right arm. "As you said, this time it's Germany's fault."

Color drained from Johan's face. "Right, Sir. Thank you, Sir."

"Germany's a long way away," the colonel continued. "You're here, so you're an easy target."

"I was born in America," Johan told him. "My parents immigrated from Germany right after they married. Both have brothers and sisters living in Germany. At least, we hope they are still alive. We haven't heard from them since before the United States entered the war. I have cousins who fought for Germany. Neither I nor my parents have met them, but they're family, my parents' nieces and nephews. Over there, when we were shooting at the enemy, I might have been shooting at my cousins. I never thought it right that Germany invaded Belgium and

France, but other Americans don't understand what they asked of German-Americans in this war. No one should be asked to make such a choice."

Glorie's throat tightened in sympathy at the pain in his voice.

The colonel's expression didn't change. "It's a nasty choice, no question about it. But remember, one of your cousins might have launched the gas shells that put you here, Lieutenant." He gave a sharp salute and left the room.

Glorie was dimly aware that the others in the room had gone back to their activities. Grace's voice picked up a news story again, the paper crackling as she adjusted it. The other nurse asked Elisabeth about her favorite songs. The officers at the chess table murmured across the playing board.

It's impossible to live in Minnesota and not be aware of the German-Americans' mixed sympathies, Glorie thought. Almost a quarter of the state's population were born in Germany or Austria, or their parents were born there.

Glorie rose to stand beside Johan and cleared her throat. "I have friends who Americanized their names after the war started."

"Denying their heritage? My family refuses to consider our ancestors shameful."

She wondered if he was turning his anger at Captain Smith on her. "They only wanted others to know they're loyal Americans," she said, "and to avoid trouble."

His gaze studied hers until she thought she would quake at the intensity. "Do you believe it's acceptable to deny your family and your history?"

"I can't judge them. I've not faced that choice, nor have I faced the awful choices you did."

"If I'd chosen not to fight for our country, for the United States, what would you think then?"

The question seemed silly to her, asking what she would think if he were someone else. She wanted to duck her head to hide her smile, but he might interpret that as avoiding his gaze. "That depends. Would you choose to support Germany because of your heritage or because you believed Germany right in invading its neighbors? Did you enlist in the American army because you live in America or because you believe the Belgians and French and all other people have the right to choose the leaders who will govern them?"

His eyebrows drew together in a frown. For a moment he looked confused. Then he laughed. "You should be a diplomat."

"I think that quality is required of nurses."

"Thank you for reminding me of the true questions."

"You always knew them." She knew it was true. Yet it was equally true that he and millions of others had been forced to make a horrible and costly choice.

"Tomorrow's Thanksgiving," he reminded her. "Will you spend it with your family?"

"No. I see my family often since they live in St. Paul. I offered to work to free someone else to spend time with their family. My grandparents are coming for the holidays. They live in Virginia. I haven't seen them in years. They arrive this afternoon and are staying through Christmas." She didn't tell him they'd decided the family needed each other over the holidays while they dealt with their fear and grief over Fred.

"I've never met my grandparents." Johan gazed out the window.

"I'm sorry. I can't imagine life without grandparents."

"We've other things to thank God for tomorrow." His cheer sounded forced. "The Armistice, naturally. But also, I've been off that liquid diet for a week and a half, so I plan to enjoy that turkey and dressing." He wiggled his eyebrows and rubbed his palms together in anticipation.

Glorie burst into laughter and pointed at his hands. The forgotten doll danced from them.

Chapter 3

Glorie glanced at the clock on the wall as she hurried down the hall toward the door; three o'clock. She'd have time for a short nap before helping get trays ready for the evening meal. She couldn't imagine that the patients would be hungry after the huge Thanksgiving meal this noon, but a hospital was nothing without a schedule.

The outside door opened just as she reached it, letting in a rush of chilly air tinged with the sharp scent of autumn leaves. "Surprise!" Grace, dressed in a khaki military-style coat, threw out her arms and grinned like a cat who'd just finished a bowl of cream. Behind her stood an elderly couple.

Glorie rushed to throw her arms around first the lady and then the slender gentleman. "Grandmother Lucy. Grandpa Jere. What a wonderful surprise." She pressed her lips to her grandmother's soft, wrinkly cheek, then to the tougher, though just as wrinkled, cheek of her grandfather. "I didn't think I'd see you until Sunday. I can't tell you how jealous I was of the rest of the family for your company."

Grandmother and Grandpa's Virginia-accented greetings were almost drowned in Grace's excited, "They wanted to see where you worked. Grandpa Jere wanted to visit some of the soldiers and thank them for their sacrifices. So I offered to bring them. I knew you'd love the surprise. Won't it be fun to show them around?"

Grandpa was tall with a lean, narrow face. Grandmother was slightly on the rounded side. She looked comfortable, the way Glorie always thought a grandmother should look. Her hair was still long; it was pulled back in a bun. Silver waves framed her face. "We haven't seen you in five years. Grace and I agree, it was the most wonderful summer of our lives, staying with you at Hickory Hill. We felt like Southern belles. Remember the way Grace and I tried to adopt your wonderful Southern drawls? We were such children. My, now I'm the one running on."

"Northern or Southern, you're both beautiful belles in my book," Grandpa Jere insisted.

"Let me look at you." Grandmother took both of Glorie's hands and stood back. Glorie beamed and waited patiently while Grandmother's gaze traveled from the pert white nurse's hat to the simple white dress to the sensible shoes on Glorie's tired feet. Grandmother's hand shook slightly as she touched a fingertip to the gold U.S. on one side of Glorie's shawl collar, and the medical department's gold caduceus with ANC superimposed in white enamel on the other side. "We hadn't such fine uniforms in the War between the States."

"You didn't have uniforms at all, my dear." Grandpa's dry remark set Glorie and Grace giggling out of all proportion to the humor, simply because it was lovely to be with the couple again and enjoy the way they were together. Grandpa teased Grandmother Lucy relentlessly but always with a sparkle in his eye and never with a cruel undertone.

"Let's start our tour." Glorie slipped one arm through Grandpa's. "Stop us whenever you feel the need to rest a bit." Grace hooked elbows with Lucy and the four started off.

The couple obviously was awed by the up-to-date equipment such as the X-ray machine. "It's invaluable," Glorie told them. "Every day we've a couple of men who take bismuth meals and then are fluoroscoped so the doctors can determine problems from gunshot wounds to the abdomen."

Grandmother Lucy pressed a hand to her waist and her eyes grew large, but she didn't comment. Glorie suspected she was remembering abdomen wounds of soldiers she'd nursed.

The two surgery rooms looked pristine today. "This is the hardest duty, but rewarding beyond measure," Glorie told them. "It takes three doctors and six nurses to handle the surgeries. Eighty percent of our patients require surgery. We're only able to do a couple each day. The Carroll-Darkin treatment is used in all operations for diseased bones. If there's the slightest chance an old infection is recurring, the doctors do another operation. That way gangrene can't do its dirty work, and the wounds heal faster."

Next she showed them one of the two lab wards, which looked barren and cold with its stark metal furnishings. The microscopes, set where the sun shone through uncurtained windows, were life-giving. To Glorie the room looked empty without the white-aproned doctors bent over the microscopes. Only a skeleton crew remained at work today. "The labs are specially equipped to keep the detailed bacterial counts necessary for treatments."

The physiotherapy ward was next. "You've a separate

ward for everything." Lucy sighed. "I wish we'd had all these modern wonders available during the War between the States."

A wave of sympathy rolled through Glorie. She wished much more could be done for her patients, but they had much better medical help available than when Lucy and Jere helped the men when their generation fought.

Glorie listed all the areas of medicine represented at the fort. "General surgery; orthopedics; eye, ear, nose, and throat; electro-hydro and mechano therapeutics; dental surgery, nerve surgery, and X-ray. Oh, and there's a separate building for contagious diseases. Of course, when the influenza epidemic was at its peak the entire hospital overflowed with cases."

"Everyone at Hickory Hill had it." Jere placed his arm over Lucy's shoulders. "So did Jinny and her husband. Lucy brought them to Hickory Hill. Lucy here nursed us all, and the servants and some of the neighbors, too, until the grippe dropped her in her steps."

"You did the same." The woman wasn't about to be put on a pedestal.

The fondness in Grandpa Jere's eyes as he looked down at his wife tugged sweetly at Glorie's heart. *All couples should love this deeply and this long,* she thought.

Tears sparkled on Grace's long lashes. Glorie wondered whether she was hoping that she and Daniel had such a long and lovely life ahead together as the couple standing before them.

Jere shook his head. "I don't know why a couple of old codgers like us made it through."

"This strain acts strangely," Glorie admitted. "The strong young men and women who usually weather the grippe with a few days discomfort—they are the very

138

ones who are most likely to die from the Spanish flu." The strain had swept the busy army posts, killing thousands of the United States' strongest men when the world needed them most. Glorie had seen more die than she cared to remember.

"Did you lose any nurses from it?" Lucy asked.

"None of the nurses at Fort Snelling. The army's training school for aircraft mechanics has its own hospital. Three nurses died there. For some reason I never caught it, despite the fact that I often worked when I was so exhausted that I wondered if I was sleepwalking."

"They say the flu hit the boys over there hard, too." Jere's jaw tightened. "As if they didn't have enough to fight."

"It spreads so easily and rapidly," Lucy said. "I'm surprised your hospital isn't closed to visitors."

"The flu is waning," Glorie reminded her. She shivered, suddenly cold, and wished she was wearing a sweater over her uniform. "St. Paul has allowed all businesses to reopen and children are back in school. The city officials feared that the way people filled the streets in their spontaneous Armistice celebration would cause a sharp rise in the flu rates. The number of cases did increase, but not at the rates feared."

"Then we can visit the wards?" Jere asked. "I'd consider it an honor, meeting some of these men."

"I'd like to meet that special young man Grace told us about, the one who's stealing your heart, Glorie." Grandmother's face was a study in innocence.

"Gra—ace." Glorie forced the name between clenched teeth.

"What?"

Glorie forced a smile for her grandparents. "There's

no special young man."

"Of course there is." Grace leaned toward Jere and Lucy and dropped her voice to a stage whisper. "The air between them positively crackles. He's a delightful man. You'll like him."

Glorie rolled her eyes.

A smile pulled up the corners of Grace's mouth. "I notice you haven't asked the name of the young man I've mistakenly identified as special, Sister."

The implication that he hadn't needed identification heated Glorie's cheeks in a telltale blush. "Don't be silly." She darted a glance at her grandparents. They didn't say a word, but their eyes danced with amusement.

Grace slipped her arm through Grandpa Jere's. "Let's visit one of the wards."

Nonchalance wasn't easy to assume when her heart raced in anticipation, Glorie discovered. It was obvious the ward Grace had in mind was Johan's.

Laughter met them in the hallway like a barrage long before they reached the ward doors. "The movie must still be showing," Glorie informed the others. "We don't have a screen, of course, so it's shown on the ceiling. It's the new Charlie Chaplin film. Charlie is a rookie soldier. He single-handedly captures the kaiser and the crown prince. I saw it earlier today in one of the other wards."

The letdown of disappointment mixed with relief for Glorie. Her spirits always lifted when she saw Johan. She'd love for him to meet her grandparents. But she and Johan were only nurse and patient. Well, perhaps a little more. After he was discharged, they'd never meet again. She hoped impulsive Grace hadn't said anything inappropriate to him, hinting a certain nurse had her cap set for him, for instance. Grace was a dear, but she didn't understand why Glorie liked to keep her life more private than Grace kept hers.

They met other Thanksgiving visitors and patients in the hallways. When the group entered another ward, they saw visitors dressed in their Sunday best seated beside many of the beds. Grace and Glorie went from one bed to another, introducing Jere and Lucy and wishing each man a happy holiday. Glorie found herself wishing they'd visited Johan's ward, after all.

Grandmother Lucy wanted to see Glorie's nursing quarters, but Grandpa Jere wanted only a chair and a cup of coffee. Grace assured him she would find him both.

Glorie and Grandmother had the quarters to themselves. The other nurses were either on duty or out on holiday. Grandmother looked about, commenting on the few personal and impersonal belongings before sitting down on the neatly made-up, narrow bed with its thin mattress. She pulled out a pearl hat pin and laid her fashionable, wide-brimmed hat down, then patted the army green blanket beside her. "Now, sit down and tell me about your life as an army nurse."

The words poured out, describing the experiences and feelings of the two-and-a-half weeks since the overseas men had arrived. "I felt cheated when I was assigned here, Grandmother. I desperately wanted to work near the front. The men there needed help most, I thought. My friend Julie is near the front. She went over with the medical corps from the University of Minnesota. She told me of her assignment when we met for dinner one evening. I was so jealous, I made up an excuse to leave early. I'm ashamed to admit it, but I did." Glorie took an envelope from her bedside drawer. "Here's her description of the first batch of wounded she saw."

She opened the letter with its familiar YMCA letter-head and read:

The injured came in a like a flood, over six hun-dred in twenty-four hours. Most walked from the battlefield, if you can call it walking, the way they reeled and stumbled. They leaned on each other when necessary, using sticks, when they could find them, for canes. Gassed men came in single file, cloths bound about their streaming eyes, each man with his hand on the shoulder of the man in front, the blind truly leading the blind. The ambulances only had room for the worst cases, usually meaning men without limbs or who were in danger of losing shattered limbs. The sheer numbers with horrifying wounds took its toll on our hearts and minds. It took stern stuff to turn from the continuing stream of wounded and concentrate on helping the person in front of you. And throughout all of it, the constant sound of guns and bombs.

I wish you could see these brave doughboys of ours. All shot to pieces yet telling us to help their buddies first, and all the time talking about getting back to the front.

The worst, for both the medical staff and the sol-diers, is knowing there are more injured boys where no one can reach them out in that awful no-man's-land between the armies.

Glorie looked up from the letter. "When I first read this, I thought how blessed she was to be stationed where she could help these men. Her work sounded so. . .noble. I wanted to be there if Fred was injured. But even though many boys I know are over there, for me the wounded she wrote about were faceless."

"And now they aren't." It wasn't a question.

"No." The word came out a whisper. "Now when I read these words I see the men in our wards struggling toward the hospital, or worse, lying helpless in no-man's-land, not knowing whether help will reach them in time. It's because some of the wounded here laid in the mud and filth so long that they've lost their legs and arms."

"It sounds like the war Jere and I were in. The weapons change, but war remains the same."

Grandmother stared out the window, but Glorie knew she saw the battlefields and hospitals of her own generation, not the bare tree branches swayed by raw November wind.

She isn't fragile, Glorie realized. *She's old but still strong.* Strength seemed to seep into Glorie's spirit at the thought of Grandmother Lucy and Grandpa Jere and thousands of others of their generation who had experienced war's carnage and survived to live happy, useful lives. *My generation will, too.*

Grandmother turned her gaze back to Glorie and took one of her hands in both her soft ones. "One of the men you see when you read this is Johan."

"Y–yes." She stared at Grandmother Lucy, too surprised to be embarrassed. "How did you know?"

"When the War between the States separated Jere and I, and I didn't know whether he was alive or dead, I saw him in the face of every soldier I nursed."

"Today you might be scolded by your medical superiors if they heard that," Glorie teased. "We're to keep our contact with the patients impersonal. Some of the nurses manage that by joking and laughing with the men. Others are brusque and businesslike, concentrating on the treatments, as though the patients are toy soldiers to be rebuilt instead of humans with emotions as well as flesh and blood.

"When I was taking my nursing course, one of the doctors invited me to dinner. I was flattered. I chattered on about how much the profession means to me, how deeply I'm affected by suffering. He said, 'If it's so hard for you to be around the suffering, why do you want to be a nurse?' Can you believe it, Grandmother?"

"What did you answer?"

"I said, 'How could I be anything else?' "

Grandmother's arms encircled her. Glorie felt the older woman's soft cheek pressing against her own. "Yes, that is the right answer. That is the answer in every true nurse's heart."

When the embrace ended, Glorie said, "I wonder if reconstruction nursing isn't by nature more personal than other types of war nursing."

"How do you mean?"

"When the first overseas men arrived, they were almost drunk on the joy of the war ending and returning as heroes. They never spoke of their wounds as anything but a minor difficulty to be overcome. I suspected much of it was bluster. The longer the men are here, and as more and more arrive, the more I see that every patient has emotional problems, too—what are called the spiritual wounds, I guess. Especially the amputation cases. The greater the physical wound, the deeper the unseen wound. The men are terribly afraid of the changes their disabilities will cause in their lives."

"Are you able to help them?"

Glorie hesitated. Were she and the other nurses helpful? "It seems the men respond best if we neither pity them or treat them like heroes beyond the reach of ordinary men. Of course, we let them know we honor them for their courage and sacrifice."

"It sounds like a difficult balance to find. And your friend Johan, does he have these invisible wounds you speak of?"

Glorie looked down at her hands. "He has deep wounds, Grandmother. His greatest wound is bitterness. He's not angry with the Germans; he's angry that he was forced to fight against them. It's not that he thinks the Germans were right to invade France and Belgium," she hastened to clarify. "It's that so many don't understand that for him and other German-Americans, they had to chose between their countries, to make war on their own people."

Grandmother Lucy nodded slowly. "Yes, that is always a hard choice."

"I. . .I was afraid you would think he's awful for feeling that way."

"Awful?" Surprise filled the wrinkled face. "Many people felt that way during the War between the States. Jere had a terrible time choosing which side to serve on. Didn't we ever tell you how Jere's father almost disowned him when he decided to serve with the Union?"

"No. I just thought. . ." Glorie paused, revelation striking. "I'm embarrassed to say that I thought it natural he was with the Union army. I suppose it seemed like the 'right' side, since I was raised in the North."

"Jere and Grace will wonder what happened to us. There is something I want to tell you before we rejoin them."

The reluctance in her tone made Glorie draw back slightly. "What is it?"

Grandmother's fingertips gently touched a small pin on her round collar. "This."

Glorie leaned forward and studied the image of a small, old-fashioned lamp. The brooch was made of metal, polished to a soft luster. "It's lovely. It looks old. Is it an antique?"

Her question brought a soft chuckle from Lucy. "I expect you would think so. Jere gave it to me sixty years ago, on my fifteenth birthday. He made it himself, fashioning it after a lamp he'd seen in a picture of Florence Nightingale. You see, he knew of my dream to follow in her footsteps."

"How special." Glorie was aware once more how deeply her grandparents cared for each other. *What a blessing it must be to find someone you love that much, and who loves you back the same.* A painful twinge of envy twisted her heart. Would she ever experience that? Johan's face with his teasing blue eyes and wide smile flashed into her mind. She pushed the picture away. She mustn't allow herself to daydream their friendship into something it wasn't.

But the picture returned, and the longing remained.

"It's the pin I want to tell you about," Lucy went on. "Ever since you went into nursing, I've planned to pass this pin along to you."

Glorie gasped softly and pressed her palms to her chest. "To me?"

"I'd hoped you would wear it close to your heart, as I have, and pass it along to your own daughter or granddaughter one day. But now I've decided to leave the pin to Grace."

"Oh." Disappointment filled Glorie's heart.

"Grace confided in me this morning that she'd also dreamed of becoming a nurse. Then she met Daniel and gave up her dream of nursing to marry him. She's not sorry for her choice, as I'm sure you know. She is completely in love with that man, and darling Elisabeth is the light of their lives. But Grace feels useless next to you."

Surprise straightened Glorie's spine. "Useless?"

"When she sees the wounded and knows you have the skills to help them and she doesn't. . ." Lucy spread her hands, palms up.

"She fills every minute with helping others. Hasn't she told you about her Red Cross work? She visits soldiers here, reads to them, writes letters for them, does shopping for them. She spent untold hours making surgical dressings. And even remade shirts for the soldiers when the army changed the uniform regulations, which was a great sacrifice, since she hates sewing."

Lucy smiled. "Yes, she's thrown her heart into helping the soldiers. That's why I decided to give her the pin. I realized you won't be allowed to wear it when you're in uniform. Grace can wear it. I hope it will be a reminder that her efforts are as much a gift as any nurse's. From your defense of her, I know you will understand."

"I think it's a wonderful idea." Glorie gave her a quick hug.

"I want to give it to her tonight, instead of leaving it to her in my will. I want to see her face when I pin it on her." Lucy stood and replaced her hat. "I would have joined the army as a nurse in this war, if they'd allowed me to." Her eyes danced with a merry smile. "Unfortunately, the army only accepts nurses between twenty-one and forty-five, so like Grace, I joined the Red Cross and made dressings. My favorite work was recruiting nurses."

As they left the room, Lucy continued, "Did I ever tell you about the time I met Clara Barton? It was one of the most memorable days of my life. It happened in Washington, and. . ."

Chapter 4

lorie was assigned to Johan's ward that evening. She saw him look casually toward the door when she entered. Then he did a double take, and a grin brightened his face. A smile leaped to her own in return, but she made herself casually stop at each man's bed until she arrived at Johan's in turn.

"You haven't had a shift on our ward for quite awhile." Johan's tone was a mixture of censure and gladness.

"I've been assigned to surgery most days. Did your parents visit today?"

"Yes. Better than last time."

She understood that he meant no one had said anything unkind in their presence, and she was glad for all concerned that it was so.

Three beds later, she discovered she was humming. Even a short encounter with Johan left her happy.

At the ward desk she filled out paperwork, then made a final check of the ward toward the end of her shift.

Johan, dressed in his uniform, showed up at the desk minutes later. "I can't sleep. Will you walk with me when you're off duty?"

Shocked at his boldness, she could only stare at him.

"It's not against the rules for an officer to ask a nurse to walk with him," he reminded her.

Like Johan, Glorie and most of the nurses were lieutenants, though most patients called them "Nurse" or "Sister." Glorie liked it that way. The men treated the nurses with respect whether they called them by the proper army titles or not. She couldn't quite imagine a patient saluting every time a nurse passed his bed.

"It's not against the rules," she agreed, "but fraternization between patients and nurses is discouraged."

His grin blazed. "Did the bachelor doctors make up that rule?" He leaned against the desk. "I won't be a patient long. I'm only asking you to keep me company on a platonic walk around the hospital halls."

In the end she agreed. She'd wanted to all along.

They chatted in low voices as they wandered the dimly lit, empty halls. He told her of his parents' visit, and she told him about Jere and Lucy.

"They sound interesting. I wish I'd met them."

She was glad he didn't know of Grace's attempt to arrange that or Grace's comments on Glorie's feelings for him.

At the end of one hall, they stopped beside a tall window overlooking a wide, tree-lined green. The moon shone brightly down, casting tree shadows across the manicured lawn. "I wonder if we'll have snow for Christmas," Johan mused. "I like a white Christmas. Do you?"

"Yes. I love snow." She leaned her forehead against the cool glass. "My brother, Fred, used to pummel Grace and me with snowballs. We'd fight back, but our aim wasn't as accurate as his."

"This is the first time I've heard about a brother. How old is he?"

"He's. . .I don't know." Glorie closed her arms tight over her chest, trying to keep back the pain gripping her.

"You don't know? What kind of sister doesn't know her brother's age?" Johan teased. He traced a frosty outline on the windowpane with his index finger.

Glorie had to swallow twice before she could explain. "Fred's birthday is November sixteen. He's twenty-one now, if he's alive."

"If. . ." Johan swung to face her.

"He. . ." She swallowed again. "He was declared missing after the last offensive." She shut her eyes tight in a vain attempt to keep back the threatening tears.

Then Johan's arms were around her, and her cheek pressed against the wool of his coat. "Oh, my dear, I'm so sorry," he whispered into her hair.

Her heart cracked open, and the tears spilled. She clung to him, sobbing. "I've tried so hard to believe he's all right, but I'm so horribly afraid."

"Of course you are. Anyone would be." One arm held her close about the waist, while a hand cradled the back of her head. She felt a kiss pressed against her hair, just above her ear. "Cry it out, Dear. It's all right."

His spoken invitation wasn't necessary. She was bawling uncontrollably, the sobs wracking her body.

When they subsided to a small shower and she'd used up both their handkerchiefs, part of her was appalled at her behavior. She always did her crying alone. She never broke down like this in front of others. Yet it hadn't felt strange or embarrassing. It felt. . .comfortable. It was too much to understand how sharing her grief with him could feel that way. She set it aside to examine later.

He led her to a flight of marble steps. She didn't resist the arms he kept about her, drawing her close when they sat down. The crying had drained her of energy. Exhausted, she laid her head against his shoulder. He rested his cheek against her hair. It felt so peaceful, so right, together with him this way. She wasn't sure how long they sat like that—not speaking, not spooning, just being together. She had the sense he was praying for her.

"Fred was with your division," she said finally, breaking the silence. "He was. . .is one of the Gopher Gunners with the 151st artillery, the Rainbow Division."

"I don't remember a Fred Cunningham. Of course, there are a lot of men in our division. We might know each other by face."

"I keep telling myself 'missing in action' doesn't mean dead. I know it might mean that, but it could mean other things, couldn't it?"

"Of course."

Had he hesitated before answering? She didn't want to believe it. "He could be a prisoner, couldn't he?"

She felt him nod, his cheek mussing her hair.

"Or wounded. Maybe he's unconscious and the people at the hospital don't know who he is. That's possible, isn't it?"

"Yes, Dear."

Glorie pressed her cheek harder against his shoulder and rested her hand on his chest. "Sometimes I don't think I can hope anymore. Other times, I don't know how to go on if I don't hope."

"Did Fred ever write you about the rainbows?"

"I know the Gopher Gunners are part of the Rainbow Division."

"Because of the division's name, we gave special meaning to nature's rainbows. We all knew the biblical story of the rainbow, how God gave it as a promise after the great flood. 'And the bow shall be in the cloud; and I will look upon it, that I may remember the everlasting covenant between God and every living creature of all flesh that is upon the earth.' When we'd see rainbows, we'd take them as a message of hope. They showed up at some pretty strategic times.

"The first was in June, when we left Baccarat and headed for Champagne and our first battle. The next was July 15, when the regiment started attacking north of Chateau-Theirry. Then September 12, when the division went over the top at the start of the Saint-Mihiel drive. We won the battles and the war."

The names were important names in the war. Like most Americans, she'd followed the troops' movements through newspaper reports. It seemed the Rainbow Division fought in all the major battles after its arrival in France.

This man beside her, with his arms around her and his uniform beneath her cheek, had been in those battles, which would be listed in history books for generations, perhaps for centuries. He'd returned injured, but he'd returned, and was almost restored to health now. If he could come through it all, couldn't Fred, even if he was missing in action?

If it's not already too late. The words hissed through her mind.

Reluctantly, Glorie pushed herself away from Johan. "I should go back to the quarters. If it weren't a holiday and so many nurses away on leave, I'd probably be in trouble. It's way past lights-out."

He walked with her down the steps and to the outside door. There his arms encircled her once more, and she leaned against him trustingly, not wanting to leave. His lips touched her temple in a soft, warm kiss. Then his fingers were beneath her chin, lifting it gently. His gaze searched hers with a question. She shyly smiled her answer.

His lips were gentle against hers. Glorie closed her eyes, welcoming the beauty in the lingering kiss. She wanted to stay in this place forever, this place of tranquillity and hope.

"When you think of Fred, remember the rainbows," Johan whispered as she stepped into the night.

✳

St. Paul citizens spent Thanksgiving rejoicing over the war's end. Victory Sings across the country celebrated "thanksgiving for the triumph of right, birth of universal freedom, and dawn of a new day." St. Paul's Victory Sing brought together almost five thousand people. Some ambulatory patients received passes to attend the sing with relatives or Red Cross volunteers.

Glorie heard about the celebration from Grace. "The people sang their hearts out, Glorie. 'America,' 'Battle Hymn of the Republic,' 'America, the Beautiful,' 'Star Spangled Banner,' and a host of our generation's songs, like 'Keep the Home-Fires Burning' and 'Pack Up Your Troubles.' The reverend from St. Mark's spoke. He said—let me think a moment, I want to get this right—okay, he said, '1776 marked the birth of the nation. 1861 marked the reconstruction of the nation. 1917 marked the birth of the nation's soul.' Isn't that beautiful?"

Glorie did think it beautiful.

So was Grandmother Lucy's lamp brooch which Grace now wore. Glorie commented on it, and Grace told her how much she loved it. "I almost forgot," she added, "Grandmother sent this box for you, Glorie."

Glorie took the box back to her quarters to open it. It

was a cedar box, hand carved. Inside were old letters and a journal. A note from Grandmother said they were letters Jere had written her during the War between the States and the journal in which she'd written letters to God. "I thought you might enjoy reading them," Grandmother wrote. "If you wish to share them with Johan, you have our permission to do so."

It was tempting to share the news of Johan's kiss with Grace. She and Glorie seldom kept secrets from each other. But Glorie wasn't ready to share this one yet. She wanted to savor the memory of it, the sweetness of it.

Glorie was glad she was assigned to surgery Friday and Saturday. She longed to see Johan, but she didn't know how she'd hide her fondness for him from other patients if she was working in his ward. It was a lesson in discipline, keeping her focus on the surgeries.

Saturday afternoon, she and the rest of the surgical team came out exhausted from a grueling eight-hour operation. A nurse met them with grim news. Five patients had come down with the flu that morning. Already fifteen were suffering from it. All were removed to the contagious-diseases building.

The staff exchanged weary glances. Fear bubbled up in Glorie's chest like chemicals in a test tube, hot and sudden and overflowing. No one said the removal had come too late. But everyone knew it.

By Monday, St. Paul and Fort Snelling were caught up in another wave of the deadly Spanish flu.

Chapter 5

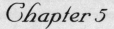

The building set aside for contagious diseases was overflowing within the week. Wards in the regular hospital buildings were set aside for flu cases also. Those who worked with the flu cases weren't allowed to work in the other wards.

The hospital, according to plan, had spread since it opened in September until it encompassed the entire fort. Now the fort was quarantined.

Still the flu spread.

Surgery cases were postponed, except in the most serious gangrene cases. The strictest care was taken to avoid exposing those who had recently had surgery. Precautions were also taken to keep gassed patients apart. As the flu spread, it became more difficult to protect these patients.

Every time Glorie approached Johan's ward, the fear she struggled to keep under control threatened to overwhelm her. She'd studied a lot about the gas used in war since the overseas men started arriving. It was believed that mustard gas didn't harm the lungs, as did chlorine and some other gasses that were common in the early years of the war. Already it was known that soldiers attacked with these gasses often had lingering asthma, and bronchial and heart problems.

She never thought she'd be grateful for anything related to Johan's experience with mustard gas, but now she
was grateful the gas wasn't considered more harmful.
Still, the knowledge of gasses' long-term effect was in its
infancy. If he caught the flu, could his lungs fight off the
resulting pneumonia that killed so many of its victims?

Ten days into the second influenza wave, Glorie stood
outside Johan's ward gathering her courage. Her hand on
the door, she sent a prayer heavenward. She straightened
her shoulders, took a deep breath, forced her lips into a
smile, and entered the ward.

She avoided eye contact with Johan while exchanging
comments with other soldiers as she walked between the
two rows of beds. She made a point to talk to a couple of
soldiers who she knew were in a depressive state.

Johan, like most of the ambulatory soldiers, was in
uniform during the day. When she reached his bed, he
was seated with his back against the headboard's white
metal bars, his sketch pad on his knees.

"May I see what you're sketching, Officer?" Glorie
hoped her tone was appropriately light and impersonal.
She always tried to act professional when in the ward
with Johan. It was a difficult task, with the comfort of his
arms and tenderness of his kiss filling her memory. She'd
had a lot of practice hiding her attraction to him. Since
the surgery ward was basically shut down, she'd been
reassigned to Johan's ward.

Now he gave her a grin that was anything but impersonal and allowed her to see the page. He'd sketched her
plumping the pillow of the patient across from him.

"I'll never understand how you capture a person or a
scene in only a few quick strokes," she complimented.

"Have you seen his caricatures?" Joe slid off the neighboring bed to stand beside her. "I like them best." He glanced down at the sketch of Glorie and the patient. "Hey, that *is* good."

Johan jerked a thumb in Joe's direction. "The resident art critic."

"At least I give you good reviews."

Glorie liked Joe's constant easygoing nature. "I agree with your opinions, Joe, but I haven't seen the caricatures."

"Show her the ones of President Wilson and Kaiser Bill," Joe urged.

Glorie raised her eyebrows in surprise. "There's a likely combination."

"Didn't you hear that Wilson's going to Paris to join the peace-treaty talks?" Joe asked.

The pages of the sketchbook rustled as Johan flipped through them. A moment later, he handed the pad to her. She burst into laughter. Joe was right. Johan had captured both the famous and the infamous with the expertise of a professional political cartoonist.

"Nurse Cunningham."

"Yes?" Glorie spun around to see which patient was calling for her. "Oh!" Her ankle twisted beneath her. She reached for the bed to steady herself. The sketch pad fell to the floor.

Joe grabbed her arm. "Are you all right, Nurse? Guess I shouldn't have left my shoes where someone could trip over them."

"I'll say," Johan growled. Glorie felt his hand at her back. "Did you hurt your ankle?"

"No, I'm fine." The ankle did hurt, but only a smidgen. All the attention embarrassed her. She knelt to pick up the sketch pad. It was lying open, upside down. Some of the pages were bent. "I hope I didn't ruin any of your drawings, Officer."

She smoothed back one of the pages. "Uuuh." The picture drew her breath from her like a vacuum. Her stomach felt as though she'd been kicked by a horse.

Johan grabbed it from her and snapped the pad shut.

Her gaze darted to his. Her breath came quick and hard.

He stared back at her, his eyes black. "A patient is asking for you, Nurse."

Glorie rubbed the palms of her hands down the sides of her skirt and tried to calm her runaway heartbeat before turning to find out which patient had called to her. The nurse-smile that was as much a part of her now as her uniform slid into place.

The soldier didn't need her nursing skills. His blankets were tangled around his feet, and with one arm it was difficult to release them. Most of the other patients in the room could have helped him. Glorie suspected he only wanted the attention of a woman. She chatted with him about homey things while straightening the bedding.

When she was done, she moved to the center of the ward. "May I have your attention, men?"

It took only a couple moments for everyone to stop what they were doing and look her way.

Glorie caught her hands behind her and gave them her most radiant smile, looking at any of them but at Johan. "I stopped in to let you all know that I've been reassigned again."

A groan went up in one large wave.

Gratitude toward them for appreciating the service she'd given them surged through her. "I'll be working in the flu wards, so I won't be able to visit you for awhile."

"Ah, no!"

"Don't go there!"

"Tell them we won't allow it."

"Now *there's* a reason to get the flu."

She held up her hands in laughing protest. "I've enjoyed working with you all. When I'm free to visit again, I'll stop back to this ward and say hello to any of you who aren't discharged."

She left the room without looking back.

She'd only gone a few feet down the hall when she heard the ward door bang open and steps falling hard on the marble floor behind her. A strong hand grabbed her shoulder. "Glorie, wait, please."

Immediately she stopped and looked up at Johan. "I'm sorry. I didn't mean to do it. The sketch. I didn't mean to invade your privacy." There was so much more she wanted to say. Her chest hadn't stopped aching since she'd seen the picture. It was only a moment, but she was sure the scene depicted was etched in her mind for eternity—the battlefield as only those who had been there had seen it. The horror of what he'd seen, what he had lived among, had leaped from the page.

He started to pull her close. A nurse passing by shot them a sharp and disapproving glance.

Johan took Glorie's arm and ushered her around a corner where they could be alone. He dropped back against the wall and pressed the palms of his hands over his eyes. "You weren't meant to see that. No one was." His voice was gruff, almost as coarse-sounding as it had been when she'd met him. "I thought if I put it on paper, maybe. . .maybe I could get it out of my head. Out of my nightmares."

She slid her arms around his waist, pressed her cheek

against the rough wool military jacket covering his chest, and hugged him as hard as she could. She didn't say anything. What could she possibly say to take away the images he lived with? She only tried to surround him with her love and prayed silently for his healing.

He dropped his hands from his eyes and wrapped his arms around her so tightly, she wondered if it was possible she might break. She felt a tear against her hair and squeezed her eyes shut to keep back her own tears.

Glorie didn't know how long they stood that way. She wasn't about to move if he needed to draw strength from her. Even if the head medical officer for the entire fort walked by, she wouldn't budge.

After a long while, Johan's arms loosened. He sighed, ruffling her hair. "You always smell like spring flowers. Much better than the antiseptic hospital odors or mess-hall food."

"Anything would smell good next to them." She forced a lilt to her voice, though her emotions were still gripped by the pain he'd allowed her to share.

His chuckle released some of the tension. A wide fingertip slid along her chin line, sending a shiver through her. Barely touching her skin, the fingertip continued its path to her eyebrow, across her cheekbone, and on to the edge of her lip. She closed her eyes, relishing his touch.

His kisses traced the path he'd blazed, his lips as light as gentle raindrops against her skin. They left her breathless. When his kisses reached her lips, they lingered there, long and sweet. They felt like a promise.

When his lips left hers, they moved again to her hair. She sighed with contentment and tucked her cheek against his shoulder.

"Do you have to take the assignment to the flu wards?"

The question jolted her back to the reality of their world. She nodded, the wool scratching against her cheek.

"You'd say so even if it weren't true. You're like one of Uncle Sam's doughboys. When duty calls, you answer, and give 110 percent."

"I won't be able to see you until the epidemic is over."

Neither spoke for a few minutes. Glorie wouldn't allow her thoughts to dwell on what might happen. Instead, she memorized the feeling of shelter in Johan's arms and the strength of his chest rising and falling beneath her cheek, so that she could keep them with her while the flu war separated them.

Johan cleared his throat. "I started reading your grandmother's journal from the Civil War last night. It's fascinating. War and people don't change much, I guess. When I first reached the front in France, I wished someone waited for me back home, a special girl, like you." His embrace tightened slightly in a squeeze. "Later I was glad there wasn't a girl to mourn if I didn't make it back. Then I came home and a miracle happened. I met you. Now we're in the same hospital, and we'll be as far apart as Lucy and Jere during the Civil War."

"God brought them through it and they found each other again." Was she assuming too much, saying that? Surely not, when he'd just told her she was special to him.

"I'll be praying for you, Glorie. Remember the rainbows."

His arms tightened around her waist. "Don't let it get you." His voice broke on the words. "Don't let that flu bug take you from me."

✳

Johan's chest felt like a shell hole when he returned to the ward half an hour later. The thought of Glorie heading into a ward filled with Spanish flu patients terrified him. His mind flashed a picture of her in a doughboy's tin hat, going over the top with a thermometer in her hand instead of a gun.

Was this what it was like for the women and families who waited at home for the soldiers who went to war? And he'd thought the soldiers were the ones who had it tough.

He flopped onto his bed, setting the springs creaking. Snoring came from close by. Joe was taking a nap.

Johan rolled onto his back, picked up his sketch pad, and started paging idly through it. He paused at a picture of Elisabeth asleep in Grace's arms. It was one of his favorites. He was crazy about Glorie. If they ever married, would their children look like Elisabeth?

That wasn't a safe path to follow right now.

He flipped through a few more pages. A flash of red, reminiscent of gory battlefields, stopped him. His heart skipped a beat. *It can't be.*

The familiar sweet yet metallic scent told him it was blood. It had only been applied to one page, the caricature of Kaiser Bill. "Hun Lover" was written across the kaiser's face in an American soldier's blood.

Johan's gaze darted about the room, searching for the perpetrator. Some men slept; some visited together; some read; three were playing cards.

Only one man paid Johan any attention. Captain Smith's dark gaze met Johan's without wavering, without smiling, without smirking. *There's nothing in his eyes but hate,* Johan thought. He was certain Smith was the guilty party. He couldn't have pulled it off without at least a couple of other men seeing him do it, but Johan doubted anyone would go against the captain to tell about it, except maybe Joe, but Joe was asleep.

Johan made his shoulders relax. He ripped out the offensive page, balled it up, and tossed it into the waste-basket beside his bed. The blood had soaked through a number of pages. One by one he removed them, the sound tearing through the deceptive quiet.

Chapter 6

The second wave of influenza was like reliving a nightmare.

The wards overflowed with sick soldiers. Most recovered after three to five days. Some died within forty-eight hours of the first symptoms. The healthiest-appearing men often were the ones who didn't make it.

Usually the onset was sudden. A headache, a general sense of not feeling well, then chills or fever. Within a few hours the temperature shot to 101 degrees or higher. Fevers lasted three to five days. A cough developed, short and dry, lasting a week or two beyond the flu itself, if the person was fortunate. Back and leg muscles and joints ached, causing the patients the most distress of any of the symptoms. Eyes watered and swelled. A few patients experienced nausea and vomiting.

The medical staff had little to offer the patients, other than to attempt to keep them comfortable. Isolating them was necessary in an effort to contain the disease as much as possible. Quinine and aspirin powders reduced some of the symptoms but didn't cure anything. Keeping the patients hydrated with water and juices and nourished with any food the patients could be convinced to eat was important.

Everything the patients touched needed disinfecting: blankets, handkerchiefs, bedclothes, eating utensils. The staff couldn't keep up with the demand.

During the first wave of influenza in October, enlisted men stationed at the fort while waiting to be called overseas were drawn into service at the hospital to help nurse the ill. Now there were no enlisted men to call upon. The overseas men at the hospital for reconstruction and convalescence were in no shape to help with flu victims. The dozen doctors and 120 nurses had only themselves and the Almighty to rely upon. And when the doctors and nurses began falling ill, the pressure increased. Neither nurses nor doctors were available from other hospitals, or even from training schools. Everywhere the need exceeded the supply, not only at Fort Snelling.

Red Cross volunteers helped out, as they did everywhere in every emergency. Even though most hadn't any medical knowledge, they could perform many of the necessary mundane procedures. Until they too fell ill and became patients.

Glorie was glad she didn't see Grace among the Red Cross volunteers. She didn't want Grace bringing the disease home to her husband and Elisabeth, or to their parents, or Grandmother Lucy and Grandpa Jere.

Even in the midst of the flu battle, Glorie always had an awareness of Johan. He wasn't foremost in her thoughts, but the knowledge of his caring was like a soothing background melody. When she allowed herself a moment to dwell on him, it was with a prayer that he be saved from the flu.

Time sheets and schedules were forgotten. Everyone worked until they were too fatigued to move and then worked awhile longer. Glorie and other nurses bandaged their ankles to help them keep going when they'd been on their feet too long. She became adept at recognizing staff members behind their gauze masks.

It wasn't the flu that killed, but the pneumonia that often followed the flu. When the patient appeared to be recovering, he was in the most danger. Glorie came to dread the cheerful patient with a heliotrope coloring to his skin. The combination was a sure sign that the patient wouldn't be alive in twenty-four to forty-eight hours.

The wards were never silent, even in the middle of the night. Even when nurses and volunteers weren't hurrying in and out, or urging patients to drink more fluids or take their medicine, or changing bedding, or bathing patients, the flu's dry cough was constant.

It was only two days before Christmas when Glorie walked into a flu ward, stopped short, and rubbed a hand across her eyes. Surely she wasn't seeing right; it was only fatigue causing the illusion that a masked Johan bent over one of the beds, sponging off a patient's face.

He wasn't an illusion.

Nausea threatened to overwhelm her. She fought it down. She'd faced so many fears the last few months, but seeing Johan in the midst of the flu victims. . .

She rushed to him, dodging a Red Cross girl whose arms were piled with clean towels.

Glorie reached to lay a hand on Johan's arm but hesitated at the sight of the patient in his care. "Captain Smith."

Johan turned. The blue eyes above his mask were heavy with fatigue.

"How long has he been ill?"

"A few hours. Complained of the headache about 0900, according to the guy in the bed next to him. He's running a fever already. He's sleeping now."

"That's probably the best thing for him."

"Joe's ill, too. I brought him down here an hour ago."

"Oh, no. Johan, we need to talk. Come out in the hall, will you?"

They walked quite far down the hall, searching for privacy. Glorie launched into her attack before they stopped walking. "Why didn't you let the staff bring him down here, Johan? It's dangerous for you to be in this ward." She hated the way fear slid her voice up the scale.

"Joe has been sleeping in the bed next to mine since Armistice." His voice was low and soft. To Glorie it sounded as though he was trying to quiet a hysterical child. It only added to her upset.

"But here everyone has the flu. Everyone except the staff, and I'm not so sure about some of them."

"The flu's everywhere, Glorie. Everyone knows we're short on nurses here now with so many down sick. I've more strength than most people in this hospital. I can't just sit up there on my bed and try to protect myself when I can do something, anything, to help."

She stamped her foot in frustration. "Don't you understand? The gas may have weakened your lungs. You mustn't take the chance of getting ill. If you develop pneumonia, you could die."

"I'm not going to—"

She covered her face with her hands. "I couldn't bear it if anything happened to you. . . ."

His hands were warm and strong on her shoulders. "Nothing's going to happen to me. I caught the flu when I was in France, before I was gassed."

Glorie lowered her hands as far as her chin. "Are you telling the truth or just trying to comfort me?"

167

He grinned. "Both."

"This is no laughing matter, Lieutenant."

His chuckle filled the hall.

It infuriated her. "Why are you laughing?"

His arms encircled her waist. "Are you always going to call me Lieutenant when you're angry with me, using that upset-mother tone of voice?"

She pressed her palms to his chest and shoved him away. "Why won't you be sensible? You shouldn't be holding me. I've been exposed. And I'm not so sure catching the flu once means you won't get it again."

"Glorie. . ."

"Oh, do go back to your bed." Frustrated, she started back to the ward. Her view of a Red Cross girl heading toward her carrying a pitcher grew hazy, cleared, and grew hazy again. *I must get some sleep soon,* Glorie thought.

She bumped into a table filled with glasses, then grasped it to steady herself.

From a great distance she heard Johan call her name, deep and slow like a Victrola record running down. Her knees seemed to dissolve. She heard something crash. Then she was falling into a deep, soft, foggy sea.

Chapter 7

A white curtain separated the cots of ill nurses from the ill soldiers. A dozen of the 120 nurses at the fort had developed the disease.

Johan refused to leave Glorie's side, except when modesty demanded, despite urging by doctors and nurses to rest. The second time the doctor checked on her, Johan made a quick trip to the ward where Joe and Captain Smith were located. Both still fought fevers. The captain ignored Johan when he stopped.

"Guess he'll never forgive you for being born German-American." Joe paused, then continued in an uncertain tone. "So, have you forgiven him? Couldn't believe you helped him down here."

Hands in his trouser pockets, Johan looked over at the captain's bed. "I've had a lot of time to think about the war. None of us were raised to kill. People think the hard thing about going to war is risking your life. They forget our country asks us to put aside everything we've been taught and take lives. It's easier to kill if you can hate the people you're fighting." He shrugged, self-conscious at opening up this way. "I expect that's what's happened to the captain. A person is an enemy or an ally, no gray lines. Easier that way."

Johan tried not to act rushed while talking with Joe, but as soon as possible he hurried back to Glorie, stopping at his ward to pick up his Bible and the cedar box with Jere and Lucy's letters that Glorie had lent him. The twenty minutes since he'd last seen her seemed like a lifetime. There was no change in her condition.

He sat beside Glorie's bed, praying for her, loving her, trying to will strength and health back into her body. Her collapse had sent fear spiraling through him, fear as strong as anything he'd experienced on the battlefields. Twelve hours passed before she slipped bleary-eyed into consciousness. She struggled to get out of bed, grabbing her hip, which he knew ached like those of all the flu victims. "I can't lie here. The men need me."

Johan pushed her gently back onto the mattress. "You can help them best by getting your strength back."

"But there aren't enough nurses."

"Take care of yourself, then you can take care of them."

The head nurse repeated his words a few minutes later, invoking her rights as a superior officer to turn the suggestion into a command.

Johan tried to temper the joy that flooded him at Glorie's awakening. He knew it was only the beginning of her fight.

He bathed her face with a cool, damp cloth.

"That feels good. Have I scolded you yet for staying with me?"

Her question surprised a short laugh from him. "Not yet."

"I must be even sicker than I feel. You shouldn't be here."

"You're too weak to chase me away. I'm staying."

"I suppose it's too late anyway. If you weren't suffi-ciently exposed to the virus before, you are now. If you get sick, Johan Baker, I'm going to be awfully mad at you."

"I'll take my chances, Beautiful."

She groaned and pushed back her hair. "I know what patients look like when they feel like this. It should be against hospital rules to let you see me when I'm ill."

Johan laughed softly, glad she had enough energy to make the feeble joke. He lifted one of her hands and touched his lips to it. "Your face is beautiful to me, but even if it weren't, it wouldn't matter. It's your beautiful heart I love."

Her feverish eyes searched his. "Love?"

He nodded.

She sighed and closed her eyes. "What a nice word." Tucking his hand against her fever-heated cheek, she fell back asleep.

It didn't matter that he grew uncomfortable sitting on the hard oak chair with his hand in hers. He wouldn't remove his hand if a bomb struck. He shifted the rest of his body as best he could time and again the next couple hours, while reading more of Jere's letters to Lucy and Lucy's letters to God one-handed.

It wasn't until morning that Johan thought to call Grace. Lucy answered the telephone. She thanked him for letting the family know about Glorie, assured him that someone would visit if allowed into the wards, and asked him to tell Glorie they were praying for her.

By noon Glorie was coughing up blood.

The tired-looking doctor stepped out from behind the curtain around her bed where he'd been examining her and spoke to the impatiently waiting Johan. His gaze focused over Johan's shoulder instead of meeting Johan's own gaze. "Pneumonia's setting in."

The fever built. Glorie drifted in and out of consciousness, sometimes hallucinating, sometimes moaning in a manner that tore at Johan's heart. Her medicine was changed to quinine. Terror at the evidence of the flu's power twisted his insides into painful knots. Johan found it difficult to concentrate on the letters, journal, or Bible.

He bathed her face repeatedly. It seemed to soothe her, and that soothed the aching around his heart a little. He combed her hair, though she remained unconscious of her surroundings, simply because he knew she disliked looking unkempt.

He almost prayed himself out. It was difficult to avoid the temptation to try to make a deal with God, even though he'd seen on the battlefields that such deals seldom appeared to work. He wouldn't let himself think what life would be like if she didn't make it.

Hours later, strains of "Silent Night" filtered through the patients' moaning and coughing and the clatter of dishes from dinner served in bed. The music startled Johan. Carolers were singing in the hallway. *It's Christmas Eve*, he remembered. A night for miracles. Would there be any miracles in the hospital tonight?

"Lieutenant Baker?"

"Yes?" Johan rose politely and held out his hand to the tall, slender old man standing with his hat in his hand at the end of the bed.

The older man's grip was firm. "I'm Jere Cunningham, Glorie's grandfather."

"Glorie will be glad to see you. I wasn't sure family would be allowed in. But, maybe it isn't safe for you to be here."

"I've had the flu. Besides, it was important to me to see Glorie tonight." His gaze rested on Glorie's face.

"She's sleeping right now." Johan was thankful she wasn't tossing and turning. He knew it would hurt her grandfather more to see her in that state.

Jere removed something from his pocket and held out his hand, palm up, toward Johan.

"Why, that's the pin your wife gave Grace, isn't it?"

Jere nodded. "Grace died this afternoon."

Shock muted Johan.

"Her husband, Daniel, died a few hours earlier," Jere continued, "right after we received the news that Fred, Glorie's brother, is alive. I guess the good Lord gave us the gift of that news to strengthen us for what came next."

"We didn't even know they were sick." His senses reeled. Bubbly, compassionate Grace, gone. *How will I ever tell Glorie?*

"When Grace fell ill, she made us promise not to tell Glorie. Grace didn't want her sister to leave the men here when her nursing skills were so needed."

"Elisabeth?"

"The flu didn't strike her hard. She's already getting past it. Getting past the other will be the fight." Jere sighed deeply. "Almost losing our grandson in the war, losing Grace. . .I had to come see Glorie. Not to hit her with the hard news, just to sit with her awhile and pray for her."

Johan understood that to the depth of his bones. He indicated the straight-backed oak chair that had been his home the last two days. "Won't you sit here, Sir?"

Johan retreated a few feet away to give Jere privacy. He watched the older man take Glorie's hand and knew he was talking to her heart-to-heart, though not out loud.

He wanted to tell Jere he'd learned so much from his letters, written during a different war. He recalled what Jere wrote near the beginning of that war, when he joined the Union army. *"I can't support the South, but neither will I fight against the South. I told the officer in charge, 'I am strong and can obey orders. I can be a litter bearer and help bind up wounds. But my beliefs will not allow me to bear arms.'"*

Johan had learned about that war in school, but he hadn't understood it was about people choosing sides against their own families and friends. He hadn't realized that other people had faced the kinds of choices German-Americans had in the Great War. Now he knew it wasn't about choosing who you'll be against; it was knowing what you are for, as Glorie had reminded him. Glorie, Grace, Lucy, and Jere all chose to be for healing, even in the middle of war.

I choose healing, too, Johan thought.

Healing of a different sort. President Wilson had a plan for a new kind of world with an organization to help nations choose to live in peace instead of war: the League of Nations. It seemed to Johan something the King of Peace would like. *That's what I want to do, help the world live in peace.* He'd try going into politics. Maybe be an ambassador one day or, better yet, part of that League if it became a reality. Wherever he ended up, he wanted Glorie beside him.

Jere left before Glorie awoke.

Johan was sitting beside the bed, turning the lamp pin over and over in his hand, when dawn's first light filtered through the windows and Glorie opened her eyes. Joy leaped in Johan's chest when he saw that her gaze was clear and true, without the haze of fever. "You had company," Johan greeted her return to the waking world. "Family. You have good news. Fred is alive."

Even the fever couldn't keep the joy light from her eyes. "What happened to him? Is he home?"

"He's staying in Europe with the occupation troops for now. He was injured in the last battle and found unconscious. Who knows why the news didn't get back to your family. He's fine now."

"What a wonderful Christmas present."

"Yes." He waited until a round of coughing passed. "Grace wanted you to have this." He placed the pin in her hand.

"Why, it's the pin Grandmother Lucy gave her."

"Yes. Florence Nightingale's lamp. A symbol of healing."

"How nice of her to lend it to me." Another round of coughing racked her.

Johan cradled her hand, kissed her palm beside the pin, and said yet another silent prayer. When she was stronger, he'd tell her about Grace and Daniel. "Will you marry me, Glorie? As soon as you're well?"

"Yes, oh yes, my love." The glow in her eyes lit his heart. "But, would you mind very much if we wait until Fred is home? I want all my family at our wedding."

"Of course we'll wait for Fred."

Glorie yawned and blinked. "I suppose it's awfully poor etiquette for a girl to fall asleep when she's just received a marriage proposal, but I don't think I can stay. . .awake. . .any. . ." Her eyes closed. Her hand went limp in his.

Fear struggled within him. The fever seemed to have broken, but it would take awhile to recover from the pneumonia. He remembered God's rainbows and made himself concentrate on the future he hoped he and Glorie would share, man and wife, raising Elisabeth, and working together for healing in the world.

※

Johan continued to pray and hold fast to his dreams of the future during the anxious days which followed. When Glorie showed definite signs of improvement, he teased, "It wasn't the fever talking when you promised to marry me, was it?"

Her lashes lowered against still-pale cheeks, then rose to reveal green eyes sparkling with love. "I thought perhaps I'd hallucinated your proposal. I couldn't ask without being immodest."

He chuckled and drew her into his embrace, rejoicing inside at the gift of this woman's love. At the sound of a nurse's voice nearby, he released Glorie reluctantly. She leaned back against the pillows, smiling in the January sunshine. "I'm so happy. It hardly seems possible the war is over, Fred is alive, and you and I found each other here."

"All answered prayers." Johan sent up another silent prayer. So far she'd accepted Grace's absence as a wise precaution in avoiding the flu. He took Glorie's fingers in his, rubbing his thumbs lightly over the back of her small hands, wishing there were a way to prevent the pain he was about to inflict. Sorrow for her burned within him. "But Grace. . ."

"What about Grace?" Her green eyes smiled in question.

"God has called Grace and Daniel home."

Glorie stared at him as if she didn't comprehend.

"It was the flu. I'm sorry." His voice cracked on the words. He gathered her into his arms.

She clung to him as he gently rocked her. After a long

time she whispered, "Poor Elisabeth. I want to raise her, Johan."

"Of course we will raise her, Dear. We both love her already."

Healing tears came. Gradually Glorie's tense body relaxed against him and she slept. Johan gently lowered her to the pillows. His vision blurred. How like her to be more concerned with Elisabeth's pain than her own. The realization that Glorie's love for Elisabeth would help heal Glorie's own loss brought him peace. And he would be with her every step of the way, from the storm of heartbreak to the rainbow God had promised.

Epilogue

May 8, 1919

L ook, a rainbow!"
   A collective "Ooooh!" went up from the crowd waiting at the railroad station for the returning Rainbow Division. The spring shower that had made the brilliant colors bridging the sky possible was instantly forgotten.

Glorie squeezed Johan's arm and met his glowing gaze. Elisabeth was held tight in his other arm. "Uncle Fred will be home in just a few minutes, Elisabeth. Watch for the train."

"I hope your parents saw that rainbow," Johan said as he stretched to look over the heads of the crowd. Many people carried flags, making it more difficult for Johan to see. "I guess it's no surprise that we've managed to lose them. There must be forty thousand people here."

A stranger saw the wound stripes on Johan's uniform and asked to shake his hand.

A whistle blew.

"Here it comes! Here comes the train, Aunt Glorie!"

Elisabeth's eyes were wide with excitement.

Glorie clung tightly to Johan's arm as the crowd jostled in anticipation.

The engine chugged into view, draped with rainbow-colored ribbons. An engineer leaned out the window waving an American flag for all he was worth. A sign stretched across one of the cars announced, "Minnesota's Gopher Gunners." The crowd let up a roar of welcome.

Everything was tumult and noise. Men in khaki almost fell from the train in their eagerness to find family and friends. A corporal threw his arms around a tiny gray-haired woman. "Ma!" An older man blinked back tears, pounding a private's shoulder and repeating, "Well done, Son, well done." Dozens of grinning doughboys shook hands with everyone they met, whether they knew them or not. A burly sergeant stopped beside a woman wearing a black crepe armband, removed his hat, and thanked her.

Tears clouded Glorie's eyes at the sight of a Red Cross girl in a broad-brimmed hat weaving through the crowd handing soldiers oranges and chocolates, which were accepted with a polite "Thank you, Miss" and stuffed into pockets while the soldiers continued looking for loved ones. Glorie touched a gloved finger to the lamp pin on the lapel of her Army Nurse Corps jacket, a strict violation of the dress code. Then she dashed her tears away. This was a day for rejoicing.

For a split second Glorie saw Fred's face on the train steps before he dropped into the sea of people. She waved her handkerchief frantically. "Fred! Fred Cunningham!"

"Fwed!" Elisabeth repeated, waving her hands in the air at no one in particular.

Their calls were lost among thousands of other calls.

"Which way?" Johan yelled in Glorie's ear. They pushed through the crowd in the direction she'd last seen Fred.

Suddenly he was there. "Sis!" His arms enveloped her, sweeping her off her feet. Their exuberant hug knocked her hat askew.

Elisabeth allowed him a brief hug, suddenly shy now that she was face-to-face with him.

Grinning, Fred held out his hand to Johan. "You must be the man who won my sister's heart." His lower jaw dropped, a shocked look on his face. "Why, it's. . .it's you!"

Mystified, Glorie looked from his face to her fiancé's. Johan's face had the same shell-shocked look as Fred's.

"You!" Johan repeated.

A moment later the men were slapping each other on the back. "I wondered what happened to you," Fred said, "but I didn't know your name so couldn't ask."

Fred turned to Glorie. "You've some man here. A group of us were surprised by a sudden shelling. Gas bombs, you could tell by the sound of them. We headed for a trench, reaching for our gas masks on the way. The area was nothing but mud. I fell, rolled a few feet, stood up, and started forward. I stepped in just the wrong place and found myself up to my knees in mud. I grabbed for my gas mask. Evidently when I fell, the mask hit something sharp, for there was a hole in it."

He jerked a thumb at Johan. "This soldier sees what's happened, pulls off his own mask, and shoves it on me. I protested something awful, but caught in the mud like that, I couldn't get away. He yanked my mask out of my hands. I saw him stuff a handkerchief in the hole in my mask, slip the mask over his head, and take off down the trench as fast as he could away from the cloud of gas that was rolling toward us with the speed of a locomotive."

Johan shrugged, his face ruddy. "I wasn't exactly a hero."

"You are in my book," Fred declared.

Glorie's gaze met Johan's embarrassed one. "In *my* book, too," she quipped lightly. A sweet peace washed over her. War and evil weren't as strong as people thought. Love was stronger. Johan taught her that in helping Fred. The nurses who voluntarily risked their lives to help the wounded proved it, too.

Nothing was as strong as love.

JOANN A. GROTE

JoAnn is an award-winning author from Minnesota. She believes that readers of novels can receive a message of salvation and encouragement from well-crafted fiction. Her first novel, *The Sure Promise,* was published by **Heartsong Presents** in 1993. It was reissued in the best-selling anthology *Inspirational Romance Reader, Historical Collection #2* (Barbour Publishing). JoAnn has published historical nonfiction books for children and over twenty historical and contemporary novels for adults and children, including several novels with Barbour Publishing in the **Heartsong Presents** line as well as the *American Adventure* series for kids. She contributed novellas to the best-selling anthologies *Fireside Christmas* and *Prairie Brides* (Barbour Publishing). Once a full-time CPA, JoAnn now works in accounting only part-time and spends most of her "work" time writing.

A Light in the Night

by Janelle Burnham Schneider

Dedication

With love and gratitude to three very special nurses,
who I am honored to call friends—
Catherine, Diane, and Cathy.
And to Mark, for all you do to help
bring my stories into being.

*"Therefore, since we are surrounded by such a great cloud
of witnesses, let us throw off everything that hinders
and the sin that so easily entangles,
and let us run with perseverance the race marked out for us.
Let us fix our eyes on Jesus,
the author and perfecter of our faith."*
HEBREWS 12:1–2 NIV

Author's Note

The Atlantic Ferry Command is a little-known part of World War II. This was the means by which men and matériel were transported from North America to England to aid on the European front. Goose Bay was only one of several locations involved in this endeavor. First the Canadians carved an airfield and supporting military base out of the wilderness of Labrador, then the Americans made their own space. Though the focus at the bases was the flights made by the Royal Air Force of England, the Royal Canadian Air Force, and the U.S. Army and Air Force, thousands of support personnel also contributed.

In *A Light in the Night*, I've chosen to highlight the efforts of the nurses who were posted at Goose Bay. Though this base was far from the front, medical services were still needed for routine ailments, as well as for the injuries sustained during the many crash landings and other accidents that occurred.

We owe just as much to those who served on this little-known base as to those who fought overseas. Without the Atlantic Ferry Command and other supporting organizations, those overseas would have had no resources for their struggle against the Axis powers.

On a personal note, this story is particularly special to me for two reasons. First, the romance between Ian and Elisabeth mirrors some of the experiences in the courtship between my husband and me. My husband, Mark, is an engineer with the Canadian forces and, as such, spends much time away from home. From the earliest days of our romance, the moon has remained our joint symbol of our love for one another.

Second, just as I was beginning to write this story, a small hero passed from this life into the Father's arms. Grifin Alexander Rochat was born to a dear friend of mine and experienced a heart transplant at just three weeks of age. Though he fought valiantly to remain with us, his body couldn't continue the struggle. He had a true warrior's spirit. His parents and his older brother have continued to display incredible courage as they adjust to their loss.

Experiences like war and like Grifin's death sometimes cause us to ask how a God of love can permit such heartache. I have no answers. All I know is that God is faithful in all His ways, and He carries us through the storms of grief.

The cloud of witnesses to which the writer of Hebrews refers has a whole new meaning for me. I find great comfort in knowing Grifin is watching with all those who have gone before and waiting for us to join him. May we, too, be found faithful.

Janelle

Chapter 1

Accompanied by chattering coworkers, Elisabeth Baker tugged her parka hood securely over her auburn hair as she stepped outside the doors of the nurses' quarters. Here in Goose Bay, Labrador, winter's chill could freeze exposed skin in a matter of minutes. The fur around the edge of her hood shielded her face from the wind as they walked to the officers' mess.

The walk did nothing to decrease her dislike for what lay ahead. She didn't enjoy these weekly "social evenings." She preferred to watch, to observe unnoticed from the sidelines. That wasn't possible here. A collection of young men always hovered around the nurses, wanting to chat or even wanting to dance. Her adopted father would tell her it was a good "stretching" experience.

She felt the affectionate smile tug at her lips while the cold stung her cheeks. Just the thought of Papa Johan, as she called him, brought a sense of security and courage. He and Mama Glorie had always understood her shyness yet encouraged her to step beyond it. Mama would remind her of her duty. Somehow, when Mama used the word, it didn't sound like drudgery. It sounded like honor, part of the honor of being a nurse, following in Mama Glorie's footsteps and those of their nursing ancestors.

The sounds of the festivities could be heard long before Elisabeth reached the swaths of light pouring from the windows. Piano music seemed to float above the roar of conversation mingled with laughter. As she and her friends passed through the doorway, welcome warmth embraced them. The sheer volume of conversation made her think briefly of retreat. Instead, her gaze searched out other nurses while she unzipped her parka and hung it by its hood on one of the many wooden pegs that bristled from the wall.

The room was large and open. The rectangular tables that usually filled it had been stacked and pushed together along the long wall across from the main doors, to open up the floor area for dancing. One of the soldiers sat at the beat-up-looking upright piano in the corner to Elisabeth's right, providing better-quality music than often graced these gatherings. Urns of hot water for tea and fragrant coffee sat on a couple of tables against the wall to her left, along with bowls of fruit juice punch and plates of cookies. Just above the tables, a large opening allowed a view of the large kitchen area, staffed tonight by two soldiers who kept the refreshments supplied.

In the far corner, beside the refreshment tables, Elisabeth spotted the group of nurses. She threaded her way toward them, through clusters of conversing men. While her small stature made it impossible to see over the shoulders of the crowd, it also enabled her to slip through unobtrusively. By the time she reached the corner where she had seen the other women, they'd already been claimed for dances.

Dancing hadn't been part of her life before she was stationed here. Though many of her Christian friends viewed dancing as immoral, Elisabeth's reasons for not dancing were more personal. She simply didn't want a stranger holding her that close. Even though dancing was one of the few recreational options here at this remote post, she still couldn't bring herself to participate. Nevertheless, she enjoyed watching others have fun. These Friday evening socials enabled them all to put aside for a few hours the grim reality of their daily lives.

The approach of a tall, blond-haired soldier in a Canadian uniform made her palms suddenly feel clammy. She hated being invited to dance. While some accepted her gentle refusal, others became insistent. When she tried explaining that she didn't know how to dance, they offered to teach her. The situation always made her feel put on the spot. Even though her job as a nurse required that she know how to assert herself when necessary, her confidence always deserted her in social settings.

"May I bring you a cup of tea?" His bass voice penetrated through the noise around them.

Having braced herself to refuse a dancing request, she was caught off balance by his less-threatening inquiry. "S–sure," she stuttered in reply. "Uh, that would be nice."

His deep-set gray eyes softened with his smile. He gave no verbal reply, making Elisabeth feel as if he didn't fault her for her social awkwardness and perhaps even understood it. She almost laughed aloud at the thought. His blue uniform and the gold wings below his left shoulder told her he was a pilot. Pilots were known for their confidence. What would she say to him when he came back? She hoped the other nurses would return soon to carry the conversational burden.

"Do you take sugar?"

Again, his deep-voiced question made her stumble mentally. "Um, well, sometimes."

He extended the cup toward her. "In that case, this shouldn't be too offensive. I dumped a spoonful of sugar in just to be safe." His twinkling eyes invited her to share his amusement.

She felt her tension ease enough to make her smile genuine. She raised the volume of her voice to be heard. "A nurse can't be too picky about her refreshments. We learn to take whatever is available."

"Contrary to common belief, pilots are the same. One has to take whatever food and drink might be offered at a refueling stop or go hungry." He leaned back against the wall, his knees slightly bent as if he were used to relaxing without benefit of chairs. He inclined his head toward her, giving the impression he wanted to be sure to hear whatever she wanted to say next.

But nothing clever came to mind. She enjoyed the warmth of the tea as it slipped down her throat, but it wasn't worth commenting on. She could hardly tell him she felt surprised to be enjoying his company. The piano player moved easily from a familiar wartime tune to a melody Elisabeth hadn't heard before. She tilted her head, letting herself absorb the music and sensing that this tune would replay in her mind for days to come. She noticed the pilot smiling at her just before he spoke.

"Is the song a favorite of yours?"

She shook her head. "I've never heard it before. It sounds like the words would be wonderful."

"They are. Would you like to go see if they're written on the sheet music he's using?"

Nerves assaulted her again. This corner felt comfortable, unnoticed. If she followed him across the room to the piano, she would be seen. But his eyes communicated quiet encouragement as he silently extended his hand, as if inviting her to trust him. The music drew her as nothing else could have. She took a step toward him. He pushed away from the wall, grasped her elbow gently, and began to maneuver them through the crowd.

At the dancing area, her steps hesitated. The open area lay between them and piano. Crossing it meant making herself conspicuous, but gentle pressure on her elbow steadied her. Her tall companion guided her along the edge of the crowd, seeming to take care not to draw her into the dancing area. Once they reached the piano, she stood just behind and to one side of the man seated there. Her companion took up a position between her and the rest of the room. The musician slowed the tempo, clearly drawing the song to a close.

The soldier quickly reached into his pocket for a quarter and made a circling gesture with his hand, asking the musician to play the song again. The man grinned and segued from ending notes back into the introduction. Elisabeth couldn't help but smile. She felt almost as if she were back home, singing beside the piano with Mama Glorie while Papa Johan accompanied them, adding his bass to their higher voices.

Now as she read the words on the sheet music, the pilot's strong, deep voice began singing along in perfect pitch.

Early in childhood, she'd learned to harmonize with her parents. Since the pilot was carrying the melody of this song, she quietly found a simple, high soprano harmony to add to the refrain.

"No matter where I go
    You'll be with me in my soul.
Though we have to part for now

191

In our hearts we're never far.
When I see the sun, I'll feel your smile.
When I look at the moon, I'll think of you."

Their voices blended so perfectly that her gaze sought his in pure surprise. They maintained eye contact throughout the refrain, then Elisabeth had to turn back to the sheet music for the words to the next verse, which they sang in unison. The din in the room slowly faded to a listening silence. Elisabeth didn't realize they'd become the focus of attention until the second verse. She hated the tremble in her voice. Her singing partner shifted slightly closer to her and put a reassuring hand at the small of her back. Somehow it steadied her. The pianist must have felt the mood in the room as well, because he didn't end the song but took them through the refrain two more times. As the final notes of music hovered in the air, applause swept through the room. Elisabeth felt a blush heat her face. When the clapping subsided, she offered a smile and inclined her head graciously. No matter how much she disliked being on display, she could do no less than acknowledge the appreciation.

To her immense relief, she felt the pilot's hand at her elbow, guiding her toward the exit. She reached for her coat, and he took it from her fingers to hold it while she slipped her arms into the sleeves. As she zipped it and slipped the hood into place, he shrugged into his own coat.

The cold struck her face like so many invisible needles as they stepped into the starlit night. He guided her around the edge of the building, where they were sheltered from the blast of the wind.

The cold felt tolerable here, even welcomed after the heat of being on display. She couldn't believe she'd followed this man into the seclusion of the dark outdoors, but his presence felt more sheltering than the noise and crowd indoors.

After a few moments of silence, he commented, "Now that we can hear each other clearly, introductions might be in order. I'm Ian MacDonald."

She had to tilt her head back to look up into his face. "I'm Elisabeth Baker."

"Too bad we already have jobs." Even in the darkness of the northern evening, she could see the humor in his eyes. "I think we could go on the road as a singing team."

"Not me." She shook her hooded head. "I like to sing, but only in private."

"I guessed as much." He reassured her with a smile that seemed to come from his heart. "You were very courageous in there."

"Courageous?" Conviction made her voice more forceful than usual. "That was just manners. It would have been rude to turn my back on the appreciation they were showing. No, courage is what I see every day at work when young men struggle to recover from injuries they shouldn't have in the first place."

"I haven't thought much about the hospital, to be honest. Is it busy?"

"It seems like we always have at least half the beds filled with routine afflictions—flu, pneumonia, frostbite, and various injuries."

"I guess this far from the front, you wouldn't see many battle wounds."

"For which I'm grateful," she responded fervently. "It's bad enough seeing the casualties from crash landings. You'd know as well as anyone about the number of planes that miss the runway, or slide off the end, or otherwise end up in a heap. One of these days, someone is going to get killed." She could hear the emotion in her own voice and fell silent. She was here to serve, not give commentary.

"Any part of war is risky, even being part of the supply line," Ian remonstrated softly. "We all know that's part of the package."

"It still doesn't make it right."

"Do you also see that it's necessary?"

The gentleness in his voice made her want to confide her distress. Their purpose here haunted her day and night. She'd come because it was part of her responsibility with the Red Cross. In no way, however, did it make her a believer in the "cause." But this wasn't the time for her to voice those thoughts. Instead, she deliberately shifted the subject. "I'd rather hear about your family."

He looked off into the distance with tenderness in his expression. "My mom, Sarah, is a widow from the Great War. My dad was killed toward the end. She supported us by working in a bakery. I have younger twin sisters, Megan and Millicent. Megan's fiancé is an infantryman overseas. How about your family?"

"I'm an only child, adopted. My adoptive dad, Papa Johan, is a veteran of the Great War and has worked ever since as a politician. My adoptive mother, Mama Glorie, was an army nurse in the Great War and still works as a nurse."

"Is that why you became an army nurse?"

"Actually, I'm not real army. I trained under the Red Cross. But when America joined the war, all qualified Red Cross nurses were automatically enlisted in the U. S. Army Nurse Corps. It's not my choice, but it is my duty."

"Which brings me back to my original question. Don't you see that our being here is necessary?"

Apparently this man could be stubborn as well as charming. "I know our governments think it's necessary. My belief is that war is never necessary. If people want peace badly enough, they can always find a way."

The pilot turned to face her directly. "May I tell you how I see it?"

She nodded again.

"We didn't seek out this war—not Canada, not the United States, not Britain. Britain was forced to defend itself, and Canada's loyalty to Britain made her a part of it as well. The U.S. suffered an unprovoked attack by Japan, and she had no choice but to become part of the conflict. We're in it because we have to be, not because we want to be."

The intensity of her feelings forced her to speak. "I'm not questioning our involvement but rather the war itself. It's so senseless. How many people are losing their lives, or their health, because of the Axis's determination to control the world? What's the point of it all?" Her voice broke. Silently, she berated herself for even opening the conversation. Why bare her heart like this when she knew he'd never understand?

He remained silent for a long time. Finally he inquired in a soft, yet respectful voice, "Elisabeth, are you a believer?"

"Yes, I am. Why do you ask?"

"I wanted to be sure we have the same frame of reference." He turned to face her and took both her mittened hands in his own. "Since we believe in Jesus as Savior, we also have to believe in God as the Controller of all things. We don't know why He allows the things He allows, but we can be at peace knowing He is in control."

She shook her head in disagreement. "That's not

good enough for me. I believe He is in control, but I want to know why He doesn't stop it."

Again he didn't respond immediately. Finally, he shrugged. "I can't even pretend to have an answer for that, Elisabeth. For me, it's enough to be doing what I can to help stop the war. I wish I could give you answers, but since I can't, I'll offer to pray until peace comes to you. In the meantime, I'd better get you back to where it's warm. Shall we return to the mess or would you rather go back to your barracks?"

"The barracks, please." She appreciated his perception of her mood. She needed quiet now, not a noisy roomful of people. To her surprise, he kept her hand tucked in the crook of his elbow and let the walk pass in silence. When they reached the nurses' quarters, she smiled up at him. "Thank you for listening and for the company."

"My pleasure." A smile lit his face once more, as if he'd just thought of a wonderful secret. He saluted her then walked away into the night.

Chapter 2

Elisabeth woke at reveille the next morning, feeling as if she'd barely slept. Her conversation with the tall pilot had replayed itself in her dreams. It wasn't typical of her to voice her thoughts, and especially not to someone she barely knew. What was it about the Canadian that had drawn such openness from her?

She thought back over the evening as she loosened the braid that had confined her long, heavy hair while she slept. The words to the song she'd learned began to replace her self-conscious thoughts, and she found herself humming the poignant tune. As always, picking up the silver-backed brush from her dresser top made her think of home. The brush had been a Christmas gift from Papa Johan and Mama Glorie, and it matched the silver picture frame that always stood beside it. The frame held a sketch of a curly haired tot and a woman smiling at one another. The love between the two glowed from the picture. Elisabeth slid her fingers over the images, giving thanks yet again for Papa Johan's artistic skill. He'd drawn the portrait of Elisabeth and her mother, Grace, in the hospital where he'd been recovering from war injuries. Just weeks later, both of Elisabeth's birth parents succumbed to the flu epidemic. She paused to say a quick prayer for the health, safety, and happiness of her adoptive parents. Then, as she began to brush her hair, her gaze drifted to the small metal brooch pinned to her dresser scarf.

Shaped like the lamp carried by every nurse's heroine, Florence Nightingale, it had been created by Elisabeth's great-grandfather. Elisabeth's adoptive mother, Glorie, had inherited the pin, and had presented it to Elisabeth just before her departure for Happy Valley-Goose Bay. More than anything, Elisabeth wanted to live up to the traditions of dedication and service it represented. How could she be worthy of it with so many questions in her soul? She wished she could replace the questions with certainty as easily as she replaced her nightclothes with her nursing uniform.

With the ease of frequent repetition, she gathered her hair into a low ponytail at her nape, then twisted the hair into a tidy bun on the back of her head. A few pins secured it in place. She set her white nursing cap in place and secured it as well.

She checked her appearance in the mirror one final time. To her relief, none of her doubts showed in her blue eyes. Instead, a competent-looking nurse stared back at her. Her soul might not be as steady as Mama Glorie's, but her appearance was every bit as professional. The thought brought a smile to her lips as she bundled into her army-issue Arctic parka and boots.

From her first day on duty she had enjoyed the short walk from the nurses' barracks to the hospital. The distance was just long enough for her to enjoy a bit of fresh air and yet short enough that walking on even the coldest days wasn't unbearable. At ten minutes to seven, she saluted her nursing supervisor. "Good morning, Captain."

"Good morning, Lieutenant." Of average height, Captain Thompson had straight, graying hair that seemed always to be perfectly ordered beneath her nursing cap. Laugh lines around her brown eyes indicated a sense of humor Elisabeth had seen only rarely. Most of the time, the captain projected an image of military precision that made Elisabeth feel like a stumbling recruit. "It was a quiet night, so I sent the night nurses home a few minutes early."

"Yes, Ma'am." Elisabeth saluted again as a third nurse, Sandra Carter, arrived. She and Elisabeth shared the same rank, so the salute wasn't strictly necessary. However, Elisabeth didn't want to neglect any detail in Captain Thompson's presence.

Lieutenant Carter had received her training through the Army Nurse Corps, so she had as much military training as medical. She and Elisabeth had become friends soon after Elisabeth's arrival, and she had helped Elisabeth adapt to the military environment. With blond curly hair, which often escaped its confining twist, and twinkling green eyes, she had an air of relaxed confidence that always put Elisabeth at ease. For the next four days, the two women would work the same shifts. Elisabeth enjoyed working with the tall nurse. When their duties allowed, they often traded confidences, which made Elisabeth feel as though Sandra were the sister she'd often craved.

But today gave them no time for confidences. They served breakfast to the six patients under their care, and by lunchtime, a series of accidents had filled the ward to capacity. Two soldiers had encountered "soft ice" on the lake and were brought in with hypothermia. A plane returning from a reconnaissance mission over the Atlantic missed the end of the runway, resulting in broken bones for all four crew members. The navigator had escaped the plane first but returned to drag the pilot from the burning wreckage. The pilot had a few minor burns on his face, but the navigator's hands were much more severely burned. A pneumonia case and two men suffering dehydration from the flu filled the remaining beds.

"The nurses on Ward A are just as busy," Captain Thompson informed them. "It looks like influenza has hit the Signal Detachment hard."

Elisabeth felt grateful for the busyness. The tall pilot and their conversation the previous evening kept returning to her thoughts. Something about him piqued her interest beyond anything she'd ever experienced. But the demands of the day forced her to focus on other things, enabling her to ignore the strange attraction. By the end of the eight-hour shift, she wanted nothing more than to prop her aching feet on a stool and just sit still. The next shift of nurses arrived, she and Sandra gave them an overview of the patients, and then the two women walked together back to the barracks.

"Any plans for tonight?" Sandra asked with an odd gleam in her eyes.

Elisabeth laughed in spite of her exhaustion. "Yes. I have a hot date with my footstool and a shower. Cynthia is away, so I have the room to myself."

"Where is she off to this time?"

"She left yesterday for Iceland to airlift some patients to Halifax."

"Hmm. Maybe you should have become a flight nurse." Sandra grinned at Elisabeth, her eyes dancing with mischief. "You might have met your pilot sooner."

"My pilot?" Elisabeth tried to stem the blush that warmed her cheeks.

Sandra winked at her. "I hear you two made quite an

impression in the mess last night. I'm sorry I missed it. I figure he has to be someone special if he got you to come out of your corner."

From anyone else, the comment could have been hurtful. But Elisabeth knew Sandra understood her shyness. In fact, the other nurse often deflected attention away from Elisabeth when she sensed Elisabeth's discomfort in social situations. Elisabeth shrugged and grinned back. "He bribed me with that song. I'd never heard it before, and the music was wonderful. He suggested we go look at the words, and the next thing I knew I was singing along with him. I didn't realize everyone was listening until it was too late to stop."

Sandra put an arm across Elisabeth's shoulders in a quick hug. "Good for you! From what I heard, you two sounded great together."

Elisabeth shrugged. "He's with the Canadian Air Force, so it's not like he'll be at our mess on a regular basis."

"Maybe so, maybe not," Sandra replied cryptically, reaching for the door of the barracks building. "Do you feel like playing some Ping-Pong later?"

"Sure. You know I'm always ready for a game."

On either side of the entry area a long hallway led to nurses' quarters. Sandra's room lay down the hallway on the left, while Elisabeth's was on the right. Elisabeth looked forward to what promised to be a quiet afternoon and evening. She opened the door and almost stepped on a folded white piece of paper that lay just beyond the threshold. She unfolded the paper to reveal small, neat printing.

Dear Lt. Baker:
Please do me the honor of accompanying me to dinner in the Canadian officers' mess tonight at 1900

*hours. With your consent, I will provide transporta-
tion at 1830 hours.*

Sincerely,
Ian MacDonald

A thrill shot through her, quickly replaced by trepida-
tion. Why did he want to seek her out? She noticed the
absence of rank in his signature, seeming to put their fledg-
ling acquaintance on a personal level. Yet, the respect in his
form of address showed he didn't want to presume anything, either. It conveyed a comfortable balance between
formality and friendship. But of all the nurses he could
have invited, why her?

She pondered the invitation while she traded her uniform for her flannel housecoat, then slipped down the
hallway to the communal shower room at the end of the
barracks. With a plastic cap covering her hair, she enjoyed
a quick but warm shower that eased the day's tightness
out of her muscles. Back in her room, she stretched out
on her bed for a rest. What would she do about the pilot's
invitation? Her impulse was to turn it down. She had no
way of making contact with him before his arrival at 6:30,
but she could easily leave a note for him taped to the
front door.

Yet just as her thoughts had been pulled toward memories of their meeting last night, so now a strange sort of
instinct pulled at her to accept the invitation. She argued
with herself that she'd already made plans with Sandra.
The strange "something" argued back that Sandra wouldn't
mind the change in plans—would, in fact, encourage it.

With a grunt of frustration, she stood up. She might
as well talk it over with Sandra right away. She wouldn't
be able to relax until she'd made her decision. Regulations

permitted the wearing of civilian clothing within the barracks, so she pulled on a white turtleneck sweater, navy wool pants, navy socks, and white tennis shoes. Around her hairline, wisps of hair had curled from the steam of her shower, but her hair remained tidy enough for a visit to the other nurse's room. She grabbed the paper off her bed and hurried down the hallway.

She found her friend lounging in her housecoat, a book in hand. "What story are you into now?" she teased.

"Nothing I can't put aside for you." Sandra closed the book and set it on her dresser. "It must be important to bring you out of your room before supper. Sit down, Honey." She patted the edge of her bed.

"I found this under my door after our shift ended." She held out the note, and Sandra took it. Elisabeth remained silent while Sandra read. At Sandra's wide smile, Elisabeth held up a cautioning hand. "Don't jump to conclusions. He's invited me for dinner, that's all. Not a one of us nurses goes a week without at least one dinner invitation. It's part of being only a handful of women among thousands of men."

Sandra raised her eyebrows. "Which explains why a Canadian pilot seeks out an American nurse and offers to take her to his mess?"

Elisabeth shrugged, willing down the blush that warmed her face again. "How do I know what he's thinking?"

"That's not as important as what *you're* thinking. The fact you're even considering this invitation tells me there's some kind of spark between you two."

"He just wants to be friends, that's all." She accepted the paper as Sandra returned it to her.

"How many dates have you had?" Sandra's gaze turned perceptive.

"You mean invitations or dates I've accepted?"

Sandra's smile was indulgent. "Ones you've accepted."

"Just here at Goose Bay or in general?"

"You're stalling, my friend." Sandra stood and beckoned Elisabeth to take the chair, then began rubbing the other woman's shoulders. "How many dates have you actually accepted in your lifetime?"

"None." She felt ashamed to admit she'd never participated in an activity that seemed a normal and frequent part of many people's lives.

"How many invitations have you received?" Sandra's fingers worked at a particularly tight spot beside Elisabeth's neck.

"I don't keep track."

"And that's my point," her friend offered. "You never lack for attention from men, but you always turn it away. For the first time since I met you, you're actually thinking about going on a date. Not only are you considering spending time with someone you barely know, but you're even willing to go somewhere unfamiliar. It seems to me your heart might be speaking louder than your brain."

Heart? What did her heart have to do with it? Heart implied affection, and affection could lead to falling in love. There was no way Elisabeth wanted to let her emotions get entangled. But if she voiced that resolution, Sandra would grill her about her reasons, and she wasn't ready for that. "How can my heart have anything to do with this? I met him just last night."

"He's obviously smitten with you. Sometimes the best things in our lives happen in mere moments. So, are you going?"

"I don't know." Elisabeth took in a deep breath then let it out slowly. "You and I already had plans for the evening."

Sandra laughed as she moved around to sit on the edge of her bed. "As if those plans were anything special. Girl, you have a chance to spend time with a man who must appeal to you in some way. Just go with it. Besides, I've decided I'm too tired for Ping-Pong tonight. After you leave to get ready for your date, I might just lay down for a nap and let myself sleep right through supper." She tried to pull her face into an exhausted expression, but her eyes twinkled.

Elisabeth couldn't help but laugh. "As if you've ever slept through any meal!" She sobered. "This must be another of those experiences that my Papa Johan calls 'a stretching experience.' I can't say I enjoy them."

"Silly woman!" Sandra leaned forward to give Elisabeth a quick hug. "It's just dinner and some pleasant conversation, not ward inspection. Go and let yourself have a good time." She stretched out on her bed. "I'm going to sleep."

Elisabeth left her friend's room, wishing her decision were as simple as Sandra made it sound. Yes, a part of her felt drawn to the tall, charismatic pilot. But she didn't want to be. She wanted no attachment to any soldier. If she fell in love then lost her love to this horrible war, she doubted she'd ever recover. Better to stay firmly unattached until the world returned to normal.

She changed back into her housecoat and lay down on her bed. Pulling a wool, army-issue blanket over herself, she snuggled down into her pillow, willing her body to relax for a nap. If she woke in time to get ready, she might just take this adventure. If she didn't, then Ian MacDonald would arrive to pick her up and would probably assume she'd had to work. But that was the cowardly way out. It would also show lack of respect for a fellow officer and, even worse, an officer from another army. Her integrity rebelled against the thought.

Two choices remained—compose a note of regret for him or get dressed to accompany him. Both options gave her the jitters. Slowly she remembered Papa Johan's advice. How often she'd seen him wrestling with difficult choices in his diplomatic career. "I just need to listen to my heart," he'd say. "The still small voice of God will tell me what to do." Then he'd lay down on the sofa in their living room and close his eyes. She and Mama Glorie knew not to disturb him when he lay in that pose. Rarely did more than half an hour pass before his eyes would open. He'd look at Mama Glorie and say, "I see the clear path."

As Elisabeth was growing up and she faced her own difficult decisions, neither he nor Mama Glorie dispensed advice. Papa Johan would always ask, "What is your heart telling you?" Her heart had led her first to train as a nurse and then to join the Red Cross. Even though service in the Red Cross had then required that she become part of the Army Nursing Corps, she still knew her choices had been right.

But now she faced a different kind of decision. This wasn't so much about her future as about vulnerability. She closed her eyes and willed her thoughts to still. She could remain emotionally safe and turn down the pilot's invitation. She imagined herself writing the note then spending the evening quietly with some of her coworkers. The prospect held appeal, except she knew she'd wonder how the evening could have turned out. What if she never experienced a second opportunity to get to know Ian MacDonald? That thought filled her with unease.

What if she "took her courage in hand" as Mama Glorie would say and accepted the invitation? It would mean unfamiliar people in an unfamiliar setting. Not her favorite way to spend an evening, but it would also mean a chance to find new friendship. As much as she felt terrified, she also felt a tingling anticipation.

Kind of like the day she started nurses' training. And like the day she boarded the plane to come to Goose Bay.

She saw a clear path. . .with Ian MacDonald as her dinner companion this evening. She couldn't predict where the path would lead, nor did she think she wanted to try. It would take all her courage to follow her heart just for tonight.

Chapter 3

I an escorted her to a small round table. Elisabeth couldn't decide whether she felt relieved or disappointed when she noticed that another Canadian officer obviously was waiting for them. He wore a clerical collar, indicating his status as a chaplain. She felt even more intrigued by her companion—an outgoing, confident pilot who shared a close friendship with a chaplain.

Apparently, the same standards of informality existed in the Canadian officers' mess as in the American, as the men did not exchange salutes. The chaplain stood as they approached, and the pilot made introductions. "Miss Baker, I'd like to introduce my friend, Don Landry. Don, this is Miss Elisabeth Baker, with the U.S. Army Nursing Corps."

"Pleased to meet you, Miss Baker," the dark-haired chaplain replied, extending his hand to shake hers. "I hope you don't mind that we don't use rank here in the mess. It's a neutral environment, so we don't have to keep track of protocol." Standing, the top of his head barely reached the pilot's shoulder. Dark eyes and a swarthy cast to his skin indicated native heritage. His gaze held a sturdy peace that intrigued Elisabeth.

She felt immediately at ease with his soft-spoken

manner. "It's the same in our mess, Chaplain. It's nice to have a place to get to know one another as people, rather than just as officers."

"Then in that case, I'd like you to feel free to call me Don. Chaplain sounds just as formal as Captain."

"Don it is, then." She wondered if she should invite him to use her first name as well, but the moment was interrupted by the arrival of their server with steaming plates of food. The server departed, and Elisabeth felt no surprise when both men bowed their heads. She joined them. Don offered a quick and quiet blessing over their food, concluding with, "And we ask for a speedy ending to this conflict in which we feel compelled to take part and for Your peace and comfort to sustain those who have already lost loved ones because of it." She added a heartfelt amen to his.

The three of them enjoyed easy conversation over the thick slabs of meat loaf which turned out to be more flavorful than she expected. The canned green beans were just as mushy as those served in the American mess, confirming her opinion that canned vegetables simply couldn't be made appealing. A well-roasted potato rounded out the meal.

Elisabeth had never felt so comfortable around new acquaintances. Before the plates had been half emptied, she discovered she could easily address each of the men by first name, and she invited them to use hers. Don's use of her name felt comforting, while every time Ian said it, a strange tingle ran down her spine. By the time dessert arrived—squares of chocolate cake accompanied by scoops of ice cream—she found herself able to voice the question that refused to leave her alone.

"Don, how do you reconcile the concept of God's love with this awful war?" She hoped she hadn't offended Ian.

A quick glance at his face showed his empathy for her quandary.

The chaplain, or padre, as she'd heard others in the mess address him, didn't answer immediately. He studied her face for a moment, then dropped his gaze downward as if looking deep inside himself for the right words. "To be honest, Elisabeth, I don't think there is an answer to that question. If I could explain everything about God, He wouldn't be any bigger than my concept of Him. As participants in this war, we simply have to hang on to faith."

The initial question had fallen from her lips as a theoretical discussion. Now she wished she'd kept her mouth shut. The food she'd just eaten turned to an indigestible lump in her middle. As much as she wanted now to change the subject, she somehow couldn't hold back the disgraceful admission. "Sometimes I wonder if I have any faith left."

"Do you still love Him?" Don's tone held nothing but kindness.

Again, she glanced at Ian to see what his reaction might be to this conversation that had suddenly turned very personal. The encouragement in his eyes made her feel as though anything she said next would be accepted and understood.

She had no doubt what her answer would be. "Yes, I do. I don't know how I'd get along without knowing Him."

"Do you believe that He loves you?"

"Oh, yes." Mama Glorie and Papa Johan not only had taught her of God's love but had lived it before her so convincingly that she was as certain of His love as of theirs. "But that's where I stumble. If He loves all of mankind as I know He loves me, then how can He permit the killing and suffering?"

Again Don fell silent for a time. When he looked back at her, there was deep compassion in his eyes. "I could talk to you about how God lets each of us make our own choices and suffer the consequences, but I don't think it would answer your questions. I suspect you already understand the concept of free will. Sometimes we can only cling to what we do know of Him and leave what we don't know in His hands."

"Leaving it is the hard part," Ian put in. "It's not easy for me to let go of something I can't understand or resolve."

"Of course it's not," Don offered with a teasing smile. "We all like to feel we understand and are in control of our circumstances, but I think you pilots have it worse than the rest of us."

Ian accepted the good-natured jab with a chuckle. "No comment."

The conversation drifted into easier topics. Elisabeth enjoyed watching the interplay between her two companions. Their rapport spoke of more than acquaintance by circumstance. "How did you two meet?" she finally asked.

They looked at each other and started laughing simultaneously. "We happened to be on a military flight together," Don explained. "We were seated across the aisle from each other, and Ian was as nervous a passenger as any I've ever seen. I finally asked him if his pilot's wings were fake."

She could hardly envision the scenario they described. "You're honestly not pulling my leg?"

"Padres don't lie," Don informed her solemnly.

"Though they might exaggerate," Ian added. "I wasn't as bad as he describes."

Don merely raised his eyebrows in unspoken question.

Ian lifted his chin and asserted, "I wasn't nervous. I

simply wasn't used to not being in the cockpit."

Don turned to Elisabeth. "What were we saying about being in control?"

"Don't you have to be somewhere in ten minutes?" Ian asked, but with a smile that assured Elisabeth he could poke fun at himself.

Don grinned back. "Honesty hurts, doesn't it, Pal? But sadly, you're right. I promised to meet someone at 2030 hours. It was good to meet you, Elisabeth, and I hope you'll be our guest here again soon."

Somehow Elisabeth didn't feel awkward being alone with Ian. In fact, it felt very right. "I enjoyed meeting your friend."

"Don is one of the best," Ian replied, his words underlined by the deep feeling in his eyes. "He helps keep me from getting that overconfidence pilots are famous for."

Elisabeth smiled, thinking of some of the pilots she'd encountered. One in particular had pestered her with invitations for weeks, unable to believe she honestly didn't want to socialize with him. The memory brought to mind an audacious question. "What would you have done if I hadn't been waiting outside for you?"

His eyes twinkled. "I wondered myself. I thought I might stand outside and serenade you until you'd be forced to come out just to make me shut up."

"Good plan," she acknowledged with a mockingly solemn nod. "One small problem—my room is on the opposite side of the barracks from the front door. I likely would not have heard you."

"Hmmm." He appeared to be thinking deeply. "I suppose I could have stormed the barracks, then."

"Even bigger problem." Elisabeth felt a full-fledged laugh building in her throat. "Captain Thompson would have skinned you alive."

"She's not in awe of pilots?"

"Captain Thompson isn't in awe of anybody but God, as nearly as I can tell." The laughter in Ian's eyes enticed a story from her. "She's the nursing superintendent at the base hospital. She was a nurse in the Great War and is as tough as an old sailor. Just a couple of weeks ago, we had a two-star general come for a base inspection. He's also a veteran from the last war, and everybody is scared of him. He's been known to strip his officers' rank for saluting improperly. He had airsickness on the way here. From what I heard, he just about passed out leaving the plane. He absolutely refused to come to the hospital for examination, so Captain Thompson went to see him. I didn't get to witness the encounter, but the captain returned with the general meekly in tow. He was badly dehydrated, and she had him in bed sipping fluids in less time than it took us to realize what she'd done. Apparently, she convinced him that Allied defeat was imminent if he didn't allow himself to be treated."

He grinned. "She runs a tight ship, then?"

Elisabeth basked in his appreciation as she nodded. "She's good to work for because we always know what's expected—nothing less than our best. She's quite strict about the rules in the barracks, but only because she feels they make us better nurses."

"Like what?"

"One example that really rankles some of the other girls is that she frowns on civilian clothes, even in the barracks. The official rules say we can wear them in the privacy of our rooms and between each others' rooms, but she prefers we be in uniform all the time."

"Does she have uniform pajamas?"

Ian's mischievous eyes made Elisabeth feel like laughing again. "No one has seen her out of uniform, so we have no way of knowing. We suspect she does, though."

He responded with a story about someone similar he had met, and their conversation flowed effortlessly from there. Elisabeth had never enjoyed such comfortable interaction with anyone outside her family.

As she lay in bed later that evening, she could still feel the warm companionship she'd sensed at supper, the feeling of absolute safety. Her last thought before sleep was, *I could even let him teach me to dance.*

Chapter 4

As Elisabeth expected, Sandra stood waiting beside the front doors the next morning. "Since we're going to the same place, I figured we might as well walk together," she announced in what seemed to be a casual manner.

Elisabeth knew better. "Besides, if we're busy at work today, this will be your only chance to find out about my dinner last night."

Sandra winked at her. "Absolutely right. So, tell all. Quick, before we get there."

"He took me to dinner where we were joined by his friend, who is a chaplain. The three of us talked. He brought me back here. The end."

"Oooh. This is good. He's introducing you to his friends already. Way to go, Elisabeth."

For the first time since meeting her, Elisabeth found Sandra's enthusiasm bothersome. She didn't want to think about last night in the context of a date. It had been a pleasant evening with friends. Nothing more.

The rest of the day and the two that followed were too busy for contemplative thoughts. No sooner did one patient become healthy enough to be discharged than two more took his place. She felt like she started each shift on the run and didn't stop until she reached her room nine hours later. Sandra seemed to sense she shouldn't push discussions about Ian, enabling Elisabeth to stay silent on the subject. Yet in the privacy of her room before sleep overtook her each night, her thoughts were anything but silent. She had enjoyed the evening with Ian and Don more than she thought possible. She thought a lot about Don's comments about faith, but it was Ian's smile that drifted through her dreams.

Monday was her last day on morning shift, which gave her twenty-four hours before she had to report for duty at 1500 hours on Tuesday. She luxuriated in the extra sleep. After waking, she stayed in her room in her bathrobe and crocheted slippers. Cynthia had returned from her overseas mission the night before, but she always took care to give Elisabeth solitude on her mornings off. Elisabeth reveled in the privacy. She pulled a chair close to her bed so she could prop her feet on the edge. Using a book as a lap desk, she wrote to her parents about meeting both Ian and Don. She carefully screened out any references to her feelings about the war in general, limiting herself to closing with a quote from Don's prayer.

> *I pray, as I'm sure you do, for a speedy end to this conflict in which we feel compelled to take part, and for God's peace and comfort to sustain those who have already lost loved ones because of it.*
>
> *With all my love,*
> *Elisabeth*

With an hour yet before lunch, she decided to take a walk. She rebraided her hair and wrapped the braid around her head, securing the end with pins. She pulled on the navy wool sweater issued for Arctic wear, as well as pile-lined trousers, Arctic boots, and her parka. Snugging a wool knit toque over her head, she then pulled the fur-trimmed hood of her parka into place.

The day was stunningly beautiful. Bright sunshine didn't occur often here at Goose Bay, but today the clouds had parted. Sunlight glinted off ice particles in the snow, creating a brightness that demanded sunglasses. She set off away from the hospital; she saw that view often enough. Today her feet led her toward the airfield before she realized the direction they had chosen. Even after she became aware, she couldn't muster the resolve to turn around. She wouldn't be looking for Ian, she reasoned, especially since she stood no realistic chance of meeting up with him. She was simply taking a walk.

She reached the edge of the airfield, which vibrated with activity. On the distant runways, she saw planes landing and taking off. Numerous vehicles maneuvered around the various buildings and parked aircraft, and even more people hustled here and there. While at first glance the scene seemed to be one of confusion, it took only moments for her to feel the sense of purpose throbbing in the air. As she watched, an awareness began to grow in her. For the eight months that she'd been here, her focus had been limited to the sick and the injured. Her profession demanded that focus.

But here on the edge of the heart of Goose Bay, she could acknowledge her world as just a small part of the overall work accomplished at this location. The bombers and fighters using the runways so continuously were desperately needed in skies far distant from where she stood. It required an immense amount of manpower to accomplish that objective. Her role was to help the personnel involved when their bodies succumbed to illness or injury. Turning back toward the base with a lighter heart, she sensed a faint understanding of a brand-new perspective. Rather than seeing her patients as victims of wretched circumstance, perhaps she'd now be able to view them as important elements in an effort much bigger than any one person or country. Her work wasn't so much rescue from misfortune as it was enabling her patients to take their part in the bigger purpose.

Those thoughts carried her through four more busy days. Though she worked with Sandra on Wednesday and Thursday, they had little time for mundane conversation. They usually ate dinner together in the dining room and enjoyed games with the other nurses in the evening, but there was no opportunity for the exchange of confidences. Elisabeth felt relieved. She'd seen or heard nothing from Ian all week. She told herself she didn't mind, that there was nothing between them other than casual acquaintanceship. Still, when Friday came, she felt a twinge of regret that she wouldn't be off duty until 2300 hours. Not that she would seriously consider going to the evening social, even if work were not a factor. She refused to start pining for someone she'd met only twice.

Still, she couldn't deny that she missed him. She kept reminding herself that it wasn't likely she'd ever see him again, stationed at different bases as they were. Saturday brought another shift change, this time to night shift. Though she felt exhausted by the time she got off work Sunday morning at 0800 hours, she set her alarm to wake her in time for the service at the chapel at 1100 hours. It wouldn't be easy to stay awake, but she needed the spiritual sustenance.

She slipped into a back pew a few minutes late. The

congregation had already begun singing the opening hymn, "Great Is Thy Faithfulness." It was a favorite of Papa Johan's and brought tears to her eyes. She felt in her soul that this was part of what Don had talked about at dinner the week before—God's faithfulness in spite of inexplicable circumstances. The chaplain's message came from the text in Joshua 1:6, "Be strong and of a good courage." After the service, she remained in her seat for awhile, mulling over what she'd heard.

"Good afternoon, Lieutenant."

The familiar voice both startled and delighted her. "Captain MacDonald! I didn't expect to see you here."

"I'm sure you didn't." The smile that had danced through many of her dreams lit his face. "I just thought I'd pop over here this morning to see if I might catch up with you."

Elisabeth's weariness fell away. "I got off night shift at 0800, so I might not be the best companion."

A throat-clearing to her left attracted her attention. Somehow Sandra had slipped up beside her without Elisabeth knowing it. "Captain MacDonald, this is my friend, Lt. Sandra Carter. Sandra, this is Capt. Ian MacDonald, pilot with the Royal Canadian Air Force."

The two shook hands, and Sandra offered, "Would you join us for lunch, Captain?"

Elisabeth looked at her in shock and dismay. While they were permitted to invite guests for meals in the nurses' dining room, she didn't feel ready to bring Ian as "her" guest. She knew some of the nurses would jump to conclusions, and she would become the focus of attention.

As if understanding Elisabeth's thoughts, Sandra added, "You can be my guest, and no one will know you're really here to see Elisabeth."

The comment made Elisabeth's face flame, even while she was grateful for the intervention.

"I won't be keeping you up when you should be sleeping, will I?" Ian inquired of Elisabeth, genuine concern in his eyes.

She managed a smile. "I have to eat anyway, and you're welcome to join us."

※

As she had expected, Ian's presence did attract attention. Worse yet, Captain Thompson joined the gathering. Everyone sat around one large table, with Captain Thompson at one end. After being introduced to Captain MacDonald by Sandra, she invited Ian to sit opposite her at the other end. Sandra quietly suggested Elisabeth sit to his left, and she took the seat across the table to his right.

Lively conversation swirled around the table as the other nurses directed a multitude of questions and comments at Ian. He fielded them all with both respect and laughter. Elisabeth watched in awe. Had she been in his position, she knew she would have been a stammering mess. Every once in awhile, he glanced her way with the slightest of winks, just enough to let her know he remained aware of her.

The meal concluded when Captain Thompson left the room. The nurses on afternoon shift departed shortly afterward. Elisabeth knew Sandra also needed to leave for her shift but appreciated her continued presence as a buffer until everyone else had left. At long last, the other nurses drifted over to the recreation room, leaving Ian, Sandra, and Elisabeth alone in the dining room.

"Thank you for the lovely lunch, ladies. I felt like a rooster in a henhouse, but it was fun." Ian turned to Elisabeth. "Thank you for keeping yourself awake. I'll leave so you can get to bed, but I'll be in touch."

Elisabeth walked him to the front door. When it closed behind him, she turned back to find Sandra still watching.

For once, Sandra's face looked solemn. "I hope someday someone looks at me the way Captain MacDonald looks at you." She held up a hand to stop Elisabeth's protest. "I know you think you don't want this. But consider carefully. What's budding between you two is too precious to throw away just because you might lose it."

Chapter 5

Pure physical exhaustion caused Elisabeth to drop into slumber, but she slept lightly. Cynthia tiptoed into their room and back out again, and other nurses murmured in the hallway. But all of those disturbances were minor compared to her inner restlessness over Sandra's parting words. Was there really something special between herself and Ian? If so, did she want it or, worse yet, did she even have a choice?

She dragged herself to the ward for duty at 2300 hours. Three nurses typically covered both wards for the night shift. As the junior nurse, Elisabeth moved back and forth between the wards as necessary. In spite of a heavy patient load, the night was quiet enough to allow her thoughts to continue tumbling over each other like pebbles tossed down a slope.

Her rest didn't improve on Monday afternoon. By the time she got off shift at 0800 hours Tuesday morning, she felt as though she were walking in a stupor. She fell into bed without a meal and slipped into sleep. When she woke, it took her a few minutes to orient herself. A glance out her window showed deep darkness. Cloud cover obscured the stars. The shadowy shape of her roommate huddled beside the window. "Cynthia?"

The other woman turned her head, her long brown hair black in the semidarkness. "Sorry to wake you."

"You didn't." Elisabeth sat up and draped a blanket around her shoulders against the chill in the room. "What time is it?"

"It's four in the morning." Her voice sounded as though she might be smiling. "Sandra stopped by around eight last night to see if you were okay. You didn't even stir."

"I was beat. So what are you doing awake at this hour?"

"Just thinking about things." Her voice now sounded distant and sad.

"I know the feeling." Elisabeth sank down on the bed and studied her hands. All the uncertainties of the past few days flooded her mind once again.

Cynthia moved to sit on her own bed, opposite Elisabeth. "If you want to talk about it, I'd love to think about someone else's problems."

Elisabeth looked toward the other nurse, even though the night obscured her expression. "A couple of weeks ago, I met a Canadian pilot." Somehow, being unable to see her roommate clearly made her words form more easily, even made her feel eager to talk.

"Ah, a man," Cynthia commented in a quiet tone. "Many a nurse's sleep has been disrupted by the opposite sex."

Elisabeth smiled. "We haven't spent a lot of time together, but he's different than any other man I've ever met. I want to be able to trust him."

"What's stopping you?" Gentleness filled the other woman's voice.

"I don't want to fall in love with someone who might not live past next week." For the first time, she voiced the crux of her fear, laid it out bold and bald.

"Do you have any idea how he feels about you?"

Elisabeth shrugged. "We've seen each other only three times, so we haven't come close to discussing our feelings, or lack of them. Sandra is sure there's something between us, though."

Cynthia sighed deeply. "Elisabeth, I don't claim to have a lot of wisdom, but I do know this war has put us all in a place where everything about life seems more urgent than it did before we became involved. We look death in the face every day—you and I in helping the wounded, your pilot in his sorties over the Atlantic. In times like this, we don't have the luxury of slow and easy courtships. More than once I've seen two people meet, and it's like their hearts recognize each other instantly. I don't know if that is what is happening between you and your pilot, but I would advise you not to throw away the possibility just because you're afraid of loss. Loss is going to touch all of us personally before the war is over. We can't hide from it, so we might as well embrace the joy that comes our way, no matter how unexpected."

Elisabeth had never heard her roommate sound so philosophical—or so urgent. Usually, she remained calm and quiet, with not a lot to say. She didn't battle shyness as Elisabeth did, but she didn't speak unless she felt it necessary. Her usual reticence made these words all the more weighty. "Cynthia, what's happening with you? Something serious is bothering you."

Cynthia sighed again. "Later today, I fly out on a cargo plane bound for England. I'm needed to accompany a planeload of wounded back to Gander. My mind has been buzzing all night with the what-ifs."

Elisabeth knew exactly what she meant. Cynthia's trips as a flight nurse had been mainly to and from the Arctic bases, as well as a couple of rescue missions over the Atlantic—but still close to the North American coast-line. This trip would take her right over some of the worst of German U-boat activity. She pushed back her covers and moved to sit on the edge of the other bed. She found her roommate's hands in the semidark and clasped them tightly. "I don't know what to say, Cynthia, other than you'd better come back."

"I'm not so much afraid of death for myself." Cynthia talked as though thinking out loud. "I know Jesus is my Savior and heaven is where I'll go. But what about those wounded men I'll be responsible for? They've already been through so much. What if we get shot down and I can't do anything but watch them drown in the ocean?"

Elisabeth didn't want even to imagine the horror of the experience. She didn't consciously think the words before they came out of her mouth. "I have no doubt you'll know exactly what to do if the worst happens. You'll do the best you can, and God will take care of the rest."

Tears seemed to hover in Cynthia's reply. "Thanks, Elisabeth. That was just what I needed to hear. The same holds for you. He'll show you what to do, as long as you're not afraid to listen."

Elisabeth enfolded her friend in a tight embrace, then returned to her own bed. Was she ready to listen for what God might say about this attraction between her and Ian? She lay down to think about it and drifted into a dreamless sleep.

When she woke at midmorning, she felt peace in spite of her uncertainties. With the rest of that day off as well as the following day, she had plenty of time for long walks, more rest, and opportunities to enjoy friendly Ping-Pong competitions in the nearby recreation hall. She'd heard nothing from Ian since his Sunday dinner with the nurses.

When her thoughts drifted in his direction, she reminded herself that there could be nothing between them. Obviously, time and circumstances weren't going to allow even a basic friendship. Before she could acknowledge the sliver of disappointment, she redirected her thoughts by saying a prayer for Cynthia's safety. She did her best to ignore the ball of fear in her middle every time she thought of the extreme danger the flight nurse would have to experience.

Her first day back on shift was Thanksgiving Day. The hospital kitchen had managed to create a full-course dinner, which Elisabeth and Sandra served to the patients at noon. Though the two of them had been on different shifts for the past two weeks, Elisabeth felt gratitude for their togetherness on this one day. Sandra's cheeriness helped alleviate some of the loneliness Elisabeth felt for her own family. One of the youngest soldiers seemed to become more despondent during the meal. She made an opportunity to stop by his bed for a quiet chat.

"Are you okay, Private Keller?"

He looked up from his half-eaten meal with naked homesickness in his eyes. "It's the dinner, Ma'am. Puts me in mind of Thanksgiving dinners at home, with both sets of grandparents there and a ton of aunts, uncles, and cousins. Since I can't be fighting, I can't help but wish I were home. Tomorrow they'll put up the Christmas tree."

Elisabeth forced a smile. "I don't have a huge family like yours, but I miss being with them today as well. Being away from them is part of doing our duty, but that doesn't make it easy."

"No, Ma'am," he whispered, looking back down at his tray.

But her words must have helped, because when it came

time to clear the trays away, Private Keller had eaten every scrap and had found a crossword puzzle to work. The rest of the afternoon was hectic as the captain opened both wards for unlimited visitors. "It's bad enough that our boys have to be away from home on Thanksgiving; I want them to be able to be with their comrades, at least," she explained to her staff. It meant that the first shift of nurses had to work an hour later, but seeing the brightened spirits of all the patients, none of them seemed to mind.

Elisabeth returned to the barracks that night with her spirits heavier than ever. As she'd told Private Keller, she missed her family terribly. But she hadn't told him about Papa Johan's Thanksgiving dinner prayer. Usually his blessings over meals or his prayers for other occasions varied according to circumstance. He wasn't given to ritual or flowery language, but every year on Thanksgiving Day, he used the same words. Elisabeth came to understand them as the only words he could find to express his gratitude for what he valued most—his family and world peace. She pondered the words now:

"On this day of Thanksgiving, our Father, we thank Thee for our blessings too numerous to count. Dearest to our hearts is the gift of family You have bestowed on the three of us, brought together by heartache and war. We also thank Thee from the depths of our hearts for the gift of peace that You have bestowed on our world. We ask Thy guidance in the year to come as each of us continues in our work to ensure continued peace. In the name of the Prince of Peace, amen."

Elisabeth's homesickness only made her more aware that this prayer from Papa Johan's heart had not been answered. What had he prayed this year? Something in her soul told her he'd still asked for peace in the world but had also added a plea for her safety and happiness.

She knelt by the side of her bed and repeated the first part of the prayer. Then she added, "Though I cannot understand why You would allow war to sunder our world again, I thank Thee for the opportunity to serve those who would do their duty in the fight. Please bless Mama Glorie and Papa Johan and keep them safe. In the name of the Prince of Peace, amen."

Tears fell onto her hands for just a few moments. Just as she was getting to her feet again, Cynthia came through the door. The two women collided in a joyful hug. "Welcome home, Cynthia! How was the trip?"

"Not bad," the flight nurse replied, her brown eyes shining. "The Germans tried to nail us, but we got our boys home. I'm supposed to leave on another mission on Sunday."

Apprehension almost forced words of protest from Elisabeth's lips, but her training held them back. As members of the Army Nursing Corps, they were trained to render service anywhere. She could not dishonor herself or the Corps by speaking of her fears. But the sick dread didn't vanish for being left unspoken. On the contrary, it finally brought resolution to her questions about Ian. She could not, must not, risk more than the most casual friendship with him. To allow herself to become attached to his companionship would only put her at risk for a broken heart. This war had already demanded more than her heart felt able to give. She simply could not give more.

With her decision made, Elisabeth plodded through her days. Cynthia once again returned safely from her overseas mission. That Friday night, Elisabeth accompanied Sandra and a few other nurses to the officers' mess for the Social Evening. Though she tried to tell herself she wasn't looking for Ian, she couldn't deny the disappointment she felt over not seeing him. She sidestepped the many offers to dance, though she did try to maintain pleasant conversations with those who approached her. Thankfully, no one seemed to remember the duet she'd sung with Ian, or if they did, they didn't mention it. For her part, she just tried to ignore the piano on the other side of the room. She couldn't look at it without remembering how well their voices had blended in song. Sandra had to leave at 2200 hours to get ready for her night shift, so Elisabeth accompanied her back to the barracks. She promised herself she wouldn't visit the mess again. The memories were simply too vivid and the uncertainties too unsettling.

The next morning she awoke after a restless night, resolved to let Ian MacDonald occupy no more space in her thoughts. Nursing was what she'd come here to do, not pine over someone she barely knew. As an ever-present reminder of her determination, she fastened the clasp of Mama Glorie's lamp pin over the chain of her dog tag so she could wear it under her uniform.

She glanced over at her roommate, who had donned her flight suit. "Where to now?"

Cynthia grinned. "Just to Gander and back on a training flight. We should be back tomorrow night."

Elisabeth hugged her roommate, relieved beyond words that she would be out of range of enemy fire. "If you get home early, I promise to let you win at Ping-Pong."

"It's a deal." Cynthia hurried out, and Elisabeth pulled on her outdoor clothing for the walk to the hospital. She reported for duty, determined to focus on her nursing duties to the exclusion of anything else. When a few moments of unoccupied time occurred between patients' needs, she helped the corpsmen with their cleaning and scrubbing.

Toward the end of her shift, she looked up from

making a newly emptied bed to see Captain Thompson talking with the other nurse on duty in Elisabeth's ward. Both nurses looked over at Elisabeth then continued their whispered conversation. After a few moments, the captain approached. "Lieutenant, I need to speak with you outside the ward, please."

Elisabeth checked the nursing supervisor's face for a sign of censure but saw none. "Yes, Ma'am." She followed the other woman out into the hallway.

"Lieutenant, I have difficult news for you. We just got word that Lieutenant Jenkins's plane crashed at Gander. All the crew, including Lieutenant Jenkins, were killed."

A horrified numbness settled over Elisabeth. The only words that would come out of her mouth were, "Are you sure?"

Captain Thompson's voice remained brisk and matter-of-fact. "Yes, Lieutenant, we're sure. I trust I can count on you to finish your shift."

Elisabeth shook her head as if to clear away the fog of disbelief.

"Lieutenant?"

The sternness in her supervisor's voice penetrated the cloud. "Yes, Ma'am. I'll be fine." Elisabeth returned to the bed she had been making and finished the job mechanically. She had no idea how she finished that last hour or even how she managed to return to the barracks.

But in her room the grief broke over her. Never again would she turn to the soft-spoken woman for advice or even just for company, when homesickness became too intense. She felt something precious had been ripped away from her. She lay facedown on her bed and let the sobs shake her. Into her pillow she cried out, "God, how could You let this happen?"

But no answer came. After awhile the tears abated, leaving only an ache just under her rib cage. She stayed in her room as the twilight deepened into nightfall. Supper would be served soon, but she had no appetite. It just made no sense. Cynthia had survived two round-trip flights across the enemy-patrolled Atlantic. How could she have died on a training flight?

Elisabeth sat by her window staring into the night, as Cynthia had just a few days ago. A hush seemed to have fallen over the entire barracks. Only faint sounds of other nurses' activity reached her ears. Then came a knock at her door. She opened her mouth to respond, but the tears spilled over and choked out her reply. The knock came a second time, and this time the door opened slightly. Sandra's worried face peered through the semidarkness. "Are you okay, Elisabeth?"

Elisabeth couldn't move, other than to nod.

"You don't look like it. May I come in?"

Again Elisabeth could only nod. She heard her friend's approach, then felt comforting arms slide around her. She tried to hold back the tears, but they refused to be denied. With her head resting on Sandra's shoulder, she sobbed afresh.

Sandra murmured quieting words, barely more than nonsense. Then Elisabeth felt a dampness on her own shoulder. With it came the awareness that she wasn't alone in her grief. There were so few of them among so many men that they were like their own extended family. This loss would scar them all.

Chapter 6

Elisabeth forced herself through the days which followed. A memorial service took place three days after the crash, but she refused to attend. Her loss only felt bearable when she focused stubbornly on her nursing responsibilities. Regulations forbade any communications home about the loss, for which she felt grateful. This way she didn't have to decide whether or not to tell her parents.

One evening, as she sat alone in her room, a diffident tap at the door startled her. When Elisabeth opened the door, a fellow nurse stood on the other side with a piece of paper in her hand. "One of the Canadian pilots asked me to give this to you."

Before her brain could absorb the information, a jolt of delight went through her. With shaking hands, she opened the note. "If you would join me outside, I have a surprise for you." It was signed simply, "Ian."

She dismissed the other nurse with a smile and a "thank you," then shut her door and began pulling on outerwear as fast as her hands could move. All the while, she reminded herself that she needed to tell Ian she couldn't date him anymore. Regardless of what she felt she had to say, her heart refused to let go of its happiness.

Well-bundled against the cold, she hurried outside. There he stood, off to one side, looking more handsome even than in her dreams. He held a basket on one arm, and with the other, he beckoned her. "I figured it's a good day for a picnic, since it's too cold for bugs."

Elisabeth laughed, the first time she'd felt any kind of joy since the awful news ten days previously. She tucked her hand into the crook of his elbow and smiled up at him. "It's good to see you."

He began walking at an easy, wandering pace. "I'm not supposed to tell you I've logged more hours in the air than I think I can count. I no sooner get one plane delivered than they whip me back here for another one. So, how have you been?"

She studied the snow in front of her feet. How much should she tell him? Since this would be the last time she would see him, she might as well be honest. "My roommate was killed in a crash landing at Gander a couple of weeks ago."

"The flight nurse?" His voice quivered with disbelief.

"Cynthia." She could barely say the name.

"Oh, no. I saw the rubble on a couple of landings before they got it cleared away. They told me a nurse had been killed, but I had no idea it was your roommate. I'm so sorry, Elisabeth. How are you doing with it?"

She shrugged. "I'm coping, I guess. Don't have much choice."

He let the silence hover for several strides. Then with a gentle nudge, he turned her toward a snowbank as high as her waist. "Let's sit for a few minutes. The snowbank will break the wind." He pulled a blanket from the basket on his arm and laid it out on the snow, then gestured for her to take a seat. She expected to be chilled quickly.

Instead, with the diminished wind, she felt cozy in her Arctic gear. He lifted an insulated container from the basket, then filled two mugs with steaming liquid.

"Hot chocolate?" she asked incredulously. "How did you come by this?"

"Connections," he responded with a saucy grin.

Not until they had finished the drinks and resumed their walk did she find the courage to voice her thoughts. "Ian, I don't know how to say this, so I'm just going to be blunt. I don't think I should see you anymore." She couldn't bear to look up into his face. If she had hurt him, she wouldn't be able to forgive herself. Still, she had to protect herself. The past two weeks had reinforced her resolution.

When he spoke, his voice remained as conversationally friendly as ever. "Would you mind telling me why, other than the fact that I'm never around?"

"I don't want to get attached." The words sounded cold, but she had to make her point.

"Are you talking about friendship or about romance?"

"Both."

"Elisabeth." He paused and turned her to face him. The intensity of his gaze, even in the gathering dusk, compelled her to maintain eye contact. "I don't have to tell you we're living in terrible times. I know better than anyone how easily I could take off on a flight and never return. Not once do I take off from a runway without thinking of my mother and two sisters and the loss they'll feel if something happens to me. I feel horrible about making them live with that. But I couldn't live with myself if I didn't do what I do."

He set the basket on the ground and took both of her gloved hands in his. "I'm not one to date just for the sake of dating. I know there's something special between us, but I don't want to try to define it. I cannot let myself become part of a romantic attachment until I know for sure that I'll be alive to fulfill any promises I make. Does that make sense to you?"

She nodded, no longer sure of her own feelings. Just to hear him say the words "something special between us" filled her with both joy and foreboding. She couldn't care about him any more than she already did. She simply wouldn't let herself.

"Are we still friends?" Once again, his gaze held hers.

Once again she nodded, incapable of further response.

"I do want to keep you as a friend for as long as God allows." He tucked her hand around his arm again and picked up the basket, resuming their walk. "I know you're going through a horrible time right now, and I hope it helps to know that I think of you often."

For some strange reason, it did help. The ache that she'd begun to think would be a permanent part of her began to ease.

"Look up there." He pointed into the sky ahead of them. The cloud cover was sporadic tonight, providing a clear view of a large, full moon. "That's your reminder, little friend. Whether I'm in Gander, Iceland, England, or someplace as yet unknown, I'll see the same moon and I'll be thinking of you." Then in the wonderful baritone she'd heard once before, he began to sing,

"No matter where I go
    You'll be with me in my soul.
Though we have to part for now
    In our hearts we're never far.
When I see the sun, I'll feel your smile.
    When I look at the moon, I'll think of you."

She tried to hum along, but emotion clogged her throat. He finished with a grin, and they returned to the barracks in silence. At the doors, he wrapped her in a quick hug. "Remember the moon," he whispered, then he stood back as she went inside. Not until she reached her room did she realize he hadn't agreed that they shouldn't see each other again. Rather, he'd offered a promise of friendship that her heart seemed determined to cherish in spite of her good intentions.

And so, each day as she trudged through the snow and darkness to and from work, she couldn't help but look upward. She was surprised at how often she could see the moon, however faintly, in spite of the seemingly permanent cloud cover. Whenever she saw the steady glow, a matching glow lit her soul.

Just ten days before Christmas, a package arrived from home. She invited Sandra to join her as she opened the treasure. Tissue swathed the top layer. She gently pulled the packing aside to reveal a small wreath woven from dried stalks of grain and decorated with bits of green felt and tiny red yarn pom-poms. Beneath that lay a box of fudge, from which they each took an immediate sample, and a tin of her favorite shortbread cookies. A cedar box lay at the bottom of the package, with an envelope attached.

Dearest Elisabeth,

the note began in her mother's tidy handwriting.

While Papa Johan and I were praying for you the other day, I felt the time had come to send you this. The letters and the journal were written by my

grandmother Lucy, your great-grandmother, while
she served as a nurse during the Civil War. Her
thoughts encouraged your papa and me during some
dark days when our circumstances were similar to
yours, and I hope they'll do the same for you.

With all our love,
Mama Glorie

Elisabeth gently lifted the cedar lid. Carefully folded within lay sheets of paper already yellowing with age. She felt startled by the unfamiliarity of the rounded writing. In the years before Great-Grandma's death, she'd often sent little notes to Elisabeth. That writing had been shaky and sprawling. But as soon as she started reading the words, she knew her great-grandmother's spirit hadn't changed a bit with age. Her courage and determination showed through each sentence.

She laid the box aside with regret. With only an hour until time to report for her shift, she couldn't let herself get involved in the story she was sure to find. But distant memories of her great-grandmother accompanied her throughout her hours on duty. It had been years since she'd thought of Lucy as anyone other than the heroic first owner of the pin Elisabeth still wore on the chain beneath her uniform.

Over the course of the next three days, she found opportunity to read the letters a bit at a time. Sunday would be her next day off, and she promised herself she would spend the entire afternoon with the little cedar box. But as she left the chapel after the morning service, she saw a familiar, though unexpected, figure in the crowd ahead of her. The top of his head was visible above those around him, and anticipation rippled through her. She pushed it away with the reminder that she'd told him they shouldn't see each other again. For that reason, she shouldn't expect his presence on the American base to mean he'd come to see her.

But as she stepped outside the chapel, there he was, a short distance away, obviously waiting for her. She didn't try to stop the grin that felt like it might split her face. No matter what she wanted to tell herself about her intentions, she simply couldn't deny her joy in seeing him. Because they were both in uniform, she couldn't greet him with anything less than a very proper salute.

Formalities out of the way, they stood facing each other in the cold winter air. "I really wanted to see you this afternoon," he explained. "I hope you don't mind."

She smiled again and shook her head. "I'm glad to see you."

"Are you?"

She knew why he asked and couldn't blame him for being uncertain. "I don't want to be, but I am." She expected him to be offended by her honesty.

Instead, he looked at her with understanding in his eyes. "We seem to have been given a gift neither of us wants. May we have lunch together?"

"Yes. I'm off today, so my time is my own. Would you like to join us again in the nurses' dining room?"

"Is there someplace where we might have a semi-private conversation?"

"The officers' mess might have a quiet corner."

He nodded, and they both turned toward the building that stood just a few doors away from the chapel. Neither said anything more until they were settled at the end of a large table with full plates in front of them. Ian sat at the end, while Elisabeth sat on the side immediately to his left.

Though there were other officers at the table, two empty chairs created a gap for privacy.

After asking a quick blessing over their meal, Ian didn't reach for his fork right away. Instead, he looked solemnly at Elisabeth. "I came over today because I need to talk with you about something. There's no easy way to say it, but since I told you I want to be your friend, I feel I have to tell you this." He studied her face as if trying to discern how she would react then took a deep breath. "I can't give you any details, but it may be awhile before you see me again. I've been assigned to go on patrols."

Elisabeth didn't need any further explanation. She had heard patients talking in the ward about "Jerry Patrols." German U-boats had penetrated partway up the St. Lawrence Seaway and were suspected between Labrador and Newfoundland. While ferrying planes took Ian right over enemy-patrolled waters, this assignment would be even more dangerous. "Jerry Patrols" meant the planes went looking for a fight. The U-boat captains were known for being relentless when attacked. The exchange of gun-fire usually ended only when either the submarine or the attacking airplane was destroyed. At that moment, she wished she could take back the evening when they met. If she had known then what she knew now, she would have walked away rather than accept the cup of tea that started their acquaintance.

Instead, she had to sit still and endure the wave of terror that broke over her. Involuntarily, she recalled the early morning conversation with Cynthia before her first flight to England. She'd felt this same clammy fear that morning, and it had proven prophetic. But she couldn't voice that thought to Ian. He didn't need her fear. Yet no heartening comment came to mind. Instead, she put a forkful of food into her mouth. It could have been straw for all she knew.

Ian looked closely at her. "I wish I could promise you I'll come back safe and whole. I'd feel less guilty if I could. All I can tell you is that we want the same thing—an end to this war. You work toward that goal by patching people up. I work toward it by flying a plane wherever they tell me to fly it. We each have to go where duty takes us."

"I know." She finally found safe words. "As long as enemy soldiers risk their lives, we have to do the same."

Chapter 7

Elisabeth reported for work Monday morning feeling as if the last bit of hope had drained from her. It no longer mattered whether or not she should care for Ian. It didn't even matter whether she felt mere affection or longed for something more. Whatever words she chose to define her feelings, they had been shredded by his announcement yesterday. Her hours on duty became her refuge. At least on the wards, others' need for her care kept her mind off her own troubles. She felt relieved that she knew none of Ian's comrades. It would have been unbearable to catch a glimpse of someone who knew him, but not see *him*.

With Christmas only six days away, activity buzzed around her. The nurses started with the barracks, decorating as best they could with a variety of handmade items. The tissue from boxes received from home became bells and lacy paper chains. Someone's mother sent popcorn, which the women threaded into long chains in the recreation room. To add even more excitement, the nurses had divided themselves into two "teams." The team that made the longest popcorn chain by Christmas Eve would be treated to foot massages and back rubs by the other team.

Then, as time allowed, the nurses on night shift created

little bits of cheer for the wards. They used green and red crayons to color mini wreaths to hang at the end of each bed. A set of paper bells hung in each doorway. Captain Thompson made no comment about the decorations, either positive or negative, so the day shifts left them in place.

Still, Elisabeth couldn't get excited about the holiday. "Joy to the World" and "Peace on Earth" were simply too far removed from the emotions with which she coped every day. Christmas Eve morning, she decided to go for a walk. She turned away from the barracks toward a trail that wound around the perimeter of the base. Approaching the main road, she heard someone call her name. "Lieutenant Baker!"

It sounded like "Left-ten-ant," which was the Canadian pronunciation. She knew only two Canadians. The exceptional height of one of them made him easily identifiable, which meant that this man could only be the padre, as the Canadians called him. "Captain Landry!" In the instant of recognition, she knew his companionship would be exactly what she needed.

Once they were within conversational distance of each other, Don explained, "I saw Ian for a few moments last night and he asked me to be sure to let you know he's okay. He had just a few hours for some sleep before he had to leave on another patrol."

Her relief lasted only long enough for her to hear that he was probably on another patrol as they spoke. "Thank you for coming."

"Ian told me of your loss. How have you been?" His tone told her he cared, but without pity.

For a few moments she considered dissembling, as she'd done with everyone else. After a week of hearing her reply

"Just fine" to every inquiry after her well-being, her fellow nurses stopped asking. Even Sandra didn't try to dig further. More than once, Elisabeth had sensed Captain Thompson's gaze on her. But no matter who asked, she simply couldn't admit that she lived in moment-by-moment terror of bad news, or that Cynthia's death still ate at her spirit. She hadn't even tried to befriend the nurse who now shared her room. "I'm struggling." She watched Don's face, alert for any sign that she shouldn't have confided in him.

But his brown eyes remained steady and watchful. "Struggling isn't a sin. In fact, it's healthy."

She shook her head. "I don't think so. My mother was an army nurse in the last war, and somehow she didn't let stuff like this bother her."

"Do you know that for sure, or is it just the image you have of her? We often remember our parents as being more heroic than they actually felt at the time. As children, we don't know the agony of heart they experienced."

"I don't think she could have made it through the war if she felt the way I do."

"Can you tell me what your worst feeling is?"

She pondered the question. It felt good to stop hiding from herself. "If God could stop the war, then why is it necessary for good people to die in it? He didn't protect Cynthia, so I can't even ask Him to protect Ian. And yet if something happened to Ian, I wouldn't be able to forgive myself for not praying for him."

"Dear girl, Ian's safety rests in God's faithfulness, not in yours. If He wills to preserve Ian's life, nothing can destroy it—not your lack of prayers and certainly not German ammunition."

"But where was God's faithfulness when Cynthia's plane crash-landed? It wasn't even enemy fire that killed her. It was an accident!" She ended on a sob. The tears poured in hot streams down her cheeks, and she buried her face in her hands. A gentle arm came around her shoulders and pulled her close. She wept against him, not caring about the cold or what anyone who saw them might think. It felt good to let out the grief and confusion. When the sobs no longer shook her shoulders, she remained with her head against him. It was foolish, she knew, but it felt, just for a few minutes, like he had absorbed the burden she'd been carrying alone for so many days.

He fumbled beneath his jacket, then handed her a crisp white handkerchief. "Shall we find some place warmer to continue this discussion?"

Embarrassment set in. She started to shake her head, to tell him she felt fine now, but he grasped her elbow lightly and turned them back toward the buildings.

"It's my job to listen and to help people work through their troubles as best I can," he said in a tone no different than if he were commenting on the latest snowfall. "Tears are part of the process." As they passed the chapel, he paused. "Shall we go in here?"

To Elisabeth, the suggestion seemed perfect. The little building offered her both a sense of safety and of privacy. No one would think twice about them being alone together there. Once inside, she sat in silence, absorbing the peace but also wondering what she should say next.

Don seemed to sense her dilemma. He didn't wait for her to reopen the conversation. "I could offer you any number of trite reassurances, such as that Cynthia could just as easily have died from a fatal illness in peacetime. But I don't think that would answer what's disturbing you most. May I ask a really personal question?"

She nodded, certain she would tell him anything if it would help unravel the knot of misery that had been tightening inside her ever since she had found herself part of the Army Nurse Corps.

"Who else have you lost in your life?"

She looked straight into his eyes in astonishment. Of all the questions she might have expected, that was not one of them. Equally surprising to her, her eyes filled with tears. She could barely push the words past the lump of agony in her throat. "My parents."

His ungloved hand touched hers. "When?"

"At the end of the Great War. A flu epidemic."

"How old were you?"

"Three. My mother's twin sister and her fiancé took me in and raised me as their own."

He honored her grief with silence, then slowly and gently began talking again. "That was a monumental loss for one so young. Though you probably can't remember the details, I would guess that at the time, you felt as if your entire world had been ripped away. You would have been too young to comprehend any explanations, so you were left with terrible confusion as to why the parents you loved disappeared."

The tears started slowly, seemingly a continuation of her mourning for her roommate. Childhood memories came with the tears. How often she'd sat in her room as a teenager, wishing she could meet her parents. Papa Johan and Mama Glorie had been wonderful about keeping her parents' memory alive for her, but she wanted to feel the hugs of those who had given birth to her, to look in their eyes just once and see their love for her. She'd never voiced the feelings aloud, much less shed tears over them. Her adoptive parents had given her so much.

Mourning would have seemed so ungrateful.

But now, a profound sense of loss rose within her, feeling as though it came from the deepest part of her soul. She felt as though it would swallow her completely, leaving nothing but the empty shell of her body. She wrapped her arms around her waist as if to hold herself together, and was barely aware of the way she rocked back and forth. This time she didn't merely sob. She keened with agony that could be released no other way. She wept until she felt limp from the emotion. Don's patient presence felt like an anchor that kept her from being swept completely away. Only when her rocking stilled did he move close enough on the bench to again put his arms around her.

"It is a huge loss, Elisabeth. You've carried this grief for so long. Now you can let it go."

When she was finally able to look at him again, his eyes were red-rimmed with unshed tears of empathy. "The book of Hebrews says that those who have died form a great cloud of witnesses that cheers us on as we continue our lives here on earth. I know your parents are watching you, Elisabeth, and I know they're proud of who you've become."

"But I still have so many questions. I can't simply accept war, sickness, and death as His will and leave it at that." She felt surprised at the lack of bitterness in her tone. Where there had been anger and frustration, now there was only a clean hurt, one that felt like it would heal, rather than fester for years to come.

"I wish I had answers for you. All I know is that God is big enough for our questions. He knows how we feel and doesn't blame us for feeling that way."

"But isn't it lack of faith that brings us to ask Him why?"

Don gripped both her hands in his. "Knowing Him doesn't mean we have all the answers. It only means we have a safe place for our questions. As long as we take those questions to Him, rather than clutching them to ourselves and running away, I believe they serve His purpose."

"That's not an easy concept to get used to. I wish you were around here every day, so you could keep reminding me." The first genuine smile she'd felt in weeks lifted her lips.

"God has promised something even better than that. Jesus told His disciples that the Holy Spirit's mission is to remind us of those things we've been taught. The Spirit is with you at all times, so there's never a moment when His encouragement is too far away for you to hear." He released her hands, then looked at his watch. "It's almost lunchtime. Would you like to join me at the mess?"

Elisabeth shook her head. "Thanks for the offer, but I couldn't handle a crowd right now. I'll get something at the hospital kitchen before I go on shift."

"Are you working tomorrow?"

"Yes. This is my first of four afternoon shifts. I don't mind, though. I came here to be a nurse, and I'd rather be with the patients on Christmas Day than anywhere else." Except maybe with Ian. But she couldn't voice that thought, not even to this wonderful man.

"Then you're just the person they need to have around on a day when they're bound to be missing home and families. I'll be praying for you."

She wanted to ask him to focus his prayers on Ian's safety, but the words wouldn't come. Instead, she stood, zipped her parka, and pulled on her mitts. "Thank you so much for taking time for me today. I know something has changed inside me, and it feels good."

He winked. "That's what I'm here for. I'll keep Ian in my prayers, too."

They left the chapel together then parted. Don went left, toward the base entrance, and Elisabeth went right, toward the nurses' barracks. Back in her room, she picked up the cedar box containing Grandma Lucy's journals and letters. The small bound book was ragged from handling and fragile with age. Gently, reverently, she opened it. From the first entry, she felt gripped by the emotions expressed by her ancestor. They were the same thoughts that she, Elisabeth Baker, in 1943, had been thinking, the same questions she'd been afraid to ask God, the same confusion. She read the girlish handwriting until so late that she had to run all the way to the hospital to be on time for work.

She felt strangely energized as she went about her duties until the end of her shift at 11 PM. Her patients were no longer symbols of families torn apart by war. As in her early days of nursing, they were once again individuals in need of the education and skills she'd gained, the solace she could give. When she returned to her room late that night, her heart remained sore from loss, but healing had begun. She lay her head on her pillow, snuggled under her covers, and fell into a dreamless, deeply restful sleep.

Chapter 8

A new peace accompanied Elisabeth during the following days. While on duty, her mind felt clearer than it ever had. For the first time since Mama Glorie had presented her with the heirloom lamp pin, she felt no unworthiness in wearing it. The pin no longer symbolized an ideal; rather, it made her feel connected with those who had gone before. After every shift, she hurried back to her room to read more in Lucy's journal. Once she finished the journal, it felt like the most natural thing in the world to pick up her pen and begin writing letters of her own. But instead of letters to God, these were letters to Ian. She wanted desperately for him to know the changes taking place in her and what had sparked those changes.

Two days after the turn of the year, Sandra caught up with Elisabeth as they were both heading out the door for duty. "Where have you been hiding, Friend?"

Elisabeth grinned. "No place special. I thought you were the one hiding. You haven't pounded on my door in weeks."

Sandra's smile faded. "I didn't want to bug you too much. You seemed to need time alone after. . .I mean. . ." Uncharacteristically, her words trailed off.

"You mean after Cynthia's death. Yes, it has been an awful time, but I'm doing better now."

Sandra studied her, then nodded. "I can see that. What made the difference?"

"It's a long story, but the short version is that my mother sent me her grandmother's journal. Great-Grandma Lucy was a nurse during the Civil War."

"Oh, wow! How does it feel to hold a journal almost one hundred years old?"

"Scary." Elisabeth laughed. "I'm afraid it's going to fall apart in my hands at any moment. When I get back to the States, I want to find someone who can help me preserve it. It's something that has to be handed down to the generations of family to come."

"Thinking that far ahead, are you? Is there something you're not telling me?"

The two laughed together as they reached the door of the hospital, and then their duties ended the conversation. Elisabeth recorded her thoughts later that evening in her letter to Ian.

Sandra's comment made me realize that for the first time in my life, I'm looking forward to the future, rather than dreading it. I feel like I've finally been able to leave the past in the Father's hands and rest in His care for the present.

She still didn't feel comfortable telling him all she held in her heart. Specifically, she held back how her thoughts continually turned to him—wondering where he was, praying for his safety, asking God for an awareness that He was with Ian as he did the duty for which he'd been trained.

Being that it was midwinter, daylight appeared for only a few hours each day. Thus, most of her treks to and from the hospital took place in darkness. She enjoyed it, though, because whenever the cloud cover allowed, she'd catch glimpses of the moon. Even while chatting with Sandra, or any other nurse who happened to accompany her, she still looked for the moon and felt a link with Ian whenever she saw it.

One afternoon, toward the end of her shift, Elisabeth found a note at the desk where the nurses did their record-keeping.

Lieutenant Baker, report to my office at the end of your shift.

Captain Thompson

A shiver of apprehension went through her. More bad news? She touched the lamp pin through her uniform, reminding herself of the divine strength that had helped Lucy Danielson through difficult circumstances.

But when she approached the nursing supervisor's desk with a crisp salute, the captain looked friendly. "At ease, Lieutenant. Have a seat."

Elisabeth sat in the indicated chair, taking care to keep her posture straight. She folded her hands in her lap to hide their shaking.

"Are you aware it's time for your fitness report?"

"No, Ma'am." Elisabeth had completely forgotten about the annual evaluation.

"You've had much on your mind."

"Yes, Ma'am."

"In fact, I was beginning to fear we might have to send you back to the States."

Elisabeth's heart rate accelerated. Two months ago, she might have jumped at the chance. Now she felt as if she had finally found her purpose here. "May I ask why?"

"Lieutenant, I know you took your roommate's death very hard. I felt concerned it might lead to a breakdown. Though we're not under enemy fire, service here is every bit as demanding as at the front. We would have sent you back for your own health, Lieutenant, not because you had failed in some way."

Not sure how to respond, Elisabeth waited for her to continue.

Captain Thompson looked through a file, which Elisabeth assumed to be her personnel record. Finally the captain looked up. "You're a good nurse, Lieutenant. You care deeply, and that communicates itself to our patients. It's exactly what they need to help them recover so far from home. But caring also puts you at risk for emotional exhaustion. We've been pleased to see that since Christmas, you seem to be recovering. Would you care to tell me what has made the difference?"

Elisabeth's mind raced. She felt compelled to say something, but it was contrary to her nature to confide in someone who still intimidated her. "I had a long talk with Captain Landry, a chaplain on the Canadian side. He helped me find peace."

The captain nodded. "I'm glad to hear it. And the Canadian pilot? What do you hear from him?"

A wave of dizzy shock passed over Elisabeth. How had the captain learned about Ian? Would she forbid Elisabeth any further contact? Granted, the stipulation against married nurses no longer existed, and thus there was no discouragement against romance. But Captain Thompson was known for being "old school." Elisabeth sent up a quick prayer for help, then gave the only answer possible. "I haven't seen him since before Christmas, Ma'am."

"Not by choice, I take it?"

"No, Ma'am."

Captain Thompson's gaze softened. "Lieutenant Baker, though some days it seems quite the contrary, this war won't go on forever. You have a lot of your life ahead of you still. Don't be afraid to let your heart plan for that day." She cleared her throat, and her voice resumed its gruff tone. "I have been very pleased with your contributions to our unit and to our hospital and will be recommending you for promotion."

Elisabeth stood and snapped to attention. "Thank you, Ma'am."

"Dismissed."

Elisabeth returned to her quarters feeling dizzied by the conversation. Not only had she been complimented in her professional life, but if she hadn't misinterpreted the captain's comments, she'd also been encouraged in her personal life. A door of hope opened ever so slightly within her. Did she dare? Even if Ian survived his missions, did he care enough about her for her to dream about a future with him?

More unanswerable questions. Her letter writing slowed to nothing. The only thing she wanted to discuss with him was something she couldn't write. It had to come in person, and it had to come from him first. She followed Lucy's example and turned her pen toward prayers. As she wrote, the peace that was becoming ever more familiar settled her heart.

Just two nights later, she left the ward at 2315 after an afternoon shift. The moon shone bright and full in a clear sky. She wandered off in the direction she and Ian had taken for their snowbank picnic, drinking in the sight of that luminous connection between them. Was he flying tonight? Was he able to see the moon?

Lost in thoughts and prayers, she didn't notice anyone approach until a pair of hands settled on her shoulders. Even before her startled gasp left her lips, she recognized the touch. "Ian!" She whirled about in his arms for a joyous hug.

He returned the embrace with equal enthusiasm and a laugh. "I didn't expect to be greeted this enthusiastically! How have you been, little friend?"

"What are you doing here at this hour?" The question fell from her mouth without any forethought. She clamped her hand over her lips. "I'm sorry. That sounded rude and didn't answer your question."

"It's okay." He hugged her again. "I know it's late. I arrived at the airfield less than an hour ago. Since I was so close, I decided to hang around and see if you might be getting off shift. Good intuition or what?"

She couldn't have stopped smiling if she'd wanted to. "Good intuition, Captain. In answer to your question, I'm doing well."

"I can see it in your face. I'm glad." Moonlight illuminated his face so clearly, she could see the expression in his gray eyes. Tenderness showed in his gaze. Her heartbeat quickened and her ability to make conversation vanished. Mesmerized by what she saw, she barely noticed his face coming closer until his lips touched hers. The kiss was brief, but their hearts touched. He drew back slightly, his arms still holding her close.

"Elisabeth?" His whisper was ragged, as if he were afraid to say more.

"Yes, Ian?"

"I haven't been able to stop thinking about you. I

know you don't want us to fall in love. I didn't want it either. But I think it's happening anyway. Do you mind?"

"Mind?" She laughed softly. "I've been hoping you wouldn't mind if I fell in love with you."

"It won't be easy, little one. I can't stop flying until the air force tells me to park my plane. I can't even promise I'll come back safely. But I also can't leave one more time without letting you know how much I care."

"I know." This time she was the one to pull them together in another embrace. "I can wait, and pray, and hope."

He pulled back again to study her face. He gazed into her eyes as if trying to see her soul. Elisabeth willed her heart to show itself in her gaze. "I'm not afraid anymore, Ian."

"I can see that. Neither am I. I've actually written you some letters to tell you what's been on my mind. I don't have long on the ground between flights, but I can meet you for lunch tomorrow if you have time."

"I have letters to give to you, too."

"Then let's each go grab some sleep. I'll come to the mess here and meet you at the doors. Okay?" He tucked her arm into the crook of his elbow as if to hold her close to him as they walked to her barracks. At the door, he touched his lips to hers again in another meeting of their hearts. "Good night, my little friend. I'll see you in a few hours."

Chapter 9

So the pattern of the next three months established itself. Elisabeth never figured out how Ian found time to write. But whenever he had more than six hours between flights, he tracked her down, even if it was for no more than an exchange of letters. She began carrying her letters in her parka pocket just in case she saw him. She also drew up a copy of her schedule so he'd know where to begin looking.

No subject remained undiscussed in their writings to one another. She opened her soul on paper, and he did the same. With each meeting and each exchange, their love grew.

Separation continued to test their love. Every parting sent shivers of fear down Elisabeth's spine. Would this be the last time she saw him? As days passed, she wavered between the joy of new love and desperation to know he was safe. During those desperate moments, she looked to the sky. Even during daylight or when clouds obscured her view, she took comfort in knowing the moon was there, whether she could see it or not.

Then in the middle of March, after a single joyous afternoon together, Ian flew out again. A week passed. Then two. Then a month. Each day, Elisabeth struggled to keep her hope alive. When it seemed she could hope no longer, she'd glimpse the moon and feel a resurgence of confidence. Somehow she would know if he'd been shot down. She had to believe that. Until she heard otherwise, she'd cling to courage. She read and reread Lucy's journal. Lucy hadn't even had brief reunions with Jere to feed her hope. If God could bring Jere and Lucy together after their horrific experiences, surely He would do the same for her and Ian.

Palm Sunday arrived, but still no word from Ian. Even Don Landry seemed to have vanished. Usually Elisabeth loved Easter. With its theme of resurrection, it had always been her favorite holiday. But this year she struggled to feel the joy of it. The threat of death seemed more potent than the promise of resurrection.

She'd just begun her night shift when she heard the sickening screech that told of yet another missed landing at the airstrip. She and Sandra were on shift together that night, and with only a glance exchanged, they began to prepare for the worst. As expected, within minutes the hospital doors banged open. "Nurse!" an urgent male voice called out as a stretcher was carried in. Through the open doors she could see two more stretchers being unloaded. "Another crash. Is the doc around?"

"He's on his way," she assured the stretcher carriers. The man they carried looked battered beyond recognition. His legs lay at awkward angles and his arm dangled loosely. She couldn't tell where his specific injuries were beneath the bloodied clothing.

So began the longest night of her nursing career. Three planes skidded off the airstrip—it was due to freezing fog, she was told later. The worst crash was a cargo plane bringing Ferry Command pilots back from England, where they'd delivered bombers to be used on the European front. Both wards filled with injured. Some merely had broken limbs. Others required all the medical skill available to get them through the night alive. She worked ceaselessly, pushing away the fear that the next patient through the door would be Ian. He wasn't, but her craving to know his whereabouts grew. She kept her mind focused on the tasks at hand and refused to think about possibilities. When the morning shift of nurses arrived, Elisabeth and Sandra made their way back to the barracks without a word. They were exhausted in every way—minds, bodies, and emotions.

Four of the injured required solicitous care through Elisabeth's following three nights on duty. She poured her longing for Ian into the care she gave her patients. On the fourth night, her last on night shift, one of the men died. He was the first patient she'd lost since coming to Goose Bay.

But her grieving this time was different from her grief over Cynthia. While she ached over the loss, she still felt a peace that defied explanation. She even found words to write a letter of condolence to the man's wife, describing his last conscious moments and the words of love that had come with his last breath.

Her heartrending duty done, she then slept around the clock, waking only for a single meal. When she awoke Saturday morning, the soldier's widow was the first thing on her mind. She wandered through the day at loose ends. She didn't even have the solace of the ward to return to until Sunday morning, Easter Sunday. She tried to occupy herself with Lucy's and Jere's letters to each other, but they only intensified her longing for Ian. She went for a walk but ended up at the edge of the airfield where the charred remains of one of the aircraft lay only a hundred feet away.

Easter Sunday dawned with sunshine. Much as she'd wished for duty yesterday, on this morning she wished she were off. How she would have loved to share in the Easter service with other believers. She arrived on the ward to find that one other patient had died, but the other two who were in critical condition were expected to live. Just as she'd grieved over the deaths, so now she felt deep joy at the others' recovery.

She pushed through her duties for the day, keeping a smile on her face as much as possible. But when three o'clock came, releasing her from the ward, she practically ran for the chapel. It had been there that she'd found comfort after Cynthia's death. Maybe there God would meet her again with comfort for the ache of loneliness and fear.

Something drew her to the front of the simple empty room, where she knelt at the bench. The dim quiet made her think of the tomb on the first Easter Sunday when the women had come to do one last service for the Lord they loved. But instead of the body, they found an empty cave. For the first time, Elisabeth understood the fear and agony that must have coursed through them. Not yet understanding the Resurrection, they thought someone had stolen the body of their Lord, removing their last tangible contact with Him.

She could identify. No contact. No means of communication. She lay her head down on her arms and wept. As the tears subsided, she began whispering into the dimness. "Father, I've tried so hard to be courageous, to be faithful. You know how much I've come to love Ian, how much I miss him. Even more than that, you know how afraid I am that something has happened to him. You know where he is, Father. Please give me the strength to keep waiting, to keep hoping. Keep him safe in Your love." Her whispering voice broke, and again the tears fell.

The peace enveloped her again. She felt loved and strengthened. Still she knelt, basking in the wonder of it. Then the creak of the door caught her attention. Silhouetted in the doorway stood the tall form she'd been craving to see. "Ian?" It took only seconds for her to be on her feet. With long strides, he met her in the middle of the center aisle. His hug left her breathless as he lifted her off her feet for a joyous kiss. His face was rough with several days growth of beard, and shadows of fatigue rimmed his gray eyes. But there was no mistaking the love shining through the dirt and weariness.

"Elisabeth, my love! I've missed you more than I can tell you."

Pure joy caused laughter to bubble out of her. "You don't need words. I've missed you the same way."

He set her gently on a bench. Then, rather than sitting beside her, he knelt before her. "Elisabeth, you've become part of my heart. I wish I could promise you forever, but all I have to give you is right now, this moment. Still, I have to ask; when this wretched war is over, would you become my wife?"

For just a moment the old terror made her hesitate. Could she pledge her heart, knowing it might be broken? But she drew again on the peace that had carried her through these past six weeks of loneliness and uncertainty. Her heart had already bound itself to this man's. She could try to protect it and wound them both, or she could accept the love that had grown between them and trust whatever the future held. Divine love would carry her through.

She leaned forward to capture his face between her hands. "Yes, I'll marry you, dearest Ian."

❋

World War II ended in May of 1945. Elisabeth fulfilled her requirement to serve six more months with the Army Nurse Corps, then accepted release back to the Red Cross. She applied for, and received, a transfer to the Canadian Red Cross. She and Ian were married in Papa Johan and Mama Glorie's living room on December 19, 1945. They then returned to Halifax, Nova Scotia, where Ian's career with the Royal Canadian Air Force continued. They had four children and visited Johan and Glorie frequently in the United States. Two of their children returned to the States as adults, where they married and raised their families.

JANELLE BURNHAM SCHNEIDER

Janelle published her first five books with **Heartsong Presents** under her maiden name of Janelle Burnham. She put her writing aside during her own true-to-life romance, wedding, and the birth and infancy of her daughter, Elisabeth. She then wrote her sixth book with lots of encouragement and practical support from her husband, Mark. A son, Johnathan, has since joined the family, but with Mark's help, she continues to make time for her writing. As a military wife, she has lived in various places across Canada, including British Columbia, New Brunswick, Alberta and Ontario, collecting new story ideas and learning much about real romance.

She says this collection is a dream come true. She began writing under the tutelage of Colleen Reece over ten years ago. That work resulted in her first novel, *Midnight Music,* from **Heartsong Presents**. She explains, "Ever since Barbour started publishing novella collections, I've dreamed of being published in a collection with Colleen. Working with JoAnn Grote, whose writing I have also admired, and Renee DeMarco is icing on the cake, as it were. God really does give us the desires of our hearts!"

Beside
the
Golden Door

by Renee DeMarco

Dedication

To my husband, Dan, and to Alexa, whose decision to sleep though the night enabled the completion of this project.

And to all of the individuals who spend their lives helping the Amandas, Carries, and Michaels of the world, I offer my thanks.

Let your light so shine before men,
that they may see your good works,
and glorify your Father which is in heaven.
MATTHEW 5:16

Author's Note

In the 1880s, New York City was the destination point for thousands of immigrants seeking refuge in the United States. Emma Lazarus, published poet, author, and native daughter of the city, championed the cause of immigrant Jews. By the time she was thirty-five years old, she was well established as a benefactor to the oppressed. She developed classes for immigrants and helped them find housing in a crowded city. She founded the Society for the Improvement and Colonization of East European Jews and wrote articles on Jewish history that appealed to both Jewish and Christian readers.

Emma Lazarus published her famous poem "The New Colossus" in 1883 for an auction to benefit the Aid to Bartholdi Pedestal Fund for the Statue of Liberty. France was bestowing the statue, entitled "Liberty Enlightening the World," to honor the United States. Funded by donations from the French, the statue was first exhibited in Paris, then dismantled, shipped across the Atlantic, and reassembled at its present New York Harbor location.

It was formally dedicated by U.S. President Grover Cleveland on October 28, 1886. He said Liberty's light would "pierce the darkness of man's ignorance and oppression." He was right. The Statue of Liberty soon became an international symbol of freedom. Emma Lazarus didn't live to understand the full impact of what she had penned. She died in 1884. In 1903, "The New Colossus" was added to a bronze plaque at the base of Liberty. The statue's torch and Lazarus's words greet thousands each year, proclaiming America a land of freedom and hope.

Renee

"Give me your tired, your poor,
    Your huddled masses yearning to breathe free,
The wretched refuse of your teeming shore.
    Send these, the homeless, tempest-tossed to me.
I lift my lamp beside the golden door."
                        —Emma Lazarus,
                        "The New Colossus"

Chapter 1

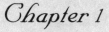

Seattle, Washington

Looking out over the sea of bobbing black-capped heads, Kiersten Elisabeth Davis unsuccessfully fought to suppress the smile that spread across her face like a run in a pair of nylons. Not that she'd had much experience with nylons. *Nature Girl,* as her sisters jokingly referred to her, had little need for the accouterments her sisters considered the basic necessities of life—namely, nylons, fancy clothes, makeup, and "hair stuff." Most days, Kiersten's beauty routine consisted of rolling out of bed, putting her shoulder-length auburn hair in a ponytail, rinsing her face—lightly peppered with freckles—with cold water, and heading out the door. She had the routine down to four minutes flat—and that included grabbing a bagel for breakfast, feeding her cat, Fido, and packing her books for school.

Today, though, she had broken the morning ritual. It took something *big* to warrant more than four minutes of personal prep time, but today certainly qualified. She had spent ten minutes this morning getting ready for the occasion: Graduation Day. Finally. Suddenly all the years of sleepless nights, endless studying, and stressful tests seemed to fade to a distant memory.

"A University of Washington *alumnus,*" Kiersten whispered, allowing the word to fill the air around her.

Boy, that word has a nice ring to it, she mused, her eyes dancing. *I wonder if Grandma felt this way when she stood with her diploma, ready to begin her career. I can't believe I'm almost free to follow my dream.*

"Hey, Kit," Dennis, her best friend, teased, casually flipping Kiersten's pink tassel over to the other side of her cap. "You aren't a nurse yet. How about leaving the tassel on the *right* side until you get your diploma. Oh, by the way, nice feet."

Kiersten glanced at her Birkenstock sandals, protruding toes painted in the alternating purple and gold colors of the university.

"You like?" she responded. "I'll do yours for my friends-and-family discount—ten bucks."

"I think I'll pass," he countered. "I don't suppose you do hair? I was thinking of going purple and gold for the occasion."

Kiersten lifted his graduation cap, revealing a scalp-close buzz cut. "With *what* hair? Purple and gold scalp is more like it."

Dennis placed his cap squarely back on his head and feigned injury. "I'll have you know I cut my hair myself, only this morning." His injured look turned to one of distinct interest. "Good thing I did; I have some ladies to impress."

Kiersten followed his gaze to where a group of four blond beauties were congregating. "Not a chance," she informed Dennis. "They're high-maintenance girls. Your beginning nurse's salary wouldn't quite cut it—especially since we have to complete three internships before you even get a real nurse job. Besides, aren't you a little old?"

Dennis dismissed her with a glance. "You are only as old as you think you are, my dear. My boyish good looks and overwhelming charm will more than make up for my short-term fund deficiency." He winked. "Wish me luck. I'm off to make my entrance."

Kiersten rolled her eyes. "I warned him. I better go pick up the pieces." She made her way through the crowd of graduates over to the group. The girls were deftly handling Dennis' pick-up lines. "Hey, ladies," Kiersten spoke, the corner of her lips displaying her amusement.

"Kiersten," they chorused, enveloping her in a whirlwind of hugs and kisses. The next few minutes were filled with four competing voices describing their trip to Seattle, their latest dating endeavors, and relaying the gossip from home.

"Dennis," Kiersten deadpanned, "I'd like you to meet my *little* sisters. These are Kylie, Karina, Kayla, and Kimberly. They all attend *high school* in Colorado."

"I think I'll make my exit now," he said, his voice revealing his embarrassment. "See you later, Kit."

Kiersten's sisters were soon joined by her blond, equally good-looking parents. "Hi, Honey," her mom greeted. She planted a kiss on Kiersten's cheek. Glancing at the sea of soon-to-be-graduates milling around, she asked, "Now, how are we going to see you? There must be ten thousand kids here."

"Look for the guy with the inflatable five-foot-tall husky dog on his head—that will be Dennis." She rolled her eyes. "I'll be next to him."

As the proceedings began, Kiersten's family excused themselves to find a place in the bleachers. Kiersten spotted Dennis, complete with new headgear, waving her over to where the nursing-student graduation candidates were gathering.

"Hey, Kit," he chastised, "if you don't get over here they're going to start this thing without you, and you'll be left diplomaless."

"Truth be told," she responded, "they don't give you a *real* diploma anyway. Most of these guys will get theirs mailed in a month or two; but we nursing students—*we* won't see ours until after our internships are successfully completed. That's another nine months at least. Oh well, I've waited this long—another nine months won't kill me."

"Have you received your internship assignments yet?" Dennis asked.

"Yeah. They arrived in the mail yesterday. Let's see—I go to the Winston Alcohol and Drug Rehabilitation Clinic in downtown Seattle for the first three months, the Pediatric Care Center for babies born with addictions for the second three, and Harborview Burn Clinic for the final three months."

"Man. Talk about depressing. I got a rotation in surgery, one in an emergency room, and my final at a physical-therapy rehabilitation center." Dennis shook his head. "I think I'll keep mine."

Their conversation came to an abrupt halt as the strains of "Pomp and Circumstance" blasted from the speakers positioned above their heads.

"Well, this is it." Dennis bent down and kissed Kiersten on the forehead. "And they said I wouldn't graduate."

The ceremonies dragged on. By the time Kiersten found her family, she was starving. She maneuvered the clan to the car and through heavy traffic to a local Mexican restaurant. After downing the first bowl of chips and salsa, conversation finally resumed.

"So, Kiersten," Kylie asked, "what is up with that hot man?"

Kiersten looked at her without comprehending. "What are you talking about?"

"You know. The cute one with the dog on his head."

Rolling her eyes and shaking her head was the only response Kiersten could muster. "Is that all you girls can think about—boys?"

"Is there anything else worth thinking about?" Kimberly responded. "Come on, Kit. If you don't start looking soon, you're going to wind up an old maid. You know, if you'd just take the time to put on makeup and do your hair, you could look great. Oh, and a change of clothes couldn't hurt. Speaking of which. . ." She reached down and pulled out a bag. "Here's my graduation gift to you."

Kiersten opened the bag to find an expensive cashmere sweater and a pair of designer black pants. Her other sisters' gifts soon followed: a makeup case, an appointment to a local spa for a makeover, and a jeweled necklace. "Thank you very much," Kiersten mustered with a half-smile before excusing herself to the ladies' room.

Looking at her image in the bathroom mirror, she didn't see her mother come in, until she stood beside her. "Mom, why am I so different from them?" she asked. "I really couldn't care less about boys, or makeup, or fancy jewelry. It's just not important to me. My aim in life has never been to get married. Or to be rich. I just want to finish my rotations and travel abroad to serve as a nurse to our soldiers and civilians in war zones."

"Well, Kiersten," her mom explained, "people are not all alike. My mother and I shared very different interests. At the first sight of blood, she would move in to help and

I would run as far away as I could, and that was only if I could keep from fainting. We all have different talents and interests. If I let the fact that I didn't want to be a nurse like my mother get me down, I never would have developed my painting talent and I wouldn't own my own gallery. You need to follow what *you* love and not worry about anyone else. God uses all our differences to help make the world a better place."

"But, Mom," Kiersten lamented, "I don't even care if I have a boyfriend or ever get married. On my list of priorities, checking out boys is dead last. Is there something wrong with me?"

"No, Honey." Her mom grinned, shaking her head in amusement. "You may find that you are extremely happy and never want to get married. You may also find that someone will come along someday and change your mind about marriage. Regardless of what you decide, remember: If you keep a close relationship with God, He will guide you to make the right decisions. And remember this, too: We'll always love you, married or unmarried.

"Enough of the serious talk. I spoke with Grandma before we left. She was sorry she couldn't be here, but with the broken hip, the doctor thought the long plane ride might not be the best idea. She wanted me to give you this package. She said to open it when you got home." Handing over the package, Kiersten's mom placed her arm around her daughter's shoulder. "Now let's go get us some of that *arroz con pollo* before the others eat it all."

After dinner, Kiersten said her good-byes to her family and headed back to her apartment. Turning down sorority row, she looked at the large old houses that lined the street. At the end of the road was the quaint, small two-story brick Tudor she called home. She smiled at the welcoming lights and recently planted flower boxes that lined the old driveway. Ascending the stairs, she paused at the doorway to the living room. Janie, her beautiful blond roommate, was engaged in a lively conversation with a handsome suitor.

I think I've had my limit of beautiful blonds tonight, she thought. Avoiding detection, she quietly stole to her bedroom. Once there, she plopped onto her large futon, put her feet up, and examined the package from her grandmother. As she took off the wrapping paper, she could almost smell the cinnamon and spices that permeated her grandma's house. Grandma Elisabeth was her favorite.

She had always known her middle name had been given her to honor her grandmother, but it wasn't until she was seven that she derived any special meaning from the name. The year she turned seven was a hard one for Kiersten. Her youngest sister, Kimberly, had been born that year, bringing the total in the Davis household to six blonds and one *very* redhead. The comments about her beautiful younger sisters were common, but Kiersten had always been proud of her sisters.

That was, until the day at school when she found a stray starving dog running around the playground. She fed it and nursed it for two weeks. She'd brought her lunch out to him at recess. After school officials noticed the dog and decided to call the pound, she determined to "adopt" it and took it home with her that evening. Her parents informed her it would be "too dangerous" to have the dog around the baby and her little sisters. They made her take it to the pound.

Suddenly Kiersten wanted nothing to do with her new sister (or any of the other ones, for that matter).

Sensing the struggle faced by their skinny, freckled, red-headed seven year old, Kiersten's parents had allowed her to stay at Grandma's house for a month. Bedtime stories about Grandma's nursing service in World War II ignited a spark in the small misfit. She liked people and animals, and she loved taking care of them. She would be a nurse, like Grandma, and would serve her country. She would go to nursing school and would seek a position as a nurse for soldiers abroad.

Kiersten smiled at the memory and resumed opening the gift. She was almost ready to fulfill that dream. Three short internships and she was on her way. As the paper dislodged from the package, an envelope fell out. She opened the seal and a small pin dropped into her hand. The accompanying letter explained.

> *Dear Kiersten,*
>
> *I cannot express the pride I feel at the step you have taken today. I remember my own graduation from nursing school as if it were yesterday. The moments I have served as a nurse have been among the greatest of my life. Today I pass to you the torch, handed down in our family from generation to generation to those who have served in the healing profession. The lamp pin was given to me by my mother, and to her by her grandmother. It is a symbol of our love for family and the healing art. I have also included a bound book containing copies of the letters and journals of your nurse ancestors. I hope you will find that the pages of their lives touch you and inspire your life, as they have mine. I love you and am very proud of you.*
>
> *Grandma Elisabeth*

Across the bottom of the page, Grandma had penned the words: "Let your light so shine before men, that they may see your good works, and glorify your Father which is in heaven" (Matthew 5:16).

Kiersten fingered the small lamp pin, marveling at its age and history. She leafed through the journal pages, bundled in a large book. The stresses she had experienced with her sisters earlier vanished, and her connection to her family suddenly felt strong. As she began to read the entries, the activities of the day caught up with her. Kiersten fell asleep, lamp pin in hand, dreaming she was serving beside her courageous ancestors, nursing soldiers back to health.

Chapter 2

Kiersten quickened her step as she passed by the unsightly group of homeless men gathered at the corner of Third and Pioneer. The stench of booze and stale urine assaulted her nose.

"Hey, Babe—can you spare a quarter for a cup of coffee?" a wizened, unshaven man voiced, stepping in her direction.

"Forget the quarter," his colleague added, "how 'bout joining me for a cuppa joe—my treat? Ain't often we see a pretty lady down in these parts."

Kiersten uncomfortably shook her head, trying to avoid their gazes. *What was it I was told?* Her mind raced along with her heart. *Something about not looking them in the eyes. Or was that wild animals?* She couldn't quite remember.

She rounded the corner with a velocity that might have qualified her for a speed-walking ribbon. *Where in the world could that medical clinic be?* She looked down at the map, tightly wadded in her clenched hands, and up to the green signs marking the intersection. *I must be close.* Halfway down the block, Kiersten warily eyed a man sporting a moth-eaten jacket as he worked his way toward her. *Not another homeless man,* she thought. *I wonder what this one will want.* She eyed him as he turned into a doorway with a rickety sign hanging above. WINSTON ALCOHOL AND DRUG REHABILITATION CLINIC, the sign read.

Kiersten's racing heart dropped to her stomach. *This is the place I'm spending the next three months of my life?* Looking around at the graffiti plastering the inner-city walls, she didn't recognize even half of the words or symbols. *I suppose a reassignment is out of the question.*

She took a deep breath, trying not to smell the air she was inhaling, and flung open the door to her first internship location. "Home sweet home," she muttered under her breath.

"Well, some of us call it home, Child." Kiersten looked up to find the largest black woman she had ever seen peering at her suspiciously, one eyebrow raised almost to her hairline.

"Oh, um, well, I didn't mean anything," Kiersten stammered.

"Everything we say has meaning, Girl. Now, who are you and what are you doing in *my* clinic?"

Kiersten tried to swallow, but suddenly her mouth was terribly dry. "I'm Kiersten Davis, from the University of Washington nursing program," she managed to squeak out.

The woman across from her towered at her full six-foot height, hands placed firmly on her hips. "I'm Lucille Carter. I own and operate this 'home.' You will report to me promptly at 6:30 AM and will leave when I say you may go. You will follow my instructions to the 'T.' Am I understood?"

"Yes, Ms. Carter," Kiersten answered with as much respect as she could muster in her voice. "I'm truly sorry for my comments before. I just had kind of a scary morning trying to get here."

"This is the wrong place for excuses, my dear. We don't tolerate them from the patrons or from the staff." Ms. Carter turned on her heel and marched her immaculately dressed body out of the room.

Kiersten felt as if the air had been sucked out of the place. *Great start, Ms. Davis*, she chastised. *I guess this will be my induction into the military.* She gathered her composure just as Ms. Carter poked her head back through the door.

"Well, Ms. Davis, did you come here to stand in the doorway as a welcome mat or are you prepared to assume some nursing duties? Follow me."

Kiersten watched in amazement as the two conducted rounds. Ms. Lucille Carter, or "Lu" as the patients warmly called her, was obviously the den mother of the motley crowd that filled the clinic. Bed frames, or in some cases mattresses, lined the facility's two rooms end to end. Nurses and clinic aides moved deftly through the maze of beds, tending to the patients, all clad in clean white T-shirts and hospital-scrub bottoms.

"Most of our clients' clothes are infested with insects when they arrive—if they have any. The local hospitals donate the pants and shirts. This fight is hard enough without having to do it clothesless," Ms. Carter explained.

"Hey, Lu," one of the patients greeted.

"Jerry, I told you I was going to wring your scrawny little neck if you wound up back in here," Lu chastised. "What happened, Baby? What went wrong?"

"Don't suppose you'd believe I just couldn't stand another day without seeing you?" Jerry shrugged with embarrassment, limply smiling.

"Come on, Honey." Lu placed her arms around his shoulders. "Let's see if we can get you clean once and for all."

Kiersten felt exhausted and overwhelmed after the rounds, watching the various faces of addiction. Lucille Carter led her back to an office with a "Boss Is In" sign on the door. She motioned for Kiersten to have a seat in the shabby chair in the corner. "So, do you have any questions for me?" she asked, sitting in her own worn chair behind a small desk.

"How do you do it? I mean, some of them are so young, and the women—and, well, there are just so many of them." The thoughts that had been plaguing Kiersten all day poured out.

Lu's face softened. "You love them. You do your best, and when that's not good enough, you do better."

"But how do you keep going? I mean, the facilities are terrible, and it's so depressing. Really, how many of them ever beat the drugs for good? If they do, what do they have to go back to—life on the streets? It seems like a lost cause."

"Well, Honey," Lu responded, "you're right. The statistics aren't great. Most of them will relapse. It's not an easy struggle. Some of them make the cycle from the streets to the hospital to the clinic again and again, all their lives. We know it and they know it. But we don't use words like *lost cause* around here. See, in the Good Book it talks about lost causes. It says the Lord is a Shepherd and if one sheep is lost, He will go after it. Just one. It also talks about how we are to be like Jesus. If Jesus will go after one lost sheep, can we do any differently? We at this clinic believe no. So no one is ever turned away. These patients become our family. We love them, and we never give up." She sighed.

"You can have the best nursing skills in the world, but if you don't have love and respect for your patients, you will never be a great nurse." Lu cleared her throat and shook her head. "Enough of that, though; there are things you need to know if you are going to continue to work here.

"One, do not leave your lunch out in the open." She glanced to where Kiersten's paper lunch bag stuck out from her purse. "Rats. We don't need to feed them.

"Two, do not ever be disrespectful to a patient. Even if the patient stinks up a storm, which many coming in with month-old body fluids caked to their clothing will—treat them with respect. If you have to throw up, walk to the restroom and do it. Never let them see anything but respect in your eyes.

"And three. Be careful coming to work. When you see a drug deal going down, which you will every week, get out of there. Where there are drugs, there are guns. Wait for someone to walk with you to your car. We always use the back entrance to leave at night. It's safer. Now, welcome to our family. It may take a little while, but you'll get your feet under you soon." Lu stood up, and Kiersten took that as her invitation to leave.

Once home, Kiersten showered for thirty minutes but still couldn't wash the sights and smells of the day away. She tossed in bed, mulling things over in her mind. *Don't they bring it on themselves by using drugs? What good does it do to help them, since most will never get better anyway? And what did Lu mean by saying you have to love the patients?*

Kiersten leaned over and grabbed her nurse-ancestors' journals that were sent by her grandma. *If I can't sleep, I may as well read.* She arbitrarily flipped to a page in the center and began to read the words written by her great-grandmother, Glorie Cunningham, during the World War I era.

Today Jon Adams was assigned to my care.

*Everyone on the unit has been talking about him—
his bad attitude and language to match. They say it's
self-inflicted—suicide attempt. On our first encounter,
I got in one word and he spoke the rest—I don't
believe I've heard so much cursing in my entire life. He
wouldn't even let me change the dressings on his
wound. I left his bedside upset. If he doesn't want my
help, what can I do? Besides, he wants to die. Every
time I passed his bed, I caught him looking up and
glaring as I walked past. I suppose part of it is the red
hair, but partway through the day, I decided I would
not let Mr. Adams get the best of me. No matter how
angry he got, I would be equally and stubbornly nice.
I'd treat Jon as kindly as he treated me badly. My first
few encounters after that went as well as the first one.
Amazingly, though, tonight as I was getting ready to
leave, Jon looked up and asked whether he would have
the misfortune of having me as his nurse tomorrow.
When I replied yes, I could have sworn he had a little
smile on his face before he turned over in bed. I think
this may be working.*

Kiersten felt a small weight lifting from her heart,
which remained heavy with unresolved questions. *I'm not
great with this love thing*, she thought, *but stubborn I can
do. Tomorrow I'll find a patient and stubbornly treat him
with kindness.*

✷

The day dawned bright with promise as Kiersten passed the
graffiti-filled concrete walls. Today she would find her pet
patient—someone who she would stubbornly and lovingly
treat back to health. As she walked the rounds, changing
bedding, administering medications, and interacting with

patients, she kept her eyes open for the one.

When she reached the corner of the room, Kiersten leaned down to cover an older man who was riddled with detoxification tremors. She wondered if the tremors were easier on him than the hallucinations he had experienced the night before. *How did life lead him to this point?* She fingered the blanket that covered his convulsing body. *He once had a mother—did she love him? Was he ever married? Did he have children?* Her questions remained unanswered as she went on to the next patient.

She was startled when she moved around to look into the patient's sleeping, unshaven face. He couldn't have been more than her age. She looked up to find Lu standing there.

"Can you believe it, Lu? I mean, what a waste. He's so young and so handsome. How did he ever mess his life up this badly? If nothing else, he could have been a model, with that curly brown hair and those chiseled features. What a terrible loss."

"Remember, Kiersten," Lu responded, a small gleam in her eye, "no one here is ever a lost cause. You have to be careful not to judge people too quickly."

"Oh, Lu," Kiersten remorsefully responded, "I'm sorry. In fact, I took what you said to heart about loving patients. I'm going to adopt this one as my special project. He won't know what hit him when I'm through. He's going to get sober if it's the last thing I do. He won't want another drop of alcohol after he gets 'loved' out of here. What's his name?"

"Brett."

Kiersten shook the man's shoulder. "Brett, it's time for you to get clean. Come on, up and at 'em."

Brett sat up groggily.

Kiersten pushed him to a sitting position. "I've got a cup of hot coffee that has your name written all over it."

Brett pushed her arm away, eyes closed. "I don't like coffee. Please take it away."

"Nope," Kiersten stubbornly and cheerfully replied. "I'm not leaving you alone until this mug is empty. It's for your own good."

"Anything to get rid of you, Merry Sunshine." Brett downed the coffee. "Good night."

"Not so fast. It's time for you to stand up and get moving. Come on, we're going for a walk."

"A walk," Brett rumbled. "You must be crazy."

"Call me what you like," Kiersten replied, thinking of her great-grandmother's journal entry from the night before. "I'm going for a walk, and you're coming with me."

Brett struggled to remain in bed as Kiersten lifted him up. Finally, he stood beside her. She took his hand and led him out into the room.

"Now," she said with concern in her voice, "tell me about your problem."

"You are my problem," he snapped. "Other than that, I'm fine."

"You know," Kiersten answered, trying her best to sound loving, "denial is a very common symptom." She paused as two staff members greeted Brett by name. "See, everyone here knows you. How can you say you don't have a problem when you've been here often enough that everyone knows your name?"

Brett just shook his head and kept walking.

"Ms. Davis," Lu's voice resounded in the room, "could I speak with you a moment?"

"Of course." Kiersten directed her newly acquired patient to wait for her.

"Oh, Lu, you were right. It feels so good to really get in there and love the patients. I'm feeling so much better," she gushed.

"Kiersten, I really appreciate your enthusiasm." As Lu spoke, the corners of her mouth quivered. "Perhaps it would be better used on an actual patient."

"What do you mean?" Kiersten's brows furrowed. "He was out cold on a cot."

"Honey, Brett just got off a twenty-four-hour paramedic shift and was taking a snooze before heading home. He brought in Larry, in bed fifteen, and when he went off duty, he lay down for a bit of a nap."

Kiersten couldn't pull her gaze from the floor. Her embarrassment was all-encompassing. She wondered how she could disappear from the room.

"Hey, it's okay. Everybody makes mistakes." Lu laughed. "Boy, though, you're right about that stubborn streak. I don't know anything that can get that boy out of bed once he goes down."

"Lu, I can't face him ever again. I need to leave out the back entrance—*now*."

"Baby, if this is the worst thing that happens to you this week you can count your blessings," Lu counseled. Then she left to tend patients.

Despite Lu's attempts to lighten the situation and make her feel better, Kiersten slipped out the back door undetected. *I can never come back here,* she resolved, *and I can never, ever face that man again.*

Chapter 3

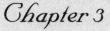

K iersten buried her head under the pillow in an unsuccessful attempt to keep the incessantly ringing doorbell from interrupting her sleep. "Can't these people find someone else to bother?" she grumped.

Her roommate, Janie, cautiously poked a head into Kiersten's drape-shrouded room. "Hey, Kit, you awake?" she whispered. Kiersten rolled over, feigning sleep. Janie plopped down lightly on the bed and spoke, concern in her voice. "That's the fifth person who's come by to see you that I've sent away today. Not to mention all the phone calls and visitors from yesterday and the day before. If you're that sick, don't you think you should see a doctor? I mean, you've been in that bed for three days running. You can't miss any more of your internship, either. I'll call my doctor for you."

Kit sat up, putting her hand to her forehead. "Oh no, you don't have to do that. I'm sure it's just one of those bugs going around. I should be fine soon."

The doorbell rang again, summoning Janie. "Okay," she answered reticently on her way out of the room. "But if you're not better by Friday, I'm calling."

Fine, Kit thought. *By Friday I'll have concocted another excuse not to go back to the center. I can't go back after what happened.*

From the living room she heard a loud voice drowning out Janie's protests that Kit wasn't up to having company. *What on earth?* she wondered, fighting the urge to go see who was causing such a ruckus.

Before she could formulate any other thoughts, the door to her bedroom swung open. Almost filling the frame, a familiar figure loomed.

"Well, Ms. Davis, rumor has it you are sick," an imposing voice boomed. "As luck would have it, I'm a nurse. I'll be staying here until you are better. Can't have you missing any more clinic time."

Oh brother, just what I need, Kiersten thought. But she voiced, "I wouldn't think of troubling you like that, Lu."

"No trouble at all, Dear," Lu Carter responded with a knowing wink. "I believe I'll have you up and well before you know it. I think you will feel like you were never sick at all."

"I'm feeling better already," Kiersten mumbled under her breath.

The bed sagged as Lu sat down. "Oh, good. I was hoping you'd be up for a little car ride. But first you'll want to shower." She took a deep whiff of the air in the room. "I'd guess it's been about four days since your last one."

Kiersten pulled herself up to her feet, her legs wobbling from lack of use. Once in the bathroom, with the door shut and the water running, she let loose with her real feelings. "How dare she! Marching into *my* home like my *mother* and threatening to stay until I get out of bed. She should understand. She saw me make a horrendous fool of myself. This is *my* life and *my* decision. I'm going to tell her to get out of my life and stay out! The nerve."

Kiersten shook with anger and headed brazenly for the door to set matters straight. Catching her reflection in the mirror, she halted. *A towel might help.* The thought that she had almost topped the most embarrassing moment of the week, caused Kiersten to reconsider her course of action. *I suppose a car ride couldn't be all that bad.*

❋

Lu headed her old yellow Volkswagen bug toward the city, contrite passenger in tow. As they wound through the narrow one-way streets marking the university district, Lu began a monologue. "You know, Kiersten, I wasn't always the poised, confident supernurse you see before you." She added a wink for emphasis. "I once was ashamed of my size, but more than that, I was ashamed of where I had come from." As they passed the low-income housing projects lining the freeway, Lu pointed. "That was my home. I grew up in the projects. My six siblings and I shared a one-bedroom excuse for an apartment. My nights were filled with gunshots and sirens. My escape was school, where I excelled.

"When I won a full scholarship to the UW nursing school, I was placed with people who looked a lot different than I did. For the first couple of months, I told them I had come from out of state, so no one would know my embarrassing secret. Then I woke up. I realized I was the only person embarrassed by my history. Holding onto the shame hurt nobody but me."

Lu pulled to a stop in front of the clinic and turned to face Kiersten. "What happened to you was great medicine for our clinic. There is not a lot to laugh about within these walls. You provided a hearty and much-needed chuckle for many of our patients and staff. What you did was minor compared to the shame these people feel every day of their lives. Their addiction has caused more embarrassment than anything you will ever experience."

Lu opened the door and ordered Kiersten out. "We're going back to work. Would you like the A-wing or the B-wing?"

Kiersten rushed through the activities of the day. With the good-hearted ribbing she received from the patients, she found her embarrassment lessening. Until she saw Brett, that is. Each time she passed him, her face turned the color of ripe tomatoes. *Boy, that man gets a lot of calls to this facility,* she thought, as she struggled to avoid him for the fourth time. She looked around to find a patient as far as possible from where Brett and his partner were pushing their gurney. Over in the corner, she spotted the older man she had tended immediately before the incident with Brett. She headed in his direction.

"Hi. I'm Kiersten, and I'll be taking care of you."

His soft Irish brogue and blue eyes startled her. "It's a pleasure to meet you, Kiersten. I'm Michael."

The next few days sped by quickly, as Kiersten intermingled conversations with Michael and her nursing duties. She found him to be pleasant company and enjoyed his recollections of his childhood in Ireland. It also helped her keep her mind off seeing Brett.

When Michael tried to talk of darker matters, Kiersten, uncomfortable, changed the subject. Michael's drug of choice was morphine, but he'd use any available substance. He explained that he had been an addict for thirty years. "Cost me my wife, my family, my home. . .everything I had." He'd lived on the street for more than twenty years, and his body showed the scars. Bad teeth. Bugs. Body sores exacerbated by lack of cleanliness. Track marks. In addition, he had extensive scarring covering his left arm.

Suicide attempt? Kiersten wondered, staring down at her patient, now sleeping. *Or a knife fight? I don't understand why he would ever decide to start using drugs. . .or why he hasn't stopped. How can he live like this?*

She headed home that evening, pondering Michael's situation. *Isn't this just the natural consequence of his bad choices? Didn't he bring this on himself when he first experimented with drugs?* Her thoughts were interrupted as she walked through the door to her apartment.

"Hey, Kiersten, you got a call from a mysterious *man*," Janie teased. "He refused to leave his name but said it was urgent that you spoke with him. He left his number."

"You can calm down, Janie. It's one of these guys who wants to offer me a once-in-a-lifetime credit card deal or, better yet, a long-distance phone plan." Kiersten grabbed the number and started to dial. "I'll just explain that I'm not interested in his offer."

A man's voice answered, "Hello."

"Hi," Kiersten droned. "I'm Kiersten Davis. I'm happy living without a credit card, and I like my long-distance plan. I don't do telephone surveys and don't need a windshield replaced. Oh, and I don't need life insurance. Is there anything else I can help you with, Sir?"

A tentative voice asked, "Do you like juice with your toast?"

Kiersten placed her hand over the receiver and mouthed to Janie, "A prank." Into the receiver, she said, "As a matter of fact, I don't like toast. I eat bagels. Now if you'll excuse me, I don't think I can help you."

"Wait, Kiersten, please don't hang up. This is Brett Lewis. You know, the guy from the clinic. I figured you wouldn't call back if I left my name, as you appear to be avoiding me. I just want to know if I could bring you some juice and bagels in the morning. No life insurance, I promise."

Kiersten blanched and hastily answered, "Yeah, I guess so," before hanging up.

"I did it again. I look like such an idiot." Turning to Janie, she asked, "What does it mean when a guy asks if he can bring you a cup of juice?"

"Sorry," Janie replied. "You're on your own with this one. I've never been asked out for juice. Could it be a peace offering?"

✳

Kiersten tossed and turned all night, wondering what the juice offer meant. Early the next morning, when she arrived at the clinic, Brett was waiting with fresh orange juice and a six-pack of bagels in hand.

"I thought we could go to this place I like and share these," he explained.

She followed his six-foot frame across the road to a neighborhood park. The play equipment had seen better days, and graffiti lined its bars and every other available surface. He pulled breakfast out, spread it over the solitary picnic table, and sat on the table's surface. Patting the space beside him, he motioned for Kiersten to sit down. "Really, it can't be as dirty as it looks," he joked.

Kiersten sat and proceeded to munch on a pesto bagel.

"You know," Brett started slowly, his blue eyes staring straight ahead, "I've been trying for the last few weeks to talk to you, but every time I got in the room, you'd take off faster than a turkey on Thanksgiving. I finally finagled your home phone number from one of the clinic nurses and figured maybe it would increase my chances of speaking with you if we weren't in the same room."

"I assume you want an apology." Kiersten stared straight

ahead as well. "I'm sorry for thinking you were a drunk. I'm sorry for waking you up. I'm sorry for making you drink coffee. I'm sorry for making you walk down the hall with me. Is there anything else?"

"How about 'I'm sorry for avoiding you when you were trying to ask me out on a date'?"

Kiersten looked at him in confusion. "A date? What date?"

Brett cocked his head, covered with dark brown, wavy hair, and laughed. "Well, this one for starters. I figured if I couldn't get you to go out with me any other way, maybe breakfast would do it." He waved his arms, taking in their surroundings. "And the ambiance can't be beat, don't you think? The fresh air, great company. . .and where else would you find this kind of art?"

Kiersten looked at the graffiti he was calling art and couldn't help but chuckle. "I think you better stick with the fresh air and company. But why on earth would you want a date with me?"

Brett's dark eyebrows raised. "You obviously have been spending so much time on the telephone getting rid of telemarketers that you've failed to look in a mirror recently. Besides, I hear through good sources that you are also a fan of the great outdoors. I could use a good hiking partner this Saturday."

Kiersten ignored his mirror remark, thinking, *He obviously hasn't seen my sisters—or roommate, for that matter.* She did take him up on the hiking offer, though. It had been awhile since she'd visited Mt. Rainier.

Saturday morning, Kiersten awakened two hours before Brett was scheduled to pick her up. Janie had offered to give her a makeover guaranteed to drive Brett crazy. Despite Kiersten's original reservations, she agreed, recognizing that Janie had a *lot* more experience in this arena than she did. Besides, for some reason she really cared what this guy thought of her. *I'm probably just trying to make up for the terrible impression I've made thus far,* she speculated.

Hair curled, makeup on, and perfumed, Kiersten hardly recognized the image in the mirror. She wasn't sure she liked it. *I look like my sisters—only in red.* Janie had insisted that she exchange her tried-and-true hiking boots for some of Janie's more fashionable leather boots. Janie had also provided the hiking outfit.

Brett met her at the door, a curious expression crossing his face. "Well, I guess we ought to get going," he said, eyebrows furrowing. "You *have* done this before—right?"

"Of course," Kiersten assured him.

Once in the car, conversation flowed. They both shared great love for nature and had passion for their work. Kiersten described her childhood dream to be a nurse and was surprised to learn that Brett's own dream to be a paramedic was fueled as a youth.

The day was perfect—bright and sunny—and the hike progressed well. At least until the second hour. Kiersten's feet were killing her. *Oh,* she groaned inwardly, *what I wouldn't give for my hiking boots.* She continued to trudge along, until she felt the sweat beading on her forehead. She reached up and wiped it off with the sleeve of Janie's white linen blouse. When she looked down, she was mortified to see a large beige makeup stain covering almost the entire forearm of the shirt. Kiersten caught her reflection in the next large pool of water on the hiking route and noticed that her forehead was a different color than the rest of her face. To make matters worse, the perfume was attracting every insect in the vicinity.

He must think I'm an imbecile. The thought was fleeting, as her throbbing feet caught her attention again. Brett stopped at the top, and Kiersten breathed a sigh of relief on behalf of her aching feet.

"So how do you like your work at the clinic?" Brett interrupted her consideration of the pain.

"It's interesting," Kiersten said. "I'm taking care of this down-and-outer. It's so sad. He's been on drugs for thirty years. I just don't understand how anyone can make such bad choices. He totally ruined his life. I know I'm supposed to have compassion, but sometimes it's like they bring it on themselves; so what do they expect? You must see that, too, with all the people you bring in there."

Brett was silent for a moment. "Sometimes you have to be careful not to judge too quickly. Things aren't always as they seem. I try to live by the 'judge not lest you be judged' adage."

"Yeah, I know. But can you imagine being related to someone who had messed up their life that way? I'd be so angry if I were Michael's wife or daughter. Besides, I hear it can be hereditary. What a burden."

Brett looked at Kiersten, realization dawning. *She doesn't know,* he thought. *She doesn't realize Michael's my father. She thinks I only go to the clinic when I'm running calls.* His mind raced. *Should I tell her? How would she react? She seems judgmental—and it took so long for me to even get her on this date. Can I risk never going out with her again? Will she think I purposely hid it from her? I really like this girl and don't want to mess it up.*

Before Brett could work through his thoughts, Kiersten stood and motioned for him to follow. "Let's head down. I'm getting a little cold."

Brett tried to find a time to bring the matter up again, but his efforts were in vain. Kiersten was subdued on the way down and not much into conversation.

The large blisters that had formed all over her feet were pressing against the side and bottom of the fancy leather boots. With every step, her feet screamed in pain. The bug bites added to her misery. She couldn't, however, bring herself to admit to Brett the error in judgment that her vanity had wrought. Upon reaching the car, she collapsed into the seat. Neither spoke on the ride home, Kiersten lost in pain, Brett lost in thought. He opened the door for her and she exited the car.

"Kiersten, I had a wonderful time. I think we should do this again, but next time you might want to lose the boots, the face paint, and the hair." Brett grinned and pointed toward the tangled mess of curls on her head. "I'll drop by some ointment for the blisters on your feet after church tomorrow. Somehow, I don't think you'll be up to going with me."

Kiersten nodded, embarrassed by his perception. *Am I going to get anything right with this guy?* she wondered, followed immediately by the question, *And why do I care so much whether I do?*

Chapter 4

The next few weeks flew by, as Kiersten dedicated herself to the clinic during the day and to Brett each evening. She couldn't remember ever having such a sense of peace. She couldn't wait to see what each new day had in store.

"I just can't believe it," Janie informed her one evening as they lounged on the living room sofa. "I would have put my eggs in the 'Kiersten will never get into a serious relationship with a man' basket. What happened to saving the world and all its inhabitants? How about the not-getting-tied-down and the traveling-abroad-to-help-the-soldiers parts? And of course, there's my favorite motto of yours." Janie put on one of Kiersten's hats and mimicked, "I don't see any need for a romantic interest in my life—*I* am doing great and don't need some male to mess it all up."

Kiersten shook her head at Janie's antics. "Are you about finished?"

Janie retorted, "If you're willing to own up to the fact that you've fallen big-time for this guy."

"It's not like that, Janie. My dreams are still intact. I just have a great time being with Brett. We share so many interests. We both love the outdoors and helping people. We enjoy practicing in the medical field. We also both believe in God."

"Last time I checked," Janie challenged, "Dennis had all those qualities, and I didn't see you spending every spare minute with him. You also didn't swoon when you came home from *his* apartment."

"Let's set the record straight," Kiersten explained. "I do not swoon—ever. Brett's just different—I can't explain it. You know how we meet for breakfast or lunch in that graffiti-filled park across from the clinic? The first few times we went there, I complained because it was dirty and ugly and I occasionally saw drug deals going down. One day, Brett pointed out a stooped man in the corner. I looked briefly and made some snide comment about him not being able to wait to find a restroom. Brett told me to look again.

"The man was planting flowers. He tends them every week. Brett showed me that if you focus on the negative, a lot of times you miss out on the beauty that is right in front of you. I learn something each time I am with him, and I've *never* trusted anyone so completely. It is so nice not to have any secrets between us."

"Boy, you really are hooked!" Janie exclaimed, then added, "I guess if I found someone like him, I might be, too."

The next morning Kiersten headed for the clinic bright and early. She was so excited. Today was the day Michael would be released. The old Irishman had come to occupy a place deep in her heart, and she felt great personal satisfaction at her role in his recovery.

She brought a card and gift that she presented before he left. Opening the small wood frame, he quietly read the words, " 'I can do all things through Christ which strengtheneth me'—Philippians 4:13." He thanked her, the tears in his eyes spilling over. As Kiersten stood in the doorway waving good-bye, a deep voice over her shoulder cautioned, "Remember the statistics, Honey."

"But Lu, this will be different. He wants so badly to stay clean, and we worked so hard together. I *know* he will be successful."

Lu just shook her head sadly, years of reality dulling her optimism.

Brett was working late that evening, but Kiersten briefly shared her news over the phone. "Michael was released today—totally clean. This is the best day since I started nursing. It feels so good to have made a difference."

Brett was silent. When his reply came, it was subdued. "Kit, you do make a difference. Every day that you go into the clinic and care for the patients, you make their lives brighter. That doesn't change, regardless of whether the patient stays clean or not. Michael probably won't stay away from drugs. He has done them for many years. He is going back to an environment where drugs are as available as water. The temptation is great. Just remember, his relapse doesn't mean your efforts were any less important."

"How dare you say he's going to relapse?" Kiersten's anger sizzled across the phone lines. "You don't know him. You don't know what we went through. He's changed—I know he has. If everyone expects him not to be successful, how can he hope to succeed?"

Brett's response was pained. "I know more than you think, Honey. And I really hope you are right." His pager went off in the background. "I've got to run—we have a call. I'll try and call you later."

Kiersten cleaned the house in a fury, trying to get rid of some of her frustration and anger. *First Lu and now Brett, Mr. 'Look for the Positive' himself. How dare he tell me to look for the beauty in ugly situations. Hypocrite. They just don't know. Michael and I will prove them wrong.*

Over the next few days, conversations between Brett and Kiersten were strained. Kiersten threw herself into her work. Tuesday morning marked her final day at the Rehabilitation Clinic. When she arrived, Lu motioned her back into the office.

Kiersten sat, searching Lu's face.

"I want to tell you what a marvelous job you have done here at the clinic," Lu started. "I wasn't quite sure when you first arrived how you would manage this internship. I didn't know if you had the attitude or the stomach for it." She reached across the table and grabbed Kiersten's hands. "I hope you will consider coming back to work here permanently after your internships are completed. You will always be welcome on my team."

Kiersten felt deep color fill her cheeks, and she rose to leave. "Thanks, Lu. I've enjoyed my time here, and you have taught me more than you will know."

"I'm not done yet." Lu's voice halted Kiersten in her tracks. "Kiersten, I thought I should be the one to tell you—Michael's back. They found him in Pioneer Square, doped up on heroin. When they picked him up, he was holding this." Lu handed Kiersten the engraved plaque she had given Michael a few days before.

Kiersten kicked the door. "How could he? We worked so hard. How could he make such a stupid choice? I guess it shouldn't surprise me." Sarcasm dripped from her voice. "If he was dumb and weak enough to start drugs in the first place, how could I have believed he wouldn't be weak enough to relapse? What are we doing here in this clinic—trying to help people who won't help themselves? It's a waste of time."

"You better hold your tongue." Lu's voice cut into Kiersten's pain-filled ranting. "I know you are hurting, but you have no business playing God. This clinic fills a very real need. I told you before, our success is not measured by large numbers. Even one life saved makes the effort worthwhile. And as for the ones who don't win their battles, we may be the only kind and loving faces they see in their lives. We are the only place many of them will receive a warm meal and real conversation. So don't you go calling what we do a waste.

"You also need to stop assuming things." Lu shook her head, like a mother at a wayward child. "I thought you would have learned with the Brett incident that things aren't always as they seem. You keep talking about the choices these people made to start drugs and how they brought this on themselves. While some of the people in the clinic did start drugs volitionally, some of them did not. Michael, for example. Did you ever bother to ask him about his story?"

Kiersten dejectedly shook her head, her gaze fixed on the floor.

"Well, I'm going to tell you. He served as a commissioned officer in the Vietnam War. He was sent overseas and left his pregnant wife in the States. He was out on the point with another man, scouting for enemies, when his partner tripped a bomb. Michael was far enough away to avoid most of the impact, but his left arm was severely injured. He experienced a great deal of pain. It took several major operations to piece the arm back together—and to help him control the pain, he was given morphine. He never got off it. He tried to kick it—went to rehabilitation three or four times back in the States—but every time he relapsed. He held it together for awhile, went back to his wife and young son and got employment. Eventually his habit got him fired and he left his home, too ashamed to come back." Lu shook her head sadly.

"After he grew up, Michael's son went looking for him. Michael was here, in the clinic, at the time. That's when I first met Brett. Brett, Michael, and I have worked together to fight this monster more times than I can count. It's a hard world out there for a struggling addict."

Kiersten stared at her in a haze. "What a terrible story; I. . .I didn't have any idea. That's how he must have gotten the scars on his arm. Oh, poor Michael." She covered her face, then looked up with confusion. "You said something about Brett helping Michael. Why didn't he tell me he'd worked with him?"

Lu responded. "He probably thought that you'd just assume he'd try to help his father."

"His *father*. . .I don't understand. Michael is Brett's *father?*" Even as Kiersten said the words, they refused to sink in. *He lied to me. I trusted him. I opened my heart to him. I told him my struggles with Michael. How could he not tell me? Doesn't he trust me enough to share? Was he just using me to get information about Michael?* The numbness that spread through her body drained her emotions with it. Her inner voice taunted, *See? That's what falling for a man will do for you.*

❇

Kiersten finished her last day at the clinic in a daze and headed for home. When she opened her front door the phone was ringing. She picked it up more out of habit than conscious thought. "Hey, Kit." Brett's voice resounded with excitement. "I just got home—I'll change clothes and pick you up."

Given the day's events, Kiersten had forgotten their

scheduled date. She forced out a wooden, "I don't think so—I'm going to lie down."

"Are you sick?" Brett asked with concern. "I could come over and cook dinner there."

"No, I don't want you to come. The charade is over. I know you are Michael's son. You can stop pretending now."

Silence permeated the phone lines. Brett stammered, "Kit I'm coming over right now to try and explain. I wanted to tell you. . .really I did. I just—"

Kiersten interrupted him. "Brett, I don't want you to come over tonight. I don't want you to come over at all. I need some space to work this out."

"Come on, Kiersten, please don't shut me out. Give me a chance to explain. I *really* care about you."

"Maybe someday. I'm just not ready right now. You need to keep your distance."

"Okay, if that's what you want." Brett sighed. "I'll call you."

"Please don't, Brett. If and when I'm ready, I'll call you." Kiersten placed the phone in the receiver and made her way to her bedroom. For a long time she stared at the wall, thinking of Brett and Michael. Finally she willed herself to pick up the bound journal Grandma Elisabeth had sent. Fingering the book, she wondered, *Did any of the soldiers my ancestors treated become addicted to their pain medication? Did any of those men leave their wives without husbands and their children fatherless?*

Kiersten set the journal down and picked up her Bible. *I don't suppose there is a cure for a broken heart in here.* She thumbed through the pages until she reached Proverbs. She had highlighted verses 5 and 6 in chapter 3: "Trust in the LORD with all thine heart; and lean not unto thine own understanding. In all thy ways acknowledge him, and he shall direct thy paths." *I don't suppose that applies to broken hearts,* she thought, followed by, *I guess at this point it couldn't hurt.*

❋

In some ways, leaving behind the memories of the clinic and going to her new three-month rotation at the Pediatric Care Center was a blessing. Learning the new routines related to caring for infants born addicted to drugs, kept Kiersten's mind and hands busy. She found that her evenings at home were the hardest. Keeping her mind off Brett was like trying to forget she had a finger shut in a door—it just didn't happen. The pain was constant.

Trying to divert her mind, Kiersten plunged into the journals. She could lose herself in their pages with the stories of patient care, life-and-death struggles, and selfless service. She felt at home reading the stories written by her relatives so long ago. She tried to utilize lessons she gleaned from her readings in caring for the infants at the center.

Her favorite patient was Carrie. She had arrived the same day as Kiersten. A two-day-old bundle with a shock of red hair and a red face to match, Kiersten instantly bonded with the child. She cried as she watched little Carrie endure the tremors, shakes, and terror of withdrawal. She held her when the high-pitched, frantic wails of pain filled the room. She was there the first time Carrie slept for more than two hours in a row, and it was Kiersten's finger that Carrie first grabbed and held. Remembering, Kiersten smiled, looking down at the now-healthy two month old sucking vigorously at the bottle in Kiersten's hand. *She doesn't look anything like the skin-and-bones little girl who was first brought here. In some ways I feel like she is my own. I wonder where she will be placed?*

Almost all of the newborns brought to the not-for-profit center were placed in foster-care settings when they were deemed healthy enough to release. *I hope she gets a loving home,* Kiersten thought. *I'd take her myself if Brett and I were married.* Kiersten immediately dismissed the thought. *Now, where on earth did that come from? Wherever it was, I'm sending it back—posthaste.* Kiersten's thoughts were interrupted as Carrie pushed the bottle away.

"Okay. Now I just need a good burp." She placed the infant over her shoulder and began patting her back. Annette, the kindly gray-haired director of the clinic, approached her.

"Nobody can get a burp out of Carrie like you, Kiersten. She will sure miss you."

"Have you found a good home for her?" Kiersten looked up hopefully.

Annette looked uncomfortable. "The Department of Social Services called and her mother has completed the requisite drug program. Carrie is to be returned to her tomorrow, under the stipulation that her mother not breast-feed Carrie if she is taking any drug or medication."

"No!" Kiersten was horrified. Memories of Michael's relapse flooded her mind. "If this woman couldn't stop when she was pregnant, what makes anyone think she can stop now?"

Annette eased into the chair beside Kiersten. "We have to do what the state directs us to do. Sometimes, when we place our babies with a great foster family, we praise God and sleep well that night. Other times, we stay on our knees and pray that everything will be okay."

Kiersten looked down at the little girl in her arms and wiped her tears as they fell on the infant's small body. "Can't anyone do anything? She's only a baby."

"I'm sorry, Kiersten. I've railed the legislative and judicial walls to no avail."

Kiersten dragged herself home, thoughts of Carrie weighing heavily on her shoulders. *I don't think I'm cut out to be a nurse,* she determined. *My services don't matter one bit. Look at Michael. He's in the same place, doing the same things he did before I came along. And Carrie...* Her eyes filled with tears. *She just fought those terrible demons only to be subjected to them again. What if her mom passes the drugs through the milk? What if she neglects Carrie?* Kiersten grabbed the age-old journals, hoping to escape her thoughts. She thumbed through the pages, penned in Lucy Cunningham's recognizable scrawl. She began reading an entry.

"Today I learned a lesson about nursing. Jack Chishom is back in my care. I had patched him and his comrades up earlier this week, and they were all sent back to the front. He was one of the lucky ones. He survived his new injuries. Many of his friends I treated last week did not. When I found out, I went to Mary and informed her I was going home to Hickory Hill. I told her what I was doing wasn't nursing—I was fixing boys up so they could go out and be killed. It was senseless. Her answer gave me pause. She told me the healing art was one of love, to be given regardless of the outcome. The lines in her face deepened as she asked, 'If you knew your patient was going to die the next day, would you ignore his pain and refuse to treat him?' I responded, 'Of course not. I'd treat him all the better, knowing it might be his last day.' Mary quietly told me, 'Lucy, that's what nursing is all about.'"

Kiersten closed the journal, pondering the words she had read. She would have loved and cared for Carrie just as hard even if the infant hadn't made it. She would have bathed and sat with Michael even if he hadn't ever left the clinic. She closed her eyes and felt a little peace penetrate her saddened heart. Mary had been right. Lu had been right. True nursing was supposed to be a gift of love—and the return did not matter. As she drifted off to sleep, Kiersten vowed to try and remember that lesson.

Chapter 5

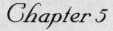

Kiersten paused before the rotating glass door marking the side entrance to Harborview Medical Center. *After the last two internships, I'm not sure I'm ready for another one.* After a moment's reflection, she dismissed the idea. *Of course I'm ready—I've been waiting for this opportunity all my life.* Squaring her shoulders, she marched toward the door, loudly humming "I Have Confidence" from *The Sound of Music.* Focused on pushing the door, she failed to notice the nurse standing on the other side until the door suddenly moved under Kiersten's weight and she was propelled into the woman's backside.

"Oh!" the bit-of-a-woman exclaimed before hitting the floor with a muffled thump.

"I'm so sorry!" Kiersten said, mortified. "I wasn't paying attention, and I didn't know the door would give way so easily. Are you hurt?"

The five-foot-two, 105-pound woman took Kiersten's outstretched hand with surprising strength. Once on her feet, she brushed her long brown hair off her beautiful cosmetics-free face and smiled. "Well, I must say, you *do* have confidence—maybe a little too much." The brown-haired lady's eyes twinkled, and she added, "I love musicals, too. Maybe not as enthusiastically as you do, but *The Sound of Music* is one of my favorites. I'm Judy; I work as the charge nurse over in burns."

Another great impression, Kiersten thought. But she said, "I'm Kiersten Davis. I'm supposed to start as a nursing intern today—in burns."

"Welcome aboard." Judy grinned. "If you are as enthusiastic in your treatment of your patients as you are in opening doors and performing musical numbers, you'll do just fine."

Judy took Kiersten around the eighth floor and briefed her on the medical conditions of the current burn patients. Kiersten tried to keep from showing her horror as she observed the damage to the patients' bodies. After the sixth room, she could contain herself no longer.

"How do you do this?" she whispered to Judy. "How can you witness all that pain day after day?"

Judy paused. Facing Kiersten, she explained, "Everyone is different. Some who work here become hardened to the pain. Their coping mechanism is to not feel anything. They treat patients as conditions. You'll hear comments like, 'How's the third-degree leg burn coming along?' or 'Order meds for the facial burn in room two.'

"Other nurses never learn to cope." Judy shook her head sadly. "They stay for a week or a month, maybe even a year, but then leave. It is too painful."

She smiled wryly. "Then there are those of us who believe that in the midst of all the pain, maybe we can ease a little of it. We do the best we can—give it everything we have—and then try to leave the pain we have seen here at the end of our shift. Some exercise rigorously before they head home. Some go to a local hangout after work to try and forget. I pray. I provide the best care I can, then turn my patients over to God when I leave.

I ask Him to watch over them and help them with the pain." She paused, then confided, "On many of the hardest days, I also ask Him to help *me* with the pain."

Kiersten shook her head in admiration. This woman could only be about fifteen years older than she, but to Kiersten she seemed a whole lifetime wiser. *I wonder if I will ever get there?* Kiersten wondered.

Judy picked up the next chart and motioned for Kiersten to follow. "Can't keep the patients waiting all day," she joked. They entered a room and Kiersten gasped at the small, dark-headed figure asleep on the stark white bedsheets.

"She can't be over five," Kiersten whispered, afraid to awaken the small girl.

"Actually, six," Judy replied, thumbing through the voluminous chart in her hands. "Her name is Amanda Cantrell. It looks like she's been to the hospital before— many times. Most have been ER visits. . .contusions, abrasions, broken arms, legs, fingers, that kind of thing. Classic abuse. She's already got a social worker assigned. It appears this is the first time she has wound up in burns. The abuse may be escalating." Judy sadly gazed at the girl and directed, "She'll need extra attention while she's here since her parents won't be allowed to visit. I'm assigning her to your care."

※

After completing the rest of her duties on the floor, Kiersten sneaked back into the dark-haired angel's room. This time, however, the girl's gaze was warily fixed upon her as she approached. "Are you going to hurt me?" she asked accusingly.

"No, Honey," Kiersten softly answered. "I'm just here to talk to you."

"Do you promise?" The girl's dark gaze penetrated Kiersten's.

"Yes, I promise."

Despite Kiersten's concerted efforts to engage the girl in conversation, Amanda would not talk. After clearly deciding Kiersten was not there to cause her harm, she did allow her gaze to wander from the nurse, but it stopped somewhere between the floor and the wall, where it stayed. No amount of questioning or coaxing would draw the girl from her shell. When it came time for Kiersten to leave, she stopped her one-way chatter and quietly whispered good-bye, but Amanda refused to look up.

I'm not giving up, Kiersten vowed determinably as she headed for home. *I'm going to get through to this little girl. She needs me.*

Kiersten struggled all night to find a way to penetrate Amanda's distrust and disinterest. *If only I could call Brett—he's so good with little kids. Yeah,* her mind added, *I'm sure he has nothing better to do than deal with the problems of a woman he hasn't spoken to in three months.*

She headed for bed, only to stub her toe. Reaching down to find the object she had struck, she grabbed her Bible. *I don't think this is what God meant by a stumbling block. Maybe it's supposed to be a hint.* Kiersten wondered where the thought had come from but said aloud, "I'm out of ideas—and God *always* seems to have one or two for me."

That night Kiersten got on her knees and prayed for Amanda. She asked God for guidance in helping her. She also prayed He would bring the small girl comfort and love. Upon finishing her conversation with God, Kiersten was filled with a peace that serenaded her to sleep. She also had a newfound plan of action for the morning.

❋

"Good morning, Sleepyhead." Kiersten glanced at the tray of uneaten runny-yolk eggs and dark brown toast next to Amanda's bed. "Don't suppose you would like some of my breakfast?"

Amanda said nothing, but her dark eyes piqued with interest.

Kiersten continued talking while bringing out large glasses of orange juice and a bag of fresh cinnamon-raisin bagels. "My friend and I used to meet for orange juice and bagels every day. We'd go to a park and sit on a table and watch a man water his flowers. Sometimes we'd go for a walk, and sometimes we'd throw tennis balls to the dogs. Once in awhile he'd push me on the swings."

A small voice questioned, "Was it a big swing set?"

"I'd say it was a pretty small swing set, as far as swing sets go. But it was one of the most colorful sets I've ever seen." Kiersten smiled at the memory of the graffiti scrawled in a rainbow of colors.

"I don't have a swing set." Amanda sank her little teeth into a large bagel. "Maybe someday you and your friend can take me to visit your colored swing set."

"I'd like that, Amanda."

After breakfast with Amanda, Kiersten felt as if her heart would burst with joy. *It's amazing that something as simple as talking about swings can make me feel so happy.* "Thank You, Lord," she whispered, glancing heavenward. "Thanks for helping with Amanda—and thank You for guiding me to nursing."

Kiersten kept her breakfast date with Amanda each morning. Kiersten supplied the juice and bagels, and increasingly, Amanda supplied the conversation. One morning, while they shared the morning meal, a nurse's voice carried through the partially opened door. "I tell you, I'd like to be there when that little girl's folks look God in the eye."

Amanda looked at Kiersten and questioned, "Who is God?"

Kiersten's astonished voice replied, "You don't know anything about God?" When the small girl shook her head, Kiersten continued. "Well, He is the Daddy to all of us—everyone on the earth. He created us and loves us more than anyone else ever will. He is always there for us and will never let us down."

Amanda's face grew expressionless as she bluntly declared, "I don't love Him and I never will."

"How do you know if you've never even talked to Him?"

"I know all about daddies and I don't *ever* want another one," Amanda explained. "I don't even want the one I have."

Kiersten was stuck for a response. She attempted to explain that this Father wasn't like Amanda's father, but her words fell on deaf ears. Nothing she could say would change the girl's determined mind. That night, wrapped snugly in a warm blanket and curled up on the couch, Kiersten searched for a way to show the child how loving God was. Each scenario she played ended up in the same place: with Brett.

He's so good with children. He could show her that not all men are like her father. He has such a great background in crisis intervention. For each reason she thought of to include Brett, she tried to think of one reason not to involve him. *It would make me uncomfortable. I would have to talk with him. What if he hurts me again? He might say no.* Somehow, comparing the potential benefits to Amanda against

Kiersten's own discomfort made Kiersten feel very small. *I guess I ought to call—for Amanda's sake. I just won't get close to him again.*

After three rings, a relieved Kiersten began to place the phone back into its cradle. *Guess he's not home.*

"Hello? Hello?" The voice from the receiver stopped Kiersten's arm. "Is anyone there?"

"Um. . ." The words caught in Kiersten's throat. *Maybe this isn't such a good idea.* "Um, well its Kiersten. Kiersten Davis. From the rehab clinic."

"Kiersten, I'm so glad you called. I've been thinking of you a lot. How have you been?"

Kiersten wasn't prepared for such a warm, enthusiastic response. "I'm fine. It's just that I have a little girl I'm working with over in the burn unit at Harborview. I've received special permission to take her out of the facility to a park and wondered if you would come with us?"

"Of course. When do you need me?" Brett responded.

"Don't you want to know why I want you to come or anything?"

"Kiersten, I've been waiting for this call for three months. I don't care why you want me there. I want to see you, and I'll use any reason. Just give me the address, day, and time. I'll be there."

Kiersten shifted uncomfortably. "You know our park. . . I mean the park we used to meet in across from the clinic. How about the swing set at eleven tomorrow morning?"

"Sounds great. I'll be there. And, Kiersten, I can't wait to see you."

After hanging up the phone, Kiersten glanced down at her still-shaking hands. The adrenaline pulsating through her body, combined with her rapidly beating heart, made her feel like running. *Why does he do this to me? This is crazy. I'm a grown woman, more than capable of having a phone conversation without having this happen. I am just going to introduce Amanda to him, and after that he can visit her in the hospital when I'm not around.*

※

Amanda left her breakfast virtually uneaten in her excitement. "You're taking me to the swings today? Will your friend be there? Can I stay for a long time? Do you think the flower man will be there?" Her questions peppered Kiersten faster than she could answer them.

After being sure that Amanda was medically stable, Kiersten transported her to the park. Brett was waiting on their bench. Upon seeing them approach, he stood. Amanda clung to Kiersten's leg, displaying her distrust of the man.

"Amanda, I would like you to meet my friend, Brett. He's the one I told you about."

Brett knelt down, looking Amanda in the eye. "I'm so glad you came. This is my favorite park. Would you like me to show you where the swings are?"

"The colored ones?" Amanda asked warily.

Brett looked at Kiersten with amusement, then responded, "Oh, yes—they are very colorful."

"Okay," Amanda replied. She followed Brett, careful to keep her distance.

Watching the retreating figures, Kiersten wondered if her plan would work. *Is Amanda so fearful of males that she won't let any of them get close to her? Is the fact her father is the only male she's ever known going to keep her from trusting Brett?*

Her fears were soon allayed as she watched Brett pushing a smiling little girl on the swings. Kiersten kept her distance when they walked over to look at the flowers that she and Brett had watched the man plant and care for. *It seems like just yesterday.* She smiled. *Boy, how I've missed this place.*

After an hour of watching Brett and the joyful girl play with abandon, Kiersten saw them back on the swings, gently swinging. She approached quietly from behind, unwilling to interrupt their conversation.

"You know," she heard Brett tell his very attentive audience, "not all daddies are like your daddy and my daddy."

"Is your daddy bad, too?" Amanda asked, wide-eyed.

"My dad hurt me when I was young. For a long time I hated him. I used to wish for another dad. When I grew up and didn't get my wish, I thought maybe all dads were like him, and I decided not to trust any of them." Brett paused and looked warmly at the little girl staring at him in rapt attention. "I was wrong, you know."

"You were?" asked the small voice.

"Yes. There are many dads out there who are loving and caring. Most dads don't hurt their kids. And I found I had another Dad—one who was more loving and cared more about me than any other dad anywhere."

"I wish I would find out *I* had another dad like that," Amanda lamented.

"You do. He's the same as my other Dad. His name is God and He is the Father to everyone. He knows who you are. He knows when you hurt. He is with you and will be your Best Friend forever. You just need to talk to Him."

"My dad won't let me use the phone. I'll get in big trouble."

Brett smiled. "Honey, you don't have to use the phone. You can talk to your heavenly Father whenever you want to, and He will be there for you. He will listen and will help you."

Kiersten wiped her eyes and sniffled, catching Brett's and Amanda's attention.

Amanda's rapid-fire recount of Brett and her "adventures" in the park left little time for conversation between the adults. While Brett helped them into her car, he mouthed to Kiersten, "Meet you at your place after work."

Her heart still full from hearing his gentle explanations to Amanda, Kiersten could do nothing but nod yes. It wasn't until she was well on her way back to the hospital that she realized what she had agreed to do. *Kiersten Davis, what on earth are you doing—inventing a surefire recipe for a broken heart?* Despite her overwhelming urge to protect her heart, glancing in the rearview mirror at a contented, sleeping child, she couldn't help thinking, *Maybe this recipe won't turn out so badly.*

Kiersten smiled and finished washing the last of the dinner dishes. It didn't seem like it had been over a month since that fateful day in the park. *I can't believe I wasted three miserable months apart from Brett. What was I thinking?* As quickly as she asked the question, she answered it, imitating her mother's delivery perfectly. "Get up and move on, Kiersten. There is no use crying over spilt milk." *Besides,* she thought, *at least I came to my senses before it was too late.*

The last few weeks with Brett and Amanda had been the best of Kiersten's life. Under her care and with Brett's frequent visits, Amanda was thriving. The once seemingly timid child had become the social butterfly on the floor. To the nurses' veiled amusement, she would "escape" from her room to visit other patients in the wing. She would inevitably be discovered sitting next to the bed of a patient, talking up a storm. Her visits were much anticipated by the other, older floor residents, and even the most hardened nurses grudgingly acknowledged that the little girl was providing some of the best medicine they'd seen in years. The doctors, after ensuring Amanda's visits weren't delaying the healing of her burns, turned their heads, hoping the visits might help heal her emotional scars.

"I don't know what you did to that girl," Judy, the burn unit's head nurse, commented, watching the mischievous, dark-haired pixie sneak out of her room again. "But it worked wonders."

"I can't take the credit," Kiersten humbly explained. "It's amazing what a little love will do. Knowing I love her and Brett loves her and God loves her and the nurses love her has given Amanda a whole new take on life."

Kiersten watched Amanda stealthily make her way through the hall toward the room of an unsuspecting patient. She couldn't believe how much love she felt in her heart for the small child with the spirited dark eyes. *I'd adopt her in a second if they'd let me. I feel like she is my own.*

She headed down the corridor to intercept the girl. "And where might you be going, young lady?"

Amanda stopped, wide-eyed, in the middle of the hall. Kiersten could see that the girl was trying to figure out how she was going to explain her way out of her predicament. "I just needed to go for a walk."

"Oh, wonderful. I was just thinking how nice a walk would be. Mind if I join you?"

Disappointment that her rendezvous with her chosen patient had been thwarted crossed Amanda's face. It was soon replaced by a large grin, demonstrating her pleasure at the prospect of spending time with her favorite person: Kiersten.

The two took off hand in hand, Amanda chatting up a storm and Kiersten listening attentively.

Later that evening, Kiersten described the events of the day to Brett over chicken stir-fry. "I can't believe how happy I am when I'm around Amanda. I learn something from her every day, and she makes me laugh constantly." She paused, then confided, "I know that when caring for people as a nurse, you're supposed to create bonds with patients, but with her it's totally different. It's so weird; sometimes when I'm with her, I feel like I'm her mom. I don't know how to describe it. I love her so much, it feels like the kind of love a mother must have for her child. I wish there were a way I could bring her home with me. Do you think I'm nuts?"

"No," Brett responded softly. "She's a wonderful kid." He continued, concern etched in his voice. "Kit, you need to be careful. It's a wonderful thing to love your patients, but you have to remember that they are *patients*. They have families and lives beyond the hospital. They will eventually get better and leave to go back to their homes." He sighed, running his fingers through his dark brown hair. "It's easy in the microcosm of the hospital to forget that these people won't stay there forever. It's also easy to forget that they have families they will need to return to."

"But Amanda *doesn't* have a family to go back to. Look what that monster did to her. No one would send her back there," Kiersten said with conviction.

Brett shook his head sadly. "Don't be so sure, Honey. Sometimes there isn't a choice. Remember Carrie at the Pediatric Care Center. And think of my dad and the others at the rehab clinic. We can't always control the environment the patients we care for are returned to—even if we think it's against their best interests."

Kiersten pleaded, "But we have all the medical records that prove the abuse. They couldn't let her go back with all that evidence!"

Brett placed his hand on Kiersten's. "Let's just pray that you are right."

Less than a week later, Kiersten wondered if perhaps they hadn't prayed hard enough. Word came through the social worker assigned to Amanda's case that the judge conducting the hearing had issued his ruling. His order dictated that the child's parents were to attend anger management classes before revisiting the custody issue but granted them supervised visitation while attending the classes.

"I don't get it," Kiersten raved. "How could he ever let them be in the same room with her again?"

"It could be a lot worse," Judy informed her. "They could have been given custody outright. This way, the majority of the time she will be with a foster family. When she does visit her parents, it will be with a supervisor."

"But can't we keep her in the hospital longer?" Kiersten begged, her eyes filling with tears.

Judy reached up and patted Kiersten's shoulders. "We don't have a choice. We've done all we can do medically— we know that, the judge knows that, and the insurance company knows that." She wearily ran a hand through her long hair. "You know, it really doesn't get harder than this. I'm sorry—maybe I shouldn't have assigned you this case. You have brought so much light into her life. Why don't you take the rest of the day off? We'll wait until tomorrow to tell Amanda."

Kiersten couldn't keep the tears at bay. She rushed to the nearest rest room, trying to stop the torrent streaming down her face. *God, how can You let this happen? How can You allow her to go back there?* The questions hung unanswered in her mind. When she finally emerged from the bathroom, it was with red, swollen eyes.

That evening, despite Brett's efforts to comfort her, Kiersten felt no better. In fact, the more she thought about it, the more upset she became. By the time Brett left for his night shift, she had herself worked into a real state. As he closed the door, Brett gently said, "I've found that no matter how dismal the situation looks, God always has a plan. Why don't you talk to Him? It can't hurt, and it might even help."

The only thing Kiersten was sure of while heading to bed was that she did *not* want to talk to God. In her anger, she might say something she would later regret. Instead, she opened her Bible, scanned the page, and began to read the highlighted portion. "And the light shineth in darkness; and the darkness comprehended it not"—John 1:5. The words caught Kiersten by surprise. She reached over to her bedside table, where the lamp pin sent by her grandmother lay. Holding the pin, she repeated, "The light shineth in darkness." *Surely when Christ came down to the earth there was darkness and evil. There were murderers and liars and thieves. . .and people who beat and injured innocent children. Yet He shone through the darkness. He triumphed over all evil.* Kiersten looked at the small metal lamp. *I am supposed to carry the lamp—a light to those who are in the darkness.*

As quickly as the thought entered her mind, she knew she had received the answer she was seeking. She pulled the bedcovers over her shoulders and sent a silent "thank You" upward.

❈

"You are all better now, so we have to let someone who is really sick have the bed." Knowing what she wanted to say and saying it were two different things, Kiersten decided, looking down at the beautiful child.

"Where will I go?" Amanda asked, her initial toothy smile fading with the news.

"There is a wonderful foster family, the Adamses, who want you to come live with them for awhile."

"So, I don't have to go back to my house?" Amanda

queried, relief clearly etched on her face.

"Not for right now." Kiersten wished she could add, *and never again.*

"But I will have to go back soon?" Amanda tremulously questioned. Then she blurted, "Oh, Ms. Kiersten, *please* don't make me go back there. *Please.*"

"Honey, I wish more than anything in this world that I could make it so you wouldn't ever go back. I'd go back in your place if there were any way I could. But I can't. You won't have to see your parents alone; another person sent by the court will always be with you—to protect you. And you'll have Someone else there, too. Remember when we talked about God, your Father, and how much He loves you? He will be there, too." Kiersten struggled to control her emotions.

"He wouldn't want to come visit at my house. It's a bad place."

"Amanda, He will come with you wherever you go—especially in the bad places. You know how, when it is really dark in here at night, we plug in the night-light and it isn't so dark anymore?"

The girl's small head nodded.

"God is like your own little night-light. No matter how dark things seem or how bad things feel or how scared you are, you can always talk to Him, and He will send you a light and make things better."

Amanda flung her arms around Kiersten's neck. "Will I see you again?"

"Of course. Brett and I will pick you up every week and take you to the park. I promise."

The little girl smiled at the thought. "Can we have bagels?"

Kiersten smiled back. "You bet."

❋

The loss Kiersten felt each time she walked down the hallway and realized Amanda was gone didn't get any better. The week dragged on endlessly. The only bright spot was the picnic Brett, Amanda, and Kiersten shared at the park on Friday. Saturday, Brett met Kiersten for dinner, trying to keep their minds off the fact that this night was Amanda's first scheduled supervised visit with her parents. Brett's effort at distraction failed miserably. They picked at their food, the unspoken worry etched on both their faces.

Finally Brett spoke. "As miserable as we both feel, I can't think of anyone I'd rather be with right now."

Kiersten smiled slightly. "I was just thinking how nice it is to be with someone who knows me well enough to understand what I am thinking and feeling without me saying anything. I don't think I could have made it through all this without you." She looked down in embarrassment. "Thanks. I really need you in my life."

An insistent beeping interrupted the moment. Brett reached for his pager and read the message. "I'm sorry, Kit. I have no choice. I've got to go to the station. They had a sick call and my name is up. I'll call you as soon as I get a chance. Will you be okay without me tonight?" He rested his palms on the side of her cheeks and looked into her eyes.

"I'll be fine. I'll probably rent a movie to try and get my mind off of it. Go on."

Brett hurriedly paid the check and rushed out of the restaurant. Kiersten gathered her belongings and put on her coat. When she looked down, she noticed Brett's pager on the table. *It looks like I'm going to be making a trip to the station.*

As Kiersten pulled out of the parking lot, the incessant beeping started again. She picked up the offending device and read the message across the screen. Many of the letters and numbers meant nothing to her, until DV @ 221 Willow flashed across the screen. Her heart leaped in her throat as she deciphered the message. The address was one she had seen on a chart enough times to memorize. There was a domestic violence call, and it was at Amanda Cantrell's home. Kiersten instinctively floored the accelerator and sped toward the address. Amanda needed help, and she was going to her.

The house appeared dark from the street. Kiersten didn't stop to think. She ran straight through the unlocked front door and into a horrifying scene. Jesse Cantrell stood there, armed with a .45 automatic pistol pointed at the three figures cowering against the paint-chipped kitchen wall. Kiersten didn't need an introduction to know she was looking at Amanda's mom, the court-ordered supervisor, and Amanda. The two women were bruised and sobbing, but Amanda was looking at her father with a fearless gaze. Kiersten's abrupt entrance produced an expletive from Jesse and a semi-welcome look from the other three.

Kiersten was instantly herded against the wall as the fourth hostage. "So nice of you to join our party," Jesse taunted. "Thought it might be a nice night to die?"

Kiersten desperately tried to recall her crisis-intervention training but couldn't remember anything on hostage situations. She took Amanda's hand and held it tightly. She was amazed at how warm it felt—when her own hand was icy. Her blood had rushed to her body's core in response to her fear. Looking into the young girl's eyes, she saw no concern, only peace. Kiersten turned to Jesse. "Why are you doing this?" she asked, hoping to start a dialogue.

"Nobody's takin' my kid away from me. She's mine and nobody's gonna tell me she ain't. I'm her father, and if you don't like it, too bad—I'm the only one she's got. 'Sides, who would want her but me? She's ugly. She's rotten. She don't obey. She ain't lovable."

Kiersten bristled at his harsh words riddled with expletives and prepared to set him straight on a lot more than his grammar. She reconsidered when a small but firm voice spoke up.

"You are wrong. Kiersten loves me, and Brett loves me, and all the nurses at the hospital love me, and my friends on the eighth floor love me." One by one the little girl named each patient she had sneaked out to visit during her hospital stay. "And you are not my only father. God is my Father. And He doesn't think I'm ugly or rotten. He loves me very much." Amanda's conviction stunned even Kiersten.

"You little. . . !" Jesse exploded. "For your information, God doesn't exist. He's just like Santa Claus and the Easter Bunny and the Tooth Fairy. All lies. None of 'em real. Nobody loves you, little girl. Your so-called friends lied to you. They're laughing at you for being stupid enough to believe 'em. They ain't got no love for you, either."

"No, Dad. You're wrong. I know my friends love me. They told me. And I love them. I know God is my Dad— my real Dad. And He loves me very much because He told me when I talked to Him. I don't care what you say. He is with me all the time—even now. He is stronger and smarter than anybody. And He's *real* mad at you."

Kiersten was stunned at the strength of the little girl's warm hand clenching hers but even more amazed by the joy and light in her eyes.

"Don't worry, Kiersten," the little girl whispered,

smiling. "Everything will be okay—God is here and He told me."

Jesse's anger at the little girl had clearly been ignited by the speech and was fanned by the lights and sound of the approaching sirens. "I'll teach you who's the strongest and smartest, little girl."

Before Kiersten could react, Jesse pointed the gun directly at Amanda, leaned his head back, laughed, and pulled the trigger. Kiersten leaped in front of her small friend and felt the heat of the bullet pierce her upper body. She fell in a heap on the girl as the police burst through the front door. Lifting her head, Kiersten gazed at the motionless, peaceful face beside her and knew Amanda had gone to meet her real Father. The last voice she heard before everything went black belonged to Brett.

Chapter 7

Brett stared at the motionless figure lying prone on the hospital bed. He glanced at his watch, trying to determine how long he had been sitting there. *The longest seventeen or eighteen hours I've ever known.* The images of the past day flashed relentlessly through his head like a movie projector on constant repeat. His mind struggled to grasp and accept the scenes, but they moved too quickly. The call coming in to the station. Realizing it was a hostage situation. Overhearing the police officer use Amanda's father's name. Wondering if he should call Kiersten to let her know. The gunshot. The panic. Sprinting toward the front door. The shock of hearing Kiersten's voice. The blood. Amanda. Kiersten.

He had rushed to help. Not wanting to let go of either Kiersten or Amanda, he desperately tried to find where the blood was coming from, holding each in an arm. When his partner announced that Amanda was without a pulse, Brett worked diligently, attempting to revive her. Willing her to live. *It wasn't enough,* Brett thought. *There wasn't anything I could do.* Even now, thinking of his small friend brought tears to the man's eyes. *I guess she can ride all the rainbow-colored swings she wants to now.*

A small movement from the bed beside him interrupted Brett's thoughts. He anxiously turned, hoping to see Kiersten's beautiful green eyes staring back. Her eyes remained closed. *Just like they were when we wheeled her out of the house.*

Brett's thoughts turned back to the panic-filled hours last night. Seeing Kiersten's bloody, lifeless body had literally knocked the wind out of him. He had insisted on transporting her to the closest hospital, leaving the other medic crews on scene to care for the injured. He'd felt a sense of relief upon hearing the bullet had only nicked her clavicle, missing all vital organs. His relief was short-lived as he paced the floor awaiting her emergence from surgery. The last few hours had been brutal. He had revisited the scene again and again in his mind while at Kiersten's bedside. She had tossed and turned, under the influence of heavy pain medications.

Thank goodness for the pain meds. At least she's not suffering. He thought of his father and *his* pain medications. *It's too bad something that can bring such relief can cause so much heartache.*

Brett struggled with how he was going to tell Kiersten about Amanda. Many times, in his profession, he'd had to be the bearer of terrible news, but never before to someone he loved. "Loved." He mumbled the word, shaking his head. Seeing her in a crumpled heap and envisioning his life without her, he had reached one unmistakable conclusion: He loved Kiersten Elisabeth Davis. There were no ifs, ands, or buts about it—this was the real thing. And he would tell her so, in due time.

※

Kiersten struggled through her drugged state to consciousness. She hurt. Everything hurt, but especially her right shoulder area. Opening her eyes, she attempted to focus. *Why am I here?* As soon as she asked the question, she knew the answer. Memories of the shooting flooded back and left her feeling as if she were inhaling too much water and couldn't catch a breath. She caught Brett's gaze as she looked around the room for an escape from her emotions. In a gasping sob she voiced, "Amanda's gone."

Brett moved across the room in an instant. Careful to avoid her shoulder, he encircled her with his loving arms. Her head found his shoulder, and her heaving cries shook his body as well as her own. Even his whispered condolences did nothing to ease the intensity of her sorrow. She cried until she was numb and mercifully fell asleep on his shoulder.

When Kiersten next awakened, she could barely open her red-rimmed, swollen eyes. The empty pit she felt in her stomach had little to do with hunger. Nausea threatened. As painful as the wound in her upper chest was, it was no match for the pain in her heart. *I don't think I can deal with this. It's too hard.* She turned over, buried her head in the pillow, and promptly sought refuge in sleep.

The next few days were filled with sleep, pain, and occasional glimpses of Brett and her family members in the waking moments. Conversations with people melded one into the next. Brett, Lu, her mom. None was important enough to earn a place in her overloaded mind. She wasn't sure whether the numbness that pervaded her was from sadness, sleep, drugs, or pain; but then again, Kiersten really didn't care. In fact, she didn't care about much of anything except sleep.

"Hey, Sweetheart," Brett said, attempting to engage her in conversation on one of his daily visits. "Where's the first place you want to go when you get out of here?

Quite confidentially. . ."—he leaned over and whispered with a smile—"this is your opportunity to take terrible advantage of me, because anything you wish today is yours."

Kiersten stared stonily ahead. She knew Brett was talking to her, but she couldn't seem to concentrate on what exactly he was saying. Hearing a pause in his voice, she automatically gave a slight nod and an "uh-huh," hoping the answer would suffice.

Brett continued, pain registering in his voice. "So you say you'd like to go for an elaborate breakfast on the waterfront, and then a plane ride around the Sound, and finally a hike up to the best sunset-viewing location in the county for a handmade picnic dinner and engaging conversation. I think you have chosen wisely, my dear."

When Kiersten gave no response, Brett took her hands in his and forced her to look at him. "Kit, I know you are hurting terribly. I know you miss Amanda. But, Honey, you're going to be released from the hospital before the week is up. You are going to have to go on living. It won't be easy, but you have to dress and eat and work. And eventually, it will get better. I promise."

"I'm not going back to work," Kiersten said in a monotone. "I just can't do it." She looked at Brett, a bit of emotion breaking through her rigid mask. "Don't you see, there's just too much pain—I'm not cut out for this. I don't have the strength."

Brett responded, "You are the strongest person I know. You come from good stock. Remember those nurse ancestors you're always telling me about? They must have faced heartache and death and misery. They found a way to move on, and you will, too. You have their blood running through your veins." He paused, squeezing her hands. "Don't you think there is a reason you have wanted to be a nurse since you were a little girl? Don't you think it's odd that you are the only one in your immediate family who has that dream? I think it is your calling. I believe God wants you to be a nurse, to help others. If I'm right, He will help you find a way to fulfill your destiny."

Kiersten pondered Brett's words late into the evening. Was being a nurse her destiny? Could God want her to serve in this manner? Could she bring herself to face the inevitable pain she would feel in the profession? She didn't have the answers, but asking the questions had lit the littlest flame in her tragedy-darkened mind.

The next day, Kiersten arose hoping to find some of her heart's lost innocence. *I suppose a walk couldn't hurt.* As she moved her feet over the side of the bed, days of inactivity registered. She slowly stood on wobbly legs and put on her light green robe. She securely fastened the belt around her waist and finger-combed her hair in the mirror. Looking at her reflection, she noticed that the little lamp pin from her grandmother was affixed to the collar of her robe. *Brett.* She shook her head. *He must have brought it from my apartment. Doesn't look like he's ready for me to give up this nursing thing.*

She headed down the corridor toward the children's wing. Instinctively Kiersten knew that if anything would bring a little feeling to her heart it would be the sound of children's laughter and voices. As she grew closer, the telltale colored drawings lined the walls. Animals. Children. Balloons. A rainbow leading to the large golden doors marking the entrance. Kiersten allowed herself a small smile, remembering Amanda's rainbow-painted swings.

Once inside the doors, Kiersten maneuvered herself through an onslaught of bright-eyed, toothless, smiling children to the patient rooms. Remembering Amanda's visits to patients on the burn ward, Kiersten moved toward the nurses' station, deciding to conduct her own "healing visits." She glanced at several charts lying on the desk and words like carcinoma, lymphoma, sarcoma, and leukemia jumped at her from the pages. *God, how is it that such small frail bodies are forced to carry such big-name diseases? How can You allow pain and death to touch the lives of these sweet frail children? I was right. I can't do this. I can't care for children, or anyone else, knowing they are just going to die.*

Kiersten turned and made her way through the small children back to the golden doors. As she reached them, the tug of a small dark hand on her robe interrupted her dismal thoughts. Kiersten bent down to the level of the hand's owner. A small girl with beautiful, large dark-brown eyes smiled.

"Señorita. Señorita con la lampara." The smiling owner of the sweet voice pointed to the small lamp pin on Kiersten's lapel.

"Lady with the lamp," Kiersten murmured. *Thank goodness for my high school Spanish teacher. And I thought I would never find a use for it.*

Kiersten returned the smile and gently patted the child on the head. Rather than heading out the doors, she sat on a bench abutting them. Looking at the multicultural children playing in the room, visions of a trip to the Statute of Liberty, the "Lady with the Lamp," flooded her memory.

The day she had visited New York Harbor had been a foggy one. She was a new high school graduate and was excited to begin her "adult life." Immigrant children played joyfully, while their parents bent to kiss the Ellis Island soil. As Kiersten stood gazing up at the torch held aloft, an ensign of hope illuminating the haze, she couldn't help dreaming of a day when she would provide that kind of hope to those who were hurting. Her tour guide, a uniformed woman with a resonating voice, had read the inscripted words aloud to the group.

"Give me your tired, your poor,
Your huddled masses yearning to breathe free,
The wretched refuse of your teeming shore.
Send these, the homeless, tempest-tossed to me.
I lift my lamp beside the golden door."

Remembering that long-ago day, Kiersten looked around at the children now playing near her feet. Slowly realization dawned, accompanied by a smile spreading across her face. She glanced up at the golden door framing the children's unit and reached out to hug the small Hispanic girl who had called attention to her pin. The depression holding her hostage for the last few days began to release its hold.

Maybe I can do this. Just as the Statue of Liberty's lamp symbolizes hope to the lost and afraid, the light we hold as nurses, our lamps, offer hope to those who are struggling in the darkness of illness and affliction. Everyone needs hope. The sick, the dying, the homeless, the drug-addicted. They all need hope to retain any joy. They need hope that someone cares, that they will feel better tomorrow, that they will get well. Even those who will not get well need hope. They need hope that they won't be forgotten. That they will be loved and made as comfortable as possible.

Kiersten's gaze took in the small, sick children in the unit. *And who deserves hope more than these little ones?*

Chapter 8

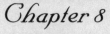

Hope filled Kiersten's heart as she rose to greet the new day. She was looking forward to another shift on the Harborview Burn Unit. It was hard to believe it had been three weeks since she was released as a patient from Liberty Memorial Hospital. She touched her upper chest gingerly. Her wound was still painful, but like her saddened heart, it was slowly on the mend. Work offered a welcome distraction from her painful memories, and she threw herself into the completion of her internship.

Kiersten affixed the small lamp pin to her uniform, a practice she had adopted after her visit to the children's ward, and headed out the door. Intent on making it to work, she tripped over a large paper bag in the entryway and stumbled. "Great," she sarcastically mumbled, picking herself up. "My favorite way to start the day. Who's the idiot who left the bag here?" She glared at the offending bag, then opened it. A dozen bagels sat innocently awaiting her. Her temper softened slightly. "Well, I don't need three guesses on this one." She looked around, hoping to spot Brett.

He was making his way up the driveway, a large carton of orange juice in one hand and three tubs of cream cheese and two glasses in the other. He grinned when he spotted Kiersten. "I see you found my surprise. Got time for breakfast?"

"I *always* have time for breakfast. Remember, I am the world-record-holder in morning preparation: hair, clothes, *and* breakfast in four minutes." Kiersten smiled, hoping he had missed her little skirmish with the bagels.

Brett laughed at her antics, clear relief at her light-heartedness etched on his face. "So how does it feel only having a week left before you are a real, bona fide, employable nurse?"

"In some ways I can't wait," Kiersten responded. "It's funny. If you had asked me three weeks ago, I would have told you it would never happen. I wanted nothing to do with being a nurse. Now I'm excited again. I've been reading the journal my grandma sent, and the more I learn about my ancestors' stories, the more I yearn to serve as they did."

"Well, as soon as you get a job, you *will* be serving just as they did. Are you going back to the clinic? I know Lu would like to have you back, and you were great with the patients there. Besides, it would give me a chance to see you on the job. You know me and my ulterior motives." He winked.

Kiersten waved her hand in dismissal. "Oh, no. I'm going to fulfill my childhood dream. I'm going to serve in a war zone, just as my grandmother and great-grandmothers did. I've been thinking of submitting my application to Mercy Abroad. They send medical personnel into war-torn areas to minister to the needs of people. I would be helping wounded civilians caught in the crossfire. I'd also be working with many children." She knew her eyes lit excitedly at the prospect. "After the last few weeks, I really believe I am being called to bring hope to those who need it the most."

Brett grew quiet. "There are people right here who need hope, too."

"Oh, I know," Kiersten responded. "But I also want to serve my country. You know that inscription on the Statute of Liberty, the one about welcoming the poor and tired and those looking for freedom. I want to be like that. I want to 'hold my lamp' for all the world to see."

"How long do you think you'll be gone?" Brett asked.

"As long as the people need me."

"Are you sure this is what's going to make you happy?" Brett solemnly questioned.

"I've thought about this a lot the last few weeks, and I feel this is what I'm being called to do," Kiersten answered with determination.

Brett remained nearly silent throughout the rest of breakfast. His bagel sat untouched at his side.

❋

"I don't get it." Kiersten's frustration oozed. "One minute it's Mr. Bagel-a-day, googly eyes, 'can't get enough of you, Kiersten,' and then it's absolutely nothing."

"Let me get this straight," her roommate Janie stated. "Brett, *our* Brett, has been giving *you* the cold shoulder?" She shook her head. "I don't believe it."

"Not a word in a week. Not a call. Not a bagel. Nothing. You're supposed to be the expert on these male creatures. What's going on?"

"I don't have a clue," Janie answered. "Did you do something to upset him?"

"No, I don't think so. I've been trying to remember all week. The last time we talked, he brought me bagels. I shared with him all the stuff I'd been dreaming about.

You know, serving others, bringing hope. I told him I was applying to Mercy Abroad. He seemed excited that I was happy." Kiersten shook her head in bewilderment.

"What did you say about the relationship between you two?" Janie queried.

"What do you mean? We didn't discuss it."

"You have been exclusively dating the man for over eight months. You're telling me you told him you are leaving to go abroad and you didn't discuss your relationship?" Janie looked stunned. "Kiersten, this isn't like Dennis or any of your other male friends. This man cares about you. You can't just take off and leave him hanging without a second thought."

Kiersten bristled. "I wasn't leaving him hanging. I care about him, too, a lot. It's not like our relationship is going to end. I mean, we'll write and fly to see each other."

"You are going to fly back and forth from Ethiopia or some other remote location?" Janie shook her head. "Kiersten, be realistic. You will maybe see him once or twice a year. Your correspondence will take weeks to reach each other. This is a major change in your relationship. You didn't mention anything to him at all. He probably thinks you are breaking it off with him. You are really a novice at this relationship thing. I'd say you better call Brett."

Kiersten tossed and turned all night thinking of Janie's words. *Could Brett really think I don't care about seeing him again? Would I really only see him once or twice a year?* Her tumultuous thoughts kept plaguing her. *There wouldn't be any early morning bagel runs or mountain hikes in full garb and designer boots. I wouldn't have a set of wide shoulders to cry on or someone to talk with after a hard day of nursing. No more long runs through the woods or spontaneous picnics on graffiti-covered park benches.* Sleep finally rescued her from the confusion in the early morning hours.

The 8:00 AM call from the director of Mercy Abroad informing Kiersten she was being offered a position didn't bring nearly the joy she thought it would. She mumbled quick appreciation but asked for twenty-four hours to think about it.

The majority of Kiersten's thoughts were not spent on the job, but on Brett. She tried to call his work but was told he wasn't scheduled to be there until the next morning. She placed dozens of calls to his home number, but upon receiving the answering machine, she hung up each time. *Where are you?* Kiersten wondered. *I really need to talk with you. Could you be out on a date with someone else? Did you find another girl so quickly?*

The hours of waiting wreaked havoc with Kiersten's mind. By the twelfth hour, she had convinced herself that Brett must have gone out with her for pity's sake and had found another woman he *really* liked. Her dreary convictions and resultant indignant anger at Brett had her in a real tizzy by the time the phone rang.

"She's not home," Kiersten bluntly stated, sure the call must be for her roommate.

"Kiersten, are you okay? What's wrong?" Brett's anxious voice resonated over the phone lines.

"Oh, it's you. I'm fine. Did you have a nice time with your new friend?" Kiersten's anger clouded her judgment.

"What new friend? I hiked up to the spot we visited last summer on Rainier. Kiersten, what is going on? Why did you call me so many times?"

"How did you know I called?" Curiosity broke Kiersten out of her anger.

"I have caller ID, remember?"

Embarrassment lit Kiersten's face like a stick of dynamite. Feeling herself turn red from hair to neck, she thought of the dozens of redials to Brett's number she had pushed. *And he knows about all of them.*

"Well, I just wanted to tell you I got an offer from Mercy Abroad." Kiersten mumbled an excuse, too embarrassed to tell him the real reason for her call. *He must think I'm psychotic.*

Brett's subdued voice expressed congratulations. "I just want you to be happy."

His words jarred her from her own humiliation. "Well, I'm not happy."

"What do you mean? I thought this was what you wanted?"

"I do. But I don't. It's hard to explain. Maybe I'd do better in person."

"I'll pick you up in twenty minutes. And Kiersten," he added, a slight chuckle in his voice, "if I happen to be running a little late, you can always leave a message on my machine—maybe even two or three of them."

Brett's car pulled into the driveway a few minutes later. Kiersten turned to Janie. "I don't know what to say to him."

"Kit, just calm down. Remember, he's your best friend—tell him how you feel."

Brett drove around before parking at a vantage point where the lights of Seattle shone magnificently in the background. He turned to Kiersten and gently asked, "Now what is this about?"

Kiersten looked at her hands, trying to formulate her feelings into words. "I have always wanted to serve my country as a nurse in a war. I've heard since I was a small girl about my brave and compassionate ancestors who served valiantly in the Civil War, World War I, and World War II. I dreamed of being just like them. They were the only ones in my family I could really relate to. They weren't blond, and they loved helping people.

"Over the last few months, I lost sight of that dream. As I faced the trials in my internships, I struggled with who I was and what I had always wanted to be. I thought maybe my dreams had been misplaced—that I wasn't cut out for this profession. After what happened with Amanda, I realized God wanted me to be a light of hope, shining for those who were suffering in darkness. I know it sounds corny, but sometimes when I put on my lamp pin, I feel like I am a beacon. You know, like Florence Nightingale and her lamp, ministering to soldiers in the dark. This Mercy job is a fulfillment of everything I've always wanted." Kiersten sighed, looking out the car window at the city lights.

Brett looked at the lights as well. "It sounds perfect for you."

"It does, doesn't it?" Kiersten dejectedly shook her head. "But it's not. I keep replaying it in my head. You know, they don't have bagels in these war-torn areas."

"No bagels?" Brett raised his eyebrows in mock horror. "How awful."

"And no good places to swing or hike."

"No swings? No hiking? You can't be serious," Brett jested.

"And the company. I wouldn't have anyone to bring me Chinese takeout."

Brett smiled. "We couldn't have that."

Kiersten sighed deeply. "I feel stuck. I have an impossible choice. I live my dream but I am not happy, or I am happy but give up my dream. I really don't know what to do."

Brett was silent for awhile. "You know, Kiersten, God

asks us to let our lights shine before men so they will see our good works and glorify Him. He doesn't tell us where we need to be when we hold our lights. Our lights can shine here in the United States or in a small Cambodian village, and the message is still the same."

Brett paused and ran his fingers through his dark hair. "If it's a war you want, it seems to me we have plenty of wars to fight here. What do you think you have been doing on your internships? You have been fighting very real wars. The wars against poverty, addiction, disease, and violence that you have been waging are just as real as those in which your ancestors served. The threat to our nation from these enemies is as strong as or stronger than any threat that has ever been posed. They may not have well-known faces, like Hitler or Stalin, but it doesn't make them less fearsome. I believe you can fulfill your dream and be happy at the same time." Taking her hands, he smiled at Kiersten. "Of course, I must warn you, I do have ulterior motives. Having you fulfill your dream here would also make me very happy."

Listening to Brett, Kiersten felt enlightened. *He's right. I can fulfill my dream right here.* She warmly leaned against his shoulder, wrapped her arms around his waist, and watched the lights illuminating the skyline twinkle in the distance.

✳

One month later, Kiersten paused in the golden doorway to the children's wing at Liberty Memorial Hospital and looked down at her left ring finger. *Almost the same color,* she thought, gazing at the encircling engagement band Brett had given her the night before.

"Are you a new nurse here?" a young girl asked, tugging at Kiersten's hand.

Kiersten looked down, amazed at the girl's resemblance to Amanda. "Yes, I am. My name is Ms. Kiersten. What's yours?"

"I'm Emily. I like peanut butter, puppies, and swings."

"Well," Kiersten said, knowing the smile on her face reflected the peace in her heart, "I just happen to know a great place with rainbow swings. Maybe we'll go there sometime."

RENEE DeMARCO

Renee is an award-winning, multipublished author. Her premedical courses in college, and the many years she spent working in both a hospital emergency room, and the University of Washington Medical Center, have augmented her medical knowledge. Serving as an in-house attorney for a hospital, before moving to her current legal practice, cemented her admiration for those who serve in the healing profession. She resides in Washington State with her husband and daughter. Renee hopes *Beside the Golden Door* will help remind readers of the tremendous needs and opportunities to make a difference that are waiting just outside their own doors.

A Letter to Our Readers

Dear Readers:

In order that we might better contribute to your reading enjoyment, we would appreciate your taking a few minutes to respond to the following questions. When completed, please return to the following: Fiction Editor, Barbour Publishing, Inc., PO Box 719, Uhrichsville, OH 44683.

1. Did you enjoy reading *Lamps of Courage?*
   ❏ Very much. I would like to see more books like this.
   ❏ Moderately—I would have enjoyed it more if _____

   _____

   _____

2. What influenced your decision to purchase this book?
   (Check those that apply.)
   ❏ Cover   ❏ Back cover copy   ❏ Title   ❏ Price
   ❏ Friends   ❏ Publicity   ❏ Other

3. Which story was your favorite?
   ❏ *By Dim and Flaring Lamps*   ❏ *A Light in the Night*
   ❏ *Home Fires Burning*   ❏ *Beside the Golden Door*

4. Please check your age range:
   ❏ Under 18   ❏ 18–24   ❏ 25–34
   ❏ 35–45   ❏ 46–55   ❏ Over 55

5. How many hours per week do you read? _____

Name _____

Occupation _____

Address _____

City _____ State _____ ZIP _____

E-mail _____

If you enjoyed

Lamps

of COURAGE

then read:

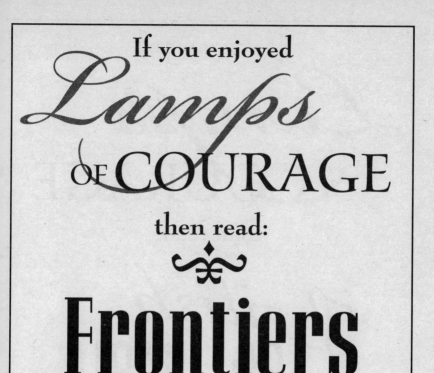

Frontiers

Four Inspirational Love Stories
from America's Frontier by Colleen L. Reece

Flower of Seattle
Flower of the West
Flower of the North
Flower of Alaska

If you enjoyed

Lamps OF COURAGE

then read:

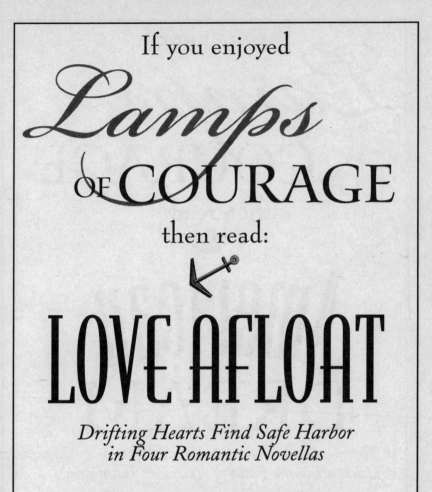

LOVE AFLOAT

*Drifting Hearts Find Safe Harbor
in Four Romantic Novellas*

The Matchmakers Kimberley Comeaux.
Troubled Waters Linda Goodnight.
By the Silvery Moon by JoAnn A. Grote.
Healing Voyage by Diann Hunt.

$\mathcal{H}$EARTSONG ❤ PRESENTS

Love Stories
Are Rated G!

That's for godly, gratifying, and of course, great! If you love a thrilling love story but don't appreciate the sordidness of some popular paperback romances, **Heartsong Presents** is for you. In fact, **Heartsong Presents** is the only inspirational romance book club, the only one featuring love stories where Christian faith is the primary ingredient in a marriage relationship.

Sign up today to receive your first set of four never-before-published Christian romances. Send no money now; you will receive a bill with the first shipment. You may cancel at any time without obligation, and if you aren't completely satisfied with any selection, you may return the books for an immediate refund!

Imagine. . .four new romances every four weeks—two historical, two contemporary—with men and women like you who long to meet the one God has chosen as the love of their lives. . .all for the low price of $9.97 postpaid.

To join, simply complete the coupon below and mail to the address provided. **Heartsong Presents** romances are rated G for another reason: They'll arrive Godspeed!

YES! Sign me up for Hearts❤ng!

NEW MEMBERSHIPS WILL BE SHIPPED IMMEDIATELY!
Send no money now. We'll bill you only $9.97 postpaid with your first shipment of four books. Or for faster action, call toll free 1-800-847-8270.

NAME _____

ADDRESS _____

CITY _____ STATE _____ ZIP _____

MAIL TO: HEARTSONG PRESENTS, PO Box 721, Uhrichsville, Ohio 44683